D0802706

# WHAT YOU CAN'T SEE

## ALLISON BRENNAN
## ROXANNE ST. CLAIRE
## KARIN TABKE

POCKET BOOKS

New York   London   Toronto   Sydney

Pocket Books
A Division of Simon & Schuster, Inc.
1230 Avenue of the Americas
New York, NY 10020

This book is a work of fiction. Names, characters, places, and incidents either are products of the author's imagination or are used fictitiously. Any resemblance to actual events or locales or persons, living or dead, is entirely coincidental.

First Pocket Books paperback edition January 2008

POCKET and colophon are registered trademarks of Simon & Schuster, Inc.

For information about special discounts for bulk purchases, please contact Simon & Schuster Special Sales at 1-800-456-6798 or business@simonandschuster.com

Cover design and illustration by Dave Stevenson, based on a photograph by Amanda Friedman/Getty Images

Manufactured in the United States of America

10  9  8  7  6  5  4  3  2  1

ISBN-13: 978-1-4165-4229-2
ISBN-10:    1-4165-4229-9

# Contents

# DELIVER US FROM EVIL

ALLISON BRENNAN

*He who does not punish evil, commands it to be done.*

—Leonardo da Vinci

*All that is necessary for the triumph of evil is that good men do nothing.*

—Edmund Burke

# PROLOGUE

ANTHONY SENSED FATHER PHILIP before he saw him on the overgrown garden path that connected the ancient monastery to Anthony's private retreat.

Gently he laid his book on his desk—a four-inch-thick, thousand-year-old Latin tome—and stood to greet his mentor on the porch.

"Good evening, Father," Anthony said. He used the word out of both respect and affection. Since Anthony had been abandoned as an infant thirty-five years ago, Father Philip had guided both his spiritual and personal growth. There was nothing he wouldn't do for the man.

"Raphael is on the phone," Father Philip said.

Anthony shut the door of his small bungalow and walked with the old priest toward the main house.

"Make any headway?"

Anthony rubbed his temples; he'd spent two days doing intensive research. "If there is a demon at work in Santa Louisa, I don't know how it is managing not to leave a tangible trail, something to track. I hope Rafe has more information for me."

When Rafe e-mailed him last week, his comments were vague and Anthony couldn't get much more from him during their subsequent e-mail exchange. The twelve semiretired priests in Rafe's charge were acting "strange." Or, rather, stranger than usual. Rafe described them as forgetful, melancholy, and angry.

"Perhaps you should go out there yourself," Father Philip suggested.

"I am not a demon hunter," Anthony replied. "I'm doing what I do best, and that's identifying the problem. Then I can send the right person to fix it." Though he certainly wasn't making headway on Rafe's situation. "Maybe this isn't a supernatural problem, but a mental one."

Four weeks ago, Rafe had been called to minister to the reclusive priests at Santa Louisa de Los Padres Mission, who had each been sent there to recover from supernatural and human evil. Most would never be able to serve in full capacity again. But even Rafe's arrival at the mission was odd; since when did a seminarian get called into such a sensitive service?

When Father Philip didn't say anything, Anthony tensed. "You disagree?"

"I don't think either of us can make that determination without going to the mission."

Seven years ago Anthony had failed in the worst way and someone died. He wouldn't jeopardize another life, preferring to work with inanimate buildings. "If it is a demon, Rico and John are the two best hunters out there."

"Rafe needs you, Anthony."

Father Philip didn't need to say more. Anthony had been the one who had sanctified the ground the mission stood on. He'd renovated the facilities five years ago, declared the mission safe for the troubled souls sent there.

That was his job—historical architect and demonologist. If a demon was there—if it could break through all Anthony's precautions—Anthony must have missed something.

The library housed the only phone in the monastery. Father Philip left Anthony in privacy. "Rafe?"

"Eight minutes it takes you to get to the phone? I tried your cell phone first."

"I had it turned off. I've been trying to research your problem, but I can't find anything in the ancient texts that addresses your specific observations. Do you have anything else for me?"

"I need you to come here."

"To America?"

"It's a feeling. I can't describe it. It's like I'm looking at these men and someone else is inside them."

"What about—"

"There are no cold or hot spots," Rafe interrupted. "No sulfuric scent. No superhuman strength or unexplainable events. I know what to look for, Anthony. We've been through the same training. It's like—they're here, but they're not here. They rarely sleep and when they do they succumb to violent nightmares."

"What about Dr. Wicker?" Psychiatrist Charles Wicker lived a few hours from the mission and made monthly visits.

"He thinks one of my men is communicating with a spirit. But he doesn't know who. We've used every test we can think of and they all pass."

"The tabernacle is still secure?"

"Tabernacle? Yes, of course, it's right behind the altar." Rafe sounded confused.

"Then you're okay," Anthony explained. "The tabernacle is embedded with the cross of Saint Peter and blessed with water from the river Jordan." There were also other protections, but Anthony didn't need to go into details now.

"You're one of the few people I trust. I need you. I don't want to lose any of them."

Suicide among those who have faced evil was unfortunately common. Like Anthony, Rafe had once failed in his mission.

The fear in Rafe's usually calm voice set Anthony on edge. They'd known each other for twenty-nine years, since the day Rafe had been left on the doorstep of the same monastery Anthony grew up in. Rafe was as close to a brother as Anthony had ever had. How could he refuse him?

Rafe said quietly, "Anthony, I think something evil has slithered inside. And I don't know how to get rid of it."

"I'll leave within the hour."

# Chapter One

Blood isn't red.

Blood goes beyond color. Rich and textured, dark and fathomless, blood was life and death. *Burgundy* didn't do it justice. If blood were wine, it would be a full-bodied cabernet, perhaps a zinfandel, certainly not something as boring, mundane, two-dimensional as *red*.

Especially spilled blood, filling the crevices of the nearly two-hundred-fifty-year-old limestone floor of a forgotten California mission. Every hole, every nook, every imperfection in the aged floor filled with blood, corner to corner, the porous stone absorbing death so dark red it was almost black, as black as the heart of the evil man who had murdered the twelve priests in this oppressive chapel.

*Evil men.* Certainly it had taken more than one person to slaughter twelve unarmed priests.

Until this morning, the most spilled blood Sheriff Skye McPherson had witnessed was a vicious murder-suicide three years ago. A man had stabbed his family to death, then shot himself, the bastard. Even the arcs of blood slashed against those white walls didn't come close to the tragedy before her today.

She'd never rid this image from her mind, never forget the stench of violence.

*Violence?* Twelve people dead. It was a massacre.

"Jesus, Mary, and Joseph." Detective Juan Martinez crossed himself as they proceeded carefully through the carnage.

They were in the chapel of Santa Louisa de Los Padres, a small mission closed to the public. Skye had hiked up here many times with her father, Chuck McPherson, a U.S. forest ranger who had known the Los Padres National Forest better than anyone and had befriended the priests who came to the mission on sabbatical.

That was before. Five years ago the diocese relocated the few who'd lived there, ended the sabbatical program, and moved in retired priests who weren't as friendly as their predecessors. But Skye was too busy now for weekend hikes anyway. And with her father dead, she didn't enjoy the wilderness as she once had.

Skye let the criminalists do their job as she surveyed the scene. So much violence in such a small room—it was as if the imprint of what happened last night would forever taint this hall. The altar drew her eye. She wasn't Catholic, she didn't care much for any religion, but it was obvious something sacrilegious had occurred.

The huge stone crucifix had been turned upside down. It must weigh hundreds of pounds, in addition to the deceptively simple six-foot solid-wood carving of the crucified Christ. Blood coated the crown of thorns on Christ's head, whether spatter from the killings or put there on purpose Skye wouldn't know until the crime scene team finished their work.

One of the dead lay on the raised altar; the remaining victims were scattered around the room, on the floor or in the pews. Not all bodies were intact.

There was good news, bad news. The good news was that they had the prime suspect in custody, along with the man who had discovered the bodies. The bad news was the suspect was allegedly in a coma. She'd believe it when she had a second opinion.

"I thought de Los Padres was for retired priests," Martinez said as he looked around. Many of the dead were too young for retirement.

"That's what the diocese has said, but they've been pretty hush-hush about this place for the last couple years," Skye said. "They did some major renovation five years ago, but I haven't been here for more than a decade." She forced herself to look at the faces of the victims. Their frozen expressions of terror gave her additional motivation to find the killers.

"The crime scene has been compromised." Head of the small county CSU Rod Fielding carefully approached, his face grim, stating what they already knew. "The guy who brought Mr. Cooper to the hospital didn't take any care about stepping in blood or disturbing evidence. I need his prints, his shoes, and a statement. What he touched, why, the whole nine yards."

"I sent a deputy to the hospital to hold Mr. Zaccardi until I get over there to interview him." Skye stared at the crime scene. "I don't expect it'll be anytime soon."

"Sooner than you think."

Skye whipped around and saw a tall, broad-shouldered man with dried blood on his white tailored button-down shirt. His naturally tan face was as hard as the stone walls that framed the mission, but his eyes were as deep and rich as dark chocolate. He looked like a pirate, not only out of his country but completely out of his element. His commanding presence caused everyone to pause a beat.

Anthony Zaccardi, no doubt.

"You're in the middle of my crime scene," she said.

Zaccardi stared at her with haunted eyes, his black hair falling to his shoulders. He wore a small dark stud in his left ear and bore a three-inch scar on the side of his neck along the edge of his collar. He was physically fit and muscular, more than capable of killing. But twelve men without a scratch? Doubtful. Besides, she had already verified his itinerary and the timeline wouldn't have worked, otherwise he'd be in lockup.

Chances were he had nothing to do with these murders. But *she* wasn't going to assume anything.

"I want my cross back."

She frowned. "What's he talking about?"

Tommy Reiner, the cop she'd sent to sit on Zaccardi, stepped into the room. He paled at the sight and scent of death. "He wanted to talk to you."

"I told you to keep him at the hospital."

Zaccardi repeated, "I want my cross."

Just what she needed, a lawsuit that she was denying Catholics their right to worship the way they saw fit.

"Uh—" Tommy hesitated.

"Give it back to him."

"It appeared to be a weapon."

"For shit's sake," she muttered. She motioned for them

to leave the chapel, then turned to Rod. "You need me, I'm outside."

"I have enough to keep me busy," he said. "But when you're done with Zaccardi, I'd like him to walk me through his exact steps."

She ushered everyone out of the chapel and into the courtyard. "This is a crime scene. I—"

"You need to know what I touched when I arrived, where I went. I understand. I need my cross, Sheriff."

Zaccardi spoke with a subtly luxurious European accent. He looked Italian, dressed well, and had an aura about him that suggested he always got what he wanted, when he wanted.

Reiner said, "It's a knife, Skye. I swear."

She snapped her fingers. "Let me see it."

The cop left through the main courtyard entrance. They'd cut the lock on the gate when they entered. With one survivor at the hospital, they had to assume going in that there were other survivors, regardless of what Mr. Zaccardi had said over the phone.

There weren't.

"So you weren't lying when you told my deputy you just flew in from Italy."

"I don't lie."

Everyone lied, but she refrained from saying so. "What are you doing so far from home?"

"Rafe asked me to come. He was concerned about something happening here. He felt something—" He paused.

"Something what?"

"He said something evil had slithered inside."

She raised her eyebrow. "Were those his exact words?"

"Yes."

"And you dropped everything and flew halfway across the world?"

"Yes."

"Why?"

"Rafe wouldn't ask for help if he didn't need it."

"Help?"

"Yes."

"What kind of help."

"I told you. Something—"

She waved her hand dismissively. "Something evil, right."

"What kind of evil?"

Skye had almost forgotten her detective, Juan Martinez, had followed them out of the chapel, until he asked the question. A few years older than she was, Juan had been one of her few close friends in the department since she became a cop eleven years ago.

"The kind of evil I understand."

"For a man who doesn't lie, you're being awfully evasive," Skye snapped.

His jaw tightened. "I'm a demonologist."

That was the last thing she expected to hear. She glanced at Martinez, who was nodding. "You study demons," he said, as if it were in the same career category as brain surgery.

"Among other things." Zaccardi stared at the chapel doors. "I was here five years ago. It had been safe." His voice trailed off.

"And now? You're saying *demons* killed those men?"

Skye snorted. "Please. We're looking for the men who helped your *friend* butcher those priests."

Zaccardi stepped toward her, aggressive. She put her hand on the butt of her gun, but he didn't so much as blink. "Rafe did not kill those men. He didn't have any part in it."

"When was the last time you saw him?"

"That doesn't matter—"

"All I'm saying is we don't always know our friends, especially those we don't see all the time." *And sometimes we don't even know our own family.* Skye steeled herself against her memories.

Zaccardi shook his head. "Rafe and I might as well be brothers. I know his heart. He knows mine. We were raised together, studied together in Europe."

"When?"

"Until he moved to America ten years ago."

"And you haven't seen him since," Skye said flatly.

"No."

Deputy Reiner came back with an evidence bag. Inside was a knife in the shape of a cross. *Dagger* would be a more descriptive word.

"*This* is your cross?" Skye took the bag from Tommy. "How'd you get this on the plane?"

"I checked my baggage. It *is* a cross."

"Right." This guy was getting weirder and weirder. But he didn't seem dangerous. Not physically dangerous, at any rate. His alibi had checked out. Between the time his flight landed in San Francisco and the four-hour drive to the mission, he couldn't have killed the priests. She handed him the bag.

Surprise lit his face. He retrieved the cross and slid it into a loop on his belt. For a moment he looked just like the pirate Skye had envisioned earlier, the dagger-cross his sword, a breeze lifting his hair, the morning sun chiseling his face.

Rod stepped into the courtyard. "Skye, you have to see this." He stared at Zaccardi. "You should come, too."

Skye didn't want to discipline Rod in front of the other cops, but he didn't have authority to bring civilians into the crime scene, even though he'd been working the job almost as long as she'd been alive.

"Do you really think demons did this?" Martinez asked Zaccardi without derision.

"Yes," Zaccardi responded. "I know they did."

"I don't know about demons," Rod said, "but something weird is going on, and if the press gets hold of this, PR will be hell."

Anthony walked through the carnage, trying to push aside the silent screams for salvation. He didn't have answers, and the panic in the pleas told him the dead knew their fate.

Did none of these cops see the evil around them? Didn't the presence of darkness terrify them as it tried to overtake their souls?

For his entire life, he'd heard the cries of the dead and cackle of evil. If it hadn't been for the wise men at St. Michael's on a small island off Sicily, he would have gone insane. He'd learned to control it, to let them inside in small doses, in order to help the dead as well as preserve his own sanity. But here, with so much evil and pain in one place, his head ached with the struggle to keep the agony of the lost souls at bay.

They entered the small, narrow sacristy on the far side of the altar, the room where the priests stored chalices, vestments, unconsecrated hosts, sacramental wine. The destruction was complete, broken glass everywhere and the scent of sweet wine.

An odd drawing was painted in red—probably blood—on the stone wall. It was the seal of a demon, but Anthony didn't recognize the crest. Four circles, one within the other, evenly spaced. Inside the first ring was a phrase written in ancient Latin. The second ring held three symbols Anthony recognized as traditional demonic marks—an upside-down cross at the top, a common symbol of the devil that has been around for thousands of years; a seven-point triangle in the lower right; and an upside-down hook in the lower left with a triangle at the top and an oval circling the bottom curve.

The third ring had markings he would need to analyze, but they appeared to be a numeric code of some sort. Some who practiced demonolatry used numerology as part of their rituals.

But the inner circle held three filled ovals that formed a fat triangle, a mark he'd never seen but filled him with an unexplainable primal fear. The image reminded him of soulless eyes, of which he had seen far too many.

Rod said, "It looks almost like hieroglyphics, but not exactly. Too much detail. The words are Latin."

" 'Summon the fires to serve in death; relinquish the soul to serve your lord; walk in the willing dead,' " Anthony translated.

"What the hell does that mean?" Skye demanded.

"I'm not sure, but it's part of a ritual."

"A satanic ritual?" she questioned, disbelieving.

"This isn't the mark of Satan."

"Well?" she prompted when he didn't continue.

"This is the seal of a demon. It's used as part of the ritual to bring a specific demon from Hell." He gestured at the crude painting.

"Demons, Satan, does it really matter? I mean, we're dealing with a bunch of violent psychos anyway."

"It matters," Anthony said. *Walk in the willing dead.* He'd never heard that phrase before. Fire was a common element to call upon, particularly when dealing with demons. To serve Satan, one had to relinquish their soul to the fires of Hell. But the willing dead? Physical death or spiritual death?

"And who is he?" Skye asked.

If he were in Italy or in some other countries, Anthony could explain in far greater detail what they were dealing with. Believers would be appeased with his explanation that someone had brought forth evil and until they knew *what* evil they faced they'd never be able to send it back. But here in America? This pretty blond cop with intelligent, sad eyes? Her entire demeanor said she wouldn't believe anything he had to say.

"I don't know," he finally said. He didn't know which demon had been called, a first for him. All those years of study, and he was at an impasse.

"Great." She rolled her eyes. "So we're dealing with some satanic cult," she said, obviously not listening to—or believing—Anthony. "You're right, Rod, the press *is* going to have a field day."

"You think we have a wacko group running around

performing satanic rituals and killing people?" Rod asked. "The crime seems too—disordered."

"Very Charles Manson-ish," Skye said with a smirk.

Anthony said, "You don't know what you're up against. These aren't satanists, and they're not disorganized. This is pure demonolatry. Someone called this spirit up and helped it kill those men. This seal is—how would you say it?—like his signature. He's gloating over death."

Skye rubbed her temple. Anthony resisted the anger that rose because of her disdain. He'd faced ridicule many times before, and he knew whatever spirit had been unleashed would feed on his anger, fear, and insecurity.

"So you think a demon killed those priests? And your friend just happened to survive the slaughter?"

Anthony chose his words carefully. "I think that a person brought forth the demon and used the power of Hell to kill those men. How, I don't know. Why Rafe was spared, I don't know. But I can tell you that *it*"—he pointed to the circle on the wall—"is still here. And more people will die if I can't find him and send him back to Hell."

Skye sighed and rubbed her eyes. "Let's get out of here."

Anthony didn't move. He took out his wallet, extracted a business card, and began to re-create the seal of the demon on the blank side. Anthony needed to find out exactly who—and what—he was up against. Maybe there was a chance to save those souls. *The willing dead.*

These men hadn't been willing. The demon would be looking for someone who was. One of those who summoned him? Did they know what the demon would demand of them?

"Look, Mr. Zaccardi," Skye said, sympathy crossing her face. "You've been through a lot today. I'm sorry about your friends, but I'm asking you to leave the crime scene. I'll be in contact later."

He finished the sketch and wrote down the Latin phrase. "You do not know what you are up against," he repeated.

"Yes I do. I'm up against a group of brutal cowards who killed twelve unarmed men."

"You are up against those who worship *him*." He stabbed his pencil at the drawing. "It is *his* strength that slaughtered those men. The people who called him—and there had to have been more than one—are tools. They may be frail old women or strong teenage boys. It doesn't matter, after bringing forth this demon they have the power of Hell on their side."

Anthony must sound crazy to the sheriff. The more she tried to dismiss what he knew to be true, the angrier he became. He had to control his temper. Not only to be able to work with this cop, but to prevent the spirits from using his temper against him.

"Sheriff," he said quietly but firmly. "You don't believe me. But you must. We don't have time for doubts."

"Please leave."

"You wanted me to tell you if anything was missing."

"Do you know where the written records are kept?"

"In the caretaker's office."

"I'll let you know if anything has been stolen," she said.

He stared at her, her green eyes never leaving his, her mouth firm, her posture rigid. She wore her long blond hair back, in a complicated French braid. But the tight hairstyle didn't diminish the femininity of the tall, athletic woman. Skye was attractive, but deliberately downplayed her assets. To be seen as a leader first, a woman second.

The men around her were watching the situation closely. This was her turf, her pride at stake. There would be another time, soon, to reason with her. When they were alone, maybe she would let her guard down, soften her heart to the reality she denied.

"We'll talk later." He pocketed the drawing and left.

Skye watched Zaccardi leave, nodded to Martinez to follow him out. She turned and stared at the hideous drawing, the eyes inside the circle seeming to look right at her. Watching her.

*Demons.*

Ridiculous. "Don't listen to him," she said to Rod. "The guy's a whack job."

Rod didn't say anything.

"What? Man of science believes in demons?"

Rod put away his equipment and stared at her. "Skye, I'm fifty-two years old. I've been a crime scene analyst in New York City, Chicago, and Los Angeles. I came here because Santa Louisa was supposed to be one of the safest places to live.

"I'm telling you, in my thirty years of law enforcement, I have never seen anything like this. I'm not a religious man, but I believe in God. And if God exists, why not demons? I just can't wrap my mind around this crime scene. It makes no sense. No one tried to leave the chapel. The killers should have been drenched in blood, but not one drop was found outside this room, except for what Mr. Zaccardi tracked out when he saved his friend. If we are to believe Zaccardi that he broke down the kitchen door, which was bolted from the inside, that means that the only two entrances to the mission were *locked by someone inside.*"

"Which means Rafe Cooper is our only suspect."

"Where are the weapons? We have searched everywhere and there are none. As far as I can see, at least four different weapons were used, all blades. Yet there is not one knife in this room, and certainly nothing that can decapitate a man."

Skye opened her mouth, closed it. She had no answer.

She walked out of the sacristy and saw Anthony Zaccardi standing next to the altar. "Reiner! Escort Mr. Zaccardi back to his car."

What the hell was he doing standing like that? What was he looking at?

He turned to her with a strained expression. "The tabernacle. It's missing."

Juan stood next to her and pointed. "It's right there."

Skye stared at a small, simple antique metal box with gold mesh wire for sides.

Zaccardi shook his head. "That's not the tabernacle I installed five years ago. Now I know exactly how the demon got in."

# Chapter Two

ANTHONY CLOSED HIS CELL PHONE and stared at the fountain in the mission courtyard. He'd called the only person who might know which demon had been summoned, the only person who knew more about demons than he did.

And if Father Philip didn't know, they were in mortal danger.

He'd stepped out of the chapel as soon as he realized the tabernacle had been replaced. Without the ancient protection against evil, these men had been in jeopardy from the moment the tabernacle had been switched. For how long? Was this a slow-working insidious evil, or a sudden awakening? Anthony had specifically asked about the tabernacle, and Rafe hadn't seemed worried. Had it been switched before he arrived last month? Or more recently? The fake looked nearly identical to the original. Only someone with Anthony's expertise would be able to tell the difference.

How long had the demon been tormenting these men?

A silent cloak of frightened whispers wrapped around the former sanctuary, suffocating the mission. The vicious imprint of what had happened inside these walls could never be cleansed.

*Help us help us help us.*

The chant wrapped around him, invisible tentacles reaching for his soul, the pleas growing in urgency as a sharp sliver of icy fear rolled down his spine and his heartbeat doubled. Sweat broke out on his brow and he leaned forward, putting both hands on the fountain, the trickle of water soothing. Breathing deeply, eyes closed, he forced his heart rate to slow and regained his internal composure. He needed all his energy focused on learning who and what was responsible for these murders.

He opened his eyes. Blood poured from the statue of Saint Jude. He gasped, blinked, and the blood was gone.

*Help us help us help me.*

The keening of trapped souls, the souls of the men being carted out of the chapel in black plastic body bags, surrounded Anthony, deafening in their persistence. He'd heard the cries of the dead before, had saved countless souls before they were forever lost. But never like this, never this strong. Never this lost.

"What's wrong?"

He turned and faced Sheriff Skye McPherson.

Needful, he soaked in her raw beauty to clear his mind of all he'd seen. She did everything possible to diminish her sensuality, but nothing could destroy what lay beneath. Her creamy, clear skin. Her sharp, intelligent green eyes. Her full, red, unpainted lips. Makeup would only have destroyed what nature had created to be pleasing to a man.

Anthony desperately needed hope. Skye's presence strengthened him. It was as if she'd been conjured from his dreams. As if he'd seen her before. As if he was *meant* to be at her side, helping her. Watching her. Protecting her.

He turned from her, unsettled by the thought that there might be a bond with a woman he did not know, a woman who doubted him and everything he believed in.

He touched the statue, water—not blood—flowing over his hand. Certainly his mind was clouded and troubled by what had happened here. The bond with Sheriff Skye McPherson was only through death.

"Saint Jude," he murmured, "the patron saint of desperate causes. The men inside were desperate, Sheriff. Desperate because of what they had lived through. I put this statue here, personally selected and retrieved it from a monastery in France that had given sanctuary to other desperate people. Jews escaping the Holocaust. Desperation and hope. Without hope, we have nothing."

Uncertainty flashed in her eyes, then the steady face of the cop he'd first met returned. She wouldn't understand, she hadn't believed him even when faced with the violence inside; why did he even try to explain?

Because of *hope*. He sensed the hope and goodness within Skye McPherson as strongly as he felt the evil that permeated the formerly hallowed grounds of Santa Louisa de Los Padres.

"All I *feel*," she said, "is that someone—most likely several someones—slaughtered twelve people. Considering they were priests and this is a place of worship, it is being looked at as a possible hate crime."

Anthony almost laughed, pulled his hand from the water and crossed himself. A faint scream from the trees taunted him. Skye didn't hear it.

"Hate crime?" he repeated. "All violence comes from hate."

She glanced at the doors of the chapel where another body bag was being removed, then looked at him. It was obvious to Anthony she had grave questions for him.

"Did you remove anything from the crime scene?" she finally asked.

"Other than Rafe, no. Why?"

She didn't answer, then suddenly it became clear. He pictured the destruction he'd walked into at dawn.

"There are no weapons."

"Someone removed them. And if you were telling the truth about breaking into the kitchen—"

"I was."

"Then they are in here, someplace."

"The killer left. He could have taken them."

"You said a *demon* killed these men." She couldn't keep the derision from her voice.

He sighed, ran a hand through his hair. *Patience, Anthony.* "Demons don't act on their own. They need human intervention. They need someone to bring them forth. Once here, they have more power, but in the netherworld, their power is only that which they are given by Satan himself. This is why demonolatry is so dangerous. It is *humans* who are giving these demons power, enabling them to walk on earth stealing souls.

"Yes, a demon was responsible, but only with the help of people."

"Then how did the *human being* leave a locked mission?"

"You're the cop, you figure it out!" Anthony turned away from Skye, angry with himself for his temper. He couldn't allow himself to fall. He leaned into the fountain, put his hands in the water, seeking peace.

*Help us help us help us*

"You told my deputy that the mission was locked when you arrived."

"Yes. The gate here"—he motioned to the courtyard fence—"had a padlock. I have a key to the mission, and went through to the kitchen door because it was closest. But the door was bolted from the inside. I broke in."

*It had been like an invisible hand, dark and twisted, holding him back. The sensation of evil slithering across his skin. Malevolence hung thick in the air, whipped his tongue, and he knew he was too late.*

"The lights were out."

"It was five in the morning," Skye said, as if his comment were ridiculous.

"For some of these men, dark is as much an enemy as Satan himself. The wall sconces are always on, and in the event of a power outage, the mission has a generator."

He saw Skye scribble a note. Of course, a sabotaged generator was tangible, something she could investigate. But who would know these men feared the night?

*Anthony held the crucifix—dagger point out—in front of him as he ran down the hall toward the smell of death.*

"I smelled fresh blood. The chapel doors were closed."

*Resisting the urge to call out, he pushed open the solid wood doors and stepped into the house of worship. A rush of burning heat came at him, then the temperature dropped and he saw his own breath.*

Anthony couldn't tell this cop about the demon he felt vacating the chapel. She wouldn't believe him.

"I checked for survivors, but it was clear they were butchered. I was too late."

*Eerily beautiful, the early morning sun filtered through the tall, narrow stained-glass windows bathing the dead in colorful rays of light. Body upon body filled the narrow chapel. Some decapitated, some without limbs, all murdered.*

*The crucifix hung upside down. It was a sign of demons, of Satanists, but this cross weighed too much for even a large group of men to invert and rehang. It had been carved from granite in Mexico and brought to the mission when it was first built in 1767.*

"I began looking among the dead for Rafe, giving blessings as I went."

*"What spirits tortured you?" Anthony whispered to the dead. Where was Rafe? He carefully crossed the floor, checking the pulse of the men he passed. All dead. As he neared the altar, he saw his friend.*

"I found Rafe behind the altar."

*He lay facedown, white T-shirt covered in blood. Anthony squeezed back tears of anger, regret, and deep sadness as he knelt beside Rafe and turned him over. Anthony wasn't a priest, but at this point he doubted God would care who gave last rites. The crying for help intensified as Anthony began the prayer.*

"After I turned him over, I saw that he was breathing. His pulse was strong and I ripped open his shirt to find the wound that had caused all the blood, but there was nothing. No visible injuries. I couldn't wake him, so I carried him out."

*The trapped souls of the dead priests cried out to him.*

*Maybe they hadn't been dragged down to Hell. Maybe they were in between worlds, like ghosts, waiting for help. Waiting for him.*

*First, save Rafe. Then he could return to save the dead.*

"I called 911 as soon as I started down the mountain."

"We have the call logged at 5:32 A.M. You told my deputy you arrived at the mission about twenty minutes before that."

He nodded, rubbing his temples as the whispers continued, scratching at his subconscious. "Skye," he said quietly, not looking at her, calling on the person, the *woman*, not the sheriff.

"Yes?"

"Do you know of doubting Thomas?"

"Vaguely."

"He had to see Jesus to believe. He had to touch His wounds to believe in the Resurrection."

Anthony turned, stronger now, faced the woman whom he needed in order to save these men. He could stop the demon, but it would be her investigation that led him to those humans responsible for calling on Hell. To the ritual that maybe, with luck, strength, and faith, he could reverse.

He reached out, touched her soft skin. "I am asking for faith from a doubting Thomas. But I am still asking."

Skye stared at Anthony Zaccardi, the dark pirate, because that was most certainly what this man was. She should be laughing in his face—demons and Hell? Ridiculous. Her own mother had left to seek God and look what happened to her. Their entire family had been torn apart. Skye didn't need religion or belief in anything she couldn't see when she had cold, hard facts that didn't lie.

But she couldn't laugh at this man whose middle name could be *Serious*. His expression when he recounted finding the dead priests would stay with her for a long time. So full of pain and agony, as if he felt what they'd gone through. Zaccardi believed everything he told her, of that she was positive, and she couldn't figure out how he had anything to do with the murders.

But the investigation was still young and she refused to let her feelings cloud the facts.

"I am a cop," she finally said, her voice a mere whisper. "I want the people who did this. Demons or not, *someone* was responsible for killing these men and I will find them."

Skye turned from Anthony Zaccardi's eyes, so piercing it was as if he could read her mind. She didn't like that, not one little bit.

She surveyed the courtyard. Two wings extended on either side, leading toward the main entrance, with the traditional rounded arches of California missions. Entirely surrounded by the Los Padres National Forest, Santa Louisa had been built by a reclusive sect of the Franciscans and dubbed the "lost mission" because it wasn't easily accessible from the Mission Trail that started in San Diego and ended in San Francisco.

The courtyard was beautiful in its simplicity. Six arches on both sides framed the buildings. Brick walkways. And roses, everywhere roses. The fountain in the center was designed as a natural rock waterfall, water trickling over gray and brown stones that looked so precariously balanced that Skye was surprised they didn't topple over.

*Saint Jude*, Zaccardi had said. Patron saint of lost

causes. She was certainly a lost cause. But one thing she *was* good at, thrived in, was being a cop. And her instincts told her that God or no God, a man was responsible for these deaths.

"I'll need your passport, Mr. Zaccardi," she said, regretting her decision when a cloud of disbelief crossed his face, but knowing a good cop would insist that Zaccardi not be able to leave the country. He reached into his back pocket and handed her the documents.

"I'm sorry," she found herself saying.

"You're just doing your job," he finished for her.

"Where are you staying?"

"I don't know."

"The Coastal Inn outside town is a nice place. I know the owners. Tell them I sent you, they'll give you a good rate."

He looked over her shoulder. What did he see? All she saw was a simple stone building. His troubled eyes told her he saw something more. She wanted to ask, but bit her tongue. She couldn't, wouldn't, be sucked into his fantasy. Or hers.

Detective Juan Martinez stepped out of the chapel, waved her over.

"I'll keep in touch," she said to Zaccardi.

A chill wind swept through the courtyard as he turned and left, as if he'd summoned the elements himself.

Or they came in his wake.


Trapped himself without a human body, the ancient demon imprisoned the twelve souls that fought for the Light, but didn't have the strength to bring each soul back to his Master.

He had failed. Black pain twisted his noncorporeal mind as he hovered in the mountains, invisible to those who did not know what he looked like, how he smelled, how he felt, in his true form.

He had never faced Zaccardi, but the human was known to all in Hades. Zaccardi was a relic from the past, relishing the destruction of that which ensured balance on earth.

If the Master of Heaven hadn't wanted them to exist, He would have extinguished Satan and the rest of them during the Great Battle. But it was a game. How many souls could they win over? How many would serve the Dark Lord? The more they won, the hotter Hell burned, the more of his kind walked the earth.

But Zaccardi was among those pathetic humans who wanted a piece of the pie. As if destroying demons would grant him a larger room in Paradise. Because of Zaccardi and his powerful friend, he'd failed. He hadn't been able to keep Zaccardi at bay and Cooper trapped at the same time he manipulated death. And in that sliver of time, the soul he'd been promised got away from him.

He burned at the unfairness of it!

Losing the body chosen for him greatly irritated the demon. That which was lost would have given him more power than he'd ever had. He'd have ruled on earth forever! He would have opened new portals for his Master, converted more humans to dark service. They would be a potent force, undefeatable. No angel would be able to destroy them. No human would be able to fight them. They'd have the numbers and strength to come and go at will among the pitiable human bodies.

What a travesty that he needed such a weak vessel to survive in this dimension!

With the remaining strength from the ritual that had brought him from Hell, he'd be able to keep the souls trapped until he could complete his mission and send them to the fiery pit. He needed another body, which his earthly servants would soon provide.

He could survive in an unwilling body, but the constant battle to restrain a fighting soul would prevent him from attaining his highest power. Sooner or later, he would need a willing human to increase his strength.

The dead around him moaned with dread of their fate.

*No one can save you. You were betrayed by one you loved, and you're mine for eternity.*

The demon laughed, and waited, and the trees of the forest groaned.

# CHAPTER THREE

SKYE LISTENED TO DETECTIVE JUAN MARTINEZ as she drove from the mission back to town.

"While you were talking to Zaccardi in the courtyard, I spoke to the delivery boy," Juan said, glancing briefly at his notes. "Brian Adamson. He delivers every Monday morning between nine and noon."

"Did he have anything to add?"

"He confirmed what Zaccardi said about Cooper being a recent transplant. Came here a month ago. The interesting thing is that Cooper recently fired the housekeeper, a Ms. Corrine Davies."

"Do you have an address?"

"Ten Seaview Lane. North of town."

"Let's go pay her a visit."

Juan flipped through his notes and said to Skye, "According to the property manager, Corinne Davies and her daughter, Lisa, moved into the house nearly two years ago when the mother took a job as cook and housekeeper at the mission. They've never been late on the rent, no complaints, not even a call for repairs. Ideal tenants."

"How old is the daughter?"

"Twenty. A college student."

"Background?"

"No warrants, no arrests. I have Ms. Davies's credit application. A widow, her last address was in Salem, Oregon, where she worked for the Catholic diocese. Her references included the bishop."

"Who hired her in Santa Louisa?"

"Bishop Carlin."

Martinez had spoken with the bishop earlier in the day to inform him of the murders and ask questions about Rafe Cooper. Skye had met the bishop only once before, when he presided over the funeral for one of her deputies. She was more comfortable with Juan handling the religious contacts. She didn't need religion, didn't understand people who sacrificed everything for something they couldn't see. People who abandoned their family, their homes, everything, for a promise only good when you were dead.

Skye pushed that all from her mind. Already, this case was eating at her and memories of her mother threatened to return. She was as done with her mother as the last criminal she'd locked behind bars.

"Why is Cooper here?" she asked.

"Raphael 'Rafe' Cooper is a seminary student up in Menlo Park," Martinez said. "The bishop doesn't have any personal information on him."

"How does he just move to the mission without the diocese knowing his history? Isn't there some sort of background check, employment verification, anything? I need Cooper's background, ASAP. But what I really want to know is, why is he *here*?"

"Bishop Carlin didn't know. The mission, though technically part of the diocese, isn't under his control."

"So who controls it?"

"The Vatican."

"As in Vatican, do you mean like the Pope and the Catholic Church Vatican?"

"Apparently. Someone in Rome, Francis Cardinal De-Lucca, sent the bishop an introductory letter a month ago stating that Cooper was being sent to evaluate the priests for service. Cooper is a psychologist, perhaps he was giving them a mental health update, I don't know."

"And?"

"And that's it. That's all he knew."

Switching gears, she asked, "Why did the diocese fire the housekeeper?"

"They didn't. Cooper did. Ms. Davies is still on the payroll," Martinez said. "Bishop Carlin told her to take a couple weeks and he'd find her a different position. He seemed angry with Cooper for firing her without consulting him."

"Maybe I should talk to the bishop."

"Are you questioning my investigative abilities?"

Skye bristled at the accusation in Martinez's voice. "No, and you shouldn't think that I would. But you're Catholic, you have respect for the office, maybe you didn't ask the right questions."

"I asked the right questions."

Skye changed the subject as she turned off the highway. "Do you know why Davies left Salem?"

"No, but her daughter is a student at UC Santa Barbara."

"She's commuting an hour to college?"

"We do what we can when we're broke," Martinez said with a half grin.

"Let's go."

The coastal cottage on Seaview Lane had an exquisite view of the ocean, almost identical to Skye's own property three miles down the shoreline. The cottage rested on a bluff with a sheer drop to the Pacific Ocean beyond.

Skye surveyed the rental house. Small, neat, functional. The perfect place for a recluse or lovers, separated from nearby homes by nature. Craggy, wind-sculpted cypress trees lined the property, and with the smell of salt water and sound of crashing waves below, the entire setting was picturesque.

She opened the door of her police-issue Bronco and they walked up the cobblestone path to the porch. The cottage looked well lived in with lots of plants, herbs, and flowers growing in pots resting on every available inch. Skye rapped on the door.

A moment later a young woman answered. She had long dark hair and large pale brown eyes. To say she was beautiful would be an understatement.

"May I help you?"

"Sheriff Skye McPherson and Detective Juan Martinez," Skye said. "We'd like to speak with Corinne Davies, if she's home."

"My mom is on vacation. Is something wrong?"

Lisa Davies would hear it from the press, so Skye said, "There's been a multiple homicide at the mission."

The girl's eyes clouded with tears and her delicate hand went to her mouth. "What happened?"

"I can't say, but we'd like to speak to your mother about

anything she may have witnessed or heard during her time working there."

Lisa shook her head. "Mom was so upset after—I hate to speak ill of the dead, but Mr. Cooper was a vile human being. He hurt my mother cruelly, fired her for no reason. She's at a health spa, trying to accept what happened and look for another job . . . " Her voice cracked. "She knows I love going to college here and she's trying to find something local."

"Where can we reach your mother?" Skye asked.

"I don't want to trouble her. She'll be heartbroken."

"I need you to trouble her. This is important."

Lisa relented. "I'll call her. I'm sure she'll come home immediately."

"Please have her call us as soon as she returns." Skye handed Lisa Davies her business card. "Did you frequent the mission?"

"I went up there a few times."

"And what was your impression of the men who lived there?"

"Harmless," she said. "Nice, I guess. I really didn't talk much to them."

"Did you meet Rafe Cooper?"

She hesitated, and Skye suspected she was about to lie. "Once."

"Did you have an impression?"

"He seemed mightier-than-thou. I'm sure my feelings are clouded by what happened to my mother. He fired her. For no reason."

"Please have your mother contact us as soon as possible," Skye said and led the way back to her Bronco.

"What are you thinking?" Martinez asked.

"There was so much wrong with that conversation I don't know where to start."

"She assumed Rafe Cooper was dead."

"Exactly. And she didn't ask who else had been killed, if we'd caught the suspects, nor did she seem fearful of her mother's life." Skye paused as they climbed into the truck. "You said the bishop kept Corinne Davies on the payroll. Why did her daughter think she'd been fired and needed to find a job?"

"Perhaps the bishop is keeping her on payroll until she finds something," Martinez suggested.

"Hmm."

"You think she was involved?" Martinez asked.

"I'm not making any assumptions at this point, but I can hardly wait to speak to Corinne Davies. I'd like you to do a deeper background check on mother and daughter."

Skye turned the ignition. "Let's go check in with Rafe Cooper's doctor."

# CHAPTER FOUR

ANTHONY SAT AT RAFE's bedside, praying over him, concentrating so hard that he was oblivious to everything else, trying to figure out what had happened.

If only it were that simple. If only he'd been blessed with second sight, like some of the others. If only he could reach into Rafe's mind and see what had happened . . .

He admonished himself for his futile plea. As Father Philip often said, accept the gifts you have and don't covet the gifts of others.

As a young child, he had found it difficult to understand what advantages he would have in the ongoing war. He'd been sheltered by the monks because of his strong empathic ability. He sensed good and evil in both people and things. When he was young, overwhelming waves of negative emotion nearly destroyed him; it was only with age and training that he learned to control his senses.

Now, his ability served him well as a demonologist. And sitting here, at Rafe's side, he knew there were no demons inside him, nothing evil that kept him comatose. Only emptiness, a void, as if Rafe were already dead.

"What happened in there, Rafe?" he whispered.

Perhaps the coma was Rafe's way of dealing with the

tragedy. Where had he been during the slaughter? Had he witnessed it? Had he listened to it? Had he been somehow trapped by the demon? Why had he been spared? What had caused him to collapse at the altar?

So many questions, and Anthony had no answers, and likely wouldn't until Rafe woke up.

Anthony was six when he first met Rafe. He'd instantly bonded with the child who radiated goodness.

But there had always been questions. Rafe was older than most, abandoned at the monastery at the age of three instead of infancy. He'd been dying until Father Philip laid hands on him. He had scars no one could explain, as if he'd survived a brutal battle, though he was still a toddler.

By the time the boys of St. Michael's reached puberty, their gifts had been revealed. Demon hunter, psychic, healer, among others. For Anthony, it was his recognition of good and evil, his empathy, his ability to purge demons from inanimate objects like buildings. But as for Rafe—his gift was still unknown. At the age of twenty-one Rafe had decided to serve as a priest. He'd been sent to America because Father Philip sensed it was right. Yet ten years later, Rafe had still not received the Sacrament of Holy Orders. It was as if God Himself was pushing him in another direction, Rafe had told Anthony on more than one occasion.

*"I go through the ceremony and I can't say the words. Something holds my tongue."*

"Why didn't you call me sooner, Rafe?" Anthony whispered. "I would have dropped the world for you, my friend."

Anthony reached for Rafe's hand and stared. His right

hand was in a cast, his left bandaged. He pulled Rafe's chart from the end of the bed and read.

Three broken fingers on his right hand and a shattered wrist. Fingernails on six fingers half torn. Wood slivers embedded in the tips, down to the bone.

There had been so much blood at the chapel Anthony hadn't noticed Rafe's hands had been so damaged. Slivers of wood? Had he been trapped somewhere during the massacre? How? Who? The demon?

"I must go to the mission tonight," Anthony whispered. "I need to find out what happened to you."

He would search not only for answers to what had happened to Rafe, but for some way to free the souls still trapped.

"I'm going to try," he said aloud. How could he not? How could he do nothing? Evil would triumph, the demon would grow stronger, Hell would burn hotter.

Anthony sensed that he stood on the edge of something big. Hell churned, working overtime. They, the fallen ones, would be coming in waves. As more human beings worshipped the darkness, more demons would rise to the surface. This, the slaughter at the mission, was the beginning of a battle that Anthony feared would last until end times.

He took out his holy water and prayer book. He blessed Rafe, then surrounded his friend with a powerful protection against Hell. Rafe was at his weakest now; Anthony refused to let Satan claim him.

Martinez was silent on the drive to the diocese's main office.

"What?" Skye finally said.

"Have you considered that maybe Mr. Zaccardi is right?"

Skye rolled her eyes. "I should *never* have told you what he said."

Martinez's light brown face tensed. "Are we partners on this case, or are you pulling rank, *Sheriff*?" he asked.

"What's that supposed to mean? You're the best detective on the squad."

"If you want me to do my job, you need to listen to me."

"I always listen to you." Skye was hurt that Juan thought she was pulling rank. "I value your opinion."

"Then take it," he said. "I think you should listen to what Mr. Zaccardi has to say."

"That *demons* killed those priests? Come on, Juan. You're not so damn superstitious to think that something not even human could slaughter those men!"

"And I didn't think you were so closed-minded that you couldn't see the possibilities."

"Please."

"You're letting your mother stop you from seeing the truth."

Skye fumed. "Don't talk about my mother. She's dead, if you haven't forgotten. And if anything, her murder should tell you that those people are all a bunch of freaks."

Juan's jaw tightened. "Is that how you think of me? A freak?"

"That's not what I meant—" It had come out all wrong. But isn't that what those people did? Promise the world as long as you give up everything you know and love? If her mother had never left, her father would never have been out in the woods that night; he wouldn't have died and left her alone.

Juan didn't say anything. She was angry with herself

for hurting him, and angry with him for being so easily swayed. *Demons.* Right.

"Dammit." She resisted the urge to pound her head against the steering wheel.

"Look, you know that one man could not have done that. Not all those priests were old. They would have fought back. Rafe Cooper has no marks on him whatsoever. No defensive wounds. No offensive wounds. His hands are bruised and scraped and Rod thinks it's from pounding on his bedroom door. The blood from the door matches Cooper's blood type."

After Zaccardi left the mission, Rod had discovered evidence in Rafe Cooper's room that suggested he'd been trapped inside. But there were no locks on the door and no plausible way he could have been locked in.

"What do you think happened?" Skye finally asked.

"I don't know. But I think you need to look at all possibilities."

She didn't want to hurt Juan—he was one of her few friends in the Sheriff's Department. But what he was saying was ludicrous. "Okay, here are the facts. Twelve men between the ages of thirty-six and eighty-one were murdered in cold blood. Rafe Cooper was unharmed. A thirty-one-year-old man, healthy, strong, unconscious for no reason?"

"Maybe he walked in on the scene after the fact, collapsed from the stress. Especially if someone had locked him in and he heard what was happening."

Skye weighed that and admitted that perhaps Juan was onto something. "Then let him out of his room when they were done? I don't know. It doesn't make sense to me, to leave a potential witness."

"Why was no blood found outside of the chapel?"

"They're still processing evidence," Skye said, "but an organized killer might wear a jumpsuit and shoe coverings. Strip upon leaving the chapel."

"Good point. But why? Why was it important not to get any blood outside of the scene?"

"I don't know," she admitted. "Maybe the vandalism occurred before the attack, while the priests were praying or something."

Martinez flipped through his notes. "Time of death is estimated at four-thirty A.M., take or leave thirty minutes." He glanced at her. "Odd time for a prayer meeting."

They were dead between four and five in the morning. Anthony Zaccardi had arrived just after five. Dawn. Right on the heels of the murders.

Skye had called ahead for a meeting with Bishop Zachariah Carlin, but the sun had long set when she and Juan arrived late that evening.

"Thank you for speaking to us," Juan said.

Carlin shook his head solemnly. He was in his sixties, with a full head of gray hair and bright blue eyes. "I won't be sleeping tonight. I'm still in shock."

"We're sorry to have to ask you these questions," Skye began, "but it's important that we have an understanding of who lived at the mission, who worked there, and any threats you, they, or the church may have had."

"Threats? Someone is always threatening the church."

"I'm talking something specific. A letter or phone call aimed at the mission."

Carlin shook his head. "The mission is its own entity. It isn't really part of the diocese."

"But you own the property."

"Yes, but five years ago the Vatican asked if they could use the mission as a home for retired priests."

"Certainly you noticed that not all the priests there were of retirement age," Juan interjected.

"We didn't want to advertise that the mission was for mentally disturbed men of the cloth."

"Mentally disturbed how?" Skye asked.

Carline steepled his fingers. "I'm not at liberty to say."

"They are *dead*," Skye said. "Murdered in cold blood. They couldn't care less if you discuss their mental health. All I want is to find their killers."

Carlin said, "I was told that the mission priests were on sabbatical after being witness to horrific acts of violence. I was given one example. Father Diego Ortega. He was serving the people in Africa. He and a group of missionaries built a church and school in a village and taught the natives how to grow food. The village began to thrive, be self-sustaining. One Sunday during Mass a rival tribe barricaded the church and burned it to the ground. Many died. Father Ortega survived without a scratch. He believed this was a sign to preach the word, but he went to two more villages and met the same fate—his parishioners died and he survived. He was recalled when he showed signs that he was not capable of serving as a shepherd."

"Well, he's dead now," Skye said, cringing at how cruel that sounded. "So he was recalled to what? Get over it?"

"To heal. To know that God's plan is not our plan."

Skye inwardly winced. What God would allow a bunch of innocent people to be burned to death? What God would allow his most faithful servants to be brutally slaughtered in cold blood?

She didn't know what she believed, but she held fast to the knowledge that bad people did bad things, and it was her job to find justice for the victims.

And no acts of *God* would stand in her way.

"Why wouldn't the diocese or the Vatican or whoever was in charge hire a qualified doctor to counsel these men?"

"Dr. Charles Wicker is retained by the U.S. Bishops," he replied. "He works up in Santa Clara and, from what I've ascertained, makes monthly visits to the mission. I don't know him personally."

Skye switched gears. "Who hired Rafe Cooper?"

"He's not an employee of the diocese," Carlin said carefully.

"Then why was he there?"

"I received word that Mr. Cooper would arrive to counsel the priests."

"You didn't like him."

"He's not a likable person."

"How so?"

Carlin didn't respond.

"Bishop, I need all the information in order to do my job." When he didn't say anything, she asked, "Who paid him?"

"No one."

"No one?"

"Mr. Cooper is a seminarian, I believe from a seminary in Northern California. He's also a trained psychologist, from what I've ascertained. He's been to medical school, but doesn't have a doctorate or medical license."

Skye made some notes. Rafe Cooper was becoming even more interesting as the day—and night—wore on.

"When did he arrive?"

"March sixteenth."

"And he fired Ms. Davies two weeks ago. Under what authority?"

"He had no authority," Bishop Carlin said, anger in his voice.

"But you didn't reinstate her."

"Under the circumstances, I could hardly put her back into that hostile situation. I suggested that she take a week or two vacation and I'd find her a position in another church. We run numerous schools and a hospital."

"Did Mr. Cooper tell you why he fired her?"

"No."

"You didn't ask?"

"He refused to tell me. All he said was that she was a threat to the mental health of his priests."

"Correct me if I'm wrong, but isn't there some sort of hierarchy here? How could he just fire a diocesan employee without your permission?"

"He can't. He told her she wasn't allowed at the mission."

"Why?"

"I don't know!"

This was going nowhere. "When was the last time you were at the mission?"

"Months ago. Thanksgiving dinner was my last visit."

"When was the last time you saw Mr. Cooper?"

Carlin thought. "Two weeks ago, after he'd banished Ms. Davies."

Walking out, Skye whispered to Juan, "You dig into Corinne Davies and contact Dr. Wicker. I'll pump Zaccardi for information on Rafe Cooper and work with Rod at the crime scene. Something is rotten in the state of Denmark."

# CHAPTER FIVE

FIVE YEARS AGO, Anthony had explored the forest surrounding the Santa Louisa de Los Padres Mission and remembered an alternate way in. The unpaved road was overgrown, but it would lead to the back slope and, hopefully, allow Anthony access to search the mission without police interference. He couldn't use the main entrance. During his earlier reconnaissance he learned Sheriff Skye McPherson had left a deputy to guard the place, either against the killers returning, or curious citizens.

He parked as far down the trail as possible, his headlights cutting harsh swaths of light against chaparral oaks and rocks. The eyes of an animal glowed against the black and gray, then disappeared with a blink. An easy wind tapped the car, the *swish-swish* of oak leaves brushing the roof.

Anthony pulled a windbreaker from the back of his rental and stuffed a small packet of tools into the pocket. He doubted the locks had been changed, but if they had he'd still be able to get in.

Rafe was no killer, and Anthony had to find proof to turn the course of the police investigation. While Sheriff Skye McPherson didn't believe a demon was at work, she was searching for human killers. Someone had used the strength of demons to murder those priests, and Anthony had to work with the sheriff to find those people. Because there were two evils in Santa Louisa: the evil of Hell itself, and the evil human beings who had brought a piece of Hell to earth.

Demonolatry was alive and well in the world, a platform for Hell to prevail. Anthony was a soldier in the fight against evil. He couldn't do it as a priest, and he couldn't do it within the rigid structure of the church. There was a place for men like him, and that was fighting against the most insidious evil of all.

That which preyed on the innocent.

People would die if he did nothing. That was *his* fate, and a charge he did not take lightly.

With a deep breath, he stepped from the car and into the cold spring night, snapping on his flashlight. He walked parallel to the mountain, the slope treacherous and overgrown with saplings that slapped him in the face. He tasted blood on his lip. The moonless sky aided his disguise, but thwarted quick movement.

*Help us.*

The whispers of the dead told Anthony he was close. The path to the mission was steep, but his years of physical labor aided his journey up the mountainside. He spied the three-story bell tower under the dim light of an ancient lamp. Faint, subtle, like everything about the mission.

He paused at the tree line, trying to sense where the guard was while catching his breath. All he sensed was evil.

*Help us help us help us*

Rafe had been extremely worried these last few weeks, otherwise he would never have contacted Anthony in the first place. Anthony wished he'd asked more questions, pushed Rafe for answers. Now, he had to think like his friend. Had he kept a journal? Where would he have hidden it? Had the police found it? Would Skye tell him if they had? The police had no weapons to fight incorporeal beings, but if Rafe had left a clue, a message, anything, it might help Anthony in this battle.

His cell phone vibrated in his pocket shortly after he crossed the tree line and walked through open space. "Hello," he said quietly, kneeling low to the ground to avoid being seen.

"Anthony, I found what you're looking for."

The voice of Father Philip gave Anthony the only sense of home and family he'd ever had. The image of the demon on the wall of the sacristy had haunted Anthony because it wasn't a common demon, one he was familiar with. He'd spent most of the afternoon trying to figure it out, but he didn't have access to his books and papers and so had called the one man who knew more about demons than he did, the one man who had never let him down, the one man who had saved him.

"Is it Aabassus?"

"No, but you are close. Ianax."

Anthony's heart turned cold. Ianax was an ancient demon rumored to be one of the most powerful under Satan until a falling out with the devil himself had sent Ianax farther into the pits of Hell.

"Are you certain?"

"I am. You were correct that three human souls are

needed to summon him. The interior circle shows the powerful connection between the three, and how that connection creates a second sight. An energy, for lack of a better word. They can use that energy to control inanimate objects."

"But only when they're together, correct?"

"They are most powerful when all three are together and the demon is at their center. But I suspect they are long practitioners of demonolatry and black magic."

Anthony feared the same. "Anything else?"

"Ianax can't survive long without a body. Are you sure he hasn't claimed Raphael? Perhaps the coma is his way of fighting the demon."

"No," Anthony insisted. "I was with Rafe this afternoon. I would have sensed the demon."

"Yes, my son, yes, you would have." Father Philip sighed. "The danger of these people is they believe they will grow stronger with the demon at their side. And for a time, that is true. Perhaps one of them offered their body to him."

"Why? Why would they willingly give up their body?"

"It is said that those who willingly sacrifice their body to a servant of Satan will be given rewards in Hell. Some believe aiding the demon will give them the key to the fountain of youth. Immortality."

*Walk with the willing dead.* The phrase took on a dangerous new meaning.

"But it's not a possession?"

"No. That's what makes this demon more dangerous, and the human immortal. If someone willingly gives up their body, the demon is not waging an internal battle. All his strength can be used for evil. Be careful, Anthony.

Now that Ianax is loose he is growing in power and seeking revenge. Soldiers like us have kept him trapped for centuries."

"I'll be careful."

He hung up and considered how the presence of Ianax changed everything. During the battle between Satan and Saint Michael the Archangel, Ianax had been Satan's strongest ally. He'd betrayed Saint Michael with lies and treachery, and had been sent with Satan into the pits of Hell for eternity. For his loyalty, Ianax wanted to rule half of Hell, but Satan's ego would not have it. A smaller battle ensued and Ianax was sent to rule the lowest pit of all, the darkest corner. He fed on revenge, betrayal, and lies, and could only be summoned by a union of three dark souls chanting the proper ritual. A ritual Anthony thought the earth had long forgot.

But it wasn't just a ritual he required. Ianax demanded human blood, and he'd be doubly pleased with the blood of God's men. Was the death of those men a rite of passage for Ianax's worshippers?

Had Rafe seen something that made him suspicious? Who were the three responsible for this evil act? Three couldn't have killed twelve people, unless . . .

Unless the priests were incapacitated in some way. Had they not been able to fight back? Had they been led like lambs to the slaughter?

Anthony wanted the crime scene report, but after his disappointing meeting with Skye McPherson, he doubted she'd include him in this investigation. The head of the crime scene unit, Rod Fielding, was too loyal to go behind her back. Maybe the detective—he might agree to help.

But at risk to his career? Anthony would have to tread carefully.

The sheriff didn't know where to look. She was suspicious of Rafe, didn't have any faith to accept—on Anthony's word alone—that Rafe wasn't involved. He'd have to prove it to her. Skye didn't seem like the type of woman to rely on faith or trust for anything. He needed to learn more about her, find a way through her emotional shields. Earn her trust. Quickly.

The cold whipped Anthony as he hid downslope of the mission, a hundred yards away.

*Help us help us help us.*

The windlike chanting grew louder, the dark whispers taunting him, begging him with fearful urgency.

Moving low and fast, he ran toward the mission.

Skye relieved her deputy at eleven that night. She dismissed his inquisitive stare. She knew what he wanted to ask: why was the sheriff staking out a crime scene?

She didn't answer the unspoken question. She wasn't even sure herself why she was here. Except that she knew, as certain as the sun would rise in the morning, that Anthony Zaccardi would be here tonight.

The generator had been sabotaged, Rod had told her shortly after her meeting with the bishop. Rod had dusted the equipment, but it was devoid of any fingerprints. Wiped.

Rod fixed the generator so the crime scene techs could finish working once the sun went down. When they'd turned on the power, every wall sconce came on. Now, in the dark of night, each narrow window glowed yellow.

Every window. What had those men feared that the dark terrified them?

She shivered in her Bronco. When was Anthony Zaccardi going to show?

After meeting with the bishop, she'd further researched Zaccardi—he was who he said he was. A historical architect hired by the Catholic Church to restore ancient buildings. He was a citizen of Italy, specifically Sicily, but he was born in a small town she'd never heard of. There were no other records for him until he'd used his passport for the first time at the age of ten, from Italy to France. She had no records of parents or guardians, which seemed odd, but she *was* dealing with foreign governments. Still, everyone she'd spoken with had been protective of Zaccardi. One high-ranking priest in the Vatican even threatened her.

"You can't hold Anthony," the man had said. "I demand you allow him to return to Italy."

"He doesn't seem to want to return right now," she'd said and hung up. Interesting.

What was more interesting, however, was the light behind the mission. Anthony Zaccardi, right on time.

# Chapter Six

ANTHONY PICKED THE POLICE LOCK.

He didn't need his flashlight; the lighting had been restored in the mission. He quickly walked through the kitchen and down the main hall.

The mission had been destroyed from within. He'd seen the destruction earlier when he'd broken in to save Rafe; now the sad reality sank in.

Beautiful artwork, hundreds of years old, had been defamed. Every statue in the alcoves had its head removed. Paintings slashed. This, Anthony thought, was the work of human hands. A demon would crush the statues; humans defaced.

Anthony found Rafe's room, accurately guessing that it would be closest to the kitchen. There was one small window facing the rear of the mission. A small night-light in the corner illuminated the room with shadows.

Anthony closed the door, looked at the wood. It was splintered and cracked, as if someone had been scratching from the inside. He shined his light on the marks, saw the damaged wood stained with dark blood. Deep gouges, likely made with something metal or hard wood had been used to pry open the door. Now Anthony knew how Rafe's fingers had been broken, his fingernails torn.

The police had obviously gone through the room. Rafe's computer was gone, only wires remaining. His files had been rifled through and many had been removed. The drawers of his desk were open.

But the police didn't know the secrets the mission held, nor the many hiding places.

Anthony traced the ridges of the stone wall. He'd been in many missions, in many ancient buildings. He could find any hiding place . . . there. Around the edge of one stone he found a small, ancient release. A façade for a stone safe.

Sure enough, Rafe had left something in the space. A leather-bound journal. Anthony removed it, put the stone back in place.

Anthony carefully opened the journal, hoping for a clue. Several sheets of paper fell out and he stooped to pick them up.

The door opened and the lights came on.

"I thought you were going to do something stupid." Skye McPherson stood in the doorway, gun drawn. "You're under arrest."

"Don't."

"Hand me those papers."

He did.

"And the book."

Reluctantly, he handed it over.

"Are you armed?"

"I don't carry a gun."

"Turn around and put your hands on the desk."

"I told you—"

"You expect me to believe you? You broke a police seal and entered this building in the middle of the night. You're attempting to remove evidence. You're in hot water, Mr. Zaccardi."

*Help us.*

Skye frowned, glanced around the room.

"You heard," he said, incredulous.

"I don't know what you're talking about."

Hope claimed a corner of his heart. "You heard the voices."

"I don't hear any voices," she snapped. "Turn around."

He complied. Her hands moved around his waist, his thighs, his ankles. He wanted to think of her as a cop; he could only think of her as a woman. A woman who didn't know what danger she was in, nor what power she had.

She removed his cross. "You're clear, but I'll keep this for the time being."

He faced her. She was close, only inches from him as she holstered her weapon. He reached up to touch her face, and she flinched. He dropped his hand and said, "You can't deny what you heard."

She swallowed, took a step back. "What's this?" She started flipping through the journal.

"I suspect it will speak of Rafe's concerns. He would have hidden his notes if he thought something was going on here."

She frowned, reading the journal.

"What?" he asked, inching closer. She smelled of pine and soap. All natural. All woman.

"It's in Latin."

Latin? Rafe hated Latin. Anthony could practically hear him groaning during class.

She tucked the journal under her arm and looked at the papers.

"What are those?" he asked.

"Copies."

"Of?"

She didn't say. He peered over her hands. *Santa Louisa Grocery.*

"Why would he keep copies of the food deliveries?" Anthony asked.

When Skye didn't say anything, he knew she had an answer. "We need to work together, Skye."

Her head shot up. "You said you weren't a cop. Has anything changed in the last"—she glanced at her watch—"fifteen hours?"

"You need me."

"I don't know you."

"But you know I had nothing to do with what happened here."

"How? Maybe you were working with your friend Rafe. Maybe you're supposed to steal artifacts while I'm trying to solve a mass murder. Maybe—"

"You don't believe that."

"I don't know *what* to believe."

"Ianax."

"What?"

"That's the name of the demon in the sacristy. Human blood was used, wasn't it?"

"I can't discuss the investigation with you."

She had a great poker face, but her eyes exposed her

soul, which told him he was right. He also had thousands of years of history to draw upon.

"Ianax was a triple agent, so to speak. He was a spirit on Satan's side, but attempted to convince Saint Michael the Archangel that he was gathering evidence against Satan, all in an attempt to find out how many were staying on the Lord's side and who were going with Satan. He gave information to both sides."

She stared at him blankly. "You're a lunatic."

He hardened. He was used to people not believing him, but he desperately wanted Skye to trust him. The dead depended on it.

"Ianax was banished to the deepest pits of Hell by Satan when he attempted to overtake Hades. He's an ancient demon, feeding on hate and revenge. It takes three dark souls and human sacrifice to draw him out."

"I've read thousands of crime reports. There's no proven case of human sacrifice by Satanists in America."

Anthony continued. "Your people don't know everything, and human sacrifice is rarely what you envision. He's here. You sense it. You heard the voices of those trapped between Heaven and Hell. But you won't open your heart."

"You can't tell me that a spirit killed those men."

"Not alone, but Ianax was part of the massacre and if we can't send it back to Hell more people will die."

"Bullshit. More will die if we don't capture the people who killed those priests."

"That's irrelevant."

"I don't know what planet you live on, Mr. Zaccardi, but where I come from you put people in prison and they stop killing innocent old men."

He'd said the wrong thing, but he persisted. "I agree, we need to find the three involved in order to send Ianax back. If we don't, he *will* grow more powerful."

"Why are you so certain there are three people involved?"

"The seal. In the sacristy." How could he convince this woman of what had taken him a lifetime to learn?

"You look so normal," she muttered.

A rare anger grew in Anthony's chest, the rage he fought to keep firmly at bay.

He grabbed Skye by the arms and pulled her close. "If you think this is a game, more innocent people will suffer. I am deadly serious, Sheriff McPherson."

Her lush mouth opened, closed, opened again. "Let. Me. Go."

Anthony dropped his hands, the anger washing away in embarrassment. He didn't manhandle women. It was Skye's total disdain of him and what he said . . .

He should be used to it by now. Few people truly believed that evil existed. They talked about it, gave it lip service, but didn't *believe* in evil spirits, that they could be summoned and used, that they grew more powerful with every moment they spent outside of Hell, feeding on the cruelty and rage and hatred of human beings.

"Trust me," he said simply, imploring her with his eyes. He saw a hint of doubt in her face, the desire to believe him. Then it vanished.

But hope was all he needed. He'd worked with far less.

"I'll translate Rafe's journal for you," he offered.

Skye wanted to say no. She didn't want to trust this man who talked about demons and demonolatry and evil spirits. Those were the fantasies of religious nutcases like her mother and the man who sold her a bill of goods under the guise of being a man of God.

But she'd walked into the crime scene today and felt odd. She could dismiss the idea that someone was watching her in the daylight, but when she'd been sitting in her car in the courtyard tonight her skin prickled and every nerve seemed to stand at attention. She wasn't a flighty female. She wasn't scared of the woods or of being alone—she'd hiked and camped for weeks with her dad or by herself. But here—this was different.

A crash echoed through the mission. Skye's gun was out as she walked through the door.

"It came from the chapel," Anthony said.

"Stay," she commanded him.

"No."

She didn't have time to argue. Cautious but quick, she darted down the hall, Anthony right on her heels.

The closer they came to the chapel, the hotter the air.

"Stop," Anthony commanded.

She didn't take orders from civilians. Someone was in there. The killer? Murderers often revisited the crime scene.

She opened the doors of the chapel and smelled smoke over the stench of dried blood. She blinked and saw the carnage of that morning, in full sunlight. Every body, every dismembered limb, lying there. All eyes looking at her.

*Help us!*

She stifled a scream. She wasn't seeing this. She closed her eyes. When she opened them, she saw a flame in the sacristy, where the drawing had been left. The bodies were gone. That had been her imagination, after all the nonsense Anthony spouted.

Someone—someone *human*—was destroying evidence. Her crime scene was on fire.

She whirled around to face Anthony. "You! You distracted me so your partner could destroy the evidence."

"You know that's not true," he said, but he was looking over her shoulder.

She followed his gaze but saw nothing. "I need to put this fire out before it takes the whole chapel!"

Skye ran down the hall to the kitchen where earlier she'd seen two extinguishers on the wall. She started back down the hall toward the chapel, but Anthony blocked her path. "Don't go back there. You'll be trapped. We have to get out of here. Now!"

She ignored him, but instead of going through the interior entrance, she flung open the side door, pushed a tank at him, and exited the building, running around to the main courtyard entrance.

The iron gates that had been locked and sealed were wide open, proof that the fire had been set by humans, not demons. The fact that she was beginning to believe Anthony, that she *wanted* to believe him, was a testament to her poor judgment when it came to good-looking men. He was sexy and handsome and *sounded* normal. She'd overlooked the fact that he was a lunatic to insist that something supernatural was at work.

She'd fucked up the crime scene because of him. She should have stayed at her post. She may have been able to not only stop the fire, but arrest the killer.

She saw the flames in the narrow arched windows,

bright against the moonless night. Running to the chapel doors, she touched them; warm not hot. She readied the canister and kicked open the doors.

A loud roar emanated from the building on a wave of flames and laughter.

She was thrown to the ground and only after her back hit the cold, hard dirt did she realize Anthony had pushed her down. He'd saved her life.

He was still standing, facing the flames. He had his hands up as he walked toward the fire, chanting something foreign and ancient. She couldn't make out the words, just an urgent, fierce rhythm. The fire whirled around him, and she could no longer make out his frame.

Anthony was being burned alive.

Skye tried to jump up to rescue him, but an unseen weight pushed her back down. Her heart leapt in her throat as she watched the fire turn bright red, twirl, and like a reverse tornado, rise into the sky with a sickly, deafening scream.

Anthony's body lay faceup on the stone path. She crawled over to him, her limbs like lead.

He was staring at the sky, his dark eyes searching. His clothing was scorched and reeked of smoke, but his hands, his face, his limbs had no burn marks. How could that be? How could he have survived the fire unscathed?

"Watch out!" He rolled and flung his body on top of hers. From the corner of her eye, she watched the fireball come back down from the dark sky, heading straight toward them. She tried to crawl away, but Anthony pinned her down, his entire body covering hers in a protective shield.

The flames hit the roof of the chapel like a comet. Glass

exploded from every window. An unreal screech surrounded them as the fire spread into every nook, every room, every corner of the building.

Except the courtyard where they lay.

Hot air filled her lungs and all she wanted was to escape, but Anthony held her still.

"Don't move." His lips were on her ear, but she could barely hear him over the roar of the flames.

What was happening? He grabbed her wrists when she struggled to escape, held them tight against his chest. His heart pounded against her hands. Power and fear radiated from his body. He completely covered her, shielding her, her face buried in his neck. He murmured something that might have been a prayer or a plea.

In the middle of destruction, she'd never felt so completely safe.

A cry surrounded them, and suddenly all the air in the courtyard disappeared with a violent *whoosh!*

She gasped, straining to breathe against Anthony's chest. He still held her, but now she fought for air. *Air . . .*

He covered her mouth with his and pushed air into her lungs.

Suddenly she was off her feet and being carried through the courtyard. She clung to Anthony's neck until he eased her into the passenger seat of her Bronco.

She looked over his shoulder at what had been the mission. Smoke rolled from the windows, out the chapel door, rose from where the roof had once been, filtering into the dark sky. Not a flame could be seen, just smoldering ruins. Yet less than ten minutes had passed since she first saw the flames.

It couldn't have gone out on its own. Could it? There had to be a logical explanation, something the fire chief would be able to explain to her.

But she had no logical explanation for what she had seen. That Anthony had been wrapped in flames, completely immersed, and yet he knelt here before her, without a mark.

He touched her face, his large hands surprisingly gentle. "You're okay." It was a statement, not a question, but she nodded.

His thumb brushed against her lips. She stared into Anthony's dark eyes and knew she had a crime she couldn't handle alone.

"I lost the journal," she whispered.

Anthony reached into his shirt and handed her the journal. "I picked it up when you ran from Rafe's room."

"Did you know what was going to happen?"

He shook his head. "But I've seen it before."

"What? Spontaneous combustion?" She tried to make light of it, but neither of them smiled.

"No, that fire was most certainly set by one of the people responsible for summoning Ianax."

Skye ached in disappointment. Not because she wanted to believe in evil spirits, but because he wasn't being consistent. "First demons, now humans? You're messing with me, Mr. Zaccardi."

"Demons can't set fires or do anything without a person to help them. They may be able to control those humans who have already given up their souls, they may even be able to temporarily control humans against their will. Possessions. And the most powerful among them can use the elements by becoming part of the element itself. But they can't set a fire alone."

"So what just happened? Someone put out that fire"—she snapped her fingers—"like that?"

"Once the fire started, Ianax became the flames. Destroyed his image and everything he touched, and disappeared."

"But he didn't kill you," she said softly.

"He couldn't, even though he tried." Anthony held her face in his hands. "But you, Skye, are in grave danger."

She laughed uneasily. "You know this how?"

Anthony didn't return her humor, his fathomless eyes drawing her inexplicably closer.

"He couldn't sustain the fire and defeat me at the same time. He is not that strong. Yet."

"But what does that have to do with *me*?"

Anthony touched her cheek. "You don't know what you're up against, Skye. You don't know what evil incarnate can do. That makes you vulnerable."

She scoffed at that remark. Typical male chauvinist. "I'm perfectly capable of taking care of myself."

"Not against this."

Skye jumped up and out of the truck, paced even though she still felt unsteady. "Dammit, Zaccardi, you're pissing me off. I don't know what's going on. I don't know how you weren't burned in the fire. But there *is* a logical explanation. And I will find it."

"It's logical, Skye," Anthony said, sinking to the ground. She frowned. Maybe he had been injured in the fire. "But you have to open your mind to see the logic." His eyes closed and he leaned his head against her truck's tire. "I saw your soul," he whispered.

"That's ridiculous." But there was no venom in her voice, only concern. "What's wrong?"

"I'm drained."

"I don't understand."

"I'll be okay. Just—let me be."

"Leave you? Here? At midnight?" She knelt beside him. "Let me help you."

Anthony rose unsteadily, stumbled, and fell against the truck. His body was solid muscle; Skye couldn't carry him if she wanted to. He climbed awkwardly into the passenger seat.

"Just take me to my car," he said wearily, his eyes already closing.

"Right. And let you drive off a cliff. I'll take you to your hotel. You can get your car in the morning."

Ianax's essence slithered along the ground in the form of black mist, losing power the longer he was without a human body.

*Fool. You consumed your energy with the fire. You should never have fought for Zaccardi's soul.*

His primal scream rang through the levels of Hell like nails on a chalkboard, and on earth with the moaning of trees. He rolled over a nocturnal rodent who collapsed dead after breathing his mist; a pair of owls fell from a tree above, landed with a thud.

He was eternal death.

Lifetimes of failed attempts to rise from the deepest

pit of Hell, giving him a taste of freedom that was taken away because of the weakness of the trio left him angry, unsatisfied, hungry. Finally, his minions had perfected the call and he'd come, with a willing body for his use. Payback for the willing was immortality. And even in the dark heat of the netherworld, immortality for as long as the earth breathed was a tempting apple.

And he, Ianax, would be able to stay, walk the earth, experience lust in everything—sex, food, death. *Power.* He would have been able to claim an infinite number of souls for his master.

He fed on souls, and the pure souls of the righteous tasted better than the black souls of the damned.

Zaccardi would have satiated him for a millennia, proven his worth. But the hunter's protective shield was too strong for one demon to destroy. Even Satan himself wouldn't be able to penetrate the barrier.

A sudden gale-force wind pushed Ianax off course. He was being pulled under, down, back to Hell.

*I'm sorry, Master. My thoughts betray me.*

The wind softened.

*I am all-powerful, lowly demon. I am your Lord and Master. Zaccardi is not yours to have. When the time is right, I will consume him.*

*When, Master?*

*Go, finish what you were summoned to do. Then bring me my due.*

*Yes, Master.*

Ianax's essence was released from the underbelly and flung over the tops of the trees, down the mountain, dead birds raining from their nests as he stole their breath.

# CHAPTER SEVEN

ANTHONY HAD REGAINED some of his strength on the drive back to town, but walking to his hotel room drained him.

He'd fought evil and won, this time. But he needed to rejuvenate. He couldn't protect Skye or save the lost souls at the mission until he regained his strength.

He couldn't let Skye leave.

What he'd seen in the flames would haunt him for the rest of his life. She didn't believe him, and if everything remained the same she would die. Horribly. Painfully. Her soul would be trapped and tortured for eternity.

Losing her was not an option. He would sacrifice himself first.

"Get some rest," she was saying to him. "I'll pick you up at seven and take you to your car."

"No!" He swallowed. "Please." She stared at him, perplexed. How to keep her here? "I need your help."

He sagged heavily onto the sofa, exaggerating his fatigue and pain. She looked skeptical. *Oh, my little doubting Thomas. You're a tough one.*

"Please—I need you to—" What? She already thought he was a nutcase. *Make something up, Zaccardi.*

"Pray with me."

Her face clouded.

*Good one.*

"In Latin," he added.

"You've got to be joking."

"I'll teach it to you. It might come in handy."

He wasn't joking. She didn't have to know what the words meant. If she remembered them, at the right time, they might protect her. At least buy some time.

She sat next to him looking as exhausted as he felt. Maybe he could get her to let down her shield a bit. Enough to lull her to sleep. If she slept here, in his presence, she would be safe. For tonight.

One night at a time.

He took her hands in his. She tensed, but didn't pull away. *You think your gun can save you. You think your smarts will get you out of any difficulty. You've never faced a demon, sweetness.*

He'd felt her soul in the courtyard when he'd covered her body with his. She was holding on to a deep regret and bitterness, he didn't know from what, but her innate goodness and honor shone through. A strong core of loyalty. Strength.

Satan would love to claim her as his own.

An overwhelming protective urge washed over Anthony. He swallowed, uncertain what he was supposed to do. What he *should* do. He'd never allowed himself to grow close to any woman, because in love he would be vulnerable. In love, he would be risking more than his own life. Already, his soul was inextricably entwined with Skye's.

The fire had fused them together, a bond he could not break.

*Save her. Save us.*

He whispered in Latin.

"What does that mean?"

He repeated the prayer and she frowned at him, but didn't pull her hands from his. Progress.

"Say it. Please, Skye. It—it would comfort me." He exaggerated a sigh.

She hesitated, then repeated the ancient words of protection, her voice quivering.

"Again."

She complied. He touched her hair, murmured a poem.

"That's French."

He hadn't realized he'd spoken in French. "The monks made sure I learned many languages."

"Monks?"

"I was raised in a monastery."

"What happened to your parents?" Skye seemed much more at ease talking about his past than things she couldn't see or touch. While he didn't like to share things about himself, he had no hesitation in telling Skye. He wanted her to know. To build trust, to strengthen their bond. And more.

"I don't know about my parents. I was left on the doorstep of a monastery on a small island off Sicily."

"An orphanage?"

Anthony couldn't tell her the whole truth, but he didn't lie. "In some ways. Women in Europe, particularly in the old country, are frowned upon if they have children out of wedlock. Some are disowned or ostracized. It can be very difficult. Many infants are left at orphanages or with the nuns. Or at a monastery. St. Michael's—we had an unusually high number of abandoned babies."

"Why?"

"The monks are among the most brilliant men in the world. Doctors. Lawyers. Theologians. Scientists. Scholars. They raise boys and send them to live all over the world."

"You never knew your parents." She frowned.

"Don't feel sorry for me. It is hard to miss what you never had."

"Is it?"

Anthony longed to know where he came from, but he'd buried those desires years ago when he tried to find his mother and came up with nothing.

"It is easier, with time," he corrected. "What about you?"

"My parents are dead."

She spoke so flatly, suppressing emotion that bubbled just beneath the surface.

"An accident?" he asked softly.

"My father was a U.S. forest ranger. He was hiking in Los Padres, fell off a cliff and broke his back. His radio got caught on a tree out of reach and he couldn't call for help. He died two days later."

"I'm so sorry." He squeezed her hands.

She shrugged. "So what was it like growing up in a monastery?"

Changing the subject. She didn't want to talk about

her mother. He should push, but he didn't want to scare her off. He needed her to be comfortable here, with him, for the night. But he couldn't share everything with Skye, not yet. If he said too much, she would bolt like a rabbit.

"Father Philip, a missionary, often stayed at St. Michael's. I'd always loved history and architecture, even as a young boy. Father Philip works with the church to renovate historic buildings. He became my mentor, my friend." And he taught him to harness his senses, to locate demons in buildings and destroy them. He didn't say that to Skye.

"So you became an historical architect?"

Anthony nodded. "I traveled throughout Europe, as well as Africa and parts of the Middle East working with Father Philip, before I went to college in England."

"You said you were raised with Rafe Cooper."

"Rafe was raised in the monastery as well."

"He doesn't look Italian."

Always questioning, always suspicious. "He isn't. He's probably of Irish descent."

"Doesn't that seem odd to you?"

He shook his head. "We have children from all races and cultures."

She still seemed perplexed, but asked instead, "How many live there?"

"At any given time, fifteen monks. We have four young ones—under sixteen. When Rafe and I grew up, there were many more. At one time twenty-two of us."

"What happened? Women start using birth control?"

Anthony frowned. The truth was, they didn't have an answer to the diminishing chosen ones. Rafe was one of the last. There had only been six since him, and none in the last ten years.

"It was a joke. I shouldn't have said anything. I'm sorry. Look, I should go."

"Please don't." He took her hand. "Do you remember the prayer?"

"Words can't protect anyone from anything," Skye said.

"Faith can."

"Please, Anthony, don't do this." Skye ran a hand through her hair. She'd lost her clip and her hair fell in creamy blond waves, no less alluring being mussed from their earlier ordeal. "Belief in God certainly didn't save your friends up on the mountain. And it didn't save my mother," she snapped.

"Your mother?"

Skye stared into Anthony's dark eyes. Why had she said anything? She didn't want to talk about her mother. But maybe he would leave her alone, stop talking to her about this nonsense. Trapped souls and demons . . .

"My mother left when I was ten. Met a guy, someone who talked all about God and salvation and dedicating your life to Jesus. And she gave him everything she owned and went away with him. Just like that. She left and never spoke to me again. Six years later a California Highway Patrol officer came knocking on the door and told us she'd been murdered. By the same kook who had talked her into joining his stupid cult."

Why had she said all that? The last person she wanted to talk about was her mother. She tried to pull her hands from Anthony's, but he held firm. She wanted to avert her eyes, but he turned her face to look at his.

"Skye."

Suddenly, his lips were on hers, consuming her.

No tentative kiss. He claimed her with a confidence she'd rarely seen, hungry but patient; determined but gentle. She put her hands on his arms, surprised at the dense muscle hidden under his shirt. She wanted to push him away. She couldn't. Her body reached for him while her mind told her to run. Heat pooled in all the right places, her heart beat triple time, her skin tingled from the electricity they generated.

All in a kiss.

His hands barely touched the back of her neck, but his presence captivated her. Anthony didn't try to dominate her, but conquered her nonetheless.

*Think, Skye! Forget the kiss, this guy is bizarre.*

*Shut up,* she told herself and wished for once she could separate her physical needs and desires from her logical cop mind.

She opened her mouth to tell him to stop, but instead found her tongue seeking his, being the aggressor. If he had carried her off to bed right then, she would have gone. Her body wanted him and no amount of logic would have convinced her to stay away.

Her own guttural moan was lost in Anthony's mouth, but the sound—too passionate to be coming from her— jolted her back to reality. She didn't sleep with strangers. She didn't sleep with men who weren't grounded in reality. What was she doing? She was the damn sheriff with a massacre on her hands.

She pushed Anthony back. Hard. He didn't take his eyes from hers. His confidence was incredible. He already looked like he'd bedded her. "Don't leave," he said.

"You're fine," she snapped, jumping up. "I have work to do."

He stood, followed her to the door. "Please stay. I'm worried about you."

"Worried about *me*? I'm a cop, Mr. Zaccardi. I'm perfectly capable of taking care of myself."

He leaned toward her. "I think we've gone beyond Mr. Zaccardi, don't you?"

He tried to kiss her again, but she averted her face and his warm lips landed on her flushed cheek. He looked more amused than insulted. Damn him.

He also looked worried. That didn't sit well with her.

"Look, *Anthony*," she said. "I'm a smart cop. It's after two in the morning. I'll be up bright and early to continue this investigation. With the mission destroyed, I have a lot more work to do."

"You need me."

"Only to translate this." She reached down and picked up the journal that she'd placed on the table. "I'll keep it with me for now, you can meet me at the station at oh-eight-hundred tomorrow morning."

"I can work on it tonight, have a translation for you—"

She held up her hand, anticipating his request.

He nodded curtly. "All right, Skye. May I have my cross back?"

What was she expecting? More protests? To take her kicking and screaming to bed? She didn't know how much she would have fought him. Damn, but Anthony was hot.

Too bad he was a weirdo. Just like the man who'd lured away her mother.

She pulled his cross—his dagger—out of her belt buckle and handed it to him. "Don't make me regret this," she said, more curtly than she intended.

She turned and left, felt his eyes watch her open the door to the stairs because she was too impatient to wait for the elevator.

All the good men were married, gay—or nutcases.

*A wall of flames surrounded him, but Anthony felt no heat.*

*"You again," the fire spat.*

*Again? He didn't remember this demon, one so strong it could control the elements.*

*The flames danced in laughter.*

*"Someday you'll remember. I won then, I will be victorious now. You can't save their souls if you're dead."*

*"You can't kill me, Ianax, spawn of Satan," Anthony said, his mouth working but no sound escaping.*

*"I can't. Humans will."*

*The flames disappeared, leaving him cold, shaking. He saw Skye standing at the edge of a cliff.*

*She was going to jump.*

Anthony fought sleep, weary, unusually exhausted. Something—a spell. Those who had summoned Ianax had made his sleep deep. Recognizing it, he shook his head violently, side to side, reciting the Lord's Prayer in clipped phrases as he rolled from the bed, landing heavily on the floor.

Every limb was weighted. With a primal growl he pulled

himself up. Unseen demons clawed at his skin. Burning. Restraining him.

"Forgive us our trespasses!" he tried to shout but a demon clawed at his throat.

His body staggered across the hotel room, stumbled, knocked over a vase. It landed with a thud on the thick carpet.

"—those who trespass against us."

Anthony pulled on his slacks, fumbling with the zipper and collapsing onto the couch. The spell was weakening. The demons tried to hold on to him, pin him to the couch. To slow him down. To stop him from reaching Skye in time.

"Lead us not into temptation!"

His voice was stronger. He found his shoes where he'd taken them off. Where was Skye? How would he find her?

A clear image came to his head and he knew exactly where she lived and how to get there.

"Thank you, Lord," he mumbled in recognition of the vision.

Please, he couldn't be too late.

He ran out the door, the bright hall lights blinding him. He hit one wall, then the other, as if drunk. But his sight cleared and he turned north on the street.

He ran, pulled by an invisible string to Skye's house. *Faster, Anthony. She's hurting.*

"But deliver us from evil!"

*Amen.*

# CHAPTER EIGHT

SKYE WOKE, glanced at the clock. Five A.M. Damn, she didn't have to get up until six, and here she was, wide awake, her mind crammed full of the crime scene. While driving Anthony from the burned-out mission the night before, she'd called Rod and asked him to get the arson investigator out there. Rod planned on meeting him at the mission to see if they could salvage anything after the fire, but he assured her they had enough evidence and photographs to hold up in court once they arrested a suspect.

"And," he'd added, "I can't say that I'm sorry that painting in the sacristy is destroyed."

First Juan, now Rod. Two strong, reasonable, smart men completely snowed by a few odd circumstances. Maybe it was the history of the mission itself, or Anthony's strange comments, or the brutality of the murders. It was human nature to want to blame some ethereal "evil" when Skye knew damn well a person had killed those priests.

Five-ten. No going back to sleep now that her mind had kicked into full gear. She padded down the hall to the kitchen and flicked on her coffeepot, which she always prepared the night before.

The night was still black. She shouldn't feel this alert, she'd only had two hours of sleep. But her mind was working double time. She stared out the breakfast nook window. She lived in her family home on the coast. It was just her now.

Intense sadness flooded her senses as it always did when she unexpectedly thought of her father. His death had been so *wrong*.

Skye poured herself coffee, adding a teaspoon of sugar. Her dad had been a quiet, calm man. Never raised his voice. Never harmed anyone, human or animal. He cared for all living things, taking his job as a forest ranger seriously. He was in those woods every day, even on his days off. He stayed in the ranger's cabin more often than at home. Skye had a room there as well, but she also needed to attend school. She'd pretty much raised herself, especially after her mother left.

"I can teach you," her father had said, asking her to live at the cabin with him.

"But I *like* school. I don't want to live in the woods with no one around."

She'd hurt her father, she knew, but not on purpose. Never on purpose. He'd hurt her, hadn't he? By loving the land more than his own daughter?

A tear escaped and Skye watched it hit the table. She *never* cried. But this was her father, and her emotions were always close to the surface with him. She'd loved him so much . . . and then he'd died. He'd never have died if she'd agreed to live with him in the mountains like he'd wanted.

The autopsy report said he'd been alive for two days

after the fall. With a broken back, he couldn't move. He'd died of internal bleeding.

She hadn't even worried about her dad until the assistant ranger called. After all, her father often disappeared into the woods. He could take care of himself. Then it took them two days to find him. Dead.

Skye poured another cup of coffee, angry with her mother for leaving in the first place. Her father had never recovered from Marjorie running away. To find herself, to find God, whatever, she'd left to join this freaky religion in the middle of Oregon. What did Oregon have on Central California? Why did any god want a mother to abandon her only child?

"Take me with you, Mom," Skye said out loud, feeling ten again. Torn. Between a father she loved, and a mother she knew.

Marjorie had said children were a distraction. "You're your father's daughter." As if that were a bad thing.

Why was she thinking about her mother? It was Anthony's fault, making her talk about the past. She'd gone to sleep thinking about her empty life, and woken up with these odd emotions she usually kept under tight control.

Feeling claustrophobic, Skye stepped out on her deck to breathe in fresh, cold air. The biting predawn salt air wrapped around her and she shivered, barely noticing she only wore the tank top she'd slept in and panties. She heard the waves crashing on the rocks below her house. The dark water topped with the glowing foam of breaking waves. They crashed in, rolled out.

She walked down the wooden stairs and across the

rough and rugged cliff, rocks sharp against her bare feet. The sensation didn't pain her, instead it made her feel alive. Her skin prickled, her hair rippled, in the brisk ocean wind.

She was alone. Her father had died because no one thought to look for him. Her mother had died because she'd run away to find herself, and ended up being murdered by a man she'd trusted. Her own husband would never have killed her, but she trusted a stranger more.

The memories of what was lost flooded her and she couldn't stop them.

Skye's body hung with despair. So much death in her life. She had no one. No family. No parents, grandparents, brothers, or sisters. She was sheriff, but what did that mean? Constantly on show. Constantly worrying that someone was going to stab her in the back. Her election was coming up. Her first election. She'd been appointed by the board of supervisors after the Santa Louisa sheriff died of a heart attack. She'd been held up to the media and community as the first female sheriff. They'd passed over well-qualified men to be able to say they'd appointed a woman.

Who was she to have this job? She didn't deserve it. She was a chess piece. A pawn. All she'd wanted was to be a cop. To stop predators from luring lonely housewives into cults. To know that when someone was missing, maybe they'd better look, just to be on the safe side. Better to be embarrassed than grieving.

Rocks shifted beneath her feet and she looked down. She should step back from the cliff. It wasn't stable here. The sandrock crumbled continually. Her house, which had at one time been one hundred eighty feet from the edge of the cliff, was now, after only thirty years of erosion and storms, one hundred fifty-two feet from the edge.

What would it be like? To be truly free? Not grieve, not regret, not constantly question her own competence, her job. Herself.

She'd always been alone, but she'd pretended. First that her mother wanted her, then that her father loved her. She was a lie. No one would miss her if she disappeared. No family, few friends, and those she had—who? She couldn't remember even one close friend. There had to be some-one . . .

"Skye."

She shook her head. Her imagination talking to her.

"Skye, stop."

Stop what? she tried to say, but her words sounded funny. Who was calling her, anyway?

"Skye!" The voice was commanding. Gruff.

*Step forward. Peace is only a foot away. Do it, Skye.*

Her father's voice, calm, quiet. *You let me die. You didn't even look for me.*

She stared at the space above the sea. He was there, right in front of her. So real she could touch him. Have him hold her like when she was little. Tell her stories, his wonderful stories about princesses who flew like the birds. Love her again.

"Daddy, I'm sorry."

He held out his hand.

She held out her hand.

"Skye, come home."

"I miss you, Daddy."

She stepped forward. The ground disappeared. She was falling, falling—

Through human eyes, Ianax watched Sheriff Skye McPherson walk along the edge of the cliff, much too close to the edge. A smile across the face of the body he'd fought to possess.

*Die, weak one. Die.*

He sent a bolt of energy across the space and created the image of her father.

She reached out for him.

Pain exploded in his head as the soul trapped inside chanted a prayer. His eyes glowed, turned inward, and he saw the human soul inside the physical body he possessed. Ianax sent a sharp snap of energy to silence the plea, and the soul went quiet.

The human had fought him fiercely, but after he had rid the body of all protective shields, he'd been able to gain a foothold. Just enough to subdue the human conscience and take over. But an unwilling possession was a constant battle, and energy surges to quiet the consciousness drained him. The momentary high of possession would quickly diminish. He needed to find another body, one that wasn't as emotionally strong, but first he had things to do.

"I need that journal. Where would she keep it?"

He searched the memories of the human trapped inside and looked in two places before he found it. He picked up the journal and his human hands burned.

"Argh!"

The bastard had protected the journal from those

acting on Ianax's command. The mild irritation at being slowed down was replaced by a spine-chilling shriek of excitement.

*You can't stop me!*

Using ancient chants from his master, he rid the journal of all protective elements. He picked it up, flipped through the pages, wanting to see what they knew of how to defeat him.

The pages were blank. The ink itself had been blessed, and with his spell he'd removed it.

In a rage befitting Satan himself, the book flew across the room, pages shredding in midair.

"I'll have your soul in my teeth yet, Raphael Cooper!"

He left the cottage, feeling around for Skye McPherson's soul. He would claim her, now.

But he couldn't find her.

Then he saw *him,* the bastard who'd interrupted his gathering of souls at the mission.

He wanted nothing more than Anthony Zaccardi's soul in his black gut. But Satan had other plans for him.

Impatience was only one of Ianax's vices.

# Chapter Nine

She began to tumble off the cliff when someone grabbed her hand.

"Skye!"

She screamed, kicked, scrambling, trying to climb up the sheer rocky slope. What had happened? Where was she?

Had she just walked off the cliff? No. *Yes.* Was she losing her mind?

"Help!" she shouted.

"I'm going to pull you up."

The wind picked up. The salty spray from the violent waves crashing below dampened her near-naked body. Her free hand, her feet, tried to grab for purchase, but rocks continued to fall beneath her kicking legs.

"Give me your other hand!"

It was Anthony. He clutched her wrist with one hand. His other hand was reaching for hers. He was lying flat on the ground to keep from falling over the edge with her.

She swung wildly, kept reaching for him. The wind blew at her, pushing her from his seeking hand.

"No!" she cried.

"Skye, focus!"

Focus. What did he think she was doing?

On the third try his free hand caught hers.

"I'm going to pull you up."

Anthony had looked strong earlier, but he proved it as he pulled her back up the cliff. To safety. She scrambled up, falling into his arms, shaking uncontrollably.

"What happened?" she cried, burying her face in his chest.

"What did you see?" Anthony asked.

"My father . . ." No. Her father wouldn't have asked her to walk off a cliff, to kill herself. She shook her head, trying to collect her thoughts, but everything was jumbled. "I don't know. Why am I out here? Why are you here?"

"Shhh," he said, stroking her tangled hair. "Shhhh." He held her tight against his chest, his warm body absorbing the cold that penetrated her bones.

She looked up at him; he stared at her. The depth of his dark eyes caught her breath. His black hair fell loose on his shoulders, the brisk wind blowing it to and fro. Anthony Zaccardi had saved her life.

*Twice.* First the fire, now the cliff.

Suddenly, their lips touched. She didn't know if she kissed him first, or he her, but neither of them were cautious or tentative. He kissed like an experienced man, a man who had a right to kiss her, to touch her, to hold her. It was the taste of last night, when they'd first kissed, plus so much more.

She opened her mouth, her tongue seeking his, the intimacy of the embrace igniting her nerves.

Anthony's arms wrapped tight around her, one hand holding her head to his, the other roaming up the back of her shirt, so hot, so rough, against her bare skin. She groaned into his mouth and he tilted his head in the other direction, the kiss diving deeper, holding her lips captive. Every cell in her body yearned for Anthony, a man she barely knew. She'd lusted before, but not like this *need* that had her wanting to make love right now.

Skye had always been in complete control of her sex life. But here, on the edge of the cliff, with this man, she lost control.

She shivered at the thought, and Anthony pulled her even closer, his hot mouth moving to her ear. "You're cold."

Cold? In his arms? *Never.*

She wasn't thinking, not like a rational woman, not like a cop. The realization that she'd almost died—had walked off the cliff because she'd *thought* she'd seen her father— hit her. She didn't want to die, and certainly didn't want to kill herself. The overwhelming sensation of being alive, whole, and safe wrapped her in such a tight cocoon that coldness was foreign to her. In Anthony's arms she was at peace for the first time in forever. She needed to feel safe. And loved. Just a little longer.

The creeping eastern sun highlighted every feature, every crevice, every shadow of Anthony and the coast, which glowed like sea foam in the rare light that came only at the edge of dawn.

She kissed him hard, pushing him back onto the ground. Touching his hard, lean body wherever she could reach. She fumbled with the buttons on his white shirt, roughly pushing it aside, ran her hands over Anthony's warm muscled chest. How could a man generate so much internal heat that her fingers burned at the touch? Her mouth found his nipple, hard and broad under her tongue. She moaned, the anticipation of sex making her writhe on top of him.

"Skye," he murmured as if in prayer. "My Skye."

*My Skye.*

She yearned to be somebody's, to belong to a person as she wanted them to belong to her. Partners. Friends. Lovers.

His hands went up under her shirt and touched her bare breasts, which had pebbled in the cold. He rubbed her nipples back and forth in each hand, warming her, heating her to the brink of combustion. Her mouth found his again, exotic and forbidden. Anthony satisfied a thirst she hadn't known she'd had. Reaching down to his pants, she fumbled with the zipper, feeling his hard, heavy weight. Wanting her as she wanted him.

"Skye," he whispered in her ear, reaching for her hand. "Skye, do you want—"

"Shhh," she said, interrupting his question. She felt his desire for her. Right there, in her hand. She squeezed.

He groaned, a deep guttural sound that vibrated within her.

"Make love to me, Anthony. Right now. I need you to love me. I need you inside of me. Make me feel alive."

Anthony swallowed, every cell in his body fully aware of Skye. He wanted her. But he didn't take women in distress. Though she was leading him, he knew something was wrong. This wasn't Skye, not fully. She'd gone from one extreme to another. His mind told him not to listen to her words, that she would regret this, but his heart—his soul—demanded that he be with her. In her. Now.

"Skye, do you—"

She clasped her lips over his mouth, hard, her tongue exploring. Her hand rubbed his cock, pulling it toward her. He groaned again, tasting her. Wanting her.

He had the strength to push her away, to demand that she think about what she wanted them to do. To insist she consider the consequences.

But he didn't use it. His mind was clouded with lust and desire and something indefinable. This woman had touched his heart earlier. At the mission in the fire. At his hotel with her quiet regrets. Her strength. Her heart. Her boundless compassion.

"Anthony," she whispered as her tongue found his ear.

It took all his self-control not to roll over and take charge of the lovemaking. But he wouldn't place her delicate body against the rough ground.

His hands found her beautiful ass and he squeezed, wondering only fleetingly when her panties had disappeared. Skye was all woman, lean and muscular, but soft and rounded where a woman should be. Her firm hips filled his hands as he lifted her up.

She clasped his cock and touched it to her moist center.

"Anthony," she gasped as she slid onto him without hesitation.

He bit back a cry of pleasure as he filled Skye. Opening his eyes, he stared at her face in the rising sun. Her blond hair was loose and wild, the breeze lifting it from her body. Her eyes were closed, her mouth open, her skin flushed, a sheen of sweat making her shine in the early light. She was a goddess, exquisite and beautiful, and his. He knew then, at their union, that she was as much his as his own mind and soul. How he knew, what it meant, he couldn't be sure, but there was no mistaking this knowledge.

"Skye," he commanded. "Look at me."

Her eyes fluttered open. Unfocused. Then they caught his, full of the same deep desire and longing that he had. He pulled her head down to his, kissed her softly as he wrapped his arms around her body.

Her pelvis rocked back and forth and she gasped into his mouth. He bit back his own release, his primitive need, in order to give her everything she wanted and more.

Her muscles tightened around his and he reached down, holding her tight against him. One of his hands found her clit and pressed firmly on the nub. She cried out in his mouth, then arched her back up as she orgasmed.

Then, he gave up his own pleasure.

She held him tight as they lay there catching their breath. "My Skye," he murmured in her ear.

When she started to shiver from the cold, Anthony sat up, Skye still wrapped in his arms, and pushed up off the ground, bringing her with him. Awkward, he pulled up his pants, buttoned them with one hand as she clung to his neck. Then he carried her toward the house.

"I'm sorry, I'm sorry," she whispered in his ear.

"Shhh, Skye, no regrets. I will take care of you." He meant it. He would take care of her until his dying day.

Suddenly she was struggling against him. "Put me down."

"Skye—"

"Put me down!"

He complied. He sensed no demon within her, nothing supernatural. Whatever had compelled her to walk off the cliff must still be tormenting her, and he had to find out what happened.

Skye shook her head, disoriented. She rubbed her temples, sudden pain beating within her. She'd just had sex with a man she barely knew. On the cliffs, after she nearly died.

What was wrong with her?

*I will take care of you.*

She didn't need anyone to take care of her. She didn't believe anyone would want to. A sharper pain jabbed at her head and she squeezed her temples.

Anthony's hands were on her, holding her up. She batted them away. "I'm okay," she said.

"I'm here to help."

"How did you know where I live?" Skye said, pulling away from Anthony, a sliver of suspicion hitting her. Her body temperature fell as soon as his arms dropped.

And the doubt grew.

"I knew."

"Oh, please." She turned back toward her house, stumbling in the rocky soil. Anthony reached for her hand. She pushed his arm away, fell to her knee and winced. "You followed me, didn't you?" she accused him as she rose unsteadily. She wrapped her arms around her body, trying to regain the warmth she'd had with Anthony, but to no avail.

"I didn't follow you, Skye. You're not thinking straight. Maybe it's a spell."

"Spell? First demons, now witches? I should call myself Alice and start looking for white rabbits."

"*Spell* may not be the right word—"

"You have no car," she interrupted.

"I ran. You're less than a kilometer from the inn."

That was true. But that still didn't explain how he knew where she lived.

"Skye," Anthony said, taking a step toward her, his arms outstretched, palms up. His shirt hung open. She'd done that. She remembered pulling apart his shirt with such clarity, when everything else was becoming fuzzy. "I had a dream you were in danger."

"You expect me to believe *that*?" She turned away from him, half running toward her house. *Why don't I remember leaving the house? How did I walk off the cliff?*

Her feelings of unease grew to near panic. Why couldn't she remember? It was as if she wasn't completely inside her own body. How absurd.

She stopped to take a deep breath. "I just didn't get enough sleep," she said out loud, as if that would convince her that there was a logical explanation for leaving the house in the cold morning wearing nothing but a tank top and underwear. That it made sense for her to see her dead father. Lack of sleep intensified her complex emotions about her parents. And all Anthony Zaccardi's talk about demons and whatnot had her thinking about her pathetic mother, leaving everything for a cult, for a god Skye didn't know existed.

*Stop it! Stop thinking about it!*

She pressed her fingers against her head as another

wave of pain crashed around her. She stumbled and tripped coming up the steps.

Anthony caught her. She wanted to hit him, send him away, at the same time she wanted him to hold her, to make her feel as loved and safe and alive as when they'd made love.

"Skye, something's wrong." His voice was low, almost a warning.

Skye squeezed back the pain, let Anthony help her up the deck stairs and through the sliding door she'd left open.

A foul stench assaulted her, as if someone had defecated and vomited throughout her house. She scowled. "What's that smell?"

"Hell." Anthony eased her into a chair.

"What—" She wanted to shower, to dress, to forget she'd thrown herself at Anthony.

Her face burned. *I practically raped him.*

"Wait." He pulled a crucifix from his pocket and thrust it into her hands.

"What's this for?"

"Trust me, Skye."

Skye nodded and Anthony turned, holding his own daggerlike cross in front him. For the first time, Skye believed that if demons really existed, Anthony could defeat them.

Confident Skye was safe, at least for the moment, Anthony walked slowly toward the living room.

An invisible, foglike warmth enveloped the house, making each step forward like walking through a swirling, resisting, unseen mist. The sulfuric scent of Hell worried Anthony. Was Ianax still here?

His instincts told him the demon had left. Already, the smell was fading, the heat dissipating. But there was no doubt that a demon had been inside Skye's house.

He searched the house, quietly repeating God's name in Aramaic, waiting for the telltale growl of a masked demon hiding in the furniture, the walls, the very air he breathed. There was none. The house grew colder.

Every room appeared untouched, except for Skye's bedroom. Inside, shredded paper filled the room, little glass jars from her dresser had been knocked over, some shattered, some spilling their sweet-smelling contents. He would have smiled at Skye's love of perfume if he didn't know what had happened in here.

Only a demon—an angry demon—could have done this.

Anthony picked up a piece of paper. Thick. Slightly yellowed with age. Then he saw the binding and knew that what had been destroyed was Rafe's journal. He picked up more torn paper—blank. Every one of them blank.

How?

He left the house. He couldn't tell Skye what he was doing, she wouldn't understand. And right now, gaining her trust was paramount. Not only because of what they'd shared on the cliffs, but because her life was in grave danger.

He took out a vial of holy water, twisted off the cap, and circled the house, sprinkling the blessed water in strategic spots to ensure a protective barrier.

It wouldn't stop a powerful demon, but it would slow and weaken it. It would have to be enough.

He returned to the kitchen, but Skye wasn't there. Panic clutched his heart and he started toward the kitchen door, fearing she'd already walked off the cliff. Someone, or something, wanted her dead. What if he wasn't strong enough to protect her? What if his faith wasn't powerful enough to save her?

He listened, heard running water, followed the sound and found the bathroom door locked.

"Skye?" he called.

"Leave me alone."

Guilt flooded him. He'd taken advantage of her. He'd known something was wrong, that Skye wasn't completely herself, but he craved her. Their shared kiss earlier in the evening had fueled a flame he'd kept under control for the better part of his adulthood. Her claim on him was greater than he'd realized, and then she lay on top of him and he saw her in all her beauty, her inner goodness, and he wanted her.

His desire had consumed him and he'd allowed it to happen, potentially damaging their already strained relationship. Worse, he'd given in to wants that he should rightfully postpone until the demon returned to Hell.

He'd let his guard down, a deadly sin in his vocation.

"Are you okay?" he asked through the door.

She didn't answer him, but the water shut off. "I'll be out in a minute," she said.

He wandered through Skye's house and saw her life as clearly as if he were a psychic. True crime books on the shelves. Furniture that was clean, but old and worn. Decorations that, while free of dust, seemed to be remnants of another generation. A lone picture of a young Skye with her parents.

A sense of loneliness assaulted him, a sorrow he understood all too well. It was a pain he lived with every day.

"I have to get down to the police station," Skye said, standing behind him. "Someone destroyed the journal."

He turned around, embarrassed to be assessing her home. She'd put on her uniform and was pulling her damp hair into a ponytail.

"Skye," he murmured.

She was still wary around him. Embarrassed, perhaps, and he wished he could ease her fear. Tell her how he loved to hold her. Of course he couldn't, she'd push him away. He understood that about her.

He noticed the crucifix he gave her was around her neck. She glanced down, shoved the cross under her shirt.

He needed to reach out. "Skye, don't feel—"

"Did you do it?"

He didn't understand. "What?"

"Did you destroy that journal? Break my things?"

Her voice cracked and he saw the strain, uncertainty, and unease in her eyes.

"No," he said.

"It's all my fault." She looked both irritated and physically ill. "It was evidence, and I brought it home, left it in my bedroom. Stupid." She ran a hand over her face.

"It was two in the morning."

"I don't care! I broke protocol and now the journal is ruined. Someone shredded it and must have bleached the pages or something while—" Her voice tapered off.

"Skye, something happened to you this morning. Tell me everything."

"Why?" Her eyes bored into his. "Did you have something to do with this?"

He quashed feelings of anger and frustration. That he

would use sex as a ruse to keep her from her house? "You know I didn't."

"I don't know anything right now," she snapped. Her voice softened, full of anguish. "I don't jump strange men on the cliff every day of the week."

Anthony tried not to be hurt by her comment. "How did you get out on the cliff?"

"Walked," she said sarcastically. Her defense mechanism.

"You know what I mean."

Her forehead wrinkled. "I was tired. I wasn't thinking straight." She avoided his eyes and crossed over to the coffeepot. It was half full. She picked up a mug from the counter and poured. As the mug touched her lips, Anthony stepped forward and grabbed it from her hand. Hot coffee sloshed over the edges, scalding them both.

"What the—" she exclaimed, jumping back.

Unmindful of the burn, he smelled the coffee, grimaced.

"What?"

"You drank some of this already, didn't you?"

"Yes, I have coffee every morning."

"Someone poisoned your coffee."

"That's a crock."

He shoved the mug under her nose, trying to be patient. "What do you smell?"

She breathed in deeply, wrinkled her nose. "It's sort of metallic."

"I think it's mercury. Deadly in large doses, but on a small scale it's a hallucinogen. My guess is that someone added it to the coffee grounds or water. The bitterness of the coffee would mask the taste."

"Why didn't I notice it before?" she asked, still skeptical. "I need to get this to the lab."

"You were tired. You'd had two hours of sleep. My guess is that something woke you up, but you don't know what. You rose, started the coffee." He pulled the tray that held the grounds from the coffeemaker. "Poured a cup." He looked at her. "Then what happened, Skye?"

She blinked rapidly, her eyes coated with tears. "I . . . I started thinking about my parents. I don't know why, it's stupid, really. I told you about my mom leaving for some whacked-out religious cult, and my dad dying eight years later. I've been on my own for a long time, I don't get all sappy about it, but . . ." Her voice trailed off and she wasn't looking at him.

"But it hurts."

She nodded, probably without realizing she was doing so. She seemed disconnected, and Anthony knew the drug was still having an impact on her.

Skye's inhibitions were down. When he saved her on the cliff, her emotions went from one extreme to the other. Despair to joy to relief to passion. He didn't stop her. They made love, but it wasn't Skye. It was the drugs. Guilt and nausea swept over him. He knew something had been wrong, but he'd ignored his instincts. He accepted her offering like a dying man would water.

"Skye?"

"Just leave me alone."

"You're still under the influence."

"How do you know? Did *you* drug my coffee? You could have followed me home, drugged my coffee while I slept, then waited for me to hurt myself so you could ride to the rescue. So that I would *trust* you." She spat out the word as if it were a curse.

"That's paranoia talking, Skye," Anthony said calmly, taking a step toward her. "That's the drug."

"Bullshit. That's deductive reasoning." She rubbed both temples with her fingers, a pained expression crossing her face.

"Come here."

She stared at him, doubting. He stepped forward, took her wrists, lowered her hands, and led her to the couch.

Her living room was sparse and functional, like the rest of the house. He sat on one end of the couch, pulled Skye down next to him.

"Close your eyes, Skye," he said.

Skye felt so out of balance, but here, sitting with Anthony, she was regaining her footing. Her bottom lip trembled. Slowly, she closed her eyes.

His thumbs pressed her temples and his fingers grasped the back of her head. For a fleeting second she pictured Spock performing the mind meld, but as soon as Anthony started rubbing, his fingers moving in firm circles, all thought ceased and she relaxed for the first time since walking into the mission massacre twenty-four hours ago.

The pain faded, from sharp and burning to dull and throbbing. She relaxed and sighed in relief.

"Turn around and put your head in my lap."

His deep, European voice sounded far away, as smooth as butter, as exotic as a tropical rain forest.

She lay on her back, Anthony turning to a forty-five-degree angle on the couch to hold her head and shoulders comfortably. He continued to massage her temples, moving down to her cheeks, behind her ears, and her body gave up all its tension from sleep deprivation and drugs.

"Do you really believe in everything out there?" Skye asked, keeping her eyes closed.

"You mean in demons?"

"Demons and Heaven and Hell and everything in between."

"Yes."

"Why?"

"I've seen the gates of Hell. I've felt the presence of evil. It's real. I can't conjure up a spirit to prove it to you, I can only tell you that you had a visitor, you smelled him, you sensed him, but you're only thinking with your head, not listening with your heart. You want a logical explanation, but there isn't one."

He paused, and she opened her eyes. His eyes held hers, strong, deep, fathomless. She whispered, "And?"

He leaned down, kissed her forehead. "I'm asking you to trust me."

Skye didn't know what to think anymore. Anthony was so ethereal and real at the same time. One minute she had everything sorted in her mind, knew exactly what she needed to do; the next, she wanted to place her entire faith in a man. In *this* man.

She'd never fully trusted anyone but herself. Even then, she doubted. Worried over her decisions. But always, she had her reasoning. It had gotten her this far in her life and career, how could she place her trust in someone else now? That would be like turning her back on herself, on the very thing that had kept her sane and whole during years of loneliness.

What would she have if she listened to Anthony? She'd be just like her mother, wanting to believe in fantasy because real life didn't satisfy her.

As if he could read her mind, he said, "You can't live in the past. Your mother hurt you, and then she died and you couldn't tell her how much she hurt you. It's easier to be angry with her and God than it is to acknowledge you miss her, that she killed your trust."

She closed her eyes, trying to trap the tears that came, but they slid out the corners. Anthony brushed them away with his thumbs.

"It's the drugs," she said, not wanting to admit that after twenty years she still ached for her mother.

"It's your heart, and it's okay."

His lips touched hers so lightly, so tenderly. Her heart skipped a beat. This quiet intimacy, the emotion, was difficult for Skye. She choked back a sob.

Anthony pulled her into his lap and held her, rubbing her back, his chin on her head. She could stay here in his arms forever.

"My mother abandoned me," Anthony finally said. "And while I knew it was for a higher purpose—that I had a calling—there were times, especially at night, especially when I was young, when I cursed God for giving me this life. For forcing my mother to sacrifice me. But in the end, it had been her choice."

"You never had a real family," Skye said, feeling a kinship with Anthony she didn't expect to have.

"We were a family, but I missed—we all missed— having a mother. Skye, I know how betrayed and hurt you feel. But you are strong, beautiful, smart. It's your mother who lost out on knowing what an incredible woman you have become."

She tilted her face to Anthony and said, "You're a miracle worker. My headache is gone." She spontaneously kissed him, then turned away. Almost embarrassed. But this felt—right.

"I need to talk to Rod about the fire, follow up with my detective about the housekeeper—"

"Let me drive you. Just until we know the drug is out of your system."

She felt herself—more herself now than she had for a long time—but she nodded.

Her cell phone rang, and she jumped up, popped the phone from its charger, and said, "Sheriff McPherson."

"Skye, it's Rod Fielding."

She glanced at her watch. "I thought we weren't meeting for another hour."

"After you called about the fire, I came back to the morgue. I've had a guard posted outside all night."

"You think someone is going to come after the bodies?"

"Possibly. But now I have a larger concern."

"What?"

"I ran the tox screen myself. Twice. These men were drugged."

"Drugged? So they couldn't fight back?"

"I don't think so. I think they were drugged to become aggressive, and it's been happening for a long time. Months, up until two weeks ago. But I'm checking their blood for more possibilities."

Two weeks. *The same time the housekeeper was fired.*

"How can you tell?"

"Hair samples. It's not a routine screening, but after the fire I decided to test for a wider range of narcotics, hallucinogens, and heavy metals."

"Test for mercury poisoning."

"Mercury? That would explain my findings. How did you know?"

"I'll explain when I get there. What about Cooper?"

"The hospital drew his blood, he had no alcohol or recreational drugs, but I'll need to broaden the panel. Now that I know what I'm looking for, it won't take long."

"Good."

"There's one more thing. I think I know what happened."

Finally, answers based on hard physical evidence. "What?"

"You need to come down and see for yourself. You won't believe me if I tell you over the phone."

# CHAPTER TEN

ON THE WAY to the sheriff's department, Anthony asked Skye about the conversation he'd overheard between her and Dr. Fielding.

"They were drugged?"

"Apparently it had been happening for months and ended two weeks ago. The same time as your friend fired the housekeeper."

"Housekeeper?"

"Corinne Davies. Know her?"

Anthony shook his head. "Do you know anything about her background?"

"Not much. Detective Martinez is working on it. She came from Oregon highly recommended from the diocese up there. The bishop was ticked off that Cooper fired her, but apparently has no control over the workings of the mission. She's on vacation."

Corinne Davies. "I can make some calls," Anthony suggested. "Someone in the church might feel more comfortable talking to me than the police."

Skye didn't say anything for a moment, and Anthony wondered if she was going to tell him to stay out of the investigation. Instead, she surprised him and said, "I'd appreciate that. Anything about her history, complaints, background. She has a daughter, Lisa, but there's no father in the picture. I don't even have his name."

She'd taken a step toward trusting him. Anthony was elated.

"What happened to the journal, Anthony? How did"— she paused—"the killer erase all those pages?"

She couldn't say *demon.* But asking for his advice was a huge step. "I think Rafe used blessed ink."

"Excuse me?"

"When the demon touched it, the ink disappeared."

"Disappearing ink."

By her cool tone, he was losing her. He changed tactics, using a cop's logic. "Rafe must have written something the killer doesn't want us to know," Anthony suggested. "Maybe evidence of who had been drugging the priests."

"Why wouldn't he have just called the police?"

"Maybe he didn't have proof. Maybe he didn't think you'd believe him." But Rafe had suspected something supernatural, that's why he'd called Anthony in the first place.

In light of the evidence of the men being drugged, everything made sense. Their odd behavior. Rafe's unease, but unable to explain why. Why hadn't Anthony seen it? He hadn't expected the trio of humans. He'd been looking at demons only, not at the ritual of summoning one. He'd bypassed the process of elimination and looked only at the obvious. Had his personal arrogance jeopardized Rafe and killed the others?

Whatever Rafe had sensed that spurred his call to Anthony was the beginning of the ritual to bring Ianax from Hell. And perhaps, in light of the long-term drugging, one of the priests had been concerned and asked Rafe to come to the mission in the first place.

"Why did he write it in Latin?" she asked. "To keep the information from the priests?"

"They all knew Latin," Anthony said. "The only reason to write in that language would be to keep the information from laypeople. Those who have reason to be at the mission. Repairmen, housekeepers, deliverymen."

Skye asked, "Do you know a Dr. Wicker?"

Anthony couldn't lie. "Yes."

"And?"

"What do you want to know?"

"You want to help, right?"

"You know I do."

"Then why were all these priests seeing a shrink?"

"I explained that to you. They've all witnessed evil." Anthony remembered the conversation he'd had with Rafe right before he left Italy.

*He thinks one of my men is communicating with a spirit. But he doesn't know who.*

"The bishop implied they were all mentally unbalanced."

"Dr. Wicker is a psychiatrist specializing in helping those who have witnessed the worst man can do to man," Anthony responded. He didn't tell Skye about what Rafe had said. She wouldn't believe him, and right now keeping her trust was his highest priority.

Skye frowned.

"What's wrong?" he asked.

"Juan was supposed to call me after talking with Wicker." She flipped open her cell phone. "No missed calls."

Had he missed something? Was the rest of Skye's team in danger? "Have you spoken to him?"

"Not since we saw the bishop yesterday, but that was late."

"Call him."

"Why?" she asked.

"This case is dangerous."

"Well, if all you need is *faith* then he's fine," she snapped. "Juan's the most devout Catholic I know."

Anthony winced at the derision in Skye's voice. He'd thought they'd been closer to a real understanding.

Skye said into her cell phone, "Hey, Juan, call me when you get this message. I'm on my way down to the morgue. Meet me there."

She hung up, concern clouding her eyes. Before Anthony could say anything, she was justifying Juan's inaccessibility. "He's probably in the shower. It's still early."

"He's married, call his wife."

"How do you know he's married?"

"He wore a wedding ring, did he not?"

Skye mumbled something, dialed. "Hi, Beth. It's Skye McPherson. Has Juan left yet?" She frowned as she listened to the wife speak. "No, I'm sure everything's fine. He's investigating a difficult case right now. I'll make sure he calls, I'm meeting him in thirty minutes. Right. Give the girls big kisses for me."

She slowly closed her phone. "He didn't come home last night. He called Beth after I talked to him about the fire and said he was working late and would sleep at the station."

She called headquarters. "Detective Martinez, please." A minute later, she hung up. "He's not there."

Anthony couldn't placate her. His fear for the detective had grown almost as much as his fear for Skye. Whoever was responsible for Ianax roaming the earth had piqued Martinez's interest.

"First things first," he said. "We need to find out what Dr. Fielding learned. Maybe it will help us find your detective."

She nodded. "Remember, you're not a cop. I shouldn't be bringing you in at all, except—" She stopped.

"Except you don't trust me," he said as he pulled into the police department parking lot and turned off the ignition.

She shook her head. "No." She looked him in the eye and he saw how conflicted she was. "I trust you, Anthony," she said softly. "I trust that *you* believe something supernatural killed those men. I don't, but I think you can help me figure out what happened at the mission. You have insight and experience. And you're not as, um, wacky as I first thought. Okay?"

It was a start. And it kept him by Skye's side, where he needed to be when the demon came calling.

He squeezed her hand. "Okay."


The morgue was in the basement of the hospital down the street from the police station. The coroner, a small wiry man in his late sixties named Rich Willem, who'd been here since before Skye was born, was preparing the first body for autopsy when they arrived. Dr. Willem, who never appeared happy, looked particularly sour. Skye would be, too, if she had to face twelve butchered men on the slab.

Rod was agitated and excited at the same time. He

barely gave Anthony a second glance. "Look at this." He shoved a printed report into Skye's hands.

She'd seen tox reports before, but she didn't want to take the time to decipher the shorthand. "What does it say?"

"The three men I tested all had evidence of being drugged with a heavy metal, up until two weeks ago."

"Mercury," Anthony said.

Rod shot him a look. "How did you know?" He glanced at Skye. "Is that why you asked me about mercury?"

Skye nodded, handing Rod a box that contained her coffee maker, coffee, a sample of her water, sugar bowl, and the remainder of the coffee she had brewed this morning. "My coffee was poisoned this morning. If Anthony hadn't—"

Anthony could tell how uncomfortable she was. "I came by early this morning to ask about the investigation and found Skye out of sorts."

"I'll test it immediately."

"Whoever poisoned my coffee also destroyed the journal." Skye explained how she had found Rafe Cooper's journal at the mission before the fire.

"I'm more concerned about you. The effects of mercury poisoning can be severe: death, suicidal depression, or extreme aggression," Rod said. "And that would be consistent with my theory."

"I thought you only believed in facts, not theories," Skye said, irritable. Her headache was returning.

"Our crime scene is destroyed. The fire chief said it started in the sacristy. Nearly everything is gone except for the courtyard."

*Where Anthony and I were.*

Anthony asked, "What do you think happened, Doctor?"

"I think these men killed one another."

"Why on earth would you think that?" Skye exclaimed.

Rod led the way into the main morgue. Dr. Willem gave them a perfunctory nod, continuing about his business without comment. Three bodies were displayed, and on the far wall Rod had put up photographs of the bodies as found. "I asked Dr. Willem to start with these three because they were found here, close together, and they tell a story."

He used a metal pointer and tapped the picture of what used to be a tall, physically fit young man. He lay across the floor. "He killed himself. When we X-rayed the bodies, we found the tip of a knife in his abdomen. From the angle, he stabbed himself and bled out. Took less than five minutes, but he was unconscious most of it. The same knife nearly decapitated this man." Rod tapped the photo of the man lying on the stone floor, his head almost completely severed from his body. "And it was used on this man, who was stabbed in the chest fourteen times. We tested the blood—the decapitation occurred first. Other than external blood spatter, no foreign blood was found in his wound. He was also, I believe, the first to die based on other blood evidence."

"Are you saying that Father Jordan killed this old priest?" Anthony said, his voice shaking in the first sign of stress Skye had seen.

"I can't prove it, but it holds with the evidence. There is blood from this priest in the stab wounds on the second man's chest. The striation marks are the same. Absolutely the same knife."

"So you think that Father Jordan killed first this man, then this one, then committed suicide?"

"Yes."

"Couldn't another attacker have killed him? Where is the knife?" Skye asked.

"That's your domain, but the angle suggests that it was self-inflicted and—look at his hands." He gestured toward the body on the table. "These cuts are consistent with an attacker blindly wielding a weapon, not defensive wounds. In virtually every knife attack, the attacker nicks himself."

"Someone else was in the room. Someone collected all the weapons," Anthony said.

Rod nodded. "Someone had to, and it wasn't Father Jordan. The knife was lodged in his rib. That's why it broke. Someone had to really tug to remove it. Father Jordan was dead for at least thirty minutes before the knife was removed."

"Maybe he had an accomplice. He killed himself out of guilt," Skye suggested.

"I don't know why, all I can tell you is that my theory is consistent. Dr. Willem and I are going to piece together the blood evidence on the victims and determine how many weapons were used. I have the lab working on the other collected evidence. I think we can put together exactly what happened, given enough time."

"How much time?" Skye asked.

Rod shrugged. "We're working on this twenty-four/seven. Three days for a preliminary report. Some tests will take a little longer."

"If the mercury poisoning stopped two weeks ago, why did they turn violent now?" Skye asked. "What about their stomach contents?"

"We're working on that. The tox screens I originally did were on blood and hair samples. I haven't received the blood tests back yet. That would show if they were drugged more recently. The hair samples are for long-term poisoning."

"Rush it, Ron."

"I'm doing the best I can," he said.

"There were no footprints," Anthony interjected. "How did the killer remove the weapons?"

"That's where I think the killer—or the accomplice— messed up. There *were* footprints, and that's why I think they burned the mission. At least that's the most obvious reason. Let's go to my office."

"Have you talked to Juan Martinez today?" Skye asked as they walked.

"No. I assumed he was working with the arson investigator up at the mission."

"I haven't been able to reach him."

Skye pulled out her cell phone and dialed dispatch. "Milt, can you plug in to Martinez's GPS and give me his whereabouts?"

"Two secs."

Why hadn't she done this before, when she knew he hadn't gone home last night? She pinched the bridge of her nose. The headache was still there, taunting her. A hand rested on her back. Anthony.

Milt said, "He's stationary on Highway 1, one-point-three miles south of Arroyo Grande."

"What the hell is he doing all the way up there?" That was halfway to San Luis Obispo.

"His radio is off."

"Off?" That was against regulations. "Keep trying to reach him on both radio and cell phone. I'm heading up there." Juan wouldn't have gone off half-cocked. He was a by-the-book cop, one she trusted implicitly.

"I gotta go. Juan's in trouble. I feel it." She was about to leave, then asked, "What about those footprints?"

"We took hundreds of photos. No one involved in the carnage left the chapel. But *someone* came in after the fact, walked over to several of the bodies, and left."

"Rafe Cooper," Skye said.

"But he didn't leave, and the prints don't match his. Cooper was barefoot when he came into the chapel. I easily traced his path. He came in through the side door, the one closest to his bedroom, walked halfway around the room, then ran up the center aisle and fell."

Rod continued. "I think one of the killers was still on the premises when you arrived, Mr. Zaccardi."

"Why do you think that?" he asked, his voice tight.

"You wear a size-twelve shoe, we matched your prints earlier. Someone intentionally slid their feet to make it impossible to match. But the individual crossed over your prints, Mr. Zaccardi, and the only way they could have done that was if they left after you."

"Which would explain how the mission was locked from the inside when Zaccardi arrived," Skye said. "And if these men killed one another, then perhaps only one person needed to be involved. But it still doesn't explain how. If they hadn't been drugged for nearly two weeks, why now?"

"Perhaps the killer tainted their food supply," Anthony suggested. "Gave them a larger dose. There must have been a purpose to the slow poisoning, and when it stopped—when the housekeeper was fired—the killer panicked."

"That certainly points to the housekeeper. I need to talk to her, dammit." Skye turned to Rod. "Please tell me you cleaned out the kitchen."

Frowning, he shook his head. "There was no reason to do so. I would have done it today, after getting the tox screen results, but—"

"The fire. Dammit."

Skye tried to piece together the facts. "The priests were all drugged for several months, up until two weeks ago. But why did they all go crazy two nights ago? If they were being drugged, why was that night any different?"

"Perhaps they were given a larger dose," Rod suggested.

Skye frowned. "This is what I don't get. Why were they killed? What is the motive?"

Anthony spoke up. "They were killed for their eternal souls."

*Not now, Anthony.* Skye couldn't accept that as a motive to kill. She said to Rod, "I need to find Juan. Call me as soon as you have something definitive."

# CHAPTER ELEVEN

THE PATROL SKYE SENT to Juan's location came up with nothing: his car was there, he wasn't, and there was no sign of a struggle.

"I'm going to talk to the Davieses," Skye said to Anthony as she slid behind the steering wheel of her Bronco. "I have some more questions."

"If this Ms. Davies has anything to do with Ianax, she's dangerous," Anthony said.

"You said the demon needs *three* humans," Skye said, exasperated. She really wasn't in the mood to listen to Anthony's religious garbage right now. Juan was missing. "If she poisoned those men, she's just as guilty for their deaths as if she stabbed them herself."

Based on the *evidence*—something Anthony Zaccardi seemed to be ignoring—the twelve priests had committed a mass murder-suicide. Coupled with the poison, at least it proved that human beings—not some fictitious "demon"— had been responsible for the deaths. That gave her a modicum of peace. Murder, she understood. Supernatural forces? She'd leave that to Hollywood.

On the way to the Davies' cottage, Skye called Dr. Wicker. It was after nine in the morning and he was in his office. "Dr. Wicker? Sheriff Skye McPherson in Santa Louisa."

"You're calling about Santa Louisa Mission."

"Yes. It's my understanding that you served as psychiatrist to the mission priests."

"I did."

"Have you spoken to Detective Juan Martinez regarding this case?"

"He left a message after hours last night on my answering machine stating he would be coming by first thing this morning, but he hasn't arrived yet."

She'd assumed that Juan had been traveling to SLO, but he could have also been heading farther north, to Santa Clara, to speak with Wicker. "Thank you, Doctor. I'll be in touch."

Anthony held out his hand. "May I?"

She handed over her cell phone.

Anthony said, "Charles, it's Anthony Zaccardi."

"Anthony? When did you arrive?"

"Yesterday morning. I was too late. Rafe told me he talked with you about the strange behavior at the mission."

"Rafe is safe?"

"He's in a coma."

"Someone betrayed him. Someone betrayed all of them."

"The housekeeper, Corinne Davies?"

"Rafe believed she was partly responsible, but he didn't know how. And even after he fired her, the men weren't right. He was looking internally."

One of the priests? Anthony didn't want to believe it, but he'd witnessed worse betrayals. "Who was it?"

"I don't know. They all passed every test I know. But one of those twelve—Anthony, one of them was communicating with demons. I know it, it's the only explanation for the fear."

"Fear?"

"Rafe didn't tell you?"

"Tell me what?"

"They couldn't sleep. They could barely eat. They were jumping at shadows. They got to sleeping in the chapel during adoration, the only time they felt safe. But after a while, even adoration terrified them."

*The tabernacle had been replaced.*

"Thank you." Anthony hung up.

"What?" Skye asked.

He told her about the abnormal fear, but refrained from explaining the significance of the fake tabernacle. She wouldn't believe him anyway, not with her focus on finding Detective Martinez.

"If they were drugged long-term with what I consumed only once, it's no wonder they freaked out." Skye's voice was laced with sympathy.

When Skye pulled up in front of a small cottage near the cliffs outside Santa Louisa, Anthony's instincts hummed.

"Something is wrong," he said.

"What?"

"I can't explain."

"Or won't?"

He took a leap of faith. "You know I'm a historical architect, but you seem to have forgotten I'm also a demonologist. I study demons. I also have a certain—

empathy—where demons are concerned. I sense evil. This house is evil."

"Houses can't be evil. The people inside, maybe, but houses are wood, nails, and glass."

"Demons can be trapped in inanimate objects," Anthony tried to explain further, but Skye's eyes darted away. She was letting him help—but she refused to listen to the truth.

As they approached the house, Anthony's body grew cold and his head throbbed painfully. A spell. He reached the path leading to the porch and his heart felt like it was being shredded. He could go no farther.

Skye didn't have a problem crossing the threshold. As his fear for her grew, he stepped forward and fell to his knees.

She knocked on the door, and when no one answered, walked around the perimeter, finally declaring, "No one's home, the house is locked up tight." She frowned at him. "What's wrong with you?"

He'd been sitting at the edge of the path, physically unable to cross the spell's threshold. He slowly rose to his feet and said, "They cast a powerful spell around that house to stop me. Don't come here without me, not until I find a way to reverse it. You're in danger."

"Stop." She spoke softly and held up her hand.

"Skye, listen—"

"No more talk of demons and spells. That's a load of crap. You've distracted me enough from this investigation. I have a missing cop, a friend. I have evidence that points to the priests being poisoned to the point that they committed murder and suicide. When I get those responsible into interrogation I will damn sure find out why. I want whoever drugged those men to go to prison for a long, long time. That's my job. Those are the facts."

She rubbed her eyes and sighed. Anthony's heart fell. He knew what she was going to say before she opened her mouth.

"I wasn't myself this morning." Skye averted her eyes. "You saved my life and I jumped you. It didn't mean anything, but I've felt guilty enough about it that I let you come with me to the morgue, to come here. That was not only wrong, it's against protocol. I'm going to take you to your car. You're not a suspect, and you can pick up your passport at the station."

"Your life is in danger!" Why couldn't she see what he so clearly saw?

"I can take care of myself, Mr. Zaccardi. I've been doing it for a long, long time."

He touched her cheek softly. As if his touch could convince her that he was right, could show her that he spoke the truth. That there were things in this world that people didn't understand, but it was his job to convince them. To convince Skye.

"I'm not going anywhere."

"You are a civilian and you will not be part of this investigation."

She said the words, and her body language told him she was serious, but her eyes—they were confused.

"You don't mean that, Skye."

She straightened. "Yes I do. Juan is missing. I have twelve victims. How do I know that Rafe Cooper wasn't involved? Because you've told me he's this noble guy? I need to ask the hard questions, and every time I do you throw out crap about demons!" She gestured toward the house. "Like a *house* can be evil? That some sort of *spell* is protecting it, against what? Burglars? *You*?

"I have a serious crime on my hands, and you're steering me in the wrong direction. I'm neglecting logic and reason for supernatural excuses. No more."

Anthony's anger built. He tried to tamp it down, but it came out in a rush.

"What about the fire last night?" he demanded. "The flames that almost killed both of us?"

"The arson investigator will have a scientific explanation for it," she said matter-of-factly.

"Can't you look beyond what your eyes tell you? Into what your heart sees?"

"I'm a cop, Anthony! What am I supposed to tell the jury? A demon made him do it? Give him five-to-ten, call an exorcist, and with some counseling he'll be okay? I deal with human beings, who are just as bad and rotten as the demons in your imagination."

That stung. This woman hadn't seen what he'd seen. She hadn't watched friends die horribly in the grips of Satan's fire, or watched an entire evil building disappear into the ground with people trapped inside. She couldn't see what was right in front of her—the fire, the visions of her father on the cliff, the evil emanating from the house in front of them.

"You would deny what you feel?" Anthony said. "What you know to be true?"

"Feelings aren't fact." Skye held fast to that truth.

Arguing with Anthony was delaying her. Just being

around him was clouding her judgment. How could she find Juan, investigate these murders, when she was being diverted by a dark fairy tale of good versus evil?

Anthony grabbed her, pulled her close, his face tight with anger. "Would you deny what happened between us?"

She shook her head. "That was a mistake. The drugs—"

"It was *not* a mistake! I will not deny how I feel."

Anthony's mouth claimed hers, hard and passionate. Skye would have collapsed had he not been holding her up. He poured his anger, his frustration, his emotions into her, making her tremble.

She pushed him away, stumbled backward, wiping her mouth with the back of her hand. "Stop."

"You cannot deny us. The power between us."

She steeled herself against Anthony's growing intensity. "I'll take you to your car—"

His entire body seemed on the verge of exploding, then he tightened his jaw and stated, "I'll walk."

She watched him leave, afraid to let him go—but knowing if she was going to get to the bottom of these murders, she needed logic and reason over supernatural delusions.

Why did she suddenly feel so cold?

# CHAPTER TWELVE

ANTHONY BOWED OUT OF RESPECT when he was escorted into Bishop Carlin's office and kissed his hand. "Thank you for seeing me, Bishop."

"Your reputation precedes you, Mr. Zaccardi." The bishop's tone was neither awestruck nor cynical.

"Rafe Cooper is a friend of mine."

"And you came out here when you heard about the murders. Tragic." He crossed himself.

"I found the bodies, sir."

Surprise crossed the bishop's face, in addition to concern. "The police didn't tell me that."

"They didn't like what I had to say."

"Which was?"

"A demon is at work here."

The bishop didn't say anything for a long time. "Demons cannot kill unless they possess someone. You know that."

"I do."

"So what is your theory?"

"First, did Rafe come to you recently about the missing tabernacle?"

"I told the sheriff that Mr. Cooper and I were not on very good terms, Mr. Zaccardi."

"Why is that?"

"He's a difficult man."

"He can be." Rafe was stubborn—sometimes to a fault—but he was intensely loyal.

"The tabernacle isn't missing," Bishop Carlin said. "I gave the mission a replacement."

Anthony couldn't keep the surprise off his face. "You have the original tabernacle? Why?"

"It's very old, as I'm sure you know. Several of the stones had fallen off and needed to be replaced. Father Hatch brought it to me nearly two weeks ago."

"Father Hatch?" Anthony didn't know him.

"He arrived at the mission a year ago. He's one of the few who leave the property. I'm sure you know that the mission had, frankly, become an asylum of sorts. The men are mentally ill."

Anthony's jaw clenched. "They witnessed evil, Bishop."

"We've all witnessed evil."

"Have we?" Anthony countered.

"Look around you, young man."

"I have faced demons. I have freed souls."

"You are not a priest."

"I am not."

"I know exactly who you are, Mr. Zaccardi. And you are given a lot of latitude because of your friends in the Vatican."

"I am given latitude because I can see demons. Where is the tabernacle now?"

"In storage awaiting shipment to Rome. Perhaps you'd like to take it back with you?"

Anthony bit back his first, angry remark.

"Perhaps I would," he said.

"I will ready it for you immediately."

The demon looked at his minions through his new human eyes, relishing with hubris the worship in their expressions. He craved adoration.

"Is it done?" he asked.

"Yes. We have the records."

"Have? Why didn't you destroy them?"

"We thought the information would be valuable," the older woman said. "The doctor was very detailed in his comments. There are prayers and protections that may help us grow stronger."

She was right. He'd been in a destructive mood ever since the journal disintegrated and Zaccardi saved Skye McPherson. That soul should have been his!

"You—" He pointed to the older woman. "Drive." He stared at the younger woman. "You, in back with me."

"I—"

His eyes glowed. "I have lusted for nine hundred years since I last possessed a human body. You will serve me."

She nodded, fear and excitement in her eyes, unable and unwilling to deny his lust.

He roared his satisfaction and ripped off her clothes.

Anthony sat in the Santa Louisa Public Library, his knees hitting the low table, hunched over a computer. He typed into the Google search engine: *"Jeremiah Hatch"*

He'd already woken Father Philip in Italy who was covertly looking into the mission records. The mentally disturbed priests were given necessary compassion by the church and cared for, but no one wanted to admit to the public that the presence of evil could break the strongest of the faithful. What hope could there be for regular people if devout priests crumbled within Satan's grasp?

There were far too many hits on the name, so Anthony narrowed the search to *"Jeremiah Hatch + priest."*

Fewer than a hundred sites came up and Anthony began clicking through.

He found an article published four years ago in a national newspaper about a group of missionaries, led by Monsignor Jeremiah Hatch, gone missing in Guatemala. When representatives from the Teach the Poor project had visited the site, they found it completely empty. Six missionaries gone, as if vanishing into thin air. The local villagers refused to talk, but by all accounts they knew what had happened. They'd been scared silent.

There was a bio on each missionary, including Hatch.

> Monsignor Jeremiah Hatch, 43, was born in Denver, Colorado. Orphaned at the age of twelve, he was taken in by the Sisters of Mercy. A graduate of Notre Dame University, he entered St. John's Seminary in California at the age of twenty-seven. Ordained three years later, he served as a priest in the Los Angeles Diocese, the Portland Diocese, and most recently in the Washington, DC Diocese. He'd been an advisor to Teach the Poor for the past ten years.

Anthony wondered what Hatch had done between the time he graduated college and joined the seminary. Was it just a coincidence that he'd attended the same seminary where Rafe was studying?

Another article published just a year ago mentioned Hatch again.

> Three years after he went missing and was presumed dead while a missionary in Guatemala, Monsignor Jeremiah Hatch walked into a hospital in Belize. Though physically healthy, he had no recollection of the last three years.
>
> Representatives from the United States Bishops came to bring Msgr. Hatch back to the States, but one unidentified nurse said, "He kept repeating, 'They're dead. They're all dead.'"

That would explain why he was sent to the Santa Louisa Mission, Anthony surmised.

Curious about Hatch's childhood, Anthony tried other search terms, focusing on Denver.

Nothing. The bad thing about the Internet was that while information over the last decade was easily searchable, the further back you went the harder it was to find anything. Archives often didn't make it online.

Why would Monsignor Hatch bring the tabernacle to the bishop? Anthony had inspected the damage, and it was minimal—a few missing stones, a few more loose. The stones themselves were replaceable.

The importance of the tabernacle was that it protected the priests against evil. Its removal put them all in jeopardy. If Davies was responsible for summoning the demon, she may have been poisoning the priests to make it easier for the demon to gain a foothold. And if Hatch was one of the three humans needed to extract Ianax from Hell, he would know to remove the tabernacle.

It didn't make sense *unless* Hatch knew of the protective qualities of the tabernacle. And wanted it gone.

And the only reason he'd want it gone would be because he knew what was coming. *Who* was coming.

Which meant he had betrayed everyone at Santa Louisa de Los Padres Mission. Just like Charles Wicker said.

But Hatch was dead. Had someone betrayed him? Or . . .

Anthony ran from the library. He opened the trunk of his rental—he'd taken a taxi to retrieve his car after leaving Skye—and inspected the tabernacle more closely.

He crossed himself. "Please forgive me, Father."

On the bottom panel an ancient Hebrew incantation was stamped in the metal. Anthony had to take apart the tabernacle to remove the inscribed prayer. This would help him break the spell surrounding the evil house on the coast. Skye would return, and if he couldn't get past the invisible barrier, she would most certainly die.

He slid into the driver's seat and picked up his cell phone. He had to get Rod Fielding to talk to him. Then he would know for sure whether Monsignor Hatch had worshipped demons.

# Chapter Thirteen

Feeling alone wasn't unusual, but when Skye watched Anthony walk away that morning, she felt lost. Almost as lost as when her mother deserted the family. When her father died.

She shook her head. Ridiculous. It was the remnants of the drugs, the long day and lack of sleep. That's why her mother and father were in her thoughts. That's why she couldn't get Anthony out of her mind. She wanted to trust him, but how could she?

*He walked through fire.*

The arson investigator told her over the phone it might have appeared as if he walked in the fire, but no one could survive unscathed. He explained the concept of backdraft, and how fire seemed to disappear, then could return more powerful and destructive, consuming everything in its path.

Skye suppressed what had happened at the mission. Her mind must have tricked her eyes, just like when she thought she saw her father on the cliffs.

She was a cop in the U.S.A. Anthony Zaccardi worked for the Vatican. A religious cult, as far as she was concerned. It wasn't as if he would stick around once the killers were in custody. He'd go back to Italy—Rome, Florence, Sicily, wherever—and that would be that.

She rubbed her face, missing him. What had gotten into her? She wanted to place her trust in a man she'd just met, a man who had an illogical but quick answer to every one of her problems? The fact that she missed him proved her judgment was damaged, as least as far as Anthony Zaccardi was concerned.

After checking with Rod and learning it would be another day before the autopsies were complete, she checked in with dispatch. No word yet on Juan Martinez. Guilt twisted her heart. She should know where her people were at all times. Instead, when Juan went missing, she was screwing a European hottie on the cliffs.

She rubbed her face. In her heart she knew it wasn't like that, but in the end she was responsible for the destruction of Rafe Cooper's journal, for Juan's disappearance, for sending Anthony away.

She went by the hospital, ostensibly to check on the status of her main suspect, but in her heart she knew it was to see Anthony. He wasn't there, nor had he been.

She drove by the inn. He wasn't there, either. She called dispatch and he hadn't picked up his passport.

Her instincts overrode her personal wishes. What was he up to?

She'd already put a BOLO on Corinne Davies and her daughter, Lisa. If anyone saw them, they were to call her. She wanted to talk to them, not scare them or send them into hiding.

Running through her mental checklist, she called Brian Adamson, the delivery driver whom Juan had spoken to the morning of the murders, asking if Juan had spoken with him since yesterday morning. He hadn't.

What Skye didn't understand was if Ms. Davies was poisoning the priests, why would the grocery records matter to Rafe Cooper? Why couldn't she have brought her own poison to the mission? Using the grocery would only heighten suspicion and leave a trail. She could easily have brought hemlock or whatever from her own garden. Unless, maybe, he first suspected the produce from the grocery was tainted.

And why had the killer removed the weapons? Perhaps to make it *appear* that something supernatural had happened when it was simply another example of human violence? The weapons probably didn't belong in the mission. Someone had brought them there. Skye's head hurt as she contemplated that someone had drugged twelve men, put weapons in proximity, and watched the brutal show. The weapons themselves must hold significance to the killers, or be traceable, otherwise why would they need to reclaim them?

She wanted to ask Anthony. He obviously understood religious nutcases.

*That's not fair.*

Skye ran a hand through her hair, messing with the ponytail, and she undid it, shaking her head.

Someone must have drugged the men after Davies left. If, in fact, Davies was involved at all. Perhaps she had been a scapegoat? Maybe the men had been drugged by someone inside, and Rafe Cooper arrived and pointed a finger at Corinne Davies. Maybe she was truly an innocent, but knew something. Could she, too, be in danger?

She'd gone off to a spa and her daughter was alone. Had her daughter reached her? Where were they now? Could they also be victims, and in Skye's exuberance to find a suspect and close this case she had put potential victims in the suspect column?

She called Rod. She had one more question for him.

"How were the drugs administered to the men the night they died?"

"All I can tell you is that they ate stew the night they died."

"Stew?"

"You know, beef, potatoes, carrots, onions, gravy. Stew."

"What about additions? Were the drugs in the stew?"

"The drugs had to have been in the stew. All but one of the men ate it. The richness of the food would have disguised the bitterness. I don't have the lab reports back yet to confirm."

Just like the sugar she added to her coffee disguised the bitterness.

"Who didn't eat the stew?"

She heard him flipping through papers. "Jeremiah Hatch. He had lettuce, carrots, onions, and bread, no stew."

"Why wasn't Rafe Cooper affected?"

"He wasn't dead. I couldn't examine his stomach contents," he said sarcastically.

"What about tox screens? Wouldn't the hospital have run tests?"

"Is this important?"

"Yes."

"I'll call over to the hospital and find out. I had the lab test his blood and he had no mercury or heavy metal poisoning."

"Didn't you say that you could see traces in the hair of the priests?"

Rod paused. "Yes, but that ended two weeks ago. And your comatose friend was only there for a few weeks before."

"Can you check, anyway?"

He sighed. "Of course."

"And don't forget the prints at my house."

"I have someone working on it."

"Thanks, Rod. I didn't mean to snap at you. This case—" She didn't have to say anything else.

"I know. Be careful."

She hung up and considered the new information. Either Cooper hadn't eaten the stew and he was involved, or as the evidence showed, he was locked in his room. A room with no locks.

If Cooper had suspected the housekeeper of drugging the priests, why hadn't he pressed charges? Nothing had come through her department. And if Davies was no longer in the picture, how was the food tainted? By this Hatch guy who had no stew in his stomach? But he was dead when the fire started—had Davies broken into the mission to set it? Had they been working together? Why? And what purpose would she have had for drugging those men and turning them into killers?

Motive. That's what was bugging Skye. There was no damn *reason* for those men to be drugged.

By the time she walked into the station late that evening, she was exhausted, but Juan was still missing and she'd get no sleep knowing he could be injured, imprisoned, or worse.

She ran the delivery guy and Hatch through the data-base. Nothing. Hatch didn't even have a driver's license, in California or any other state. Which made sense because there had been only one car at the mission, a ten-year-old Chevy Suburban registered to Raphael Cooper.

Deputy Tommy Reiner dropped a thick file folder on her desk. "Background on the dead priests," he said.

She opened the folder. "Anything pop out at you?"

"Lots of holes. Only three were United States citizens. The other nine were from all over the world. Got one guy from Argentina, another from Nigeria, another from Denmark. A regular melting pot up there."

"Why's the folder so thick?"

"I pulled medical records, at least what I could get without a court order. They were all under the care of the same doc, a shrink named Charles Wicker."

"I spoke to him this morning." And then she'd let Anthony talk to a potential witness. How could she have done that?

She had more questions for Dr. Wicker. Because it was after hours, she dialed his home number first.

After four rings: "Wicker residence."

"This is Sheriff Skye McPherson from Santa Louisa. I'd like to speak with Dr. Wicker regarding a patient of his."

A long pause. "Badge number?"

She didn't expect that, but she recited the number from memory.

"Sheriff, this is Officer Timothy Young from the Santa Clara Police Department. Dr. Wicker was shot earlier today. We arrived on the scene an hour ago after his daughter discovered him and called 911."

"How?"

"Gunshot to the head. He apparently surprised a burglar. We think his attacker may have been after drugs."

"Why do you think that?"

"Dr. Wicker was a psychiatrist. His garage was converted into an office. We believe it happened between one and two when he returned from lunch."

"Will he make it?"

"Touch and go. He's in surgery now."

"Do you know what was taken?"

"Not exactly. The file cabinets were broken into, drugs all over the place, the room is a mess."

"I need you to do me a favor," she said. "Can you check for a specific file?"

"Is this related to a case?"

"I'm working the murders at Santa Louisa Mission. Dr. Wicker was the psychiatrist for the men who lived there."

Skye could almost see Officer Young nodding. "I'll have to talk to the detective in charge; he arrived a few minutes ago. I'll have him get back to you. What are you looking for?"

She read him the list of names of the dead priests, Raphael "Rafe" Cooper, and asked for any files related to Santa Louisa.

She hung up and told Reiner what she'd learned. "I don't think Wicker's shooting was a coincidence."

Reiner was reading her report from her meeting with the bishop. "Hey, I don't know if this means anything, but it says that the housekeeper, Davies, had worked in Salem. One of the dead guys, Hatch, was in Salem about five years ago. Think they knew each other?"

*Hatch hadn't eaten the stew.*

"Maybe," she said. "I made a call to the diocese earlier today, but haven't received a call back." She called again, but it was after hours. She wondered if Anthony would be able to get information from them tonight, but again she hesitated to ask for his help. She could just as easily make the call in the morning. "Let's assume that Davies and Hatch knew each other, what does it mean?"

Reiner shrugged. "Dunno. Maybe they had a thing going on. Maybe they hated each other. Maybe she wanted to kill him, but poisoned everyone so there wouldn't be a connection."

"Let's go out to the Davies property again."

Her phone rang again. It was Rod.

"What do you have for me?"

"Hello to you, too." His words were slurred.

"You okay?"

"Never been better," he said sarcastically. "Just came home from the morgue to shower the stench of death off my body."

"You're drunk. Let's talk in the morning."

"I have the report from my team who went to your house."

"And?"

"The only fingerprints are yours, Juan's, and Mr. Zaccardi's."

That made sense. Juan was a regular visitor, they often had drinks after work, especially when his wife took the girls out of town to visit their large extended family. And Zaccardi had gone through her entire house.

"What about the coffeepot?"

"Yours and Zaccardi's. You told me he's the one who checked the grounds."

"What about the jar I keep my coffee in? The back of the coffeepot where the water goes?"

"I know how to do my job. The entire coffeepot was checked. Mercury-laced grounds, a borderline lethal dose. You're lucky Zaccardi was there."

Lucky? What if he had poisoned her to begin with? To distract her while his accomplice searched her house? Destroyed the journal? Or replaced the journal with blank, torn pages? She'd told him to leave the country; what if he had helped the killer? What if he was part of a larger conspiracy?

Her head pounded. "Thanks," she said quietly and hung up.

It was Anthony all along. He'd poisoned her coffee, his were the only fingerprints on the pot. There was no other explanation.

How could she have been so wrong about him? How could she have screwed him? He'd filled her mind with doubt and confusion, steering her away from the truth, giving her hope through trickery. She'd wanted so much to believe him when he told her he never lied. Even her heart lied to her, telling her she was safe in his arms.

Anthony was a master of deception.

"I want an APB put out on Anthony Zaccardi," she told Reiner. "Call the front desk sergeant. I told Zaccardi he could pick up his passport. When he does, I want him arrested."

# CHAPTER FOURTEEN

ANTHONY FOUND ROD FIELDING at his house. The head CSI was three sheets to the wind, and still drinking.

"Hey, preacher," Rod said, opening the door wide, looking like an old man.

"I'm not a priest."

Rod shrugged. "What can I do for you?"

"Can I come in?"

He shrugged again and Anthony stepped in, closed the door. "You're done with the autopsies."

"Eight of them. Four more tomorrow. Then tissue analysis, blood work to follow up on, body parts to catalogue. Fun." He drained a tall glass that looked more rum than Coke.

"I—"

Rod interrupted. "We found the eyes, by the way. Skye was upset about the eyes, but I found them."

"Where?" he asked quietly.

"In the hands of another victim."

Anthony swallowed thickly. "I need to ask you something."

"I can't tell you anything, you know that."

He raised his eyebrows. "But you can share the information about the missing eyes?"

"Where's Skye?"

"Working."

"She booted you off the case."

"I'm not a cop."

"She can be prickly, but she's a good cop."

"I know."

"She doesn't believe your theory."

"Do you?"

He rose, mixed himself another drink—rum with a splash of Coke. He sat down across from Anthony, leaned forward, face flushed but eyes surprisingly sober. "I don't know what the fuck to believe, Zaccardi. This shit doesn't happen here. I'll never get rid of these images. I *want* to believe that something supernatural did this, that no human being could be so vicious. But I know we can. I saw what a man did to his family last year. Stabbed them to death while they slept. But nothing, nothing like this."

"Who was on the altar?"

"Why?"

"I need to know."

"Does this prove your satanic ritual theory?"

"I never believed it was a satanic ritual," Anthony said. Not in the way Rod did.

"Altar." He closed his eyes as if mentally going through files, then opened them and said, "Hatch, forty-seven, six foot even, one hundred eighty-six pounds."

A sick feeling crept in.

"Does that mean something?"

"Yes." Anthony frowned.

"What?"

"Do you have the time of death for all the men?"

"Time of death is an inexact science. We established they all died between four and five Monday morning."

"Do you know in what order they died?"

"Three or four fatal fights broke out at once. I can tell based on blood spatter and foreign material in each body who was stabbed first, for example, but I don't know the exact time they died. Not until we finish the autopsies, and even then we're talking about minutes apart."

"What about the man on the altar?"

"I can look it up at the office. Why? What do you think happened?"

"I need to know if he was the last to die. I need to know how he died."

Rod stared at him for a long minute. "Skye would have my job if she knew I was telling you this. The guy on the altar had been stabbed in the shoulder, but that's not what killed him. The wound was superficial. He died of a heart attack."

"He was young."

"Forty-seven isn't too young for a heart attack. I've had victims as young as thirty-five on the table. But—" He stopped.

"What?"

"He had a healthy heart. No sign of an attack. His heart just—stopped."

*Because the demon tried to possess him. And something happened.*

Had Rafe interrupted the process? Did Hatch have a

change of heart? Right now, Anthony believed Jeremiah Hatch was intimately involved in the massacre. He had to have been one of the three. He sat on the altar watching the violence. Waiting. To willingly give up his soul. If Ianax has a willing human possession, he becomes twice as powerful than if he has to fight his way in. A willing human gained the immortality of the demon as long as they were united.

*Walk with the willing dead.*

A willing possession always ended in death once the demon was exorcized, but it was much more difficult to defeat the demon when the possessed soul wasn't fighting.

It was no coincidence Rafe had been on the floor next to the altar. He would have been dead or possessed had Anthony not come when he had. Rafe must have known what Hatch was doing. Stopped the ritual. But he'd been too late to save the others. He'd been held captive in his room—evidenced by the scratch marks and wounds on his hands—until the actual possession began and the demon couldn't hold Rafe off.

Why hadn't Rafe been poisoned? Was it as simple as the fact that he wasn't a priest? Or that he'd never seen evil incarnate? Or—

"Do you know how the poison was given to the priests?"

"I know how they consumed the last dose. In stew served late the night before."

"Stew."

"Everyone but Hatch and your friend Cooper. There's no evidence of heavy metal poisoning in Cooper's body."

"Rafe is a vegetarian," Anthony said.

"Since you and Skye are on the outs right now," Rod said, "you probably haven't heard. But it might be important. The psychiatrist treating the priests was shot today. All files related to the mission are missing."

Anthony froze. "Someone tried to kill Charles Wicker?"

"Yep, he's in surgery." He drank half his rum. "I heard through the grapevine that Skye put out an APB on you. She thinks you're the one who poisoned her coffee."

"Why?"

"Your fingerprints, and hers, were the only ones found in the kitchen."

Skye was looking at the facts, the evidence—and thought he'd planned to kill her. That she had such a low opinion of him ached, but he didn't have time to wallow in self-pity or indignation.

"If I'm supposed to be in prison, why did you talk to me to begin with?"

Rod drained his rum and said, "Because I've been in this business a long time and something doesn't add up. Hell, a lot of things aren't making sense to me." He stared at Anthony. "I don't think you're a killer, and God help me if I'm wrong, but I think you're the only one who can stop whatever's happening."

Anthony sat in Rod Fielding's personal car outside the sheriff's department watching Skye's police-issue Bronco. He'd talked Rod into swapping cars with him, though he wasn't confident Rod wouldn't let it slip if Skye called again that night. He could only hope the scientist passed out before that happened.

It hurt and angered him that Skye thought he'd poisoned

her. Her doubts—or guilt—told her he must be involved. He couldn't convince her with words; only seeing would lead her to believe him.

He called Father Philip. "What do you have?"

"Not much, I'm afraid."

"Give me everything." He told Father Philip about the altar, Jeremiah Hatch, and his theory.

Silence.

"Father?"

"I fear you are right."

"What do you know?"

"Monsignor Hatch was never supposed to be at the Santa Louisa Mission. He returned to his home parish in D.C. after Guatemala and then one day asked his local bishop for a sabbatical. He asked if he could spend time at the Santa Louisa Mission, but the bishop felt he'd be better served at a retreat in Canada. He never showed up, and the bishop filed a missing persons report with the police department."

"How'd he get into the mission?"

"You know they were very reclusive. They wouldn't have turned away one of their own who was hurting."

*Hurting.*

"What about Hatch's childhood?"

"I spoke with the Mother Superior at Sisters of Mercy and she couldn't find his records."

"Missing records?"

"It happens, Anthony. But—"

"It's suspicious, given what we know now."

"It's a theory."

"How did his parents die?"

"I don't have that information."

"It should be in his seminary records." *The same seminary where Rafe was studying. Had he learned something about Jeremiah Hatch? Or had he been ignorant up until the final hour?*

"I'll check, but they may not talk with me."

"This is important, Father. Maybe Cardinal Ciccoli can ask."

Silence again. While Father Philip was satisfied to be considered a relic in the church who saw demons on every corner, Cardinal Ciccoli wanted to uphold his image as a statesman. He had helped Anthony on several occasions, though as quietly and discreetly as possible.

"I will ask him," Father Philip finally said. "If it is truly important."

Anthony watched as Skye left the sheriff's department with a uniformed deputy. They jumped into her Bronco and left. He followed.

Anthony couldn't say for sure Hatch's past was important, but the more information about how Ianax had been summoned from Hell, the better. He already feared he wouldn't be able to save Skye.

"It's important, Father."

"Very well."

"Assume that Hatch was a willing participant for the demon, but the ritual couldn't be completed. What would Ianax do? He didn't go straight back to Hell. I felt him in the fire."

"He must have a human body. The longer he is without one, the weaker he becomes."

"But he needs a willing participant."

"He needed three people to draw him out of Hell, but now that he's here, he'll take anyone he can. And remember—he can move in and out of souls at will. He may have used people without them knowing it. Protect yourself."

Anthony watched Skye turn toward the coastal highway. Fear gripped him. He stayed far back. He now knew where she was going; he couldn't let her see him.

"I have more important things to protect."

# Chapter Fifteen

SKYE HAD TAGGED Deputy Tommy Reiner to join her in the stakeout of the Davies house that night. Though it was only nine when they settled into their hiding spot in a cove of trees to the north of the house, she was beat. There was a connection and she kept circling her mind around possible answers. Everything went back to the Davies and the poisonings. But why? Was Corinne Davies a serial killer? One of those mercy killers? Women serial killers were more likely to use poison or another less "violent" method of death. Male killers usually stuck with knives and guns and hands-on strangulation.

She watched the house and sipped lukewarm black coffee from a thermos she had picked up at Starbucks earlier in the evening. The house was dark and the car registered to Corinne Davies wasn't in the carport. More than that, the place felt as empty as it had when she'd been here this morning with Anthony. Was she wasting her time?

What was Anthony up to? Was she wrong to have put an APB on him? How else to explain his fingerprints all over her coffeepot?

*He'd checked the grounds when you came back from the cliff.*

Whoever poisoned the coffee would have worn gloves, wouldn't they?

Was Anthony himself in danger? Dr. Wicker was fighting for his life. Perhaps the killer would go after Anthony if he—or she—thought Anthony had damaging information. She should have put him in protective custody instead of sending him off.

She rubbed her head. It was going to be a long night.

Anthony hid in bushes on the far side of the Davies house. Skye was in a grove of trees, but he could barely make out a glint of moonlight reflecting off the Bronco. He could, however, see the road. He needed to get into that house without Skye knowing, before the Davies women returned home. But first he had to break the spell protecting the cottage.

His cell phone vibrated in his pocket. He answered with a quiet, "Yes, Father."

"Twelve-year-old Jeremiah Hatch found his parents murdered in their bed. Stabbed to death."

"Did they catch the killer?"

"A drug addict claimed demons made him do it. He committed suicide his first night in jail."

"And?"

"He choked on his own tongue. He'd apparently smuggled in a razor blade, severed his tongue, and attempted to swallow it."

"A razor blade. Are American prisons that poorly monitored?"

"I doubt it."

"Someone brought it to him. Forced him to do it."

"That would be my guess."

"And Jeremiah? Where was he during his parents' murder?"

"Asleep. In his bed down the hall."

"That would be enough to traumatize a child. Enough to be interested in demons."

Silence.

"Father?"

"Maybe he was interested in demons before the murders," Father Philip said quietly.

The realization hit Anthony hard and he swallowed. He heard a car on the highway.

"Pray, Father."

Anthony hung up and walked the long way along the cliff to the back of the house. There was a twenty-five-meter open stretch. The moonlight decreased as filmy clouds moved rapidly overhead.

*Thank you, Lord.*

He ran low across the ground whispering the prayer he'd memorized off the tabernacle. The cliff moaned and the house swayed in front of him.

It was working.

He took out holy water and sprinkled it in front of him as he ran toward the back of the house. Steam rose from the ground where the blessed water fell. But it cleared his path and, aided by the Hebrew incantation, he reached the back of the house without pain. A swath of light cut across the house as he flattened against the back wall.

He used his tools to quietly break the rear window—a bedroom—and eased himself in, just as the side door opened down the hall.

• • •

Skye had a great hiding place, but she couldn't see anyone approach the Davies cottage until the car was practically in the drive.

It was a dark Ford minivan, similar to the one Corinne Davies drove. She couldn't make out the exact model or color, but it could easily have been the black Windstar registered to the elder Davies.

A plump female exited the driver's seat. There was no porch light and Skye only made out her shape in the moonlight. Corinne Davies's driver's license had her at five foot six and two hundred pounds. It could have been her.

A shorter, slimmer woman exited from the sliding rear door. Her lithe frame reminded Skye of Lisa, the daughter. The woman appeared half clothed and limped to the side door. Skye frowned. Had she been assaulted?

"Okay, we'll go and just talk. Take my lead. Watch them. If they poisoned those priests, we need to be cautious. No food or drink, don't touch anything they hand you. Got it?"

"Yes."

She was about to open her door when the sliding door of the minivan opened again and a man exited the car. She stared. She recognized the build, though she couldn't see his face or features. He walked like Juan Martinez.

Why was he with them? Why hadn't he called in? Didn't he know she—and his wife and the entire sheriff's department—were frantic? Maybe he'd found the younger Davies injured and brought them home. Why hadn't he called in the assault?

Maybe it wasn't Juan. Just someone who had the same short, lanky build.

She glanced at Reiner. He didn't seem to think anything of the man. "Boyfriend?" he asked her. "Looks like he had his way with her while Mommy drove."

*Sick.* Definitely not Juan Martinez.

She radioed in where she was and who she was interviewing, then left the Bronco.

A cold fog had crept in from the ocean. It hadn't been there earlier in the evening, but seemed to roll in quickly as often happened on the Central Coast. Skye cut through the mist, the house fading behind the fog even as she approached.

The occupants still hadn't turned on any lights, the porch was dark, but candles flickered behind the blinds.

The door opened before Skye raised her hand to knock. Skye couldn't hide her surprise that Juan Martinez stood in front of her.

"Right on schedule," he said.

Juan's voice was flat, with a hint of humor.

"What's going on?" she asked.

He turned to Reiner. "You can go."

Reiner glanced at Skye, looking as confused as she felt.

Skye put her hand on her gun. Reiner attempted to follow suit, but froze.

His body shook as it rose from the ground. His head moved back and forth quickly, too quickly, and suddenly the snap of breaking bone filled the air, along with the sudden stench of sulfur.

Reiner collapsed on the porch, dead, eyes wide and full of fear.

Skye had her gun in hand, but suddenly her gun was on fire and her hand burned. She screamed in pain and surprise as the gun pulled itself from her grip and flew across the lawn, landing beyond her eyesight.

She turned to run but could not move.

"Come in, Skye. Let's get this nasty business over with," Juan said, arms open, palms up.

She stared at his hands. They were burned, but he didn't seem to notice what looked like painful blisters.

What was happening? Reiner—her gun—Juan?

For the first time she believed. Everything Anthony had told her was the truth. And she'd sent him away.

"You've been making friends with the enemy," Juan said, "and you'll be the one to kill him."

# Chapter Sixteen

Skye was a cop willing to stand against bad guys when necessary to save innocents, but she wasn't stupid.

Juan had no weapons she could see, but that didn't mean he wasn't armed. She dove to the right, toward two metal chairs. She toppled them, hoping they would provide her with a shield so she could jump off the porch and buy time to call for help.

She leaped over the railing like a horse, twisting her ankle as she fell to lower ground. She winced, knew it was sprained but not broken, and endured the pain as she ran limping in a zigzag pattern toward her Bronco.

She thumbed her lapel mic in Morse code, sending an SOS to her department.

Her radio broke under her thumb. The mic smoked around her neck and she pulled it off, coughing at the fumes.

Her chest tightened and she had no air. Maybe she'd broken her ribs when she fell and hadn't noticed. They didn't feel broken. Only tight. Tighter. She couldn't breathe.

She collapsed on the ground, gasping for air that would not fill her lungs.

"Foolish daughter of Eve," Juan said, standing over her. "You are alone. No one is coming to help you. No human can save you."

He picked her up as if she weighed but a feather. Her attempts to struggle left her fatigued.

"Juan, what happened to you? Why are you doing this?"

He laughed. And it was in his laugh that Skye knew this wasn't Juan. Not the Juan Martinez she'd worked with for eleven years. Not the Juan Martinez who stood by her when she'd been elevated to sheriff, when others in the department snubbed her.

This man looked like Juan, but he was possessed.

By something . . . evil.

*By a demon.*

*Anthony, I'm so sorry I didn't believe you. Forgive me.*

The demon in Juan chuckled as he walked up the porch steps. "Is it ready?"

"Yes, sire."

It was Corinne Davies who spoke, her eyes lit with excitement. Juan dumped Skye on the couch inside the door, which slammed shut behind them.

The dead bolt slid closed with a sharp metal click. Skye watched—no one touched the lock.

It. Moved. By. Itself.

She looked around the room, trying to contain her panic. She could think like a cop, but how could she reason with an entity that knew no human bounds? That not only didn't have a conscience, but had no soul?

The blinds were drawn tight. Candles burned on every available surface. Someone had carved odd symbols in the walls. Painted shapes on the hardwood floor. The symbol she'd seen at the mission had been burned into the back of the door.

Corinne Davies, late forties, overweight, wearing her long dark graying hair down, looked like the witch out of Hansel and Gretel. She glared at Skye with hateful eyes that seemed to glow, her lips parted as if she would bite. An image of Corinne and Lisa and Juan dancing and howling naked, wearing a jackal's head and hooves for feet, clouded her vision and Skye feared she was losing her mind.

Trapped in this room. Unable to move though no ropes bound her. These lunatics—as wild-eyed as her mother had been when she told Skye she was leaving—had controlled forces that no human should be able to control.

They'd brought evil into her town, and if she didn't end it here, more people would die.

She didn't want to die, but if that was the only way to stop them she would.

Lisa Davies sashayed into the room. She wore a long, see-through white gown and nothing underneath. "The bedroom window is broken."

Juan whirled at her. "So?"

"I don't know who might have come in."

"Didn't you do as I commanded? Protect the ground?"

"Of course—"

Juan closed his eyes, held up his burned hands. "No one is here." But his face twisted in pain. "He's fighting me. Prepare the ritual."

Juan sat cross-legged on the floor, in the middle of the painted symbol.

"What are you doing?" Skye demanded.

Corinne slapped her across the face and Skye tasted blood. Skye couldn't control her movements and the older woman easily pulled her up and dragged her into the circle with Juan.

"You drugged those innocent men," Skye said, spitting out the words, each one a chore as she fought to breathe. What were they planning on doing with her?

Skye focused on the older woman. "What did you hope to gain by killing those men?" she asked.

"I didn't kill anyone. They killed each other." Her face glowed with pleasure.

Skye said, "You poisoned them."

Corinne laughed, put her hand on Skye's neck and squeezed. "You have never experienced true power until you give up your soul. I have immortality. I will live forever. But you will die. The worms will eat your flesh, the earth will claim your bones. But I will dance on your grave in a hundred years!"

"Quiet!" Juan hissed.

He chanted under his breath in a language Skye had never heard, but it sounded vaguely like what Anthony had spoken earlier.

She had sent him away, ridiculed him, accused him of awful things, and yet something was going on here that only Anthony would understand. Only Anthony would be able to stop this . . . this evil.

*Anthony, I'm sorry. I should have believed you. You were right. Forgive me.*

"Juan, how could you do this to me? To Beth? Your girls are going to grow up knowing their father is a killer."

Juan's face wavered in front of her, as if a million bugs

moved just beneath the skin. His brown eyes glowed red. Her stomach rolled and she nearly choked on her own bile.

"*Shut up, human!*"

A burning filled her from the inside out and her vision faded.

"Don't!" Lisa screamed. "We need her alive!"

Juan's fierce anger turned on Lisa. Her body flew against the wall, her feet inches from the ground, her mouth open to scream but no sound escaped.

Then she collapsed, gasping for breath.

"Get the knife, stupid girl," Corinne told her daughter. "Don't make him punish you."

"Yes, Mother," Lisa whispered hoarsely.

"What are you doing?" Skye whispered.

"Both Lisa and I are willing to give up our bodies. Jeremiah would have been better because of his experience in these matters. He's been a willing host before. But then Rafe Cooper somehow got out of his room before the ritual was complete. We lost Jeremiah."

"It was your fault," Juan said. "You didn't cast a strong enough shield. I told you Raphael was a threat!"

"I did exactly what Jeremiah told me," Corinne snapped.

"Then it's a good thing he's dead if he's that stupid."

Whatever internal battle waged within Juan, the other presence—the demon—appeared to have control again.

"Why didn't you just kill him?" Skye asked, her breath coming in short gasps. The room grew hotter and she began to sweat. She felt like she was breathing in a thick, hot mist.

Corinne frowned. "We planned on it, but he didn't eat

the stew. He's a damn vegetarian! And he was already suspicious."

"You could have put him in the chapel," Skye said. "It was a massacre."

"He would have stopped the ritual."

"What I don't—" Skye took a deep breath, but it grew more difficult. She struggled to get free, but she'd been caged in an unbreakable, invisible bubble. "Why did you poison them for so long?"

"We had to put them in the right mind-set. Bring back their past. Show them their culpability, their guilt, their pain," Corinne said. "They were weakening. And then, when the time was right, we would have increased the dose and the result would have been the same, except that we'd have a greater reward. But that intruder nearly ruined everything. He had me removed from the mission." She smiled and glanced at Lisa. "I almost had him, too."

Skye closed her eyes. She was tired. Very tired. Her limbs felt heavy, and she found herself lying down in the circle.

Juan's chanting continued.

She had a million more questions, but couldn't find her voice. With great effort, Skye reached into her shirt and pulled out the cross Anthony had given her. She recited the Latin phrase he had had her repeat the night before, her words a mere whisper.

Juan screamed in pain and every candle flared simultaneously.

Corinne grabbed the cross and jerked off the chain, breaking it and drawing blood across Skye's neck. She threw the cross into the fireplace and chanted something that sounded like no language Skye had ever heard. Corinne's hand was in flames and Lisa wrapped it with a blanket.

The fire behind her roared to life. Juan leaned over her prone body, looked down at her, his face full of broken blood vessels.

*"I will not be defeated!"*

His eyes glowed and his mouth opened in a deep roar that vibrated every cell in Skye's body.

Juan began to chant again, looking into her eyes. She couldn't draw her gaze away, as if someone held her lids open. Corinne and Lisa joined in the ritual. The heat in the room increased until sweat poured from Skye's body. The foul stench that had permeated Skye's own house that morning seeped in, filling her nostrils, her lungs, until she wasn't breathing air, but thick sulfur. Her eyes drooped; she was on the verge of passing out.

On the ceiling, over Juan's shoulder, she saw flames. Bright, hot, red. She saw eyes, everywhere eyes, glowing, howling, laughing, shrieking. She tried to scream but no sound came out.

Her father stood in front of her, consumed by fire.

*You forgot me. You let me die.*

*No, Daddy! I loved you.*

He ignited in front of her, his flesh turning black, falling off his bones, raining down on her.

She screamed.

Her mother—her beautiful, elegant mother—floated in the flames. Her face twisted, her cheeks hollow. Skye watched the fire dance in the large hole in her chest.

"Mom," Skye muttered, her voice distant, as if she was hearing a poor recording of herself.

*I left because of you. I never wanted a child. You should never have been born.*

She was so alone. Dead to the world. No one to love. No one who loved her.

They were going to burn her alive. The whole cottage was on fire and she was going to die . . .

. . . then she saw the knife in Lisa's hand.

*Anthony. Help me.*

Ianax had one common trait with every demon Anthony had encountered.

Arrogance.

Ianax couldn't sense him because in his arrogance he'd believed he'd taken care of Anthony by erecting a protective circle and making Skye doubt him. Ianax also had to battle to keep Juan's soul imprisoned, which consumed a huge amount of satanic energy.

Anthony knew exactly what the three were doing. They were destroying Skye from the inside out in preparation for the purging of Juan's soul to the netherworld. Juan was an unwilling host and fighting the possession, so they needed to weaken Skye so she wouldn't fight Ianax when he claimed her. If that failed, they would sacrifice her.

Skye had been worn down to raw nerves, her grief and guilt and loneliness being used to destroy her.

*Anthony. Help me.*

Anthony heard Skye's plea, didn't know if she had screamed it or thought it. He peered from his hiding place into the living room where the demonic ritual was unfolding. Skye writhed on the floor as if in pain, but nothing was touching her. Skye's eyes were wild, unseeing—at least not seeing what was in front of her. Something was scaring her, something that made her believe. Believe in him. And that was all Anthony needed.

Juan and the Davies women stood over Skye, chanting, drawing out her soul.

Corinne's speech to Skye made sense to Anthony. The two women and Hatch had summoned Ianax, and had he successfully possessed Hatch's body, the demon would have been far more powerful on earth. He would have finished the ritual and dragged the other souls down to Hell. A huge victory for Satan to have God's own men in his domain, and as a reward Ianax would walk on earth in human form but with inhuman power, the goal of every demon.

But Rafe had interrupted the process, possibly begun an exorcism, and Hatch died before the possession was complete, his soul already damned. And Rafe—

Anthony remembered the rush of heat followed by icy cold when he'd entered the chapel and saw the carnage.

Rafe was unconscious; he would have been a perfect vessel for the demon. Tortured, unable to save his men. Guilt had consumed him. Ianax could have taken him, used his anguish against him, but Anthony had interrupted.

Where had the women been?

*In the sacristy.*

He hadn't searched the chapel, he'd been so intent on saving Rafe.

He could have stopped it two days ago. But he'd been blind in his own fear and failures. And now Skye was going to die because of him.

*No.* He shook his head. *I will not let her die.*

He brought out his dagger-cross and held it in front of him as he said in a loud, deep voice, "By the power of the heavens, of the Holy Spirt, by the order of Saint Michael and all the angels and saints, Ianax! You are dismissed!"

The demon in Juan screamed. Corinne stepped toward Skye while Lisa jumped at Anthony with her long nails outstretched.

Anthony pushed aside all notions that hitting a woman was wrong, and put all his strength into a right hook that stopped Lisa in her tracks. The girl crumpled at his feet, knocked cold.

"Bastard!" Corinne screamed, holding a knife at Skye's neck, crouched over her like a wild animal. Skye was sweating profusely, her body jerking as if being poked and prodded.

*She's dying.*

"Fight, Skye!" he shouted.

Corinne couldn't kill Skye because Ianax needed her.

Anthony hoped he was right. He hadn't faced such an ancient demon, nor one who was so powerful that he could survive on earth without a body, which he'd done for hours after Hatch's death.

Anthony held his cross high, chanting ancient words of exorcism.

Juan twisted, his body rising from the ground. The demon stared at Anthony.

"YOU!" he howled, his mouth straining. "I will not go back!"

The screech hurt Anthony's ears, but he continued. The demon held up his hand and Anthony was slammed against the wall, his body inches from the ground. Pain hit him like a million pinpricks. He couldn't draw air into his lungs.

Skye was pinned to the floor but looked right at him.

In her eyes, Anthony saw her pain and love and loneliness and, mostly, her trust.

Suddenly she screamed, *"NO!"* as her body arched in pain.

The demon's hold on Anthony slipped. Anthony pushed back from the wall. Corinne grabbed Skye's hair, held the knife to her throat.

The demon's horrid face could be seen in Juan as he touched Skye. "Blood for my Master and two souls."

Corinne brought the knife up and, chanting with the demon, aimed the tip for Skye's heart.

Anthony tackled Corinne, threw her from the circle. The tip of the knife sliced his side. He grabbed her wrist, slammed it against the edge of a low table, hearing the bone crack.

The smell of smoke grew. In the struggle, candles fell and both the couch and the curtains ignited.

Anthony grabbed the knife and pulled from his belt a vial of holy water from the river Jordan. He poured the water on the knife; steam rose and the knife burned his hand. It was a demonic knife, one used in many deadly rituals.

And very likely one of the knives used in the massacre at the mission.

Anthony had one chance.

The demon grabbed Skye and held her to him. Her face twisted in pain. She struggled to breathe.

Anthony glanced to Skye's right. She blinked once.

He raised the knife. "Let her go, Ianax!"

An unnatural voice rose from Juan's throat. "Mine."

Anthony felt his chest tighten. He threw the knife at the same time as Skye pivoted right. The demon's hold on her was tight and she couldn't get away. The fire grew around them, feeding on the fuel that was the house.

The knife missed her by an inch, landing exactly where Anthony aimed in Juan's thigh.

The demon screeched, his head thrown back, and Skye fell to the floor. Thick black smoke shot out of Juan's mouth, up to the ceiling, then with a shriek that made Anthony's ears ring, the demon disappeared through the fire.

He would be back. Anthony had to get them out of the house.

"What have you done?" Corinne shouted.

As soon as the demon was gone, Skye could breathe. But the smoke was thick, the fire hot. She crawled over to Juan's prone body.

"Juan!" she cried. The knife was in his leg and she knew it would be even more dangerous to attempt to remove it now.

"We have to get out now," Anthony said, staggering toward her.

Blood soaked through the side of his shirt.

The ceiling began to collapse around them. Skye stood unsteadily, grabbed Juan under his arms, and dragged him toward the door.

Corinne blocked the door. "You will die with us!" she said. "And I'll drag all your souls down to Hell!"

Anthony lunged at her, knocked her to the side. They fought and Anthony shouted, "Get out, Skye!"

Skye couldn't leave Anthony. But Juan was unconscious.

She struggled to open the door, an ungodly scream echoing around them in the night sky. Coughing out smoke and taking in as much air as possible, she dragged Juan off the porch.

The house was engulfed in flames. She couldn't see the sky through the smoke, but something looked off. The fire itself was red, the flames dense. The house seemed to be shrinking in front of her.

*Anthony.*

She ran up the steps and through the open door. Anthony was lying on the floor, unmoving. *No, no, no!* He'd saved her life. Again. She wasn't going to let him die, not when she had so much to tell him.

It took all her strength to drag him out. The smoke weakened her, the fire burned her skin. She glanced at Corinne Davies, unconscious. She couldn't see her daughter Lisa through the smoke, on the far side of the living room.

She couldn't save them. She didn't even know if she could save Anthony and herself.

*"You are mine!"*

The flames danced and whispered, a cacophony of heat and flames and burning wood and falling timber, but all Skye heard was the call of the demon.

*"You are mine. You are mine. You are mine."*

Skye didn't stop. She used strength she didn't know she had to drag Anthony from the burning house. The porch collapsed as they crossed it, and Skye rolled down the stairs with Anthony. He grunted when they landed on the sandy soil.

"Anthony!" She crawled away, dragging him, feeling the house pulling her back. She glanced over her shoulder and saw the face of evil in the flames as an inhuman scream echoed through the night.

With a deafening roar, the house collapsed into itself, and nothing but the smoldering foundation remained.

Sirens pierced the air. "Anthony, Anthony, talk to me," Skye whispered, her voice hoarse and dry from the smoke.

"Skye," he murmured. "My Skye."

She cried with relief. She kissed him, her hand touching his chest.

The blood.

She ripped open his shirt. A deep cut sliced open his lower abdomen. He'd lost so much blood already. It coated his shirt, her fingers. She pressed her hands on the wound, but it didn't stop the bleeding.

"No, no!" She couldn't lose him. "I'm sorry."

"Do. You. Trust me?" His speech was labored.

"Yes, of course. I'm so sorry I didn't believe—"

"Water in my pocket."

"I don't—"

"Hurry."

She reached into his pockets. In one was a plastic bottle half full of a clear liquid. Water?

"Pour it. On the wound."

"I don't think—"

"Trust, my Skye." He coughed.

Hands shaking, she unscrewed the cap. She smelled the liquid. Nothing.

She poured it over his wound. Before her eyes, the wound stopped bleeding. It seemed to . . . shrink.

"I don't understand," she said.

He reached for her, pulled her into the nook of his arm. "My faith, your trust."

She relaxed in his arms. The sirens were closer, the lights of the rescue vehicles cutting across the cliff where the Davies house used to stand.

"Don't leave me," she whispered.

"Never."

She took his hand in hers, brought it to her lips. "I thought I'd lost you. I'm so alone, Anthony."

"Not anymore."

She turned her head, looked at his face. "What is this, Anthony? I feel complete. With you."

He smiled. "We're complete together. I love you, Skye."

"You live in Italy."

"I live with you."

Realization hit her, but she didn't want to believe. Didn't want to be hurt. "But your life—"

He kissed the top of her head. "My life is with you. My soul belongs to you while I walk this earth. I am what I am, warts and all, but I am a man who believes in fate, a man who believes I came here for a reason. To save you."

He kissed her again, his lips stealing her loneliness.

"I was a lonely man," he whispered in her ear. "Until I saw you."

Skye had never felt truly at peace, until now, lying in the nook of Anthony's arm, being held, and holding.

Maybe, maybe she could believe in love.

# CHAPTER SEVENTEEN

*One week later*

Skye watched Anthony from afar. He stood in the middle of the rubble that had been the Santa Louisa de Los Padres Mission. His dark hair was pulled back into a leather band, his white shirt billowed in the wind, and his hands were outstretched.

He was the most beautiful creature who had ever walked on earth, and the knowledge that he was *hers,* that he loved her, that he wasn't going to leave, had finally sunk in.

She'd had a lot of work this past week, rarely saw him, but he waited for her at her house each night. He made love to her with passion and tenderness, heat and softness, showing her a love she had not believed existed. Because Anthony was in her bed and in her heart, she could put aside the questions from her colleagues, the lawyers, the threats of lawsuits by Corinne Davies's surviving family in Oregon, the forensic evidence that was still a puzzle because—except for Rod Fielding—she'd told no one about the demon, or her belief that supernatural forces were responsible for so much of the destruction.

As far as the public was concerned, Corrine and Lisa

Davies had worked in conjunction with Jeremiah Hatch to poison the reclusive Santa Louisa priests until they committed suicide. The press had implied that it was a Catholic hate crime aimed specifically at the mission, and Skye did nothing to dissuade the rumors.

But there were still so many questions and evidence to sort through. Fielding and his team were scouring the ashes at the Davies house to identify remains. And even though Skye had heard the motive out of Corrine Davies's own mouth—immortality—she had a difficult time accepting it. Without Anthony by her side, she would have believed everything she'd seen had been caused by drugs. But her eyes hadn't deceived her.

With Anthony, she would not only survive but heal. She hoped Juan could as well. A very weak Juan had finally been released from the hospital that morning. He remembered everything that had happened, was tortured by his actions.

"It was the demon." She had finally said it. And believed. She had seen the face of evil, and doubting Thomas was no more.

Juan still tortured himself. Anthony was talking with him daily. If anyone could help Juan, it was Anthony.

The funeral for the priests had been that morning, and Anthony and Skye were the last to leave. Anthony had insisted that the men, except Jeremiah Hatch, be buried at the mission. No one argued. Hatch's body had been shipped overseas, for what purpose Skye didn't know.

Anthony saw her watching him and waved. She stepped over the stones, to the rose garden that had—miraculously—been spared in the fire. Something else unexplainable that Skye was beginning to simply accept as part of her new life.

"Is everything all right?" she asked.

"The demon didn't get their souls, but I don't know if they are at peace."

"I'm sorry." She didn't know what Anthony meant exactly, but he was upset and that, in turn, saddened her.

"They may have a message, but they're not sharing with me."

"Like ghosts?"

He shrugged. "I should be grateful they're not in Hell."

She leaned up and kissed him. "You did everything you could."

"Not everything."

He was thinking about his friend Rafe Cooper. "The doctors said there's nothing physical keeping him from making a recovery," she said.

"I thought—I thought when Ianax was destroyed that Rafe would come out of the coma."

She touched his handsome face, her finger gliding over the dark stone in his ear. "You did everything you could."

"It wasn't enough."

"He'll recover. Have faith, Anthony."

He opened his mouth, closed it. Smiled. "I love you, Skye."

"I love you, too, Anthony Zaccardi."

He pulled her to him. "I spoke with Father Philip earlier. He's going to convince the historical preservation committee at the Vatican that I need to oversee the rebuilding of the mission."

"You're going to rebuild?"

"Yes."

"And you'll need to stay in town."

"I don't have a place to live. I suppose I could go back to the inn." His mouth turned up in a half grin.

She kissed him. "You already have a place to stay. As long as you want."

He rubbed her back, ran a hand through her hair. Made her feel warm and loved and whole for the first time in her life.

"Is forever too long?" he murmured into her lips.

"Sounds just about right."

# Reason
# to Believe

## ROXANNE ST. CLAIRE

# Prologue

FROM: catburd@connectone.com
SUBJ: you don't fool me
DATE: 01.19

great show tonight, ari. you did it all, sweetheart. you threw out bait and reeled in fish like the pro we both know you aren't. you even got that bald fool to cry over his dead cousin. fucking amazing, that's what you are. all sparkles and smiles, TV's darling. you might get a raise. then you can move out of that little house and get a big mansion like all the other phony deadtalkers who hit the big time. oh, yeah, i know where your house is, ari. i've been there. 9302 hillside avenue. right above the place where john belushi died. but you know that. you probably talk to him all the time, don't you? ha ha.

it's only a matter of time until the truth is out, ari. you're a fake. how long can you fool everyone? not much longer. your days are numbered. then the truth will be out and you will be finished.

# CHAPTER ONE

HOW COME SCIENTISTS could build a fully functioning laboratory eighty miles above the earth, but couldn't figure out a way to fix the L.A. freeway system? Chase Ryker had been on both, and the space station ran smoother than the 405—whose bumper-to-bumper congestion extended onto another freeway and all the way into Burbank.

He finally whipped the Porsche into the studio lot and announced himself to the guard, though he wasn't scheduled to arrive until the next day.

"You're on the list," the young man said. "Tomorrow's list."

"I'll wait at Ms. Killian's trailer," Chase said with the authoritative tone he'd perfected in the military.

The guard looked dubious, checking Chase's ID a second time as if this had never occurred at his gate before. "Listen, I can't let you go to her trailer, but this'll get you into sound stage four and you can sit in the audience." He held out a bright red pass.

Good man. He *shouldn't* let anyone go to Arianna Killian's dressing trailer, especially after dark. Security like this made his job easier. But could he push the kid? "I'm not that interested in the show, and I have an appointment."

"For tomorrow," the guard said. "Anyway, her show is great. People wait eighteen months to get tickets. You won't believe it."

No, he wouldn't—that was certain. "All right. Thanks." He took the map of the lot the guard offered and waited for the mesh gate to open.

Chase slid the map behind the visor, not needing it. He'd memorized the layout of the MetroNet studios, along with the roads in and out of the hillside neighborhood where Arianna Killian lived, the gym where she did Jnana Yoga, the natural-food restaurants she frequented, and the Santa Monica home of her widowed father that she visited almost every week. There wasn't much he didn't know logistically about the TV psychic, and he'd learned all of it on the plane down from San Francisco that morning. A photographic memory helped a lot in his job.

Another guard let him into the sound stage where the black and red logo for the show *Closure* hung over the door. Chase declined to sign a taping release, which the guard noted but didn't question. Good thing. He had no intention of being on camera.

When a perky college-aged page took him to the audience seating area, he made a mental note that there was no metal detector to spot the Glock 19 that rested on his hip, hidden by a sports jacket. How many other people in this room packed? He scouted the crowd as the young lady escorted him to an empty seat at the end of the third row.

"There's nothing in the back?" he asked.

"Oh, you'll like it up here," she assured him. "You have a better chance of getting her attention. Who are you here to talk to?"

"The host."

"I mean, who have you lost? Who do you want Arianna to talk to?"

"No one."

That earned him a surprised look. When she walked away, he covertly checked out the audience. These weren't the celebrity-starved tourists who waited to see Jay Leno down the road. All around him, the audience wore expressions that ranged from expectation to raw pain. Many held hands, a few mumbled prayers.

All of them were there because they actually believed in the chance to have that final chat with someone on the other side. They all wanted *closure*. Talk about exploiting a ripe market.

Suddenly the stage blackened and a lonesome piano hit a few slow notes. When the lights came back up and the New Age music died down, the sound stage had two occupants—one, he had to admit, quite riveting.

No doubt about it, the woo-woo girl was pretty.

Not stunning by the extreme standards of Los Angeles, where even the garbage collectors harbored dreams of stardom. But she had an earthy, wild beauty that came as much from the playful glimmer in her emerald green eyes as the cascades of copper waves that fell over her shoulders.

"David," she said, leaning toward the young man sitting across from her. "Don't look so serious. This is supposed to be totally fun." She trilled the *totally* and added a saucy wink. "I promise."

David damn near melted.

She wore a wireless mic clipped to the V-neck of a

buttercream-colored sweater that amplified her soft, feminine voice, and soft, feminine cleavage. All part of the carefully crafted package that had made her a media favorite. Charming, witty, adorable Arianna the TV psychic. But underneath the clingy clothes and sweet curves, despite the whimsical curls and the musical laugh, he'd bet there was a very shrewd businesswoman who knew exactly how to exploit human frailty.

The male guest on the set nodded, leaving his handprint impressions on the leather armrest when he released his grip and wiped his palms on his trousers.

"Are you ready, David?"

"Oh, I'm ready," he said. "I've been ready for two years."

"Okay, then." Arianna closed her eyes and inhaled deeply. "Let's talk to Mary Jo." A long moment of silence passed before she opened her eyes, a hint of a smile so sweet and subtle it had to be practiced a zillion times in front of a mirror. A smile that could sell anything. Even the idea of talking to the dead.

"She wants you to know that she appreciates what you've done for her dog."

*Oh, brother.* For this, he left the side of a Nobel scientist doing top-secret research on particle physics? But that was the nature of his job. And he'd do this one exactly like he'd done every other assignment: thoroughly.

She clasped her hands, twirling a ring on the left middle finger, her face serene and trancelike. "I'm getting something . . . with food. In the kitchen. Did Mary Jo like to cook?"

"God, yes. She was an amazing cook."

Arianna held up her hand as though to silence him, but

of course that just made it look like she was getting all her info from poor dead Mary Jo, when all she was doing was playing an elaborate game of Twenty Questions that would lead her exactly where she wanted to go.

*Did Mary Jo like to cook?* That basically covered half the female population. Talking to the dead, according to the quick research he'd done this morning, was little more than a sophisticated form of Q&A and black magic.

He'd also learned that *Closure* had been running on MetroNet for eight months, and judging by the cost of a minute's worth of advertising, plenty of people were tuning in to witness strangers have those last few words with the dearly departed. Of course, who wouldn't pay big bucks for that last conversation? Even he could think of a few things he'd like to say to someone now gone.

The thought hit him hard, and he forced himself to concentrate on the woman he'd come to watch.

"Mary Jo wants you to know that . . ." She tilted her head up, no doubt to look like she was hearing voices from the grave, but it gave the camera a nice view of her face, oval and symmetrical, with a slightly upturned nose and a little cleft in her chin. A television face, smoothed by the hand of a makeup artist. She wore the creamy color from head to designer toe, no doubt to give her an angelic, ethereal look. It worked.

"There's definitely something about the dog . . ."

"Skippy. Our spaniel. She adored him."

"Skippy." She cooed the name, as if the animal were right there begging for a treat. Then her expression turned compassionate and she leaned closer to David. "Was Skippy with her when she passed?"

David looked down, nodded, fighting tears. She reached over and touched his hand. "She wants you to be happy."

The reading took fifteen excruciating minutes, but by the time she was done, David was persuaded that his dead wife condoned, even supported, his next marriage.

Arianna Killian was a fraud, no doubt about it. Charismatic, infectious, and really, really good at her game. But as fake as her cinnamon hair and long eyelashes.

When David joined his family, who all shared tearful, happy hugs, Arianna stood. The lighting changed, the atmosphere grew charged. All around him, people leaned forward, stared at her, silently mouthed words.

They all wanted to get picked. They all wanted their chance at *closure*.

Psychics who claimed to talk to the dead had been around for centuries, but few had turned the parlor game into a business this big. And very few, Chase thought as he watched the silk of her slacks slide over narrow hips and slender legs with every step, made it look so good.

Or fun. She bantered with an audience member. She made a joke to the cameraman following her. She teased, winked, giggled, and then, without warning, she stopped.

Not far from his section, her body language changed from lighthearted to serious. She began to scan the seats, giving him a chance to notice that under all that makeup, she probably had a dusting of freckles. And her curls had thin strands of gold woven into the red, just enough to look like she'd been sprinkled with glittery bronze.

She placed her hands on her hips and bit gently on a full lower lip. "Is there a . . ." She frowned, searching for a word. "A pilot here?"

He fought the urge to draw back in surprise at the bizarre, but lucky, guess.

A man one row in front of him sat up straighter. "I have a pilot's license," he said eagerly. "You must want me."

Thank God there was a sucker in every crowd. Or in this case, in every seat.

She regarded the man for a moment, her eyes narrowed in thought, her index finger tapping the dip in her chin. "I don't think so. It's over here." Her gaze moved to Chase's section. "Something like a pilot? I'm getting . . ." She played with her ring again, as into the part as any method actor. "Someone inside a missile? A rocket? Is that possible?"

Years of training response control allowed him to maintain an absolutely blank expression. Someone had gotten to her first. They had to have.

"I see a person sitting at what looks like the controls of a plane . . . but he's on his back." She looked his way, massaging her temple, shaking her head as though nothing made sense.

And son of a bitch, it didn't.

"He's wearing a helmet, a visor." She shot a demanding look at the crowd. "And I'm seeing something . . . military or quasi-military."

A young lady in the other side of the audience stood. "Ari, my sister was killed when her helicopter went down in Iraq."

She glanced toward the slightly desperate voice, but gave her head a definitive shake and returned to a study of the people around Chase.

"No, it's not a woman. And it's not a helicopter." She raked a hand through her curls, messing the stylist's careful work, but her practiced expression said she didn't care. "Is it a rocket ship?"

That elicited a light, surprised laugh from everyone.

Everyone except Chase.

"Something's definitely wrong," she continued.

Yes, it was. Very wrong. Who told her he was coming? Who briefed her? There was no other explanation.

"There's an explosion. A fire. It's so hot. Hotter than— things are actually *melting*." She burned the crowd with a frustrated look. "Surely this is coming from one of you."

Chase mentally swore, running through every possible paradigm for how she could have gotten this information. There were a few ways—none of them feasible. Or appealing. Or possible.

She had no way of knowing he'd be in the audience, or who he was.

Their gazes locked and for a minute, he thought he'd sworn out loud. The man next to him turned, and the licensed pilot a row down swiveled to get a look. He could feel the power of numerous stares, but none as direct or unwavering as Arianna Killian's.

"Sir? Have you lost someone in a fire? Someone in the military, perhaps?"

She wanted a nod, some simple assent, and then she'd make a few more educated guesses, ask an open-ended question, redirect the information if she didn't like what she heard. She would hunt and peck, blinding any skeptic with a dazzling smile and pretty green eyes, until she hit a mark. She already knew way more than was possible.

"No," he answered, emotionless.

"I'm getting three initials. STS," she said, as though she

didn't hear the denial. "Someone you lost? Someone you cared about?"

Could she know his name? His face? Could she know that every space shuttle mission started with the same three letters? *Highly improbable*, screamed the pragmatic scientist who resided firmly inside him. But possible.

"These initials mean something to you, don't they?"

Blood roared like an afterburner in his head. Still, he said nothing. It was not the time or place to reveal himself to her, and he'd obviously made a strategic error in coming here.

"I'm getting a lot of blue," she told him, taking slow, deliberate steps closer. "But not sky blue. A dark royal blue. Is that a uniform?"

He didn't nod, didn't move. But he could tell she was reading a response in his eyes. Yeah, she was way past good at this.

"This is someone sitting . . . where you should have been, isn't it?"

Chase felt his fingers tighten around the armrest of his seat. Just like the poor bastard who'd started the show twenty minutes earlier.

Yes, someone had been sitting, launching, and dying . . . where he should have. Gone because Chase was doing something so . . . trivial.

"You can tell me." Her eyes were warm and inviting. He imagined most men did exactly what this woman wanted. But he wasn't most men.

"Save yourself the trouble, Ms. Killian," he said softly, and cocked his head toward the anxious pilot in the row below him. "Try someone who believes."

"He wants to tell you something," she continued, undeterred by his suggestion. "About the . . . incident."

*Incident.* She even used the right euphemism, as NASA did. He maintained a blank expression as she climbed the two steps to his row, vaguely aware of the red light of the camera over her shoulder, the black lens pointed at his face. Her wide green eyes speared him with a look so intense, it felt like she was peering right into his soul. Which, damn it, she was.

"I didn't sign a release," he said quietly.

A smile tipped her lips. "He doesn't care. He's here."

"Ms. Killian." He leaned forward and put his hand over the microphone, brushing her warm skin with his knuckles. "You can stop now. I'm only here to observe."

Her laugh was as soft and feminine as her perfume. "Sorry, but Michael's not."

The name hit him like a lead slug. "Good guess," he said coolly, letting go of the mic. "One of the most common names in America."

"But not a common man."

"We don't have a release for that seat." The announcement, heavily accented and harsh, came from a dark-haired woman wearing a headset and waving a clipboard as she marched across the set. "You can't do a reading unless he's signed a release."

Arianna straightened slowly, giving Chase's arm a gentle squeeze. "He wants to tell you something," she whispered. "He wants you to have closure."

Chase opened his mouth to speak, but she put her fingers to his lips, the warm touch surprising him.

"Don't fight it. Closure is good, it's healing."

He didn't need to be healed, and gave her a hard look that he hoped sent that message.

As she walked away, he decided someone had definitely briefed her. It was the only explanation for her having such private, personal, and painful information.

The only explanation that fit into his absolute knowledge of what was—and what wasn't—possible.

He had to get out of there.

He slipped out of his seat to head backstage and do what he'd been hired to do.

# CHAPTER TWO

"WHAT THE HELL were you thinking with that guy, Ari?" The clipped Australian accent matched the snap of Carla Lynch's high heels across the sound stage.

"Sometimes I don't think, Carla. I go on instinct. That's the whole idea of the show, right?" Arianna remained facing away, one hand down her bodice, the other up her sweater as she snaked the microphone pack free.

"It was a waste of time and tape, neither of which are free."

Arianna handed the mic to a waiting grip before turning to the production assistant who didn't have a clue what a boundary was, and how not to overstep it. "You are also responsible for making sure that every person in the first five rows has signed a release, Carla. Then I can choose who I will read and who I will not."

"Girls, girls, girls." Brian Burrough's baritone chuckle preceded his arrival on the set, his brown wavy hair perfectly matching the silk of his Melrose Avenue shirt. "No catfights now. We'll just edit around that business with the spaceship."

"I didn't say *spaceship*," Arianna shot back. "I was getting a rocket ship."

Brian flashed a look over Arianna's shoulder, directly at Carla. She didn't have to turn to know that the little bitch had just rolled her eyes.

"The message was too strong to ignore," Arianna said, yanking a tissue from the stylist's box on the side of the set to wipe off the thick lip gloss they'd slathered on her.

"No one in those seats was on our preapproved list, Ari," Carla continued.

"You don't need a preapproved list," Arianna replied, looking at Brian, preferring to fight with the show's creator and producer, rather than the assistant with delusions of grandeur. "Just releases. I can do this without your spies sniffing out clues during the warm-up."

"You never know when—"

Arianna held up a hand to stave off Brian's "what if you go dry one day" speech. He'd never believed her. Not when they first started dating, not when he dreamed up the idea for this show, not even when she suggested someone was knocking on his telepathic door and she offered to give him a reading. He'd never believed. And that was at the root of their breakup, not his claims that he loved another woman. How could she love a man who didn't believe her? Hell, how could she work for one?

"Believe me, Brian," she said after she'd eliminated most of the goo on her lips, "I know who and when I can read."

"Hey." Carla put her hand on Arianna's wrist to stop her from the automatic mascara picking she'd already started. "Don't take the eyes off. We'll have pickups before the crew hits overtime. Especially for that David scene."

She made it sound like David's reading was a disaster. Before Arianna could respond, Carla had swooped Brian away and was whispering something about scripting and editing. And Brian seemed mesmerized by whatever she was saying.

Well, he was the executive producer, the moneyman with five hit shows to his credit, so he called the shots. And evidently, one of the shots he was calling was to give Carla Lynch way more authority than she deserved.

That, along with his thinly veiled disdain for Arianna's gift, was getting very old, even though the ratings of *Closure* got higher every week.

She rounded the craft services table laden with snacks, snagged a chip and popped it in her mouth as she headed down the dimly lit corridor to the back exit. Before she reached it, the door whooshed open.

The yellow security lighting that should have spilled into the darkened hallway was blocked by a tall, broad silhouette. Arianna slowed her step and then stopped, hit by a force of energy so powerful and warm, all she wanted to do was . . . feel it.

She knew exactly who it was.

She waited for him to enter so she could see his face, but he didn't move. The light caught black hair, cut short but thick enough to tempt a woman to finger-comb it. His shoulders damn near touched both sides of the doorjamb, and a sports jacket hung over his muscular frame.

Raw kinetic energy shimmered around him, drawing her in. Something else pulsed in his aura, too. As hard as he'd tried to radiate cynicism a few minutes ago, she'd seen right through it.

This man was safe, good, and right. Some things, she just knew.

"Does this mean I won you over?" she asked, purposely

keeping her voice light and maintaining some distance.

"Not exactly." He entered the hallway, finally giving her a chance to see his face again. A jolt of attraction zipped down her tummy, even stronger than the one she'd had when she first saw him.

"But you *do* want to continue the reading." God, she hoped so.

"Not particularly."

Then why was he here? "The studio audience was supposed to leave at the end of the taping," she said, unable to look away from eyes the color of the Pacific Ocean after a Santa Ana wind cleared every cloud. "And this exit is for cast and crew only."

"I was waiting at your trailer," he said, as though that were a perfectly logical explanation. "But a studio page said you'd have more taping to do."

"Do you have an appointment?"

His eyes narrowed. "You can drop the act. You know who I am."

She did?

"Arianna Killian." The loudspeaker crackled through the studio. "Ready for pickups on sound stage four."

"Damn." She gave a quick glance back toward the set. "I don't really do private readings anymore, but if you want to wait a—"

"Arianna, there you are!" Carla's adorable Aussie accent thickened, as it always did when there was a good-looking guy around. "We're ready to go. *Now.*"

"I'll be there in a second," she called over her shoulder, but kept her gaze on the irresistible stranger. "I won't be too long—"

"I'll be here," he said.

"Arianna!" Carla insisted. "The crew hits overtime in sixty minutes."

Arianna winked at him. "Guaranteeing we'll be done in fifty-nine."

"Don't worry. I'm not going anywhere."

Gorgeous *and* confident. Even better. "I'm not worried." Intrigued. Interested. But not worried.

She headed back to the set, unable to resist taking one last glance. He watched her with an intensity that sent a crazy little zing through her whole nervous system.

She still felt zingy when she let the tech rewire her for sound and the stylist replaced the lip gloss, but tried to temper the sensation with a reality check. Regardless of how attractive he was, he made it completely clear he didn't believe a word she said. Hadn't she learned her lesson from the last man who thought she was a fraud?

Another production assistant pulled her out of her reverie. "We're going to get four reaction shots on the reading with David first," the young man announced, kneeling in front of her with a light meter.

The stylist picked at Arianna's curls, while a page approached waving a pink script sheet. "Updated lines, Ms. Killian."

"Why do I need new lines?" Her lines were perfect. They were *real*. Arianna skimmed the words and moaned. "Oh, please. These take *suck* to a whole new level. Brian!"

He stepped out of the shadow of a robotic camera, where he'd been checking the shot. "These have more kick, Ari. Honestly, it's all about entertainment. Remember?"

How could she forget? Now she had to pretend to be

speaking to a man—and his dead wife—who were long gone from the set and her head. "I hate this part of the job," she said into the camera, tempering the words with a TV smile.

"Ari, we're rolling in five, four, three, two . . ."

She centered herself with a slow breath, staring at the empty chair where David had finally come to terms with his wife's death.

It didn't matter that this part was acting. She'd given David some peace. Did it matter how it came across on TV? She'd still given him her gift, nothing more complicated than that.

Nothing like what her mother had done with *her* sight.

"Mary Jo is reaching out for you, David," she said to the chair, sticking to the script on the pink paper. "She thinks you're about to drink from the cup of happiness." She choked softly, then looked directly into the camera. "I'm sorry, Brian. I just can't say that with a straight face. I know you want to be entertaining, but whatever happened to integrity?"

For a moment, the whole set was eerily silent.

"Brian?"

"Uh, he stepped out, Ari," someone said.

The AD moved forward, mumbling in his headset. "Joel wants to talk to you, Ari." He took off the headset and handed it to her. The invisible director, who worked exclusively from the booth, was going to chime in with an opinion? Amazing.

"I know you hate this part, Ari." Joel's voice in the headset she held was soft, calm, and kind. He was so against type for a director. "You're right about the 'cup of happiness' line. I'll edit it out. But could you just give us one take, so we have it in the can?"

She never said no to this guy. He was so nice, so unlike every other viper on the set. "Sure, Joel. I'll give it my best shot." She inhaled a few times, recentering herself. "All right, gang. Give me a second."

Instantly, everything changed.

The vision grabbed her with enough force to double her over with the impact. Wicked, clammy fingers closed down every sense . . . but the sixth. As if she'd flipped on a wide-screen TV in her head, an image blinded her brain, blocking out everything else.

White headlights pierced a black night. Silver sheets of rain cascaded over the windshield. Dark, menacing shadows threatened to close in. A seat belt squashed both shoulder and breast, frightened fingers clamped over a steering wheel. Arianna began to shake from somewhere so deep and dark and secret, it felt like her bones might crack.

In front of her, a cat leaped, tiny, silver, glinting in the headlights. Then metal scraped against metal and she was jolted, rammed by a deliberate hit.

Blood slammed through her veins, pumping violently as everything spun and whirled and twisted. A flash of lightning illuminated a guardrail as she made impact, her teeth cracking, her neck snapping, her whole being lost in a free fall over the edge.

Then there was only blackness. And the soft rush of rain, the drenching, soaking kind that bleeds into the California earth and drags homes and hillsides into one another.

Rain that washes away everything . . . including evidence.

"Arianna? Ms. Killian!"

The image faded. The rain stopped. All she could feel was that full-body numbness she'd experienced any time she'd seen a vision in black-and-white. The icy knowledge that she'd just witnessed something utterly and purely evil.

"Ms. Killian? Are you all right?" A man crouched in front of her, covering her body, shielding her with one powerful arm over her chair, and in his other hand, a gun.

Not *a* man. *That* man. The good man who radiated safety and security underneath a layer of smoldering sensuality. That man who claimed she knew who he was. What was he doing here, holding a gun?

"Who are you?" she rasped.

"I'm Chase Ryker. I'm your bodyguard."

Oh. *Oh*. Of course. She'd called for a bodyguard days ago, the last time this vision exploded in her brain. But he wasn't supposed to . . . "You're early."

"Usually."

She closed her fingers over his, lifting his hand from her arm and using it to cover the microphone clipped to her sweater. "Come closer," she said, her voice barely audible.

He did, still exuding all that power and energy, emitting something that felt protective. Well, that made sense. He was a bodyguard. And not just any bodyguard . . . a Bullet Catcher.

With her other hand she touched his chin, turning his face away from hers to place her lips directly against his ear.

"I just witnessed a murder." She felt his whole body

stiffen. "And when I figure out who the killer is, I'm going to be next."

Denial vibrated through him, his disbelief as obvious as the menacing weapon in his hand. Was he going to dismiss her vision and deride her? Or would he wrap her in the safety net she'd suddenly needed so desperately when she'd called for someone just like him?

What was he made of, this skeptical, fearless, handsome man who'd come to keep her safe?

"Not as long as I'm here."

She dropped her head on his broad, strong shoulder and gave in to a rolling wave of relief.

Her trailer was a mess. Clothes strewn over chairs, a cluttered makeup table that lined one whole side, shoes cast about the sitting area. Yet Arianna's dressing area was inviting in its chaos, like the wild red-gold curls around her face, and it drew Chase in just as effectively.

The disorder did make it more difficult to secure the premises, and to determine that the trailer was not only empty, but unbugged. He explained that to her when she asked why he was turning over chairs and opening drawers to root through her belongings.

"You think someone bugged my honeywagon?" At the vanity, she dipped two fingers in an open pot of white cream and started smearing it on her face. "Are you serious?"

"Most of the time," he said. "But until I clear us for conversation, don't tell me anything substantive."

As he continued his search, she disappeared into the powder room, turning the water on and leaving the door open.

"Then how about you tell me something substantive," she called out, her voice muffled from a towel. "I thought your firm didn't have anyone available until tomorrow."

"Lucy Sharpe did some juggling." Juggling and maneuvering being his boss's greatest strengths.

He crouched down to run a hand along the bottom of the wardrobe rack, found a stray high-heeled sandal and placed it to the side. "Didn't she tell you that when you talked to her today?" he asked, locating the mate and lining it next to the other one.

"I didn't talk to anyone from the Bullet Catchers today." She stepped out of the powder room, stuffing something in her backpack before she dropped the bag on the floor. "I spoke with Lucy a few days ago, and she said she'd have a bodyguard available by tomorrow. She couldn't tell me who it would be."

He stood, brushed his hands on his pants, and surveyed her face, which looked entirely different with the sprinkling of freckles and the arched brows no longer darkened by pencil. Why did they put so much junk on her face? She was a natural beauty.

"If Lucy didn't tell you I was coming, then how did you recognize me in the audience?"

"I didn't recognize you," she said indignantly. "I've never seen you in my life." At his look of disbelief, she added that saucy smile, the bright and pretty invitation he'd gotten in the studio. "Believe me, I'd never forget you."

He smirked at the compliment, certain she was lying. She hadn't pulled the rocket and Michael's name out of thin air. "Why don't we start with looking at the e-mails you've been getting," he suggested. "Lucy indicated you have a cyber stalker, and that's why you need protection and an investigation."

She turned to the vanity and riffled through a stack of papers, slid a coffee cup out of the way, and presented a pack to him. "Yeah, I do. There's no shortage of people who like to dis what I do. There are whole Web sites devoted to dismantling my every word. But this guy is elevating it to something scarier. Here."

He took the papers.

"Each one gets a little nastier," she said, tapping the page in front of him. "Look at that last one—he knows exactly where I live. He describes my view, which you have to get behind a big wall to see." She gave a dramatic shudder. "That totally weirded me out."

"I can see why," he said, rereading the message slowly. "But what makes you so sure it's a he?"

She drew back, surprised. "Because chicks don't send disturbing e-mails to other chicks that say things like 'I'm always watching you.'" She thought about it for a moment. "Although this is Hollywood. You think a woman wrote that?"

"There's not a single overt sexual reference."

"Maybe he's . . ." She squinched up her face in a charming scowl. "Lowvert?"

He couldn't help it. He smiled. "Covert."

The scowl bloomed into a grin, and her eyes sparkled with a little victory. "Oh, there is a sense of humor in there. I like that. Anyway, you're right. These notes are more about my job than me. Still creepy, though."

"A competitor?"

"Maybe." She kicked off her shoes and lost three inches,

putting her at about five four, and not an ounce over a hundred pounds. And still a force field of solid energy.

"Any phone calls?" he asked, flipping through the notes for key repeated words. *Phony. Scam. Fraud. Liar.* "Letters? Any contact other than e-mail?"

"Nope." She played with the hem of her sweater, thinking. "Nothing unusual or that sounds like these." In one move she yanked the top up, revealing a thin white camisole, a tiny waist and the source of that sweet, feminine cleavage he'd been admiring.

Well, it was her *dressing* room.

He didn't even bother to pretend to look at the paper; the words weren't nearly as interesting as the half-dressed woman they were sent to. "Do you have any enemies?"

She snorted softly as she walked to a clothes-laden wardrobe rack. "Enemies? This is Hollywood. Of course I have enemies."

"Ex-boyfriend, husband, or jilted lovers?" With that body, hair, and face, she probably had a dozen. More.

She threw him a look over her shoulder as she stepped behind the rack of clothes. "An ex who doesn't have the time or inclination to write anything like that, no husband, and not a single lover, jilted or otherwise."

"Have you attempted to trace these e-mails?"

He heard the soft whoosh of her silk pants hitting the floor, the sound as enticing as her shadow on the wall. "Yes—at least, the computer people at the studio did for me. They said all the messages came through free servers, and that whoever sent them was probably using an Internet café or something."

A bullshit answer from someone who didn't feel like

doing a little work. Every e-mail could be traced. "My firm can get something more definite," he said. "How many times have you changed your e-mail address?"

"Three. But then a day later, he sends me another message."

That took a certain amount of expertise. Or access.

She stepped back into the open area, holding her hair up with both hands, a silver clip in her mouth. The camisole was pulled high enough to reveal the dip of low-rise jeans. Very low. A lavender and violet tattoo—something with wings—floated in the concave between her navel and her pelvic bone.

Yeah. This was Hollywood.

"Vadyousinkof . . ." She popped the clip out of her mouth and stuck it into her hair. "Catburd? That's what he uses on every e-mail."

"Could be a power play. Could be a reference to something else. Could be nothing."

"A power play, huh?" She plopped onto a love seat and propped bare feet onto the two inches of coffee table space that didn't have a magazine, earring, or Styrofoam cup. "Like somebody who sits in the catbird seat. Hadn't thought about that."

"Or he's a geek."

She looked up at him, from under lashes that were thick even without the mascara. "How's that?"

"A reference to General Catburd, a character from the Bonzai Buckaroo film. Real popular with science geeks. You know any?"

She snorted softly. "Not really." Then she shot forward like a little bird in a cuckoo clock, pointing her finger at him. "You know, there was this guy, this graduate student at Cal Tech, and he was just weird enough to do something like this. He said he'd prove to the world I'm a fake. That's the last thing he said to me. I totally forgot about him."

"When did you talk to him?"

"About three months ago. He was doing his doctoral thesis, trying to 'disprove the paranormal.'" She finger-quoted the phrase. "I did a phone interview—just to be nice, mind you—and he was so obnoxious. He wouldn't listen to me, he was closed-minded, and his whole attitude really torqued me. Then, the best thing happened." She grinned at the memory, leaning back and crossing her arms with a cocky smile. "Right in the middle of his ranting that paranormal doesn't exist and psychics are really psychopaths, his dead sister shows up."

"His dead sister." Chase took a seat across from her, using everything in his training not to react. "Showed up."

"You know—she started talking in my head. And I told him he had a sister who passed away of leukemia and that she was describing their house—it was yellow with a green tin roof, I remember distinctly—and he went absolutely postal and hung up. I never heard from him again." She pointed to the e-mails. "But those started around the same time. One every couple of weeks at first, then weekly."

Chase just lifted one brow. "And his sister? Has she popped in for any more visits from beyond?"

She grabbed a purple velvet throw pillow and hugged it to her chest, her eyes lit and her color high. "Let me make something clear. I do *not* talk to the dead."

"No kidding."

"*You* do."

He just stared at her.

"*I* wasn't the medium in there, when we talked to your friend Michael," she said, dropping the pillow to point at him again. "You were. I was hearing what he was saying through *you*. See the difference?"

"No, but I'm not here to buy what you're selling. I'm here to protect you and help you find and eliminate the threat. That's my job."

She shot to her feet. "I'm not selling anything. And what do *you* think happened in there? You think someone told me there'd be a tall, hot guy in the third row who has a dead friend named Michael?"

"I think," he said calmly, "that Lucy Sharpe mentioned my NASA background in your discussions about a bodyguard. I think you made a brilliant guess that I would know another astronaut killed in one of the very few high-profile incidents involving the space shuttle. Maybe you remembered one of their names. And then you took a very lucky guess. I think that's what you do, and, frankly, you do it quite well."

She half choked and stuttered over a few words, as if she didn't know where to begin her argument, there were so many possibilities. "Listen to me," she finally said. "I didn't know you were an astronaut. And I don't have time to run Internet searches on bodyguards I hire; that's why I went to a reputable company." Her eyes shone as she looked at him. "I *heard* Michael. Well, you did. And I heard him from you. It was not a lucky guess."

"It's a common name."

She threw her hands on her slim hips, adding a theatrical sigh of exasperation. "We have a big, fat problem, because if you don't believe me, then you can't protect me."

"Of course I can." He indicated the love seat. "Calm down. We need to focus on the tangible problem. These e-mails."

She shook her head slowly, dropping back to the sofa to get eye level with him. "No, you can't. Because those notes may be tangible, but the real threat to my safety isn't coming from the person who sent e-mails."

He frowned, waiting for an explanation.

"You were there. You saw what happened to me in the studio. I told you, I witnessed a murder."

He reached out and put his hand on her knee. "I don't believe in visions, Arianna." Her mouth opened and he quieted the protest with a squeeze. "But I do believe in instinct. Maybe what you think you saw, was a manifestation of something else that's making you feel insecure. These e-mails could have that effect on you."

"Oh, for God's sake." She threw herself back on the love seat with another drama queen exhale. "I am not *manifesting* anything and this isn't something I *think* I see. Images are sent from someone who has crossed over to the other side: sent directly to a person in the room where I am. I pick it up from them, and only them." Her voice rose in frustration. "You have to believe me."

No, he didn't. But he did have to listen. "Okay. Why don't you tell me what you saw and why this is making you so scared."

"It's making me scared because I can't pick up something like that, unless it is coming from someone very close. Usually in the room."

Usually. There was always a caveat with her.

"So whoever is acting as the medium, whoever is send-ing the message—and this one is quite vivid and always, *always* in black-and-white, which means it is evil through and through—is going to figure out very soon that I know they committed murder."

"And you think that person is worried that you will ex-pose them. Even though there isn't a body. Or a crime. Or any evidence of anything but your . . . vision."

"Yes," she said, shooting him a look that said he failed in hiding his sarcasm. "And it *will* become clearer. It already has. It's just a matter of time before I see their face."

"But not the body of the victim? Which, you have to admit, would be helpful."

"I don't know if I'll ever see the body. Right now, my perspective is from inside a car that's being forced over a cliff. I'm inside the head of whoever died. But every time, I see more details. And once I know who's in the other car, who the killer is . . ." Her voice quavered. "They might do anything to keep from getting caught."

"But there is no crime. Just your . . ." Imagination. "Vi-sions."

She stood, pushing back a strand of hair that had es-caped the clip. "That can be enough to scare a killer."

"I appreciate your concern, but these e-mails—"

"No, you don't." She widened her legs and stared down at him, as threatening as a hundred-pound woman in a flimsy tank top could be. "You don't appreciate my con-cern. You want to take those e-mails and figure out who sent them and stop that guy. Fine. So do I. But I mostly want to figure out who's sending me the visions in the studio, and expose them before they kill me. They might even be related. Have you thought about that?"

Actually, he had. He stood to take away the slight advantage she had by looming down at him, with her nipples six inches from his face. "I promise you that we'll investigate every possibility, and use the very best resources to get information. We will be vigilant and careful, but you need to live your life as you normally do, with the added assurance that you have protection."

"I intend to. But you need to know this: I'm seeing a murder. And I know, firsthand, that seeing it is enough to scare the hell and sense out of the person who committed it." She reached over and touched his hand, her fingers warm on his skin. "Didn't *you* run an Internet search on *me*? Because if you did, you'll see my mother was shot when I was seventeen."

"Yes, I saw that in your file. I'm sorry. There were no details."

"Then let me tell them to you. My mother was shot on the freeway, on her way to a crime scene where she was about to identify the killer. Murderers are scared of psychics. We know their secrets. *That's* why I called Lucy Sharpe for a bodyguard." She gave him one last finger-point to the face. "Not because some whacko student wants his graduate thesis to be accurate."

She strode toward the other side of the trailer for the perfect exit. A second later, he heard the powder room door latch. He sat back, staring at nothing, his brain cataloguing the facts.

Now he knew why she'd called the Bullet Catchers, and not one of the dozens of ordinary security firms that provide protection to the stars. Because this was not an ordinary case of celebrity stalking. But why had Lucy yanked him from the job at Stanford to handle this? Why did she think a rocket scientist was equipped to handle the woo-woo girl who had visions of murders dancing in her head? Had she sent him because she knew he'd be the skeptical voice of reason and logic, or just because his boss loved nothing more than finding the chink in the armor of every Bullet Catcher?

Lucy may have been in a bind to staff this assignment, but she never did anything arbitrarily.

He pulled out his cell phone. It was after midnight on the East Coast, but of course Lucy answered on the first ring. "Chase? Are you in L.A.?"

"I am," he confirmed. "And with the principal."

"How is she?"

Theatrical. Beautiful. Nuts. "Interesting."

"I've known Ari for a few years," Lucy said with a soft laugh. "It's impossible not to like her, isn't it?"

Oh, he liked her. From the tangle of copper curls right down to her pink-tipped toes and every curve in between, she was imminently likable. "She's certainly . . . lively," he said vaguely, glancing over his shoulder to make sure she was still in the bathroom.

Did Lucy, a former CIA agent who ran one of the best security and protection firms in the world, buy into clairvoyants? "Luce, did she tell you that she's worried about more than just threatening e-mails?"

Lucy was quiet before she answered. "Yes, she did."

But, being Lucy, she had let her Bullet Catcher get the pertinent information on his own. That was a hallmark of her style and they all knew it. "I'm interested in what you think about it," he said. "And how her . . . concerns impact what we're doing here." *If* they impacted what he was doing here.

"I think she has powerful intuition and I suggest we listen to it."

He raked his hands through his hair. Intuition wasn't clairvoyance, that was just a hunch. A guess—exactly as he had suspected. "How much did you tell her about me?"

"You? Nothing. I wasn't even sure you were going on this job until late last night, when I talked to Max. I've been in meetings all day."

Maybe Max Roper, the head of the West Coast operations, divulged the background info. "Did he talk to her?"

"No, I've handled this one directly. Why?"

"You knew I'd be skeptical of what she says she does, so I'm curious why you sent a scientist for a job that requires someone willing to suspend disbelief in order to help the principal."

He could have sworn Lucy chuckled. "Don't suspend anything, Chase. I'm sure a little skepticism is as healthy as a clear head on the job. Just do what you are supposed to do."

He got the message. "All right, Luce. Can you trace some e-mails for me?"

"Of course. Forward the e-mails to me and I'll get an investigator on it first thing tomorrow morning. Anything else?"

"That's it for now. But you're sure no one gave her my name or background before I arrived?"

She laughed a little. "Absolutely. Just go with the flow, Chase. You might be pleasantly surprised."

In his experience, surprises were rarely pleasant. Chase clicked off the call, staring at the phone until a soft scent told him she'd made a soundless entrance back into the sitting area.

"What is it going to take for you to believe I'm for real?" she asked.

"What I believe isn't important," he said, standing to look at her.

She grabbed a white hooded sweatshirt from the back of a chair and put it on. "Yes, it is. If you don't believe me, you can't help me figure out who in that studio is a killer."

He folded the e-mails into a crisp, clean square and tucked them in his jacket pocket. "I can help you figure out who sent the threats. And we'll start by investigating the source."

She scooped up a backpack and then flung it, unzipped over her shoulder. "I know how to make you believe."

Ignoring the comment, he opened the trailer door to the lot that had grown deserted, holding a hand behind him to keep her back as he scanned the area.

"I'll just have to figure out your weak spots," she said, so quietly he almost didn't hear her.

He stepped down to the asphalt and peered into the shadows between the buildings around them. "I don't have any."

Her laugh was light, but her touch was a sudden jolt of warmth as she slid her arms around his waist from the back, her fingers brushing the bump of his holster. He reacted instantly, whipping around and grabbing her under her arms, raising her a foot off the ground before she could so much as make a sound. "Don't do that unless you want to get shot."

"I was just looking for your weak spot," she said, catching the breath he'd stolen.

"And you found my weapon instead." He held her aloft, his gaze holding a serious warning. "This isn't a game." Slowly, he eased her back to the ground.

She tried to laugh it off, but the sound caught in her throat. "Sorry," she whispered. "I didn't mean to . . . I just thought I could sort of break the ice."

The little force field of energy and spunk suddenly looked very small, very vulnerable, and very scared, and the impact was as strong as if she had managed to get her hands all the way around him and squeeze her body against his.

"There are much less risky ways," he said, his voice sounding gruff, wanting to let her off the hook for the minor infraction, but not wanting to let go of the warmth of her.

"Sorry," she repeated, a tiny shudder making her quiver.

"You know . . ." He reached down to the zipper tab of her jacket. "For a girl who promotes 'closure,' you don't really ever finish anything, do you?" He slid the zipper up, the teeth grinding slowly as his hand followed the feminine line of her body. When he reached the hollow of her throat, he let his fingers brush her skin.

He could feel her struggle to swallow.

"Then I guess I should be careful what I start," she said.

"That's the first completely sensible thing you've said."

She closed her hand over his. "Sensible is boring."

"Sensible is safe."

The instant he spoke, a gunshot cracked the night and the trailer rocked with the impact of a bullet.

# CHAPTER THREE

ARIANNA LET OUT A SHRIEK, and Chase shoved her down. Her pack went sailing, the contents spilling to the ground as he pushed her, low and fast, around the back of the trailer.

Her heart clobbered her ribs, the sound of her pulse so deafening she could barely hear his orders.

"Stay down. Move. Now!"

In seconds, he had them hidden deep in the darkness between her trailer and another, then flattened her face forward against the cool metal using his entire body to shield her.

"Someone shot—"

"Shhh!" His demand was harsh, and indisputable. In the distance, she heard running footsteps, then the sound of a golf cart engine revving and fading across the deserted lot.

"They're gone," she whispered, her chest heaving against the ridges of the trailer with every tight, terrified breath.

He didn't move, one hand locking her against the trailer, the other holding a gun. "Maybe."

"What do we do?"

"Leave. Fast."

"But . . ." Her *stuff*. "My bag. The keys to my house. My wallet, my phone." The *ring*. "My whole life is in that backpack." That wasn't even an exaggeration. Without the ring—

"Then you should close it."

She swallowed a retort, but only because he'd just saved her ass, and was on her like a human bulletproof vest. "I can't leave without . . . my things."

"Yes, you can. We'll break into your house and we'll cancel your credit cards and you can get another phone."

"Someone will have my keys and my ID." And her *gift*.

"But you'll be alive," he growled into her ear, his insistent breath tickling the hairs on the back of her neck.

"Please." She tried to catch his gaze over her shoulder, but he held her immobile against the trailer. "I can't leave it here."

"You can, and you will. You'll do exactly as I say, when I say it."

"Chase, please. There's something . . . something I can't live without in that pack."

His body tightened in response. "What is it?" Even his jaw sounded like it was clenched.

"It's something that belonged to my mother."

"Sorry, sweetheart. Real life outweighs sentimental value. When I count to three—"

"It has far more than sentimental value," she insisted.

He squeezed her a little as if that could emphasize his point. "Money can be replaced, Arianna. Human life cannot."

"As if I, of all people, don't know that." Damn him. She'd get it herself. She gave her whole body a good shake, trying to throw him off. Totally fruitless.

"Nothing is that important."

Fury, and fear, gave her enough strength to whip partially around, finally getting to see his face. "I can't live without it."

Even in the dark, she could see his eyelids shudder. "Without *what*?" Suddenly, he looked left, then right. "Shhh."

She heard the soft hum of a golf cart motor in the distance, far enough away that there were no lights, but it was definitely getting closer. "Don't make a sound," he said. "Don't move."

"It might be security," she insisted.

"It might not." He yanked her down, pushing her against hard, cold asphalt. "Go under. Now."

He thrust her into the eighteen-inch wheel space, cinders stabbing her palms. She held her breath as he half dragged her into the darkness, blinking into the gloom, smelling earth and grease and whatever grew under there. He stopped when they were fully underneath the trailer floor.

Arianna peered into the dim light on the other side, where she could see her bag and half its contents scattered around the metal stairs. There was her wallet. Her cell phone. Her keys. And good Lord, there was the tiny velvet pouch she'd stuffed in her pack, right out in the open, where a truck would smash it or someone would find it!

*Oh, Mom. I'm sorry.*

She'd thought about leaving the ring on, but, as always, she took it off unless she needed it. Now she might lose it. That couldn't happen. It *couldn't*.

The golf cart was still far enough away that she couldn't

see any headlights. She had time. Without a glance of warning to the man beside her, she shot forward, getting no more than two feet before he seized her thigh.

"What the hell are you doing?" he demanded, dragging her back, her jacket and tank top sliding up so that the asphalt scraped her bare skin.

"You see that little bag, right past the stairs? I'm going to get that. And yes, I am willing to die trying."

He swore softly. "Don't move." He slithered forward like an army guy in the trenches, a gun in his right hand as he snaked toward the stairs.

She tried to swallow, but her mouth was bone-dry. Hope grabbed her heart and squeezed as she watched. She *knew* she was right about him. Good all the way down to the bone. Pissed off and pessimistic as hell, but good.

In one graceful move, he grabbed the keys and the wallet. But he still didn't have the ring. He inched out of the protective covering of the trailer just as the golf cart rumbled from the access road behind sound stage four, a few hundred yards away. In seconds, it would turn the corner and its lights would shine directly on him.

*Hurry.* Terrified to look, but unable not to, she glanced in the direction of sound stage four. High beam lights danced on the strip of asphalt she could see from under the trailer.

Chase dove at the bag, seized it, then pivoted without getting up from his crouch. Lunging back under the trailer, he twisted into the tiny space the very second that yellow lights spilled all over the spot where he'd just been.

She reached to him, an exclamation caught in her throat.

"Quiet!" he ordered, shimmying next to her. "I didn't have time to get the backpack," he said, the tiny note of apology in his voice touching her more than the act itself.

"Thank you." She closed her hand around the velvet bag, sending a silent message of apology to her mother. She didn't dare take the ring out and risk dropping it in the dark, so she pulled the zipper of her jacket down enough to stuff the pouch into the bra shelf in her tank top.

Next to her, he jockeyed for position in the tight space, shoving her wallet and keys in his jacket pocket. The heat of his body and the closeness of the trailer caused her clothes to stick to her skin and her neck to prickle.

There was just enough light to make out a grease stain on his cheekbone, the treacherous set of his jaw. He cut his gaze from the lights to her, his blue eyes penetrating. She touched his face, thumbing the hollow of his cheek, rubbing the streak of dirt. "That was really—"

He slapped his hand over her mouth and shook his head.

*Heroic.*

"Shhh." He mouthed the order, his expression serious, and heated. For one second, she thought he might replace his fingers with his mouth, and kiss her.

The lights grew brighter, the engine louder.

In an instant, he slid his whole body over hers, sandwiching her between him and the ground. The impact pushed a shocked breath out of her, but she clamped her mouth closed to stop any sound.

He swept his right arm forward to aim his gun, and the

movement gave her a sliver of a view between his shoulder and chin, offering a glimpse of golf cart wheels as they came to a stop directly in front of them.

It had to be security.

Then she remembered the gunshot, the explosive pop as it hit her trailer, so close it had to have been meant to hit her.

It might *not* be security.

At the sight of her dropped backpack and the open trailer door, a studio guard would radio for backup. Any second, they would hear the static, then the voice of MetroNet security requesting assistance at Arianna Killian's trailer.

But this guard . . . this *visitor* . . . said nothing.

She modulated her breaths, taking in her bodyguard's distinctly masculine scent and the musty stink of the trailer.

Still no radio static.

She could feel the steady, solid beat of Chase's heart, and his chest rise and fall with each breath. His body pressed as hard on her back as the asphalt that jammed into her hipbones.

She saw the driver's boots and dark pants as he climbed out of the cart. He reached down to lift her backpack, then her phone, but not low enough to give them a look at his face. He kicked something—her lipstick?—then started toward the trailer.

Chase lifted the gun a millimeter.

At the foot of the stairs the man paused for a second, then the familiar squeak of the trailer door broke the silence of the darkened studio lot. Above them, footsteps moved from one end of the trailer to the other. Slowly at first, then faster.

Was he looking for her? From the sound, he was near her vanity and powder room, then he moved to the seating area in the middle, then all the way to the back, to the wardrobe racks and cot.

Was it the security guard? Or someone else?

The velvet pouch slipped a little between her breasts, and Arianna's whole body clutched. She inched her left hand toward her chest, dipping her fingers into the sliver of space in her bodice. She could barely get in there, he had her so smashed on the ground, but she managed to find the opening of the pouch and worm one finger into it.

The smooth, familiar band touched her skin. Then she closed her eyes, and waited.

The footsteps pounded right overhead. What was he doing in there? She forced herself to be calm. If it was a security guard, then nothing would happen. If it wasn't, then something would. At least, in her head.

She rubbed the gold of her mother's ring and focused on its power.

Five, ten, fifteen seconds ticked by. Each footfall sounded a little more desperate as the intruder clomped back and forth over their heads. Something dropped with a thud and Arianna jerked, but Chase held her still.

Glass shattered, and a chair leg scraped.

She slipped her finger deeper in the ring. Who was it? What did they want?

A fine, familiar chill snaked down her spine. She arched into it, vaguely aware that the man on top of her responded by grasping her tighter with every unrelenting muscle he had.

She ignored him, stroking the gold and coaxing her sixth sense forward.

Like a black-and-white slide show, the images came as stills. Rain. Asphalt. Tires. Not a cat, a silver hood ornament. Darkened windows. The crash. A guardrail giving way. The free fall into blackness. Glass and rain and blood. The end.

She slipped her finger from the ring and the slide show stopped.

But she had the answer she sought. Directly above them, tearing her trailer apart, was a murderer.

"Chase," she whispered, but he smacked his hand over her mouth again, forcing her desperate breaths from her nose. In a minute, the trailer door closed and booted feet appeared again, jogging down the steps.

She had to know who it was. She squirmed and made a tiny moan into his hand. The feet froze. He'd heard her! She squeezed her eyes shut, bracing for gunfire.

Suddenly, the intruder jogged to the golf cart, flipped the ignition switch, and in less than two seconds the beam of headlights disappeared into the darkness of the studio lot.

Only then did Chase release his seal over her mouth.

"He's the murderer." Arianna blew out the words. "That's what I was trying to tell you."

Slowly, he rolled off her. "What?"

"I had the vision. That person is a killer, and you just let him drive away."

"Yes, I did. Because my job is first and foremost to keep

you alive. What was I going to do? Leave you here? That won't happen, Arianna. Ever. You never risk a principal to get an assailant. Protection 101."

"He's a *murderer*," she insisted.

"You don't know that."

"Yes. I. Do." She bit the words out.

His expression melted into disbelief and disgust. "Let's get out of here."

She opened her mouth, but he placed his hand gently over her lips, to make a point. "We do this my way. No debate."

"You aren't going to go into the trailer? He tore the place apart."

"It won't look much different," he said. "But, no. I'm not. I'm going to check to see if the area is clear, then I'm going to get you off the premises as soon as humanly possible."

"But what was he doing in there?"

"He was looking for something. That was obvious. Copies of the e-mails, maybe. Something incriminating. Something of value. Do you have something someone might want enough to shoot at you, so that you run away and leave your trailer unlocked?"

Her heart pounded against a soft velvet pouch. "No," she lied. "Nothing I can think of."

"Brace yourself," Arianna said as she pushed open the six-foot-high wooden gate that led to the steep stairs along the side of her house. "It's eighty years old, tiny as a shoe box, but it's—"

"A bodyguard's nightmare."

"Home," she finished.

He reached the edge of her pine deck, looking at the surrounding brush and the direct drop down the hillside that overlooked Chateau Marmont and the never-ending stream of car lights that snaked along Sunset Boulevard.

"It was good enough for Judy Garland," she said defensively, sliding her fingers into her front jeans pockets. "She lived here when she was starting out."

He didn't look impressed. In fact, he shrugged as if only an idiot would take up residence somewhere so precarious. "There's no railing and a direct drop down a steep hill. One drink and somebody could topple right over."

"I keep my drunken guests inside," she said. "And avoid the edges."

"The brush should be cut back. It's a fire hazard."

"It gives me privacy."

He pulled her keys from his jacket pocket. "Alarm code?"

Oh, boy. "It's, um . . . I keep meaning to get it changed. It kept going off in the middle of the night, and it's disabled right now." Stupid for a woman getting nasty e-mails, but she had hired a bodyguard. She wasn't a total fool.

"We need to get it a new code ASAP."

When he unlocked the sliding glass door she waited for a moment, letting him enter, imagining her three-room hideaway through his eyes. What she saw as an inviting and warm sanctuary, all celery silk and cream velvet, a precious collection of crystals and candles, Mr. Look at the Bright Side probably thought was a tinderbox.

When she followed him in, she flipped on a single uplight over the fireplace. He prowled through the tiny living room, set his duffel bag on an end table, and continued past the kitchenette, following the narrow hall to the only other room in the house. Had she made her bed?

Once, last year.

Maybe she *didn't* finish anything.

When he returned, she'd already started water for tea and leaned against the counter, picking dirt from her jacket and jeans.

"Cute house," he said.

"But fraught with danger," she added.

He stepped into the kitchen, his expression more relaxed as he slipped out of his sports jacket, revealing the holster and gun, and that muscular chest that had flattened her so efficiently from behind. She could only imagine what it could do from the front.

Awareness curled through her and mixed with that spark of hero worship he'd lit under her trailer. "Would you like some tea?"

He shook his head. "Never touch the stuff."

"You sure? It's African rooibos."

He laughed softly, a low, sexy sound that tingled her already raw nerve endings. "Like I have a clue what that is."

"It's tea with an attitude and no caffeine. Try it. It's all vanilla and spice. I promise you'll never go back."

"I prefer no attitude and plenty of caffeine, but all right—you sold me." He turned to peer through the wall of plate glass to the world of West Hollywood below. "That's some view."

"But a landslide waiting to happen, right?"

"No kidding." He strolled to the sofa that lined one wall, picking up a massive amethyst on the table. "And just for the record, this could be a lethal weapon in the right hands."

"Stop it, will you?" She twisted the top to the rooibos tin. "You're scaring me."

"That's my job," he explained, setting it down carefully on the glass table and looking across the room at her. "Hypervigilance."

She leaned on her elbows and dropped her chin on her knuckles. "Did anyone ever tell you what a nice aura you have?"

He fought a smile. "No, I can't say anyone's ever mentinoed my aura."

"Well, you do," she continued, undaunted by his mocking tone. "You have a lovely golden aura of goodness all around you."

"A lovely golden aura." He laughed, a little self-conscious. "Please don't tell my colleagues."

"But you are in the perfect job for someone who wants to take care of people. You are very . . ." Kind, protective, sweet. He was, but that wasn't his color. It was liquid amber. It was warm and sensual and . . . "Safe."

"I guess that beats dangerous, in my line of work." He studied her for a moment, that smile still there, but not quite as cynical as it was a minute ago. "Let me ask you something, Arianna."

She leaned forward, drawn to him, sparked by the possibility of what he might ask her. "Anything."

"Does the studio keep a log of every person who leaves the lot, as well as everyone who arrives?"

She shifted her attention back to the tea to hide her disappointment in the impersonal question. "I think so. And the security cameras run all the time, but could you do me a favor and drop it for a minute? I need to decompress after tonight. I don't want to talk about who ransacked my trailer. It makes my head hurt." And her heart, to think someone might be after her ring. "Do you mind?"

He shrugged. "We'll have to figure it out eventually."

"Eventually," she agreed. But not now. She rounded the counter that ran between the kitchen and the living area, and perched on the arm of a club chair. "Isn't there anything else you wanted to ask me? You can hit me with anything, and I'll answer. We should get to know each other, don't you think?"

"All right," he agreed. "How well do you know my boss?"

The reading she'd done for Lucy Sharpe had been unforgettable, and so powerful it had rocked them both. "We met through mutual friends a few years ago." That wasn't a lie, nor did it break Lucy's confidential reading. "How about you? How'd you get a job with her? Astronaut to bodyguard isn't your typical career path."

"I'm not typical," he said.

"No weak spots, not typical." She cocked her head, giving him a teasing, analyzing smile. "Hmm. I like those qualities in a man."

"Do you flirt with everyone? The camera, strangers, your bodyguard?"

"I'm not flirting," she replied. "This is my natural personality. And you just deftly changed the subject." She twirled her finger in a counterclockwise circle. "Back we go now. Astronaut to bodyguard? How did that happen?"

"I got to know one of the Bullet Catchers when I was

on a high-profile assignment for NASA a while ago," he explained. "Good man by the name of Dan Gallagher. He's close to Lucy, recruits a lot of new hires." He draped his powerful arms over the back of the sofa, making her want to climb under one for a few hours. "Mostly I handle the jobs that require someone who can snip government red tape."

"Were you ever in space?"

"Yes, I piloted the space shuttle twice."

She drew back, her jaw loose. "Wow. How totally cool is that?"

"Like very totally." He added a wink to neutralize the tease.

She pointed at him. "You know, you're cute when you loosen up, Rocket Man."

"Cute?" He made a disgusted face. "Don't you know it's rude to point? And call grown men cute and safe?"

She chuckled. Not cute. Totally hot, when he relaxed a little. "So why'd you quit being an astronaut?" she asked as the teapot sang.

He didn't answer until she was back with two steaming mugs, the vanilla teasing her nose as she carried it across the room.

"I quit because of changes in the space program that I didn't like," he finally said.

For the first time since she met him hours earlier, she had the feeling he wasn't being honest. "What kind of changes?" she asked.

He took the tea she offered, a glimmer of distaste in his eyes. Either he hated the smell of vanilla, or the turn of the conversation. "Lax safety."

It was only partially true, she could tell. He avoided her gaze, his whole body had stiffened.

"Let me guess," she said, finding a little space among the candles and crystals for her cup. "It had something to do with Michael."

He sloshed a drop of hot tea over the edge of the mug, swearing under his breath as it hit his thumb. He wiped his hand on his trousers. "Like I said, you're a very good guesser."

"Sometimes I guess," she admitted. "Sometimes I read body language. And sometimes I really know."

He sipped the tea, and winced at the taste. Or the idea that she really knew.

"So, tell me about him," Arianna said. "Good friend? Fellow astronaut? School buddy?"

The smile disappeared; the relaxed attitude was instantly replaced with rigidity. "No, Arianna. Don't go there."

She curled a finger into the handle of her mug to lift it. Part of her wanted to push, but her gut told her not to. She knew which part to listen to.

"Then let me go somewhere else." She leaned back, and looked into his eyes. "I really appreciate what you did tonight. It was brave and kind and I know you didn't want to do it, but it meant a lot to me."

He put his cup down, obviously done with his one and only taste of African tea. "What was in the bag that you were willing to risk both our lives to get?"

"Something that belonged to my mother, something she gave me when she died."

"That ring you're wearing?"

This time she spilled *her* tea, gasping softly when it splashed her thigh. He was up for a cloth instantly, grabbing one from the kitchen counter.

"How'd you know?" she asked.

"You didn't have it on in the lot," he explained, placing the towel on the wet spot on her jeans as he sat down next to her. "Now you do. I'm just putting two and two together."

"So you're a really good guesser, too."

His hand made the tea spill even warmer. "I'm a scientist. We like to call it a hypothesis."

"Yes, it was my mother's." She placed her hand over his, closing her fingers over his much bigger ones. "Let's make a deal, Chase. We won't talk about my ring, and I won't channel your friend Michael. That way, neither one of us will make any more guesses or hypotheses." At his dubious look, she added, "And, yes, you were right. Going after my ring was dangerous and maybe stupid, but I am eternally grateful to you."

"You don't have to keep thanking me. It's my job." He removed the tea towel, folding it into an exact square before he set it on the table. "But don't do anything stupid again, because I don't like risking my life."

"Yeah, right. You've gone into outer space in a tin can and you throw yourself in front of bullets to save strangers, and you own a car built to cruise at two hundred miles an hour. You like risk very, very much. It's quite a dichotomy, a man who exudes safety but lives for risk."

"I don't live for risk," he countered. "And the car's rented. I drive a . . . plane."

She laughed with him, then leaned forward to touch his

chin with her thumb, rubbing the sexy stubble. "So, do we have a deal? No ring talk, no Michael talk." It would work well, because without the ring, she couldn't really do anything but guess about his lost friend.

"On one condition," he said, taking her hand off his face, but holding on to her fingers. "You stock this place with coffee."

"What? You don't like my attitude and spice?"

"I like *your* attitude and spice," he said. "But this tea tastes like dirt and water."

She slipped out of his grip. One more touch, and she was going to give in and kiss him. Then she had a feeling she'd get shot down, and have to listen to a little lecture on why bodyguards shouldn't kiss the women they protect.

"Sorry about the dirt and water. We'll buy coffee tomorrow. And now . . ." She stood, and he, being a gentleman, did the same. "I'm going to take a shower and wash the underside of a honeywagon off me."

"You do that," he said. "I'll set myself up out here."

She gave him a wistful smile, her fingers already on the zipper of her hoodie. "I guess I'm wrong, then." She lowered it three inches, slowly enough to pull his attention to her chest. "You don't like risk that much, or you'd follow me into the shower." One more inch, just to see what he was made of. "You know, just to be sure I'm safe."

He put his hands on her shoulders, turned her toward the hall, and gave her a very gentle nudge. "You're safest if I stay out here."

# CHAPTER FOUR

"I'VE GOT NEWS," Lucy announced. "A lot of it."

Chase flipped the cell phone to his other ear, glancing at the bedroom door that had remained firmly shut since Arianna had disappeared behind it the night before. It was eleven A.M. but she still hadn't emerged, giving him plenty of time to work, and ache for a cup of coffee he didn't yet have.

He ached for a lot of things, to be honest, including food that wasn't organic, natural, or made with tofu. But after a sleepless night on a too-small sofa, the need for caffeine had nearly won out over hunger—and the more basic, masculine needs that had tortured him ever since Arianna's not-so-subtle suggestion that they shower together.

"What is it, Luce?"

"We traced the source of those e-mails with what you sent this morning. They were from a server at Cal Tech University."

Bingo. The science geek. "That makes sense. Some student interviewed her and she said it got nasty. Got a name?"

"We have a few, all from the same department. But one of them, interestingly enough, matches a name on that list of studio guests you sent me this morning. Eric Scheff."

"Really. He was there? I'll talk to security again and find out what time he signed out," Chase said. "Let's run background, and see if he's licensed to carry concealed. This could be easier than we thought."

"We have a student ID picture that I'll send you to show to Arianna. We can match it to the tapes, if she doesn't remember seeing him in the studio."

Chase stepped away from the mesmerizing view of Hollywood to the laptop he'd opened on Arianna's kitchen counter, tapping into his Bullet Catcher e-mail box. "How many people have access to the server?"

"A lot, but we're getting closer to pinpointing the computer that generated the e-mails." He heard Lucy's keyboard clicking in the background. "California online stalker laws say you have to prove beyond a doubt who the sender is; then you can get a restraining order, or even a year in prison and a fine. There. I just sent you what I have on him so far, including a home address and his class schedule."

He opened the e-mail to a grainy photo of a pasty-faced, sharp-featured twenty-something. "Got it. Maybe I'll pay him a visit and scare him off."

"Then your problems would be solved," Lucy said.

"Possibly." There was still the matter of Arianna's visions. "Let me ask you something, Luce. Do you truly believe Arianna is the real deal? As a psychic?"

"Yes." She didn't hesitate, not a nanosecond.

"How do you know that?"

This time, a good many nanoseconds passed before she answered. "I just do."

Like every one of the Bullet Catchers, he trusted Lucy Sharpe implicitly, and he'd rarely known her to be wrong about anything. "Don't you think she's just a sharp guesser? A woman with strong instinct and a good sense of what makes people tick? That doesn't make her psychic, just intuitive. I think there's a big difference."

"She is intuitive, but she's also an excellent psychic."

Lucy's instincts couldn't be ignored. And there was something about Arianna that made him want to throw away logic, reason, and common sense. "Why don't we run those checks on all the members of the *Closure* production staff while you have your investigation squad working on the Cal Tech guy?" he asked.

"Of course. We'll do that right away."

The bedroom door creaked open and he signed off, flipping the phone closed as bare feet pattered along the tile floor. At the sight of Arianna, caffeine and food slipped back on the physical-needs scale. *Way* back.

"Hey." She half yawned, blinking at him and running her fingers through a wild mess of bed head, the gesture tugging a skimpy top, revealing the winged whatever under sleep pants that barely managed to hang on to her hips.

"Hey yourself," he said. "Another hour and I was going to send up emergency flares."

She smiled, a glorious, sexy grin that matched her glorious, sexy hair and her glorious, sexy . . . "Is that Tinkerbell?"

She followed his gaze south and inched the loosely drawn string even lower to reveal the contour of her pelvis. "Yep."

"You go one millimeter farther, sweetheart, and that constitutes official flashing."

"You stare one second longer, darling, and that constitutes official ogling." She brushed a single finger over the tattoo. "My mom used to call me Tinkerbell." She snapped the drawstring back in place and squinted up at him, as if the sunlight suddenly seemed too bright. "Who were you talking to?"

"Lucy Sharpe. I think we've found your cyberstalker."

"Wow, you guys work fast."

"It's two o'clock in the afternoon in New York."

While she made tea, he told her about their target at Cal Tech. She studied the picture on his computer, then shook her head. "He wasn't in the audience yesterday."

"There were about a hundred people there. You could have missed him."

"Not likely. I see every single person, and I don't forget faces. I would have noticed him. We can pull yesterday's tapes and look, but I don't remember him."

"Maybe he disguised himself."

"Possibly." She clicked out of his program. "Can I check my e-mail from here?"

"Go right ahead."

She tapped a few keys, absently lifting her hair to reveal a long, pale, slender neck and something fuchsia on her well-toned back. Another tattoo?

He took a step closer, inching down the thin fabric of her top.

She didn't even flinch, just clicked the computer and acted like it was perfectly normal for him to examine her back. "It's a butterfly. My favorite creature."

This one was so beautifully drawn, it looked three-dimensional. "Pretty," he said, resisting the urge to touch it.

"My mom used to build butterfly gardens when I was a kid."

"Do you have any tattoos that are not inspired by your mother?" Not that it wasn't a sweet touch, but the constant reminder of Mom might take some of the fun out of tattoo-hunting.

"I have a great one that's all mine. But you'd have to go a lot farther down." She tapped the curve of her backside lightly. "I'd show you, but you'd call it flashing." She threw a dead sexy glance over her shoulder. "But you're welcome to look."

The invitation shot heat to a body already charged just from being around her. His fingers itched to slide those sleep pants right over her butt, but her gasp and sudden change in posture erased the playfulness of the moment.

"Shit. He's back. Look."

He read over her shoulder. Unlike the others, this message from catburd was very short.

*sorry i missed you tonight, ari.*

She turned, her eyes clouded with worry. "Missed me? With a bullet?"

"Let me arrange to get prints on Eric Scheff. And get them taken from your trailer."

"All right." She slipped away from the counter and went back to work on the tea she'd abandoned. "But is that going to stop him?"

"We have two choices, once we nail him. We can scare the crap out of him, if you want."

"I want. What's our other choice?"

"Legal channels. Restraining order. Take him to court. Get him in jail for a year, fine him. Could be enough." He inhaled the vanilla as she poured, and considered just how desperate he was for something warm in a cup.

"I'd rather avoid the legal channels," she said, bouncing a silver tea strainer on a chain like a yo-yo, and looking up at him with just enough sleep and sweetness in those green eyes to make him feel like he was on the end of the chain.

"Why?"

"Because my dad's retired LAPD, and he'd find out faster than you can say in-junc-tion."

"He's a cop, and you haven't told him about these e-mails? Or about hiring a bodyguard?"

"He's retired." She pulled the strainer out of the cup and rained tea drops all over the counter. "But he's a dad first. It would worry him."

Chase thought of his own father, a burly engineer who hid his emotions well, but who had cried openly with relief when Chase left the astronaut corps. Of course, he knew the real risk better than most. "I understand," he said, picking up the tea towel she'd left crumpled on the counter. "Here."

For a second she frowned, like she had no idea what to do with the towel. "Oh, yeah. Finish the job, Arianna," she said in a singsong voice.

She wiped the drops and hung the towel neatly over the lip of the sink, giving it a little pat when she was done. "There. You could be a good influence on me."

"Oh, I don't know. Did you make your bed before you got up for work at noon?"

She snorted as if the idea were utterly preposterous. "I don't work today, unless the studio calls for pickups." She planted her hands on the counter behind her and hoisted her backside up, swinging her legs like it was her favorite seat in the house. "They do all the editing and sound stuff on Fridays, and I don't have anything to do with that particular kind of make-believe."

"No, you handle the other kind of the make-believe."

She wrinkled her nose. "Not funny."

"Come on, Arianna. I was there at the end, remember? You had *lines*, for God's sake."

"Pickups are different." She leaned back on both hands, the position jutting her breasts just enough to accentuate the tiny, hardened nipples in yet another ridiculously thin tank top. "You know, I was thinking about you in the middle of the night."

*That makes two of us.*

"You know what I find amazing?" she continued. "That a man who has been into outer space, seen the world from far away, who has actually touched the sky, doesn't believe in the afterlife."

"Sorry, sweetheart. Too weighty a question when that man has been denied coffee."

"What do you believe in, then?"

"Laws." He stood a foot in front of her and crossed his arms. "Einstein's law of relativity, Newton's laws of motion, Kepler's laws of planetary motion, Bernoulli's law of lift. I didn't get into that tin can, as you so eloquently put it, on blind faith. I got in it because I understood the hard, cold facts of science that got it there and back. When

you understand science, there's no room for the paranormal."

"But what if you're wrong? What if you're thinking with
your head, and not your heart?" She reached out and flattened her palm on his chest. "What if your friend's energy
really was in that studio, and he really did want you to have
closure, or to know something about his death? Are you
willing to take a chance and ignore that life-changing possibility?"

She had to feel what that did to his pulse. "He wasn't
my friend. And you and I had a deal." He put his hand over
hers and lifted it, but she just gripped tighter, pulling him
toward her, spreading her legs enough to ease him into the
space of the counter where she sat.

"The deal was I wouldn't try to read you and talk to
Michael. Not that you wouldn't talk to me. What happened to him?" She curled her fingers around his, lifting
his hand to her mouth. Very softly, she kissed his knuckles, a featherlight air kiss that tightened the band around
his chest. She added pressure with her knees on his hips.
"Tell me."

It was impossible to look at her and lie. Or hide. That
was her magic. She was as powerful as gravity and just as
undeniable.

But he could deny it, and he would. "No." He shook his
head, feeling her soft breath on his hand, losing himself in
the pull of her grass-green eyes, the urge to climb right on
top of her and inside her and exchange his reason for her
magic.

"You need another law to believe in, Rocket Man," she

whispered, brushing his knuckles with her lips. "Killian's law." She turned his hand over to graze a kiss on his palm. "Which states that no matter how big a mess you make in life . . ." Another kiss, and a flick of her tongue. "With enough love and faith and positive energy . . ." She opened her mouth, suckled the skin at his wrist. "It can be completely cleaned up."

The band around his chest slipped as all the blood flowed far away from his brain, instantly swelling him. But the erection wasn't what forced him closer, it was her. Her eyes, her mouth, her tempting, charming voice.

She was pure magic.

"Eventually," she said, releasing his hand to slide her hands up his arms, slowly enough to explore every muscle, "you will believe me." She locked her hands behind his neck, never taking her eyes from his, inching him closer to the inevitable meeting of the mouths.

The kiss was entirely mutual. She parted her lips, and he tasted the tea she'd originally promised: sweet and spicy and hot with attitude. He slanted, deepened, and tongued her thoroughly, closing his hands around her hips and almost lifting her off the counter so the body contact was total and intimate.

She inched back, lifting her head to invite further exploration of her throat and chest. His hand ached to slide over and touch those nipples he'd just admired. One touch. One taste. One thrust against her. That's all it would take, then he'd be all over Tinkerbell.

"Chase," she whispered, squeezing her knees, arching toward him as she sensed his hesitation. "It's okay."

He didn't know if she was referring to his memory of

Michael, or the offer of sex. But neither one was okay. Not really.

"Arianna." He put his hands on her shoulders, pinning her in place with a serious look. "Don't you think that you would be better off sleeping with a man who completely believes in you, in what you do?"

"Probably," she said dryly. "My last man was a total nonbeliever, too. I seem to attract skeptical guys."

He tunneled his fingers into her nape, sliding around helplessly in the silk of her hair. "You attract . . ." Everything. Everyone. "Me," he finished gruffly, kissing her hard again.

His heart slammed, pumping blood to the only place it could possibly go. He ached to explore her with his hands, but used only his tongue to curl into the recesses of her mouth, fighting a groan as she shimmied closer on the counter, enough for her legs to enclose his hips, and his erection to automatically seek and find the heat at her center. Enough for her breasts to press against his chest. Enough for anything resembling reason and control and logic—his most trusted companions—to vanish while want and need and lust took over.

He palmed her breast, and she responded with a shudder that rocked her harder against him. Her nipple budded and he lowered his head to kiss her throat, the rise of her chest. He pushed the tiny strap over her shoulder, his mouth already watering to taste her.

The jarring sound of a ringing phone froze their tight, panting breaths.

She swore softly, and he slid the strap back up. With her eyes still closed, she reached behind her to a cordless phone sitting in a charger. The groan she let out when she read the ID sounded nothing like the whimpers he'd just caused.

"Speak of the devil," she said. "My ex is calling now."

"With timing like that, maybe he's the one who knows what you're thinking."

"No. He's the one who's calling me into work." She thumbed a button and held the receiver with her shoulder, immediately returning both hands to her exploration of his chest. "Hey, Brian."

*Brian?* The executive producer of her show was her ex? That relationship was definitely not in her file.

"Oh," she said, unbuttoning Chase's top button with one flick of her finger. "I saw the ID and figured Brian was calling. Okay, well, what can I do for you?"

She listened for a second, undid another button, and smiled at Chase with the minor victory. "All right." She drew the words out in dissatisfaction. "I'll be there in . . ." She finished the third button and dipped closer to the tent in his pants. "A few hours." She listened for a second, then curled her lip. "Fine. One hour. Bye." She threw the phone on the counter, and half pouted as she leaned back. "I'm afraid duty calls."

"The executive producer is your ex-boyfriend?"

"Was. Over." She lowered her hands and offered her mouth. "Can we finish?"

"In under an hour? No." He eased her off the counter. "Go get dressed."

Blowing out a breath of frustration, she grabbed her teacup. "So I'm going to work and you get to hunt down the Cal Tech geek all by yourself? That's not fair."

He shook his head. "You weren't paying attention to Protection 101. I go where you go. The geek will be there later, or tomorrow." He caressed her bare arm, sliding down the silky skin until he reached her hand. He lifted it and kissed her knuckles. "You're messing with the laws of nature, you know."

She arched one brow. "Where do you think those laws will take us, Rocket Man? Over the moon? To the stars?"

"Right into that unmade bed."

Lifting up on her toes, she kissed him. "Then I've got a surprise for you." She disappeared down the hall, leaving him hard and sweaty, and curious.

But not about her surprise. Something made absolutely no sense to him.

The show's creator and producer didn't believe she was a real psychic? That struck him as very, very odd.

Something wasn't right at MetroNet Studios.

The first thing that tipped them off was the look on Gary's face when the good-looking young guard leaned into the window of Chase's Porsche and frowned at Arianna. "I didn't know you were coming in today, Ms. Killian."

"Brian's office called me in for pickups," she said.

His frown deepened. "On sound stage four?"

"Of course."

"Your set is closed today." He checked his computer, then looked around his desk for a note he didn't find. "Sound stage four is locked tight. Mr. Burroughs is on the lot, but no one is taping on that set today. No stylist is here, and no crew, no director."

She sent an uneasy look at Chase.

"Who called you?" he asked.

"I don't know. A woman in Brian's office. He has a couple of shows that tape on this lot, and I didn't recognize her name." She leaned lower to look up at Gary. "I'm just going to go to my trailer, then."

"But don't touch anything," Chase told her softly. "I want to have it dusted for Scheff's prints. And we'll stop in to the main security office and see if we can verify what time he left last night."

When the guard opened the gate and tapped in salute, Arianna settled back in her seat, tamping down concern. Why would someone call her in for pickups that weren't scheduled? "We should go to Brian's office, too," she said when he parked. "I want to find out what happened."

"Someone locked your door and picked up your handbag," Chase noted as they neared the trailer.

She'd wanted to go back to do that last night, but he would have none of it. She'd been upset enough to agree, but now she wanted answers.

As soon as she unlocked the trailer door, she knew she wouldn't get them. "Damn," she said, turning to Chase. "It's been cleaned already."

That had never happened on a Friday, but Arianna recognized the distinct touches of Carmen, the cleaning person assigned to her. The pillows were plumped and angled perfectly on each of the love seats, and her wardrobe hung neatly on the rack, sorted by color and style. A dozen shoes stood sentry along one wall, her vanity looked like a makeup display counter, and there wasn't a speck of dust, a half-empty teacup, or a crumpled-up script note to be found. Forget fingerprints, she thought dismally. They'd disappeared with Carmen's overzealous dust rag.

In one corner sat the abandoned backpack, all zipped and neat, her cell phone tucked in the front.

She plopped on the sofa in disgust. "She never comes on any day but Monday. She hasn't been here on a Friday the entire time I've been in this trailer."

"Maybe it wasn't her."

Arianna picked up a pillow and dropped it. "I recognize her signature."

"Come on." He reached for her hand. "Let's go talk to security and see if we can find your ex . . . ecutive producer."

She let him pull her up, but teased him with a smile. "You jealous?"

"Curious, not jealous."

"Curious about what?" she asked. "How long we were together? How serious it was?"

"Among other things." He led her out and locked the door behind them. Before they walked away, he stopped to examine the side of the trailer, running his fingers along the front.

"Looking for the bullet?"

"Or a mark of it." He found something, grazed his fingers over the spot, and turned as if he were imagining where it had come from. "I didn't see the flash, but my gut says it was over there. Whoever shot at you missed by a mile. My guess is that was deliberate, or they're a total amateur. Either way, it served a purpose."

"To get me to run."

"Yes. And to leave the door unlocked so he could get in and look . . . for something. Any ideas?"

She made a conscious effort not to touch the ring she wore. "I don't keep much jewelry in there," she said vaguely. "I don't wear anything too expensive on the show because it's offputting to people. I never have any cash."

No one on earth knew what the ring meant to her. No one knew what she was—or wasn't—without it. It certainly had no street value, since it was just an inexpensive gold band.

If Chase suspected the prize was her ring—since she had risked both their lives to get it last night—he didn't say anything or even glance at her hand.

"What's closer?" he asked. "Brian's office or security?"

"Burroughs Production on-studio office is right around the corner. If he's not on the set of another show, he'll be there."

As they walked, Arianna nodded to a few familiar faces, including one of the cameramen from her show. Instinctively she rubbed the ring, hoping. But Larry the cameraman, if he was her target, wasn't thinking about a car he pushed off a cliff on a rainy night.

"So what came first?" Chase asked, pulling her from her zone of concentration. "The show or the affair with the executive producer?"

"It wasn't an affair," she said defensively. "Neither of us is married. We dated first, about a year ago, introduced by mutual friends. After we'd been together about a month he saw me do a reading, and bam, he had the idea for the show."

"What were you doing before that? Just private readings?"

"I was . . . floundering about. Looking for a purpose."

She'd really been struggling with an inner battle: the desire to do what her mother had done, versus flat-out fear of death. Fear of death had won hands down. "And his idea seemed smart."

"It's certainly profitable."

She glanced up at him. "The show's doing well, yes. But Brian has the Midas touch. Every show he creates makes money. You wouldn't know it by these humble offices," she said as they arrived at an older building, "but this is just a tiny little part of his empire. He has two shows that tape here, and two at Paramount. He's really, really successful."

He held the door for her. "So what happened? Why'd you break up? Professional differences?"

"I guess you could call it that." It was easier to blame it on the fact that he didn't believe in her, and that had certainly added to her irritation. But the real reason they broke up was the reason Brian broke up with every woman after six months.

No one could compete with the woman he really loved.

"He handles the day-to-day production out of these offices. Out on Sunset, he has a dozen people who handle casting, syndication, and all the minutiae of his business. But you can usually find someone here. An assistant, who changes depending on the day of the week or the temp agency we're using, and Carla, his PA—production assistant—on *Closure,* and another PA on the game show *Spare Parts.* Joel Zotter, our director, and some other crew members come and go."

But no one was around when Chase and Arianna walked into the little front office at the end of the hall.

The three desks were cluttered with scripts and memos, but vacant. One computer was on, with a MetroNet logo screen saver dancing around.

"I guess everyone's out to—"

Chase put his fingers over her mouth. "Shh."

She heard nothing. "What is it?"

He shook his head hard, frowning as he listened for something.

Then she heard a low, muffled grunt, a groan, a whimper. Coming from the closed door of Brian's office. Was that . . . what she thought it was?

She looked at Chase, and could tell he was thinking exactly the same thing. She wrinkled her nose. "I don't think I want to walk in on that." She glanced around at the desks. One was Carla's, for sure. Were they . . .

A guttural groan of pleasure came from the other side of the door. The distinct uncontrolled call of a man about to have an orgasm. Arianna's stomach tightened and she drew back, embarrassed.

"Let's go," she whispered, tugging at Chase's arm. "I really don't want to hear the grand finale."

Brian moaned again, calling out *baby* or *lady.*

"Come *on.*" She pulled Chase, disgust and panic rolling up her middle.

He nodded, staying with her as she broke into a light run down the hall to the front entrance. Outside, she sucked in air and lifted her face to the warm California sun.

"Well," she said, with an uncomfortable laugh. "I certainly wasn't expecting *that* from an unscheduled visit to his office."

Chase seemed unfazed, his focus on her. "You okay?"

"Sure," she said, feigning a casual voice. "Just heard a little bit of the nasty, but, hey, this is Hollywood."

"It seems odd that a man that busy and important would pleasure himself in the middle of the business day."

She blinked into the sun, the strobe effect as jumpy as her brain. "He wasn't in there jacking off, Chase. Someone was doing it to him."

"I only heard one person."

"Maybe she had her mouth full," she shot back. "He's not the kind of guy to shut his door to spank the monkey— women throw themselves at him. It was probably Carla. She'd do anything to get ahead in this business."

"And is he the kind of guy who'd exchange sex for a promotion? You don't strike me as a woman who would be attracted to someone like that."

Somewhere in that statement, there was a compliment. But she was still too caught up with what she'd just heard in Brian's office to dissect his comment.

"He just . . . he isn't like that." She knew she sounded lame, defending her ex-lover. "We never . . ." Well, they had, but not in his office, for crying out loud. "Believe me, he's a workaholic. If I know Brian, we probably overheard an audition tape for a show he's casting." Oh, wouldn't that be nice. She started walking, clinging to that pathetic hope. "I bet that's what it was."

"Maybe someone wanted you to walk in on that," Chase said.

The thought brought her to a stop. "Whoever called me! Yes, that's possible. Someone wanted to set me up. But why?"

"Maybe to get you to quit?"

"Why would that make me quit?"

"Someone who thinks you're still in love with him?"

"I never was. We're friends and we parted on great terms, but Brian . . . well, he'll never have room for anyone in his heart but his first love." She pointed across the lot. "The security offices are over there."

"You know," Chase said, "all those e-mails do have that same subtext in the message. Like someone wants you to be exposed as a fraud, and then you'd have to quit. Are you sure there isn't another psychic waiting in the wings to take over your job? Maybe that's who was auditioning in there."

She considered her response, walking again. "At the risk of sounding like a total egotist, I'll just tell you that Brian says it isn't what I say, as much as how I say it. I don't like to think that's the only reason people watch my show, but I do like to think I offer . . . something special. He has me play it up, with lots of personality and way too much makeup. Some people have suggested rotating me with another psychic to build even more ratings, maybe a man like John Edwards. But Brian said I have . . . enchantment."

She stole a look at Chase, expecting a big eye roll. But he was just smiling at her. "He's right. You are magic."

Her heart did a free fall at the sweet compliment. Or maybe it wasn't a compliment, maybe that's just how she heard it. "It's not magic, what I do," she said, still drinking in the look on his face.

"I didn't say you performed magic. I said you *are* magic. Big difference." He draped his arm around her. "Come on, Tinkerbell. Let's go see what else can go wrong today."

• • •

When the head of security handed Chase a list of every vehicle that had come and gone from the MetroNet lot the day before, including the name of the drivers and passengers, it was obvious that plenty more could go wrong.

"No Eric Scheff," Chase said to Arianna. "He must have come in using a different name."

"We check photo ID on every single person who enters this lot," the man insisted. "We don't check the ID when they leave, but we do log each license plate, and there's a camera at every gate. You're welcome to match every car to every log entry on this list, and you will not find a discrepancy. I'll stake my job on it."

Chase instinctively believed him and turned down the offer, mulling over the ill-fitting puzzle pieces. An Eric Scheff appeared on the list of studio guests, but not on the vehicle log.

"I told you I didn't see him in the audience," Arianna said as they returned to the lot. "We could look at yesterday's tapes."

"I think we should," Chase said. "Just to confirm that he was there. Or not. Who has them?"

Her face fell. "We have to go back to Brian's office and find out which editing studio is being used today. It could be one of about six, even off the lot."

"Could you call?" he asked, his hand already on his cell phone.

"I could, but . . ." She squinted up at him. "It's been long enough for him to . . . I want to face him, maybe see who he was with. I like your idea that it was a setup. Maybe . . ." She absently stroked the ring she wore. "I just want to go over there one more time."

He did, too. He was curious to get to know the man who'd hired Arianna even though he thought she was a fraud, and now that he knew they'd been lovers, he wanted to make a closer inspection of the guy.

But it wasn't to be. When they reached the office, a woman Arianna didn't know sat at one of the three desks. Unless Brian's taste ran toward fifty-year-olds with bad face-lifts, he hadn't been catching a little afternoon delight with this lady.

"He left a couple of minutes ago," she told them. "Pretty agitated, I might add. Never even said goodbye."

And she was clueless about where they were editing, and confirmed that she hadn't called Arianna in for pickups.

"I'm a MetroNet temp, Miss Killian," she said. "I've never worked in this office before. They called me this morning, but Mr. Burroughs didn't have anything for me, and he was too nice to send me back to the temp agency. He told me to go kill a few hours in the cafeteria, which I did. I was hoping he'd just sign my time card and let me go, but he shot out of here before I could ask."

Arianna gave Chase a confused look. "Is Carla Lynch around? She'd have some answers."

"She was here this morning, but then she had to go to the office on Sunset." Her face brightened. "Want me to call there? They might know where you can find the tapes."

"Um, okay." Arianna's attention drifted to the office, looking again to the room where Brian had been behind closed doors not so long ago. As the woman picked up the phone and started dialing, Arianna slowly took a few steps toward the darkened office as if she was drawn into it.

"While you call, I'll just check his desk to see if he left any notes about the editing."

She didn't wait for permission or a response, but continued right into the office, Chase close behind. As soon as she was in the office, she spun around and looked at him, her eyes bright.

"What's the matter?" he asked.

She didn't say anything, but shook her head, like she was thinking or unable to speak.

"What is it?" he asked again, putting a hand on her shoulder.

She pointed to the door. "Close that. Quick."

He did, noticing that her complexion had turned pale and she'd started to shake. "Arianna, what's the matter?"

"I don't know." Her voice was tight and breathy as she turned in a slow circle, her gaze darting around the room, over a wide flat-screen TV that took up most of one wall, a scarred and ancient oak desk, a round conference table with two mismatched chairs, one tucked in tight, the other turned to face the TV. "But there's something in this room. Something I never felt before. There's a very weird aura in here."

Despite himself, the hair on the back of Chase's neck rose. She wasn't faking this, whatever *it* was.

"Is it the vision? The one you had in the studio?"

She shook her head. "No."

"Is it . . . what was going on in here a few minutes ago?"

"No."

He waited while she closed her eyes, and, trancelike, touched her ring and swayed slightly left to right.

The door popped open with a bang loud enough for Chase to spin and reach for his weapon.

"What the hell are you doing in here?"

He recognized the venom-mouthed production assistant from the set the day before, so he kept his gun in the holster.

Arianna opened her eyes slowly, like a woman being pulled out of a deep sleep. "Looking for Brian," she said. "Why is that a problem?"

"It's not," Carla said quickly, throwing a glance at Chase. "It's just that nobody expected you here today."

"I was called in for pickups," Arianna said, shoving a fistful of curls off her face. "Do you know who called me?"

Carla screwed up her face. "Pickups? Nobody would call you for those. The show's in the can. We were finished last night."

"I need to see the raw footage," Arianna said. "I need to get a good look at everyone in the audience."

"I can get you the log, and all the releases. Why?"

"No, I want to see the tapes. I'm looking for someone who was on the log, but not in the studio."

Carla's dark eyes flickered, and again she threw a curious look at Chase. "I don't think we've met," she said, sticking her hand out toward him. "I'm Carla Lynch. And you are?"

"Chase Ryker." He purposely didn't identify himself, even though she obviously waited.

After an awkward beat, she looked at Arianna. "There

is no more raw footage, hon. Just the show, which you are welcome to see, of course. Everything else has been destroyed."

There was a hint of arrogance and challenge in that accented voice, as if she had an overblown sense of superiority, but that might just be posturing.

"Destroyed?" Arianna asked. "Why?"

She shrugged. "Boss's orders. So, are you leaving now?" She held the door open in an obvious invitation.

"No," Arianna said, shooting back with just as much authority and superiority. There was definitely some posturing going on between these two. "And we need some privacy," she said, pointing to the door. "If you don't mind."

Carla looked piqued at the dismissal, but she backed out. "Whatever."

"Something's not right in here," Arianna said softly the second the door latched.

"What is it?"

She rubbed her arms, and fiddled with her ring again. "I don't know. It's not like anything I've ever felt."

"What do you feel?" He couldn't believe he was even asking, but nothing in her demeanor said she was pretending.

Again, she turned around, stopping this time at the TV. "I know what we heard, or think we heard. But the energy in here is full of . . . hate. That's the only way I can describe it." She picked up an oversized remote and glanced at it. "What was he watching?" she asked, half to herself, as she clicked it on.

The screen lit with a familiar, beautiful face. She gasped softly at her own image. It was obviously not footage that would ever be on air, but something pulled from when she sat in her chair, getting made up, chatting lightly with the stylist, lifting the sweater she wore yesterday to be miked.

"Guess he didn't destroy all the footage," she said softly.

Had the guy been in here jacking off to her image? "Is that the only disc in the changer?" he asked.

"There are others, but . . ." She turned it off and carefully set the remote on the conference table. Once more, she touched her ring, staring at the blank screen. "I've gotta get out of here."

# CHAPTER FIVE

"YOU GET BIG POINTS for not asking a million questions." Arianna leaned back in the deli booth, pushing away a barely eaten green salad. "About Brian, and our past, and what I was feeling in that room. I know you want to know all that."

"As much as I like getting big points, those aren't the questions I want to ask." He reached across the table and touched the thin gold band she wore. "Why do you handle this thing the way you do?"

She jerked her hand away, staring at him. "How . . . when did you notice that?"

"The first time I watched you on the set." He ate one of his French fries. "It's kind of hard to miss."

Was it? "And what did you think?"

"That you had a nervous habit." He wiped his mouth, and set the napkin on the table. "But then you proved that the ring has an inordinately high value to you. And back in Brian's office, you practically broke your finger yanking on it while you were . . ." He paused, and when she didn't offer a word, he said, "Thinking."

"I wasn't yanking on it," she replied. *Or thinking.*

"I'm exaggerating for effect. You were playing with

it, twisting it . . ." He pushed the ring a little, turning it on her finger. The act of letting someone else touch it was as intimate as if he'd touched her body, and it sent the same kind of shiver through her. "You were *using* it," he said softly.

She felt her jaw drop, then snapped it closed. "You're right. A nervous habit."

"You need it, don't you? It gives you . . . whatever you need to do what you do."

Her whole body sagged with the shock of his observation. "You couldn't know that."

"But I do know that."

She covered the ring protectively, as if she could keep the secret to herself. "I've never told anyone," she said, looking hard at him so he understood the magnitude of the statement. "Not even my father knows."

She considered, and discarded, various forms of the truth. Why lie to this man? For the first time that she could ever remember, she utterly trusted someone. It was that golden aura. And those intense blue eyes. His pure heart and raw courage and unfettered intensity. She trusted him. And here, in a crowded deli in the San Fernando Valley, she decided to reveal her innermost secret to a man she'd known for less than two days.

"My mother gave this ring to me when she died. On her deathbed, in the hospital, if you want the whole melodramatic truth."

"I do."

She took a deep breath, and barely realized she'd threaded her fingers through his. While she talked, he gently turned and twirled her ring, stroking her knuckles, soothing her, eliminating her fear. That was *his* gift, and it was powerful.

"My mother was a well-known crime psychic who helped the LAPD solve some of their most unsolvable crimes." She watched his fingers on the ring, strong and clean and gentle. "In fact, that's how she met my father. He was a detective, and if you think you're skeptical . . ." She laughed lightly and pointed at him with her free hand. "You haven't *met* skeptical until you've met my dad."

"He didn't believe in her?"

"Oh, he believed, all right. Once she dragged his ass to a dead body in Woodland Hills, then gave him enough information to bring in one of the county's worst serial killers, he believed so much that he married her a month later." She smiled, thinking how he loved to tell that story. "But then—well, I told you. She was killed by a man who had something dark and sinister to hide, a man who knew she'd figure him out."

"Was that man ever caught?"

She shook her head. "She was on her way to a crime scene and someone got to her, told her that my dad needed to meet her. And she went, and . . ." Arianna closed her eyes, her head suddenly filled with the smell of the antiseptic hospital, the ice-cold chill of the ICU, the barely whispered final words of a mother to a daughter as she handed over a legacy. "No, the crime was never solved. But before she died, she gave me her wedding ring and told me to continue her work."

"As a psychic."

"As a crime psychic," she corrected. "Which was pretty amazing, because at the time of her death I hadn't even a whisper of psychic ability. Then she gave me her ring, and *wham.*" She wiggled her eyebrows. "I hear dead people."

She appreciated that he didn't laugh, that he got the seriousness of what she was telling him. Even if he didn't believe a word of it, he got props for being such a good listener. That golden aura warmed her as effectively as the sun through the blinds.

"And when you're not wearing the ring?"

"Nothing happens. Ever. I . . ." She tried to say the hard, ugly truth. "I can't do anything without this ring. It's the only way I ever see or hear anything. And that's why I was willing to risk everything—my life and yours—to get it. Do you understand?"

"I do," he said. "But I don't understand why you didn't do what your mother asked, when she said to continue her work."

Oh, Lord. Did he have to know absolutely everything about her? A lesser man wouldn't have even thought about that. Another man would focus on the gift, the power, the curious ability. That tingle started through her again. The tingle of trust. And . . . more.

"I'm terrified of being killed," she admitted. "I'm scared of the ability to know who bad guys are, and what they will do to me to shut me up. I'm a total chickenshit. And that, my friend, is why you are here today."

He smiled. "You're not a chickenshit, but I'm glad I'm here."

"Me, too," she admitted. Really, really glad. She decided to push it one step further, just to see. Now that he knew, if he believed, then maybe this could be more than trust. Maybe, if he believed her . . . it could be . . .

She took a breath and jumped into murky waters. "So, why don't you go ahead and think about your friend Michael, and I'll show you what I can do."

The slightest bit of color drained from his face and he almost let her hand go, but she grabbed his fingers. "Or not—it's okay," she added quickly. It didn't have to be love. Lust and trust worked for her.

"He wasn't my friend."

Something in his voice squeezed her heart. "I just mean the person you knew. The one you were thinking about when—"

"He was my brother." The words fell hard, and his expression matched.

"Your brother?"

"My younger brother, by eighteen months. We joined NASA at the same time, in the same class. It was a first for the agency, and a real kick for my parents." He half smiled, as though that memory held a lot of happiness, however tainted. "It was his first mission, and it was supposed to be . . ." He closed his eyes for a second; blew out some disgust. "I was supposed to fly that mission. Not him. But in typical NASA fashion, they decided to use me for some stupid PR program that lasted a whole year, and he got my slot. He sat in that shuttle where I should have been, and . . ." He couldn't even finish the sentence.

"He was killed and you weren't."

"He wasn't the only one killed," he said. "But I should have been piloting that thing."

She remembered how that third loss of a shuttle had rocked the space program. She tried to remember the names of the lost astronauts, but couldn't.

"You have survivor's guilt," she said. "It hurts."

"I have grief," he shot back. "It hurts more." He tapped her ring. "And don't suggest closure. I don't want it or need it."

She knew better than to try. Yet she felt something warm, and lovely. She felt so close to this man, it almost stole her breath.

"Chase," she whispered, rubbing her thumb on his callused palm, "will you take me home?"

He searched her face. "You don't want to go to Cal Tech and rattle that geek who's sending you threatening e-mails?"

"No. I want to go home and show you my surprise."

He looked intrigued. "Another tattoo?"

"I made my bed."

He laughed softly and picked up the check. "Too bad we're just going to mess it up again."

Chase woke hard, desperately wanting her for a third time. But Arianna's soft, even breaths stopped him from doing more than nestling her warm body into his and inhaling the delicate smell of her, the lingering essence of their lovemaking almost as dizzying as the scent of her hair and skin.

Hoping it didn't wake her, but half wishing it would, he stroked the silky thigh that curled over his leg, slid his hand over the roundness of her backside and smiled, thinking of the angel tattooed on her rump. Tinkerbells and butterflies and angels. Wild hair, a wicked mouth, and the tightest, hottest, sweetest envelope of womanhood he'd ever known.

Under the covers, he found her hand, and turned her magic ring.

Did he believe her? Or had he kissed and touched and tasted and entered this extraordinary woman under false pretenses? He never said he believed her story about her mother's ring, but he never said he didn't, either.

Did that make him a hypocrite? A pragmatic, hard-headed scientist? A man who just wanted to get inside the sexiest woman he'd ever known?

His aching hard-on certainly proved the last one was true. He wanted to be inside her again, that minute and all night. And all day.

He exhaled, ruffling her hair, and she curled closer to him. Did it matter if he believed her or not? What would it get him? Oh, right—*closure.*

His gaze moved to the moonlight reflected in her mirror, making him think of Michael. The man who still had enthusiasm when Chase had grown cynical, the teenager who idolized his high-achieving big brother, the boy who once woke him in the middle of the night to ask if *shit* was a bad word.

*What about* shit, *Chase? Is* shit *a bad word*?

Arianna stirred suddenly, and sucked in a breath. In the moonlight, he could see her eyes were open, and locked on him.

How long had he been thinking about Michael?

How much did she . . . hear?

"Hell, yeah," she whispered. "Now go back to sleep, kiddo."

He felt like he'd been punched. That was the exact answer he'd given his little brother when he asked if *shit* was a bad word. *Hell, yeah. Now go back to sleep, kiddo.*

"Oh, man," he groaned. "I can't do this."

"And you shouldn't have to." She sat up and pulled off her ring. "Don't torture yourself, honey," she said softly, then set the ring on the nightstand with finality. "Just relax." She burrowed her fingers into his hair, slipped back into her warm nest against him, and slid her heavenly thigh between his legs. "Don't think, Chase," she crooned. "Don't hurt. Don't regret. Don't."

She was magic—really, truly. Sexual, sensual, psychic healing magic. She kissed his mouth, splayed her fingers over his chest, then traveled lower to close her hands around his erection. Slowly, with so much tenderness it almost made him cry out, she stroked him, soothed him, suckled his tongue in her mouth, and let her whole body rise and fall against him, using her breasts, her hands, her legs for every imaginable, insane, impossible form of body-to-body contact.

Without a word, just murmured sounds and whispers of breath, she climbed on top of him, letting her hair tickle his face and chest, feathering kisses on his forehead and eyes.

He held her hips, helpless as she took ownership. Before, she'd been under him, conquered. Now he was hers. She rose up on her knees and, with two hands, she took his erection and placed it between her legs. Then she eased him in, all comfort and heat and deep, warm enclosure. She cooed and spread her legs, taking him all the way, as far as he could go, until he touched the very deepest part of her.

"There," she whispered gently, "Now, don't think about anything but this." She rose and fell, squeezed and released.

The effect was mind-boggling. His cock ramrod hard, his heart thumping with desperate effort, blinding pleasure pushed him deeper. He thrust and plunged into her, his thumbs digging into her body.

The need for release burned and welled in his balls, shocking him with the sheer force of it. His chest hurt, his back hurt, every muscle was on fire with focus. She arched, her hair tumbling down her back, her breasts pointed up like some kind of goddess, his name on her lips like she purely loved the sound of it.

There was no build to his release, just a furious, fierce, fast explosion. He shot everything into her, his juice erupting farther and harder with each helpless, uncontrolled thrust. Finally, when there was nothing left at all, she fell on top of him and rocked until he could breathe and think again.

"If that's closure," he whispered, "I'll take some every day."

She gave a soft little laugh, and kissed him. It was only then that he realized her face was wet with tears. And he knew why.

"Arianna," he said, wiping her cheek. "I'm sorry I didn't believe you sooner."

She didn't answer, but laid her head on his chest and quietly cried for both of them.


Arianna was certain that Chase believed her; he'd proven that the night before. Deep into the night, after they'd made love, she told him about the black-and-white visions she'd had in the studio. She'd used her hands to show the placement of two cars, explaining that one disappeared over a guardrail on a dark, rainy night, pushed by the other. He'd coaxed her for details until she finally remembered the hood ornament on the car that went over the cliff.

A Jaguar, he was convinced. It was a very distinct and stylized decoration. Pushed further, she decided that the blanket of lights she could see from inside the car was possibly Studio City, and the road was almost definitely Mulholland Drive.

So when she heard Chase call Lucy and ask her impressive investigators to look into accidents involving Jaguars on Mulholland, she knew with absolute certainty that he believed her.

Just as she knew with absolute certainty that she loved him. Some things, she just knew.

She kept both revelations to herself as they drove to Cal Tech, timing their arrival at the Pasadena campus to coincide with the end of a class in behavioral biology, run by a teaching assistant—Eric Scheff.

On the way, they played out a few different scenarios, depending on where they found him—in a lab, in an office, in a classroom—and Arianna almost giggled with anticipation as Chase formulated various plans.

"You like this," Chase said, shooting her a look from the driver's seat. "You're having fun."

She patted her backpack—neatly zipped and tucked under her feet—where the e-mails were folded into the front compartment. "I want this bastard to stop bothering me. And I want to know if he was at the show. And if he shot at my trailer."

"And if he didn't?"

"Then we keep hunting." She kicked off her clogs and folded her feet under her. "You're right, it's fun taking down bad guys. Of course, it's easy to be brave when I've got my own personal bodyguard packing big-time heat."

"You can pack heat," he said, chuckling at the phrase. "All you have to do is get some training. I'd be glad to help you."

"Yeah?"

"And then, you might feel safe enough to . . . do what your mother suggested. Assuming you want to," he added.

It still stunned her when he knew her so well. "I do," she admitted. "I always have, and my father has encouraged me—even though you'd think he'd hate the idea. But, now I have this show . . ."

"Do you like the show?"

"I like the idea of helping people," she said. "But there are so many elements about it that I hate. The acting, the pick-ups, the aspects that make it 'entertainment.'" She touched her hand, ready to say that wasn't what her mother had intended, but she sucked in a quick breath instead. "Dammit! I left my ring at home."

She could see it on her nightstand, where she'd taken it off last night.

"Do you need it? You're planning to read this guy?"

"I like to have it. Just in case." In case the freak was the one sending the black-and-white messages. In case someone needed her. In case her house burned to the ground. Even if she didn't wear it, she always had it with her. "I feel naked without it."

He reached for her hand and she half expected a comment about liking her naked, but he was sensitive enough not to make light of her ring. Another thing she loved about him.

They pulled into an underground parking lot on campus with a few minutes to spare. Before they got out, she tugged her hair through the back of an L.A. Dodgers cap and slipped on a pair of reflective Oakleys.

"Cute," he said, tapping the brim of her hat when they came out into the sunlight.

"My standard disguise."

"And I bet no one notices this." He pulled her hair gently, then glided his hand down to give her backside a pat. "Or this."

"Hey, this is California, Chase. Girls in tight jeans are everywhere."

"Trust me, not at schools like this." Glancing at his watch, he urged her forward. "Let's go."

He knew exactly where he was going, so Arianna just held his hand and checked out the student body as they headed toward a creamy, geometrically shaped building that had probably looked ultramodern when it was built in the 1950s.

As they approached, the main glass doors opened and a pack of students came pouring out, most wearing caps like hers, and almost all with various forms of earbuds firmly installed. Chase easily navigated through the crowd, parting the way to go against the flow. Arianna could feel him pick up the pace, as anxious as she was to get this over with.

Plan A was to ambush Eric Scheff in the classroom. And not to tip anyone off that they were on the hunt for him, in case it scared him off.

When they arrived at the auditorium-style classroom, there was no sign of Scheff, although a group of students sat in the back rows, deep in animated conversation using a language that might have been English, but was peppered with so much science jargon it could have been Greek.

Chase eased into the conversation, as natural as any grad student on campus. "Hey," he said casually after a moment. "Anyone seen Scheff around?"

"He never hangs after class," one of the kids said. "He's so far behind on his thesis that he disappears the minute he can. Check his office."

"On the second floor?"

"Yeah," another said. "Two sixteen, right next to the lab."

Back in the hall, Chase leaned close and whispered, "Plan B."

That meant he would try to get Scheff out of his office—hopefully while on his computer—by claiming Chase was undercover security for MetroNet Studios. Then Arianna would go in his office, and check to see if he'd sent her the e-mails.

She hung outside, a few feet away from room 216, pulling the cap low and dropping her head to pretend to be talking on her cell phone. Chase knocked on the glass panel, then pushed the door open without waiting for permission. Her heart thumped as she squeezed the silent phone against her ear, mumbling, "Yeah, uh-huh," when someone walked by, inching closer to the office to hear what was being said.

Something thudded hard against the wall, and Arianna's eyes grew wide. Were they fighting? She heard a grunt, and another. Surely that little geek hadn't overpowered

Chase? She stood to the side of the door, the phone forgotten.

"Okay!" a man's voice yelled, choked for air. "Stop!"

She threw the door open. Chase had Scheff pinned against the wall of the closet-sized office, dangling off the ground and struggling to breathe.

"Please, please," he groaned, squirming like a helpless, trapped animal. "Let me go!"

"You don't have to check the computer, Arianna. He sent every e-mail to you." Chase shoved the guy harder.

"Why?" Arianna demanded. "Why did you try to scare me?"

"I want you to quit. I want the world to know you're a fake."

Chase's expression darkened and he slammed the guy's gut with a fist. "She's not."

Scheff moaned in pain, doubling against the wall. "Then my whole damn thesis is shot."

"You're doing this for a *grade*?" She choked. "Are you serious?"

He closed his eyes and whispered, "Yeah."

She didn't believe that, and from the force in Chase's next shove, he didn't believe the weasel, either.

"Okay, okay," Scheff pleaded. "Please, c'mon, man. Put me down. I'll stop bothering her. Put me . . ." He looked down at a small wet spot in his pants. "Aw, c'mon."

Chase glanced at Arianna and she nodded. Slowly, as if it really hurt to do it, Chase slid him down the wall. Then he slammed his hands on either side of the guy's head, getting so in his face, they almost touched. "Tell me the truth, you little motherfucker."

Scheff held up his hands, as if that could stave off a

six-foot-plus human wave of fury. "Okay, okay. There was some money involved."

"Who?" Chase's hands closed in, squeezing the narrow shoulders. "Who is paying you?"

"I don't know." At the look on Chase's face, he shuddered. "I swear to God I don't know. I got anonymous e-mails back after I sent her a few. I don't know who it was, or is—I erased every one. But this guy started putting money in my PayPal account for every e-mail I'd send. And—" He clamped his mouth shut.

"And what?" Chase demanded, shaking him so hard his teeth cracked together. "And *what?*"

"And he-he s-s-said he'd give me ten grand if I could get her ring."

Arianna gasped. "What? *Who?*"

"Was that you in her trailer?" Chase demanded, thrusting Scheff's shoulders against the wall. "Did you shoot at her? Search the trailer? *Did* you?"

"No!" His terrified look darted from Chase to Arianna. "I swear to God!" His voice cracked with a sob. "I'm not lying. I've never been to your show, I swear. I don't own a gun. I don't even know how to shoot. And I don't know anything about your ring. And I don't know who's been contacting me." Tears ran down his face. "You gotta believe me. I didn't ask who it was."

She closed her hand over the gold band, only to be smacked by the reality that it wasn't there. And another reality, just as scary: Someone knew about her ring. And wanted it. Badly.

"We have to get home," she said urgently. A horrible, black intuition swamped her. *"Now."*

Chase stepped back from Scheff, who remained quivering against the wall. "You better not be lying—because I would really enjoy ruining your life for what you did to hers."

"I swear," Scheff repeated. "I don't have any idea who sent the e-mails. I didn't save any. I just hit delete, delete, delete."

But there was a money trail, Arianna thought. Before she could voice that thought, Chase whipped out his gun and aimed at Scheff's forehead.

He cowered and covered his face. "Oh, God, no!"

"Turn around!" Chase ordered.

He did, sobbing and falling to the ground. "Please don't kill me. *Please.*"

"Shut up." Chase yanked the power cord and tucked Scheff's laptop under his arm. "And don't even think about moving for half an hour, because I'll be right outside your office, waiting to shoot holes in both your hands so you'll never send another e-mail as long as you live. *If* you live," he added.

Arianna pushed the door open, checked the hall, and ran with Chase. As soon as they were outside, all she wanted to do was throw herself on him and kiss him until she couldn't breathe anymore.

No doubt about it. She was madly in love.

But first, she had to get home and make sure that ring was safe.

# CHAPTER SIX

"COME ON, ARIANNA," Chase urged as they zipped down the on-ramp, only to come to a dead stop on the freeway. "Who do you know who would pay big money to see you fail?"

"I have no idea. None." She slapped the dashboard. "Look at this traffic! I have to get that ring before someone else does!"

"Think," he said calmly. "I'll handle the traffic. You start going through those enemies you said you had. Who could get to Scheff?"

She whipped toward him, closing her hand over his arm. "You were unbelievable in there. You annihilated him, but didn't really hurt him. God, you were awesome!"

He almost laughed at the unexpected compliment. "Thanks."

"I have to say, that was . . . very hot."

He did laugh at that. "Hot? What happened to my safe golden aura?"

She made a soft, sexy sound. "It turned . . . dangerous and crimson. *Very* sexy."

"I was just doing my job. Yours is to think."

"I am," she assured him, rubbing her temples. "You

know, Chase, whoever it is, I bet it's the same person who's sending me the black-and-white image on the cliff."

He silently agreed.

His phone beeped to the tune of "Lucy in the Sky With Diamonds." "Maybe she has some information." He put the phone on speaker and held Arianna's hand. "Talk to us, Luce."

"In the last ten years, there have been sixteen incidents of fatalities on Mulholland between Coldwater and Laurel Canyon. One Jaguar, driven by a woman named Katherine Childress, in 2003. It was ruled an accident."

Arianna released his hand and rubbed her arms as if she was freezing. "Katherine Childress? I've never heard of her."

"A police file is being e-mailed in the next half hour," Lucy said. "Will you be able to pick it up, or do you want me to call and read you my copy?"

"If we're not back at Arianna's in half an hour, I'll call you." He zipped through a hole in the traffic and floored the Porsche into a rare stretch of open freeway, receiving another squeeze of gratitude from his passenger.

They made it back in under thirty minutes, and Arianna practically threw herself out of the car before he had it in park.

"Wait!" he ordered, reaching over to grab her arm and stop her. "Let me go in first."

Everything seemed normal. The gate was locked, the alarm was set even though he hadn't been able to get the alarm company to change her code yet, and the door was still double-locked. He opened it and literally held her back from tearing through the little house to get her ring.

He pulled his weapon and held her a step behind him. As he passed his laptop on the counter he tapped a key to get his e-mail going, then continued down the hall, checking the bathroom, then opening the door to the little bedroom.

Everything was as they'd left it, the closet door open, showing him it was empty, the bed disheveled from their lovemaking, Arianna's underwear and a T-shirt were scattered on the tile floor.

Unable to wait one more second, she barreled past him, leaped on to the bed, and threw herself at the nightstand.

"It's *gone*," she groaned, dropping her head in agony on the pillow. "Oh, my God, it's gone."

"Are you sure? Maybe it fell on the floor, or on the bed."

"It's gone," she repeated. "Some things, I really do just know."

Arianna made him leave the room, her pain was too intense. She appreciated that Chase wanted to help, wanted to search drawers and tear the bed apart to somehow make the damn ring appear, but she needed to sit on the floor next to her empty nightstand, and wallow in regrets. She should never have taken it off, she should never have left it home, she should never have accepted it in the first place.

She should—

"Arianna." Chase opened the bedroom door, his voice low and quiet.

"What?" She wiped her nose and looked over her shoulder. "Please don't ask me to think about who. I don't know who."

And without the ring, she never would. She'd never

read anyone again. She'd never have a chance to fulfill her mother's wishes—just when she'd stopped fighting the paralyzing fear and realized that they weren't just her mother's wishes, they were her own. Now she'd lost the power.

Chase sat next to her on the floor, draped his arm around her and opened his laptop. "I need you to look at something, sweetheart." He tilted the screen toward her. "You need to read this file. It's important."

She sniffed, blinked back a tear that made the screen swim in front of her, and forced herself to read the digital reproduction of an LAPD accident report.

According to the file, twenty-four-year-old Katherine Childress, the daughter of a Beverly Hills plastic surgeon, had been driving a car that careened off Mulholland into a brushy, muddy area and was killed instantly. The accident happened on a rainy night in April 2003, one week before her wedding. The night was so rainy police were unable to find any evidence of what caused the accident. There were no witnesses.

When she finished, she looked up at him.

"Keep going." He paged down to an obituary from the *Los Angeles Times*, with the picture of a pretty blonde. Something clicked in her head and she squinted at it, trying to think where she'd seen that face before. Her gaze darted over the words describing the brief life of Katherine Childress, a student intern at a movie studio, an aspiring filmmaker, a part-time actress. Then she stared at the last line, unable to breathe as the words sank in.

*Childress is survived by her parents and by her fiancé, Brian Burroughs.*

"Oh, my God," she whispered, her hand over her mouth.

*That's* where she'd seen the face before. The picture on Brian's dresser. In his wallet. "Katie." The only woman Brian ever loved. "She was his fiancée, who died in a car accident four years before I met him." She'd never heard him say her last name. Just *Katie.*

Chills exploded all over her. Was Brian sending the message? Had he killed his fiancée?

"It can't be him," she said, as though Chase was following her thoughts.

"Yes, it can."

"No, no." She held out her bare hand. "He's not worried about my abilities—he doesn't believe I'm for real. He thinks the staff gets information to me from secret interviews." She looked at Katie's picture again, trying but failing to reconcile any role Brian could have had in her death. It was impossible. It defied logic. "It's not him."

"I'm not so sure of that," Chase said. "The boyfriend or husband is always the number one suspect. Surely you know that, as the daughter of a cop."

"He's still grief-stricken. He couldn't have killed her. And even if he did, he doesn't believe that I could figure it out."

"But he could be thinking about her death, sending you the message."

She grabbed his arm, pulling him up. "Let's go find him. He's probably home by now. If he's guilty, you're the man to get him to confess. But if he's not, and someone else on that set killed her, he has the right to know."

"How far away does he live?"

She stared at him as realization hit even harder. "He lives on Laurel Canyon Boulevard. Right off Mulholland."

• • •

A call to Burroughs Production confirmed that Brian was at home, as Arianna suspected. He was a creature of habit who always left the sets late in the afternoon, and returned if they taped with a studio audience at night.

"I just have one question," Chase said as they wound through Hollywood Hills and turned onto one of the steepest and curviest sections of Laurel Canyon Boulevard. "When you were dating this guy, did his ex-fiancée make any appearances in your mind?"

"No, she didn't."

"Didn't you think that was odd?"

"Well, I didn't always wear the ring with him. And sometimes people who have passed don't communicate with loved ones left behind. If they do, it's usually because there's unfinished business."

"You don't think there's unfinished business when someone's murdered, or even dies in a horrible car accident?"

It was a fair question, and she couldn't answer it. "I don't know," she said, watching for the high brick wall that surrounded Brian's property. "I was always relieved she never had a message to get to him. It's right around the next corner. There's the gate. Oh . . ." Arianna leaned forward as they pulled up to the wrought-iron opening tucked between thick foliage and the wall. "The gate's open."

Just as they pulled up, a huge SUV rumbled out of the driveway, so close that Arianna gasped as Chase swerved to avoid it.

"Was that Brian?" Chase asked, looking in the rearview mirror.

"I don't think so," Arianna said, turning to look. "Brian wouldn't drive away without stopping."

Chase zipped into the driveway that rounded to the front of the house. "Would he leave the gate *and* front door open?"

"Never." Arianna was pulling at her door handle before he stopped. Chase parked and came around the car, meeting her at the steps, his gun drawn.

"Wait." He stepped into the two-story foyer, looking from side to side. "Brian?"

Arianna entered in behind him, peering into the formal dining room on the right, and the living room across from it. And then she saw him. Sprawled on the floor, faceup. Covered in blood.

"Brian! Oh, my God!"

She dove toward him, but Chase grabbed her arm and held her back, bounding to the body in two steps to feel for a pulse. "He's alive. Barely."

Shaking, she started to reach for her bag, but Chase already had his cell out and was dialing. She dropped to her knees by his head, smelling the blood oozing from his stomach. She'd seen only one other gunshot wound in her life—in the same place, on her mother.

She automatically reached for him, but Chase stopped her, so she braced her hands on either side of Brian's head, leaning closer. "Brian, it's me, Ari."

His lids moved, almost opening, his eyes rolling back a little. "Go." The word was little more than air.

Go? He wanted her to leave?

"Get."

She stroked his hair. "Shhh. We're getting help."

"Your . . . ring."

She jerked at the words. Her ring?

"Go," he growled, using every ounce of life on the one syllable. "Must have it . . . for . . . the truth . . ."

She pushed her hair back, looking up at Chase. "Chase, whoever just left shot Brian. You have to go find him."

"No."

Oh, God. Protection 101. He wouldn't leave her. "Please!" she begged, her voice cracking. "He can't have gotten far; there's no turn for a mile. Please, go." She half stood, "Chase, please. Otherwise we'll never know who shot him."

He looked at her like she was crazy. "I'm not leaving you alone for a ring, Arianna."

"I don't care about the ring, Chase," she pleaded. "I want to get whoever shot him before they escape."

He spoke into the phone, giving an address. Then he gave the phone to Arianna. "Keep them on the line."

When he left, she transferred every ounce of concentration to Brian. "Who did this?" she asked softly, brushing his wavy hair off his forehead. "Who shot you?"

His eyes opened again, unfocused under hooded lashes. "Katie." The word was no more than a tortured breath.

*Katie.* "Whoever did this killed Katie, didn't they?"

He took a slow, labored breath, which pushed more blood out of his wound. From the cell phone on the floor, a woman repeatedly said, "Stay on the line," but Arianna ignored her, sending all her power to Brian, willing him to stay alive. "Who shot you?"

"Katie." This time the word was urgent, harsh. Demanding.

She stifled a frustrated moan.

"He's trying to tell you, Ari." Behind her, a gun cocked, clear and deadly, as a vaguely familiar woman's voice said, "I shot him."

*Katie?*

Chase had gone a half mile when he saw the SUV hidden in a grove of trees in front of the next house. Swearing, he pulled up next to it, jumped out, and tried to open the locked door.

Could the shooter have parked it and walked back to the house? He ran back to the Porsche, squealed into reverse, threw it into a three-point turn and slammed on the accelerator. The engine screamed around the last hairpin turn as Chase threw it into a lower gear and headed for the driveway.

He flatfooted the brake pedal and fishtailed just in time not to hit the iron gate that was closed and locked, separating him from Arianna.

"Son of a bitch!" Stupid, stupid! But how had someone got past him? He'd been on the only road.

He vaulted from the car and threw himself against the fence, which was at least twelve feet tall and well designed to stop intruders, with no horizontal bars to scale.

Sweat rolled down his back and his heart hammered. Whoever got in there to lock him out hadn't run back up Laurel Canyon on foot. There had to be a back way.

He ran along the wall that rimmed the property, looking for any little chunk of brick that would give him a foothold. He'd get over that wall or die trying.

When he heard a gunshot, he didn't wait for a foothold. Raw adrenaline and determination pushed him up and over the wall. He had to get to her before it was too late.

At the sound of the second shot, fear choked in his throat. Then he heard a third, a fourth, a fifth—and he knew for certain that someone in that house was dead.

If it was Arianna, there'd never be *closure*. There'd be hell to pay.

# CHAPTER SEVEN

CARLA LYNCH LOOKED NOTHING like Katie Childress, yet she claimed to be her. When Arianna accused her of lying she fired her gun in anger, just to make her point, and Arianna knew she'd better pretend to believe her. Otherwise she'd be lying next to Brian, long before Chase got back or the ambulance arrived. Someone would come. Chase would not let her die.

Some things, she just . . . hoped were true.

"I thought Katie was dead," she said simply.

"But you love to chat with dead people." She reached into her pocket and pulled out the ring. "When you've got this." The Australian accent was gone.

"It's not a trick, Carla."

"The name's *Katie*." She threw the ring on the floor, where it bounced a few feet from where Brian was bleeding to death. "Katherine Childress."

"I read your obituary." Arianna kept her gaze on the deranged woman while flipping through every option of how to escape without getting shot. She came up with none.

"The obit." Carla gave a dry laugh. "My dad covered every frickin' base, didn't he?"

"Your dad?" The plastic surgeon. She remembered that tidbit from the police report. "How? Why?"

"How? With power, money, and influence—the coin of the realm in this town. Why?" She shrugged. "Daddy's little girl was in trouble, and he understood I had to kill or be killed."

"Who did you kill?"

Carla drew back, looking a little bemused. "If you don't know, then I've been losing sleep for no damn reason. I thought she was whispering in your ear, all these months."

The vision. The Jaguar. The cliff.

Carla waved the gun toward a chair. "Go over there. I want this to look like a murder-suicide. That'll be good for *Closure* ratings, don't you think?"

"That's what this is all about?" Arianna kept her voice, and her shock, well modulated, moving slowly to the chair. "Ratings?" Could Carla be that ambitious? Did she want Arianna's job? "Is that why you paid Eric Scheff to send me e-mails and steal my ring?"

"Hey, you handed him to me. Somebody had to go trace your nasty notes from whacko fans and even more whacko enemies. When I read them, it was too easy to track him down and set him up. Plus I figured if I had to get rid of you, I could direct the police to him. And no, this is not about ratings."

"Then why? Why did you shoot Brian? Why did you . . . why did Katie die?"

"Katie died because I was stupid enough to let myself get blackmailed by an underbelly of this city you probably don't even know exists. I had information and access at my internship at a studio. But they kept wanting more, and then . . . I got in that inevitable place you get with those people. I just beat them to the job and made it look like an accident."

So Katie wasn't in the Jaguar when it went over the cliff. She'd faked her own death. "But who died?"

"Some prostitute no one will ever miss. And my father ID'd 'my' body, after he'd put my ass on a private plane to Australia to have his med school cronies make me into a new person." She touched her face. "They're just a little too good down there."

Arianna heard the crack in her voice, and instantly knew it was also the crack in her hard shell. "Brian didn't recognize you, did he?"

She paled. "Makes you wonder, doesn't it? Was he in love with me, or the outside of me? I freaking *killed* myself getting back here, getting this job, getting in his face. I was sure that he'd fall in love with Carla—because underneath, I'm still the same person."

Oh, yeah. She was cracking. Now Arianna just had to figure out how to widen the gap until she broke. "He'll never love anyone but Katie," Arianna said sadly.

Carla's laugh was bitter. "I realized that today, when I walked in on him stroking a hard-on while he watched old videos of our engagement party. Funny how a man can be so in love, he can whack off just looking at a picture of a girl—yet when she's standing right in front of him, he doesn't even know it's the same person." Her voice wavered again, and Arianna grew hopeful. "So I decided I ought to just come over here tonight and tell him how I feel about him." She looked at him again, her face contorted as she fought pain. "He didn't take it so well."

"Why did you want my ring so bad, if you were going to tell Brian?"

Carla looked at Arianna as if she was insane. "I wasn't planning on telling him the truth! And I sure as hell didn't want you blurting it out to camera two. You've always been the wild card, Ari. Ever since I realized you were the real deal, I've been scared. I've tried so hard to get rid of you, but I know that ring is the key. I finally lucked out today, when you left it at home. I've been in your house so many times looking for it, I feel like I should stock your fridge."

The thought sickened her. "How did you get in?"

"Brian had your key and alarm code in his desk for months." She smirked. "You don't really think your ring was some big secret, do you? It's so obvious." She imitated Arianna with an exaggerated motion of playing with her ring.

It didn't matter. Nothing mattered but that gun, and Brian's terrifyingly still chest. "Why did you shoot him?"

"He wasn't interested in Carla."

"So you *killed* him?"

"No. I told him the truth." She swallowed. "You're right. He didn't care who I am. He blames me for Katie's death, even though I *am* Katie." She laughed, but it was a sob. "He wanted to turn me in. I had to stop him."

*Where is that ambulance? Where is Chase?* "You'll never get away with this," Arianna said. "I wasn't alone."

"I know. I ditched the car, 'cause I figured you'd go after me. Then I sneaked in the back to wipe out my fingerprints, not expecting you to stay behind."

Her voice hardened. "I locked your bodyguard out. Now, should I shoot your temple to make it look like suicide? Or maybe in the mouth? Something close, 'cause I suck with this thing. I must have missed you by fifteen feet the other night."

There had to be some way to buy time. She had to have *some* power over this unstable woman, some way to turn this around. She thought about the tough, ruthless man she'd watched in action that day. What would he do?

Chase had power. He had size. He had a gun. She had . . . nothing. Her gaze slid to the spot on the floor where her mother's ring lay. She didn't even have that anymore.

With a shaky hand, Carla lifted her gun.

Suddenly, a forceful ping hit low in Arianna's spine, and she sat straight in surprise. A swift and familiar chill ran up her body, blossoming into a vision. A face.

A scared young girl with a delicate voice and hollow eyes whispered softly in Arianna's head. *"My name is Taylor."*

*This* was her power. This was her gift. And this was going to save her life.

Arianna looked over the gun and met Carla's gaze. "Her name was Taylor." She paused, listening. "Taylor O'Neill."

"Stop it," Carla hissed. "You're a total fake."

"She wants you to know she wasn't really a prostitute."

"You can't do this without your ring!"

Evidently, she could. "You offered to help her, Carla. She trusted you."

She swung the gun to the floor where the ring lay and fired. The ring catapulted in the air, then landed, split and useless on the floor.

"There. Now you have to stop."

But the image and the power were very much intact. "She was a runaway. Did you know that?"

Carla paled and her arms trembled, shaking the gun she held with both hands. "What I know is that you *can't* do this without that ring on!"

"She was a runaway from . . ." Arianna closed her eyes and listened. "Seattle."

"Stop it!" Carla's voice cracked. *"Stop it!"* She fired directly at the ring, leaving another black hole in the smooth oak floor. "I don't care about her!" she screamed.

One more time—if she could just get her to turn to that ring one more time . . .

"Listen, Carla. She wants to tell you something. She says that—"

Carla fired at the ring three times in rapid succession, loud enough that she didn't hear the chair scrape as Arianna leaped up and jumped her. She knocked the gun to the ground and pushed Carla off balance, but she threw her weight forward on top of Arianna. Immediately, Carla started to crawl them both closer to the weapon.

Grunting, Arianna tried to stop her, to claw her eyes, to bite her shoulder—but Carla was much stronger and pulled them both within range of the gun. Arianna yanked on a handful of black hair and Carla thrust her knee into Arianna's stomach, the blinding pain taking her breath away.

Carla pinned her with her chest and legs, reaching with a loud grunt toward the gun. Arianna thrust her arm out to her side, patting frantically on the floor, knowing it was there . . . it was right . . . *there*!

The jagged edge of the ring scraped her fingertips. Closing her fist over the metal, she whipped her arm back, scraping a long, vicious swipe on Carla's cheek, making her howl. The unexpected attack gave Arianna the advantage, and she flipped Carla off her and scrambled toward the gun.

Just as she seized the weapon a blast rocked the room, silencing Carla's cries. Arianna spun around, the gun in one hand, her ring in the other.

Chase held his weapon over Carla's body, his shirt torn, his face filthy, his hands bleeding, his chest heaving.

Arianna dropped the gun, and the ring. Silently, she stepped into his strong, protective arms, with no intention of leaving for the rest of her life.

THE HOUSE SAT HIGH ON A HILL, a spectacular castle of blue-gray fieldstone and leaded glass, at least six chimneys jutting toward a cloudless sky, surrounded by an endless valley of spring-green trees curling toward the waters of the Hudson River.

"Welcome to Lucy's lair," Chase said, throwing the Viper into a lower gear to climb the mile-long drive that led to the house. "Also known as the headquarters of the Bullet Catchers."

"Great place for staff meetings," Arianna said, lowering her sunglasses to drink in the magnificent estate. "Or job interviews."

"You've got the job, sweetheart," Chase assured her. "This is just a formality. You're not nervous, are you?"

She felt the hammered metal that hung around her neck. She didn't need the ring anymore, or even the remnants of it, but every once in a while she liked to touch the symbol of her power. Just like she occasionally brushed her fingers over the butt of the baby Glock at her hip—another symbol of power.

"Not nervous about seeing Lucy, but meeting all these other legendary Bullet Catchers."

"No legends allowed," Chase said with a smile. "Well, Romero thinks he's a legend, but he's off in the rain forest on an assignment with Jazz, his wife. And you met Max Roper out in San Francisco, and he's a pussycat."

"He's a grizzly bear."

"That's an act. Ask Cori, his better half. And today you'll meet Sage Valentine, since she'll officially be your boss."

"Has she worked for Lucy a long time?"

"She used to be an investigative reporter in Boston, but gave it up to move here and learn the business as Lucy's right hand. She lives with Johnny Christiano, who, if we're really lucky, is in the kitchen cooking. Although he might be on an assignment; I'm not sure."

He curled around the last big bend to the circle in front of the mansion. It was even more impressive up close, a stunning blend of old-world Tudor and sleek, modern design.

"Dan's here," Chase said, indicating a late-model sedan as he parked close to the house. "That's no surprise; he's the closest thing Lucy has to a partner, although she'd never admit it."

Arianna quelled a little shiver of anticipation and, yes, nerves. "I thought I was going to be alone."

"You're never alone." He leaned across the console and kissed her cheek. "You may be the Bullet Catcher's official crime psychic, but you travel with me. That's the deal."

"I love that deal." She slid her hand around his neck and pulled him closer. "And I love you."

This kiss was long, deep, and wonderfully familiar. "I love you back," he murmured against her lips.

A hard knock on the window startled them both, and her door was pulled open before they broke the kiss.

Arianna turned to the intruder, who crouched by the car, grinning. A mane of honey hair brushed wide shoulders, and golden-brown eyes twinkled above the slant of chiseled cheekbones and two outrageous dimples.

"G'day, mate." He stroked the tuft of golden hair that grew under his full lower lip, the move revealing a glimmer of gold in his earlobe. "Guess nobody told you that window right there"— he nodded toward a second-story gable—"is Lucy's library. She's watching, and I happen to know she frowns on her employees pashing around in the drive."

Chase laughed, leaning forward to reach out his hand. "Hey, Fletch. This is Arianna Killian, our newest recruit. Arianna, meet Adrien Fletcher, the wild and reckless Tasmanian devil."

Fletch winked at her and stood to an impressive height, opening the door wider for her. "None of that is true, except the geography. Welcome aboard, Arianna. I heard you're bringing a completely new capability to our arsenal. You'll love us all."

Chase climbed out and sent a meaningful look over the roof of the car. "She'll love some more than others."

"Dan, probably," Fletch said. "He's the heartbreaker."

Arianna smiled. "I imagine you've shattered a few."

"But they've enjoyed every minute of it. C'mon, now." He cocked his head toward the house. "Mustn't keep the mistress waiting."

Flanked by the charming Tasmanian flirt and her very

own Rocket Man, Arianna headed toward the house. As they reached the entrance the door opened, and Arianna actually had to stop.

She'd forgotten that Lucy Sharpe was flat-out breathtaking.

She stood almost six feet tall, probably more in her signature mile-high heels, with thick, straight black hair draping over her shoulders, nearly to her waist. With the hint of an Asian tilt, her eyes nearly took over her exotic features, but it was the snow-white streak in the front of her hair that made Lucy not only beautiful, but distinctive.

"Arianna," she said, reaching both hands out. "We are so happy to have you join the Bullet Catchers."

Arianna touched the precious metal around her neck, glanced at the man she loved, then accepted Lucy's warm embrace. On her back, she felt Chase's solid, comforting hand as he guided her forward, into her whole new life.

"Thank you, Lucy. I'm going to be very happy here."

Some things, she just knew.

# Redemption

### KARIN TABKE

*To Josie Brown, Tawny Weber, and Poppy Reiffin.*
*You ladies showed me the true meaning of friendship.*
*Thank you.*

*Thank you, Kim, for putting this anthology together,*
*and to Allison and Rocki for agreeing to have me*
*along for the ride!*

*Lauren? You rock, girl!*

*And always,*
*to my husband, Gary, my rock.*

*East Oakland, California,*
*sometime after noon*

Zᴀᴄʜ ᴡᴀʟᴋᴇᴅ ɪɴ on the bloodbath that was Sanjeet Kamal's rat-infested apartment. Every shred of patience, every fiber that was his conscience, and every cell in his body screamed injustice. The combination of the three shook him to the core. He'd never experienced a single one of them before.

The minute he entered the dank putrid room he smelled the copper stink of blood so thick in the heavy air it was like breathing lead. Zach should have smelled trouble the instant he let his partner go up first.

He looked hard at Mark Santos. "I'm not taking the fall for you, Santos," Zach told his soon-to-be-ex partner.

He'd never liked the way the guy had an excuse for every wrong turn, pointed the finger away from himself, or the way bodies popped up behind him. And that was saying a lot considering Zach had done his fair share of skating under the Internal Affairs radar. He'd made his own very conscious choices throughout his personal and professional life. And the consequences that came with them were his alone to live with, but no fucking way was he going to be a consort to unadulterated murder.

Mark looked up from the body, blood on his hands. Fresh blood. Warm blood. "The guy came at me." Santos grinned, shrugged his shoulders, and slowly stood. "I was in fear for my life."

"Bullshit. He's unarmed," Zach said, looking down at the bloody body. There was nothing threatening about Sanjeet. For all that he was, he was a gentle man. He had a wife and two girls back in India he sent money to. The neat slice across his throat gaped open, the blood saturating his beige shirt and pooling on the linoleum floor beneath him. Zach felt like a piece of shit.

His quest to save the world from rapists, pedophiles, and murderers had backfired. He glared at his partner. He was no better than Santos. He was a hypocrite. Only he'd justified it by killing only the bad guys. His anger swelled. Not only at Santos but at himself. It had to stop. Here. *Now.*

It was past time Zach maneuvered his partner into an ironclad IA. The guy was lethal to citizens on both sides of the law, and Zach was tired of dodging his haphazard bullets.

"Zach, the guy was nailing babies. I slit his throat. He deserved worse."

"Oh, really?" Zach sneered. He'd used the same lines to justify his own misdeeds to himself. He stepped up close to Santos. They were nose to nose, less than a foot separated them. "You stupid asshole, this guy was my CI, not the perp!"

Santos shrugged, backed away, then squatted down next to the body again and casually wiped his bloody hands, then the six-inch knife in his hand on the white turban of the man who lay dead at his feet. "I guess next time you need to clarify."

"Don't lay that shit on me. I told you we were looking for a two-hundred-pound five-foot-two Latino male. Not a seven-foot-tall Sikh with a damn turban!" Zach turned in disgust, wondering how the hell he would clean this mess up without getting dirty himself. He'd run his minor streak of luck with IA into the ground. They had his badge number on their target, smack-dab in the middle of it, a bull's-eye. And everyone in the PD was taking their best shot.

Before Zach could formulate more thoughts a shout outside the window caught his attention. "Let's get the hell out of here before someone sees us."

He gave Santos a quick contemptuous glance over his shoulder to make sure the bone dick was following, then headed out of the suffocating heat of the apartment and down the infested carpet of the narrow stairwell. As crack houses went, this one was a five-star deal.

Mark followed close on Zach's heels. "So what? I made a mistake. That guy was a piece of shit like the rest of the addicts. I just saved the taxpayers of Oaktown a pretty penny by taking that guy out, and you know it. I should get a medal of valor for it."

Zach stopped and turned around; Mark's shoulder hit him hard in the chest. Zach didn't budge against the impact. His hands fisted and it took every bit of self-restraint he possessed not to send Santos to hell where he belonged.

Where they both belonged.

Instead he pushed back. His hands open, palms forward, he shoved Santos hard away from him. He could forgive a lot of things in a lot of people, including killing a dirt-bag piece of shit child molester by accident or on purpose. But he could not forgive sport killing. "I'm not going down for you."

Zach's radio beeped three times in alert, then dispatch announced, "All units, four Charles thirty-two in pursuit southbound Bancroft, last cross Ninety-second Avenue, following black late-model Ford Taurus. Suspect vehicle wanted in Wells Fargo two-eleven. Shots fired at scene. Suspect is armed and dangerous."

"They're headed our way," Zach said, hurrying toward the unmarked car, and for the moment dismissing the fact his partner just slit a guy's throat for sport and let him bleed to death.

"All units available please switch to channel six."

"Let them know we're around the corner!" Santos shouted to Zach over the roof of the Crown Vic. Zach hesitated only a moment before he pulled the radio off his belt and turned to channel six.

"Detective seventeen, copy."

"Go ahead, seventeen."

"Detective seventeen in pursuit of suspect vehicle." The minute the words left Zach's mouth the wailing sound of the sirens crescendoed and a black Ford Taurus sped by.

"What's your Twenty, seventeen?"

"Westbound on Ninety-sixth at Olive, directly behind suspect vehicle."

Santos hit the gas as Zach slammed the door shut.

The cruiser sped up behind the Taurus. Zach tried to untangle the radio from the strap of his seat belt and put it on at the same time. He looked up just as the Taurus took a hard right into oncoming traffic. Santos made the cut behind the getaway car, the impact of the maneuver sending Zach slamming into the side of the door.

"You son of a bitch!" Santos yelled at the getaway car. "You're gonna wish you hadn't done that." He pushed his foot to the pedal and roared up behind the Taurus.

Zach grabbed for the seat belt.

Santos rammed the bumper of the suspect vehicle and whooped loudly as the Taurus fishtailed before quickly righting.

Zach's head hit the dashboard with a hard thud, pain speared to his temples. "Jesus, Santos, not on a crowded street."

Santos flashed him a malevolent smile. Shaking his head, Zach reached for his seat belt again, just as the premonition of what Santos's intentions were hit him.

His partner laughed, the sound demonic. He gunned the gas pedal again and slammed into the bumper of the Taurus just as it slammed on its brakes.

Zach put his arms out to break the inevitable impact. Pain shot up his arms, he felt his elbows buckle and his body rush forward to meet the windshield, and the world went dark.

As Zach's body bounced back from the shattered windshield with a hard thump from the impact of the hit, Santos stopped smiling. His brows crashed together and his jaw set. He turned the car sharply to the right and gunned it again, snagging the corner of the Taurus before hitting a parked car on the street. The Crown Vic shot into the air, and turned 180 degrees in the air, landing on its roof before sliding dozens of yards down the street to a hard stop against another parked car.

Long seconds passed. Santos hung upside down in his seat belt. He shook his head and laughed, the triumphant sound reverberating against the damaged interior of the car. He resisted the urge to yell out a loud *Whoop!* His pain was minimal and lasted only a fraction of the time it had when in his mortal state. He laughed again. The sound deeper, richer, full of victory. Never once since his decision four years ago to give up his soul for immortality had he regretted it. On the contrary. He thrived. His strength and his senses heightened the moment his adrenaline quickened.

He glanced at his partner, and his body surged with energy. He smiled at Zach's crumpled form up against the shattered passenger window. Small shards of glass punctured his brow. Thin lines of blood dripped, giving him a bloody halo. Santos smiled. He would be rewarded handsomely for this kill. His stock continued to rise among the cell of Immortals assembling in the Bay Area, and his time for ascension was near.

He reached to Zach's neck and felt for a pulse. Despite the obvious injuries, it beat strong beneath his fingertips. Zach Garett had more lives than a damn cat.

Easily fixed.

In a quick chop, Santos struck Zach in the throat, the sound of crunching cartilage indicating his aim was dead-on. Zach moaned and coughed. Santos grinned in satisfaction when his soon-to-be-dead partner began to struggle for breath. His grin widened as he watched, transfixed as Zach's unconscious body gasped for air that could not pass through his smashed larynx.

The face women swooned over lost color, turning ashen. Zach's chest heaved in a mighty effort for breath. Failing, it trembled, the wheezing echo of his laboring gasps turning to mere whispers of sound.

Adrenaline surged through Mark's veins with the knowledge Zach was on his way to hell. With each kill he became stronger. Possessing his victim's life force. Soon there would be few who matched his strength. There certainly were no others like him who possessed his cunning.

The overwhelming sound of booted feet stomping on asphalt mingled with the shrill sirens infiltrated the perfect moment of silence that was Zachary Garett's death. Santos grunted in annoyance. His brothers in blue to the rescue. But too late for the one they called the Grave Digger.

"Help! Garett's crashing!" Santos screamed.

# CHAPTER ONE

HE WAS FALLING—hard, fast, and headfirst. Heat scorched Zach's skin, oppressive air clogged his lungs. He tried to spread his arms to slow his descent, but his limbs didn't respond. He fought to open his eyes. They wouldn't open. He wanted to call out to someone, anyone, but his throat was constricted, his body felt like stone. The heat intensified to unbearable. He couldn't scream his agony.

His spine snapped when a force took hold of his feet, halting the velocity of his wild descent. His body hung suspended, the heat suffocating, pain searing his lungs with each breath. Then by an unknown force his body turned upright and shot up. The heat cooled to warm as his body continued to rocket away from the incinerator below.

To hurry his ascent his feet moved in a jerky scissor-kick motion. Just as suddenly as the pull began, all motion stopped. His eyes opened—to darkness.

And silence.

No, deeper than silence. Utter nothingness with just the distant roar of rumbling air engulfed him. He hung suspended, like a puppet floating in a pool without strings.

A sharp force tugged at his foot, jerking him downward. A greater force from above yanked him free. A screech like a wild animal caught in a trap echoed through the dark, searing straight into his heart. Fear flashed into his consciousness. His body shuddered

Then—nothing. His body grew heavy. His breaths slowed. He drifted . . .

A sharp pull from below jerked him back into awareness. An equal pull from above pulled back. He felt like a bone in a tug of war between two pit bulls. He was powerless to stop it. He tried to blink his eyes but in his suspended state he could do nothing. Except listen. And feel the dark and light forces of energy swirl around him, battling for possession.

In a forceful jerk, his body catapulted upward. The screech below resonated in his ears before it abruptly ended.

He must be dreaming . . .

Time stood still.

Oddly, while conscious of his surroundings, he felt no emotion, no pain, just a sense of being. It occurred to him at that moment, he could not even feel the dull rhythmic thud of his heartbeat.

The distant ring of a telephone shattered the moment.

*Where the hell am I?*

The phone continued to ring. Louder now. High, shrill rings. He envisioned an old-fashioned black dial phone, the same kind in the Perry Mason shows.

His body lurched, an invisible force guiding it. He felt like a side of beef on a conveyer hook being led to the butcher.

The ring increased in pitch.

Far ahead the glow of light in the form of a rectangle illuminated the darkness. The ringing came from somewhere beyond it.

Zach tried to move his head to look around, to get a sense of place. His sharp instincts failed him. He had no feeling of good or evil, safe or dangerous.

How did he get here? Where *was* here?

He swallowed.

No pain from the collision.

*Collision!*

His recent memory flashed. Anger flared when he remembered Santos's reckless driving and the last malevolent smile before he tried to kill him! *Son of a bitch.* He was going to let that fool have it when he got back. Zach's skin flashed hot. He welcomed the sensation. The light became brighter and as he approached he saw that it came from behind a door. The shrill ring of the phone continued, demanding attention.

A dull throb knocked on his temples.

His feet touched a floor.

He reached a hand to the handle illuminated by the bright light.

Miraculously it obeyed his command. Sensation filled his limbs, the rush overloading his nerves. He shook it off.

Slowly he turned the knob. It gave easily under the pressure of his fingers. He pushed slowly, and as it opened, bright light rained down on him. The warmth of it penetrated to his bones. Instantly he raised his face to it, like he had raised his face to the sun as a child. Sharp pain stabbed at his head as he remembered his childhood days. Memories he had pushed far and deep into his consciousness, too ugly to bear. Yet, here, they raged out of control like the screeching goblins from his childhood nightmares.

Zach closed his eyes and shook his head. Demons from his past swirled and dove at him, snapping at him with sharp fangs. Their crazed laughter rising to a fevered pitch.

He put his hands over his ears to drown out the sound, but the gesture only brought them closer. Just as quickly as the demons appeared, a sweet rose-scented breeze swept them away. Warmth filled his heart. He lowered his hands and smiled. She came for him?

"Danica . . ." he whispered. He could feel her loving presence everywhere around him. It drew him up, gave him strength. His skin tingled, every hair on his body rose.

He opened his eyes wanting with his entire being to see her face. The light dimmed to normal. He was greeted instead by the ringing phone sitting on a desk in the middle of the room with a single chair in front of it. He scoffed back a laugh. The phone *was* the old black desk type just like in Perry Mason.

Tired of the incessant ring, he hurried across the white tile floor and picked it up. "Garett," he said.

"Take a seat," a deep, authoritative voice commanded, "I'll be right with you."

Zach opened his mouth to argue but the dial tone told him he had no audience. He replaced the handset in the cradle, looked beside him to the straight-backed wooden chair. His gaze traveled the perimeter of the room. Maybe fifteen by fifteen. In the corner to his right, another door. As he sat down the door opened.

A man about his age stepped through. He wore black jeans and a black T-shirt, but Zach could see it was damp and there was a hole, like a gunshot to his chest. The man's dark eyes swept across Zach's face. He nodded imperceptibly, and said, "He'll see you now," then exited the door Zach had just walked through.

Unhurried, Zach stood. He swallowed and for the first time felt the hard burn of his throat. He touched his fingers to it and winced. Pain exploded under the pressure. What the hell?

He took a deep breath, the whistling sound of air fighting for passage through what he was sure was a crushed larynx.

Zach didn't bother to explore the depth of his injuries. The fact he was alive, standing and breathing, was good enough for him right now. He had worse things to consider. Like was this some new IA mumbo-jumbo tactic? Were they trying mind games to get him to cop to the dead CI? Or why the hell he'd totaled another city vehicle? Hell, why his partner had tried to kill him?

Zach stepped into the room he was directed to. The man standing behind the white desk in the benign room was a stark contrast to it. He was taller than Zach's six-three frame. He was dressed in black from his head to as far down as Zach could see from where he stood in front of the man's desk. Dark blue eyes flashed beneath dark slashes of brow framing his face. Full lips, set in consternation, hovered over a square chin. Long wavy black hair flanked his broad shoulders.

"Welcome, Detective Garett." The man reached out a long arm, and pointed to the chair in front of his desk.

Zach shook his head. "I'd rather stand if you don't mind."

The tall one nodded. "I do mind. Have a seat so that we may begin."

"Begin what?"

"Our chat. About what happened to you today."

"I'm not answering one question until my POA rep gets here *and* my attorney."

The man sat, the gesture slow and fluid. He reminded Zach of a jungle panther. Steely control and the ability to pounce on its prey and deliver a fatal strike in less time than it would to blink.

"Who are you?" Zach demanded. He'd let his union rep know about this bullshit tactic. He turned to walk out the door. He gave the guy two seconds to come up with info. The man remained silent. "I'm outta here."

Zach strode toward the door and snatched it open. An enormous draft of hot air sucked him forward into raging flames just outside the threshold. *Holy shit.* Zach jumped back and slammed the door shut. *What the hell?* He turned, warily narrowing his eyes at the stranger.

"Where the hell am I?"

The man's face turned to granite. "Only heaven knows."

"Who the fuck are you? Why am I here?" Zach moved closer to the center of the room. "Where *is* here?"

"Can I get you a glass of water or something, Detective?"

"No, thanks. Just tell me how to get out of here."

"Have a seat, and I'll explain your choices."

"Choices? You're giving me choices? I don't even know who you are and you're talking about giving me choices?"

"My name is Michael."

"Michael what? Sergeant, LT? Captain?"

Michael smiled and inclined his head toward the empty chair. "Please, sit and hear what I have to say before you leave."

Zach didn't trust the guy's tone. He smelled a setup. Despite that, he walked the remaining way across the room and sat. "Make it quick." But he wasn't sure where the hell he would go if he didn't like what Michael had to say. It wasn't like he had an option two.

"I've watched you for a very long time, Zach. You've made some very bad choices with very serious consequences. Have you heard of the Ten Commandments?"

"Cut to the chase, *Mike*."

Michael opened a black folder sitting on the desk. Zach blinked in surprise. He was a paid observer and he was damn sure the folder wasn't there a minute ago. Michael smiled at him, the gesture neither friendly nor challenging. More like knowing.

"At the tender age of ten you broke twelve-year-old Billy Kershaw's hand after he stuck said hand down your sister's panties."

Zach's back went rigid. "How do you know that?"

Michael shuffled a few papers, appeared to read one, then turned those incriminating eyes on him. "A year later when Billy retaliated by strangling your dog Sheba, you broke both of his hands then removed his right thumb and shoved it down his throat and told him the next time he touched anything you loved you'd kill him."

Zach pushed back in the chair, the legs scraping on the floor. No one knew about his encounters with Billy, except

Billy, and Billy couldn't talk, because he was anchored off the Farallon Islands.

"I don't know who the hell fed you this bullshit, but unless you have proof, I don't need to listen to this crap." He stood.

"Sit, Zach."

The commanding tone of Michael's voice stirred the air in the room. As if there were a hand on his back pushing, Zach sat.

"Six years later, after Billy raped your baby sister, and you beat him to a pulp, you left him to die."

"I came back."

"After he bled out. Why?"

At that moment, Zach didn't give a shit who knew the truth about Billy. When he'd made the decision to out Santos he knew his career would be over, and he didn't care. He was tired of who he had become. "Kershaw was a piece of shit. He'd robbed, raped, and bullied his way into running our neighborhood. When he raped Kimmy, I snapped. He had to be stopped, and he had to disappear. It sent a message."

"And so the savior of the neighborhood became a cop to continue his vigilante rampage and up the body count."

"Our justice system is ass-backwards."

"So you took it upon yourself to clear the earth of criminals."

"I like to think of it as saving the taxpayers some of their hard-earned cash."

"What about Danica?"

If Michael had hit him in the chest with a sledgehammer

it would have hurt less than the pain the mention of her name invoked. "Leave her out of this."

"That will be difficult. She is a very integral part of why you're here."

"You got it all wrong, boss. She hates me. And she should."

"Because you set her up and then betrayed her?"

"Why ask me questions when you already know the answers?"

"I'd just like to hear it from you."

"I don't discuss Dani with anyone. Now tell me why I'm here. I have a case to wrap up."

"Zachary, in less than three minutes you will be dead."

The warmth drained from his body, leaving his skin feeling cold and damp. Like a corpse.

Michael pulled a remote from a drawer and pointed it behind Zach. He turned to see a white flat screen emerge from the wall behind him. In slow motion the car chase he was just involved in came into view and played out. He cringed as the car flipped then landed with a crash on the asphalt. The picture freeze-framed.

"What do you remember after the crash?"

"Nothing."

Another picture flashed up on the screen. Zach's temper soared when he watched Santos shatter his larynx and laugh about it. Instinctively he touched his fingertips to his neck. Pain flared.

The frame froze. Zach turned back to Michael. "Who are you?"

"I am the guardian of humanity, Zachary Garett, and

humanity is about to engage in a battle with a force so strong no nuclear weapon can stop it."

"What does that have to do with me?"

"Your Danica is the key to keeping the scourge from reaching earth, and you are the key to her understanding her destiny."

"Danica hates me! She'll shoot me the minute she lays eyes on me. Find another stooge to save the world."

"Don't you care?"

"I'm going to be dead, remember?"

"Do you know where you were headed before I snatched you from your fall?"

Zach remembered the oppressive heat from his dive bomb south and the unbearable weight on his chest. His body shuddered, and he suddenly felt like he was going to puke.

Michael extended a hand to the door. "You're free to continue your descent. Just walk through that door."

"As opposed to what?"

"I send you back to earth. Get Danica to understand her destiny by any means necessary, and together you save the world."

"Funny."

"I'm serious."

"*You* go kill the bad guys."

"I cannot take a human life, but I can give one back—conditionally."

Zach sat back in his chair and crossed his arms over his chest. "Of course, now here comes the rub."

"It's quite simple, really. I want the Trinity. And you and

Danica have the power together to retrieve the two missing pieces."

Zach eyed Michael as if he'd sprung two more heads.

Michael smiled. It wasn't a cockles-warming one either. Zach's temples pounded and his body burned from pain. He swallowed hard and nearly gagged. It seemed each moment that passed his pain became more acute.

"In three days' time the artifacts from the ruins of Caladia will be delivered to the Hope museum. A certain benefactor, Mr. Zao, an Immortal of the lowest order, is paying a sizable sum for the privilege of a private showing of several of those artifacts. Specifically an ancient scabbard that cradles the Star of Moria. If he gets his hands on either one, we lose."

Zach didn't dare ask what a freakin' Immortal was. He didn't want to know. "How does Danica play into this?"

"She is the last of the known Starkeepers on earth."

Zach laughed, the sound cynical. "Okay, I don't know what the hell you've been smoking." He stood, then walked to the door, jerked it open and looked down into the fire. His pant leg ignited and the hot sear of fire burned him.

He jumped back, slapping his pant leg. "Son of a bitch!" Angrily he turned to look at Michael. The man or whatever he was hadn't flinched.

Since this bizarre journey had begun, for the first time he felt as if there would be no escaping it. If he played along and listened to this crazy-ass hippy he might buy some time. Otherwise. He glanced over his shoulder. The choices weren't too attractive. "Okay, I'll play along. What's a Starkeeper?"

"Several thousand millennia ago there was a faction of beings sent to earth to watch over humanity. Without going into details, I'll just say they didn't do their jobs very well. My boss got angry and he put them away. He has refused these watchers freedom until he feels they have learned their lesson. Which to date they have not. Quite the contrary. But because the watchers had done such damage to humanity, the boss gave humans the Trinity; the sword, the scabbard, and the Star, or together as one unit, the key to their prison, and the responsibility to guard it with their lives. The matriarch of the Magori tribe, the people most defiled by the watchers, was entrusted with the key. She separated the Trinity, hiding each piece in a secret location, and passed the secret of their resting places to her only daughter. And so the secret has been hidden for scores of millennia."

Michael paced the small room, his presence filling it. Zach could feel his passion, his anger. He stopped beside Zach and looked hard into his eyes. "The secret of the key was lost through time because of complacency. Your Danica is the daughter of the last Magori matriarch. Rachel. And with Rachel's death last year, there is only Danica."

"So? Why do I have to get the key? Why not you?"

"My boss told the people he would not save them a second time. Only a human descendant of the keeper of the Trinity could ensure the safety of humanity."

"So this Trinity or key was dug up? The archeologists have no clue what they have?"

"Indeed, over the years the Immortals, Sephora's henchmen, have made it their life mission to discover the whereabouts of the key. There are whispers that the key is among the artifacts being delivered to Danica's museum."

"She has no idea about her mother?"

"None. The secrets have died with the years. It is unfortunate."

"What prevents the bad guy from just taking the key?"

"It has no power unless freely given by the keeper."

"Freely given as in, here you go even if I have no idea what the hell I just gave you?"

"Unfortunately, yes. And once Danica understands her role in humanity, she will need to begin the legacy again."

"How does she do that?"

"She must bear a daughter of Caladian blood."

Zach's hackles rose at the thought of Danica with another man. "What is that?" he bit off.

"Caladians are descendants of the children born as the result of the watchers mating with mortal women."

"So what's an Immortal?"

"An Immortal is a human on his or her way to hell and given the choice of selling their soul to Sephora or continuing the descent." Michael manufactured what could be construed as a smile. "Much like your situation."

"Who is Sephora?"

Michael's eyes flashed angrily. His hands fisted. "Sephora is the Queen of the Watchers."

"How is it, if she's one of these *watchers*, she isn't locked up?"

Michael's scowl deepened. "Sephora is not only beautiful, she is cunning and possesses power matched by few. She has chosen now to make her stand and hunt down the Trinity *and* those who stand in her way to free her people."

"So how the hell—if what you say is true about Danica—is she supposed to survive an attack by that bitch?"

"So long as there is Magorian blood mingled with that of a Caladian, the keeper can survive attacks from Immortals, and with my help a direct attack by Sephora. For reasons I will not explain, Sephora will not show herself on earth." He paused a moment to let the information sink in. Zach was having difficulty understanding it all, and even more believing it. He must be dreaming. Michael continued, "While the Immortals cannot kill the Starkeeper, they can and have killed her chosen one. They hunt Caladian warriors down like dogs." Michael reached into the left breast pocket of his jacket. Slowly he withdrew a golden short sword. His blue eyes glowed in reverence. "The Sword of Caladia, the final piece of the Trinity."

Zach had a physical reaction to it, as if it were a cherished childhood toy rediscovered. Instinctively he reached for it. Michael placed it in his hand hilt first. Zach slowly wrapped his fingers around it. It felt—familiar.

"You will know an Immortal when you meet it. They stink of sulfur. Their eyes turn to onyx when they are in kill mode. They are powerful. But then so will you be. They will show you no mercy, show them none. Slice an artery with that." Michael pointed to the weapon in Zach's hand. "And they will return to hell forever. Immortals can only be killed by a Caladian, the Starkeeper, or myself." Michael continued, "Or by Sephora herself."

Zach stood for a long silent moment with the sword in

his hand. Its warmth infiltrated his body, chasing the pain to the outer reaches of his nerves.

"Okay, Mike—you tell a fascinating story. But why am *I* here?"

"You are Caladian."

Zach smiled, truly amused, and with regret he handed Michael the sword. "Sorry, but you have me mixed up with someone else. I'm Irish, and Italian with some Greek thrown in."

Michael's dark brows furrowed. When he spoke his voice boomed like thunder. *"You are Caladian."* Just as quickly the storm cleared, and his eyes changed back to clear blue. A sly smile hovered over his lips. He thrust the sword back into Zach's hand. "You will take Danica."

Zach narrowed his eyes. What the hell—realization dawned. He backed up a step. "No way, man. No way am I doing daddy duty."

"While there are several other Caladians on earth, none of them have the . . . history with the Starkeeper you have. Either you step up or I will send for your brother. Or if you force my hand, another Caladian. There are others who would be more than happy to have your Danica."

Rage infiltrated every fiber of Zach's being. The pain swelled but his anger quashed it down. He shut his eyes as the image of another man, hot and panting and thrusting into Danica, filled him. Gritting his teeth, he said, "My brother is in jail, for God's sake. He can't father a child!"

"It is my understanding there are such things as conjugal visits."

Zach swiped his hand across his mouth, his frustration taking hold. "Not when you're in for murder."

"I have many avenues at my disposal."

"So you can get my brother out of prison to fuck my ex-fiancée so they can have a Starkeeper child? Or if that doesn't work out, some other guy? *Bullshit!*" Zach shook his head as the words left his mouth. Was he really having this conversation? Or was this some weird-ass dream? Holy hell, the one time he did LSD in high school, and it was coming back to haunt him. He stood and began pacing.

"Zach, time is running out. The paramedics just gave you a tracheotomy and they are getting ready to paddle you."

"I can't do this!" In frustration he hurled the sword across the room. It sang in the air, hitting home in the wall behind Michael's desk.

"You can," Michael calmly said.

"How?"

"Possess the Trinity *and* the Starkeeper."

"The hell I will." Zach moved toward the door. He stopped and looked at Michael, who stood as calm and collected as a marble statue. "I've fucked up my life and everyone else's, and I'll be damned if I'm going to go fuck up again."

Michael's voice boomed against the walls and reverberated in Zach's brain. *"Sephora is building an army of Immortals. They will wipe out humanity for the Trinity!"*

Zach blanched at the power of his words. He swallowed, the pain in his throat nearly unbearable. "What happens if I choose not to go back?"

"You walk through that door."

*Fuck.*

"What if I go back and fail?"

"Then you live life on earth knowing you are responsible for the release of hell on earth."

"Great. What happens if I succeed, but screw up after that?"

"Succeed and stay clean, you go north when your human life is up. Screw up?" Michael inclined his toward the burning door. "You'll go to hell."

"I've been living in hell."

"*Silence!*" Michael roared. "You have been a bad man. A vigilante cop, a liar, and a cheat. Go to hell or do what you were born to do."

The flames curled around his ankles, the intense searing a welcome replacement for the crushing pain in his heart. He raised his hands, welcoming it.

Dani's sweet face appeared in front of him. Her smile sincere, loving. He reached out to touch her, to tell her goodbye forever.

"Choose now, Zach. There is no more time."

# CHAPTER TWO

DANICA STOOD IN THE CORNER of the room, staring at the motionless body in the hospital bed. The man she'd loved and trusted, the man who knew every intimate secret clear down to her soul, the man who had sold her out so he could keep his job.

Zach Garett.

Emotions swirled so violently inside her body she felt as if a superhuman force were pushing from the inside out. And that if one more ounce of pressure was exerted she would explode into a million pieces.

Her skin tightened, her lungs constricted. Her hands balled into fists. Her jaw clenched hard against her teeth. And her heart? Her heart felt the full weight of Zach's betrayal again as if it were the first time.

In IA she had not only gone to the wall for him, but dug up a witness who could prove the murder charges against Zach were trumped up. What she didn't know was she'd been set up. By Zach himself. The case *and* her, tossed. She caught a sob. Not only had he set her up to get himself off, in the end she realized he *had* committed murder, and by her actions alone, he was allowed to walk.

It was the final nail in the coffin of what had become a hollow life.

When Mark called three days ago to tell her about the accident she fell to her knees and sobbed. Her emotions startled her. For three days she'd convinced herself she didn't care if Zach Garett lived or died. And in her heart of hearts, she believed his death would finally give her peace. With it she would no longer feel the hate, the contempt, the utter disdain for the man in front of her. The one person on earth who could—no, who *had* so completely destroyed her life.

Hot tears welled in her eyes. She fought them back, unable to comprehend why she had such an emotional reaction at this moment for the man she despised. After three years her life was finally back in order. She'd been promoted to head of security at the Hope. While she did socialize on a superficial level, she had no interest in dating. She was in all aspects of her life comfortably numb. And content to keep it that way.

Then Zach had to go and get himself nearly killed!

Damn him for tearing her in half a second time! Damn him for everything he was! Damn him and all his lies and smiles and—she sobbed—damn him for making her love him and hate him as passionately.

She didn't want to feel any more. Especially for Zach.

She stepped closer. His handsome face was swollen and bruised. Small cuts dotted his forehead. His right hand was wrapped in a soft cast. Several different bags hung from a pole and dripped into the IV stuck into the back of his right hand.

Jammed into his throat was a life-giving trach tube. All she had to do was reach over and slowly pull it out. Take his life. As he had hers. Watch him slowly suffocate. As she had.

Could she?

Three years of pushing down her anger, her frustration, her heartbreak, reared. Yeah, she could do it. She welcomed the opportunity to stand by and watch him die a slow agonizing death just as he had stood by three years ago and watched her die. Watched the career she'd worked so hard for yanked out from underneath her in one simple, selfish tug. He could have stopped what he'd set in motion, but he stood silent. The final blow was the day he turned his back on her and walked away. No heartfelt goodbye, no reason for his actions. He'd just simply cut her out and moved on.

*Bastard!*

She laughed, the sound brittle. And to think she was engaged to him at the time. Danica took another step closer and glanced at the monitor that began to beep faster.

So, he knew she was there.

Good. Perfect payback. Attached to tubes and machines, he was completely at her mercy. She'd be happy to give back. An eye for an eye. He sold out their love and the life they built together. She reached out to his throat. He'd suffer as she continued to do.

He sensed her presence long before he heard her short caustic laugh. Zach struggled to open his eyes. It felt like bags of sand weighed them down. The ache in his throat burned. His right arm throbbed. He tried to swallow but the agony of the pain was too much to bear. He groaned. His hands fisted. Pain shot up his arm. His chest heaved as he tried to gulp in air but the pressure in and around his throat was excruciating. His pain so thorough he ached to his marrow.

Her soft rose scent wafted to his nostrils, the antiseptic odors of the hospital room fading. He moaned. Despite the pain it caused, his hand opened toward her, where he knew she stood.

Had he died? Was Danica here with him? His angel of mercy?

His heart quickened. It didn't matter if he was dead, so long as she was by his side. And she was. Here. Now. She must still care.

Zach forced his eyes open, the grainy scrape of his lids over his eyes agonizing. He pushed harder, wanting to see his sweet Dani. He could see her as she was in his dreams. Soft and golden. Her thick chestnut-colored hair haloed in the sunlight. Her big blue eyes smiling at him with love.

Walking away that day had been the hardest thing he had ever done in his life. And it was also his biggest regret. Yet, he'd had no choice.

His eyelids slowly opened, his eyes mere slits in his swollen face. The Danica who stood beside him was not haloed. Her once bright hair was darker, pulled back into a snug bun. He hated her hair like that. He loved it long and thick between his fingers. Dark circles framed once brilliant eyes. Her golden skin looked sallow, taut. The dark sweep of her eyebrows drew heavily over her eyes. Her lips pulled back from her teeth, the gesture adversarial. Her hand hovered near his shoulder. Slowly she lowered it.

"I had to see for myself you were alive. How unfortunate for me, you are."

Zach closed his eyes and swallowed, the pain jarring his senses. He wanted to speak, to tell her he was sorry. To ask for a second chance. He opened his eyes and stiffened. The hard edges of her face, the rigid set of her jaw, and the flash of her eyes told him she meant each word she said. He opened his lips, and hoarsely whispered, "Dani—" He grabbed her hand, flinching in anticipation of the pain it would cause. Instead, warmth radiated from her skin to his.

She gasped and pulled her hand away, stepping back. "I hope you burn in hell."

She turned and walked away from him. He reached out, and called to her, the effort severe. He started to cough, his chest tightened. His throat flamed in pain. She didn't hesitate. When the door closed behind her Zach pushed his head back into the pillow and winced. Gritting his teeth he carefully swallowed, this time welcoming the pain. It didn't compare to the devastation in his heart.

The door opened and he flinched. She'd come back! Instead, from beneath swollen eyelids he watched a man dressed in green scrubs walk in. Intuitively Zach knew he was not a nurse. He squinted and tensed.

"How are you feeling, Zach?" the man asked, the voice rough. Familiar. He'd seen him recently. Was he a collar? A snitch? Was he here to finish Zach off for putting his ass in jail? Zach didn't care. He welcomed death. He closed his eyes. Heat infiltrated his body, like flames licking at his skin. Sudden realization dawned. Zach's eyes flashed open.

"I'm Raiden," the man said. "We met at Mike's?"

He shook his head. Denial hot on his lips. *No.*

Images crashed in his brain. Hot, warm, cold, more heat. A man in black. A white room. A video of the crash.

It was a dream!

He'd dreamt going to hell then to where? Not heaven, he'd gone to—

"Michael sent me to keep an eye on you. We need to move fast, there isn't much time, and you're one broke fuck."

Zach only nodded in stunned silence. Maybe this was the continuation of the dream. Maybe he hadn't woken yet. That would sure as hell explain Dani's presence.

He closed his eyes and relaxed back into the pillows. *Go back to sleep, man, and when you wake up you'll see the light of the real world.*

"It doesn't work, man," Raiden said. "The longer you hide in denial the more miserable you'll be."

Zach opened his eyes, the pain of the movement secondary to his dread. "It wasn't a dream," Raiden told him. He moved closer to Zach's side. He reached out a hand to Zach's face. Zach flinched. Raiden laughed. "Stop being a girl." Then for a man so big and menacing, he gently pressed one hand to Zach's throat and the other to his right hand.

A soft tingle began at the points of contact. It went from cold to warm to hot. It intensified, then eased into soothing warmth that infiltrated his skin. His bruised and battered body lightened, the throb of pain lessening.

Raiden removed his hand and stood back, a half smile twisting his lips.

"Say something," he said.

"Something," Zach said, shocked he could speak and more shocked there was little pain involved. "How the hell?"

"Company secret. Get some rest. The docs will be amazed at yet another miracle. Get them to sew up that hole in your throat and get out of here ASAP."

Before Zach could respond Raiden started for the door. He turned abruptly and walked back to Zach's bedside. "You forgot something, man." He reached behind his back and withdrew the golden sword Michael had given him. The same sword Zach had thrown across the room.

"You're going to need it." He set the hilt of the blade in Zach's repaired right hand. Zach hesitated to accept it. His gaze swept the sleek lines of the weapon, admiring the damage it could do in the right hands. Michael's words reverberated in his brain. "Only in the hand of a Caladian warrior can this blade destroy an Immortal." His fingers wrapped around the handle, he looked up to Raiden, wanting reassurance, but he had disappeared.

Zach lay quiet for a long moment. Images and emotions swirled in his head. His brain was telling him it must all still be a dream. He was a practical man. A man of action. He'd never been a religious person, hell, with the exception of funerals he'd never set foot in a church. So, how had this happened? Was he being played for a fool? Had someone drugged him, and this was the result?

He looked down at the sword. His heart pounded. The sword warmed in his hand. He tried to let go of it, but it cleaved to his fingers, heating up, as if in protest of his thoughts. It felt real. His hand tightened around the warm metal. And with clarity he knew it was all real.

The sword cooled, and his fingers opened around it; releasing it, he slid it beneath the sheets and sat up. He needed to get the hell out of the hospital.

Tentatively he swallowed, anticipating the pain, and was surprised there was only a faint dull drag along his throat.

Zach looked down at the soft cast around his arm and IV in his hand. He pulled the useless cast off then yanked the tape and needle out of his vein. The tube flopped to the floor. Fluid puddled. Before he disconnected himself from the machines and had every doctor and nurse on duty rushing into his room, he rifled through the drawers next to his bed looking for his clothes. Empty. *Shit!*

Realization hit him. He wouldn't have any clothes. Fire would have cut them off.

He stood motionless for a moment, and thought. The last thing he remembered was being in the car with Santos and trying like hell to get his seat belt fastened. They'd hit another car and then the lights went out. The bastard had tried to kill him! Why? Did Santos know Zach was going to see to it he not only lost his badge but did jail time?

Zach sat back on the edge of the bed. He moved farther back, then sank into the pillows. It occurred to him he was in no rush to get back to the job. For the first time since he'd decided at the age of ten to become a cop it didn't hold any attraction.

It had tarnished. But so had he. He was not the

supercop he'd dreamed of becoming. The one who was bigger than life, who delivered damsels in distress from evil villains. He wasn't a stand-up cop putting the bad guy behind bars the old-fashioned way—by following the justice system. No, he had more than strayed across the line. He'd sold out when the system didn't do its job. He'd had no regrets at the time, and if he were honest with himself he had no regrets now, except one. And from what he'd experienced, it would take hell on earth to make it right.

He pulled down the hospital gown and ripped the heart monitors off his chest and flung them away from him. He touched the tube attached to his throat. It was the only thing keeping him from walking out the door.

Zach pressed the call button. He needn't have; the machine tracking his vitals started to furiously beep. The door to his room was flung open. A rather attractive blonde, who back in the day would have spent more than one night in his bed, rushed in. Panic distorted her features.

Zach pointed to his throat and hoarsely said, "Get this out and sew me up."

"Mr. Garett, you need to get back in bed, you've had severe trauma to your entire body. Please!"

Zach put his hand to the tube and wrapped his fingers around it. He started to pull. "Stop! Please," the nurse shrieked. "I'll get the doctor." She scurried out of the room, giving him a quick look over her shoulder to make sure he had released the tube.

Zach nodded, grabbed the stand the damn thing was attached to, and started to walk himself but was pulled up short by a tug on his dick.

*Fuck!* A catheter. Just as he was about to yank the

damn thing out a tall thin man in his early fifties hurried in. "Mr. Garett, you are in no condition to have the trach tube removed. Your larynx is too swollen for air to pass through."

"If I can talk, enough air is getting through."

The doc's jaw fell open. "How?"

Zach shook his head and sat back down on the edge of the bed. "I don't know how or what or why, all I know is if you don't take this thing out of my throat, and this hose out of my dick right now, we'll have a bigger problem." While the words came slowly and his voice was husky, his words were clear.

"Lie back in the bed and let me examine you."

Zach obeyed.

After some poking and prodding Dr. Samuel stood back and shook his head. "Fucking amazing."

"Fucking get the tube out."

"There is more involved than sewing up the hole."

"Whatever it takes."

"I'll have to schedule surgery—"

"Do it here. Get what you need, or I'll walk like this."

"But you're signing your life away. I won't be responsible for any relapse. Your throat can swell up in less than thirty seconds and you'd be up shit creek. It'll be the end."

"So noted, now get these tubes out."

Less than thirty minutes later the tubes were removed and the hole in Zach's neck and trach sewn shut. "Take it very easy, Mr. Garett. I want to see you in my office tomorrow, the nurse will give you the info." He went on to give Zach a list of dos and don'ts.

As he listened to the doctor's droning voice it occurred to Zach for the second time he didn't have any clothes. "Where are my clothes and belongings?"

"I—" The good doc looked at the nurse.

She hurried to answer. "You went to the ER then to ICU before you came down here. I'm not sure what happened to them. I'll go look."

Zach nodded.

Zach just wanted out, and would have put on a dress if that's what it took. After the doc left with stern warnings, Zach jumped into the shower in his room, brushed his teeth, and just as he wrapped a towel around his waist the nurse came in with a plastic bag.

"All I could come up with was scrubs and a pair of size thirteen plastic clogs."

Zach nodded. The nurse's gaze ravaged his body and he felt a heat begin at his groin. But it wasn't for the buxom blonde standing in front of him with hungry eyes drinking in his body. No, it was for the haggard-eyed woman who was devastated he wasn't listed in the weekly obit.

Zach smiled, the gesture tugging at his lips. Another time and another place and he would have nailed Nurse Betty right then and there. Now? He had no interest.

"I get off in about twenty minutes, I'll be happy to drive you home," the nurse offered.

Zach nodded. "Thanks." He took the bag from her, dropped the towel, and walked naked into the bathroom and shut the door behind him. He heard her sharp intake of breath, and his dick flexed in response. Maybe he wasn't as dead as he thought he was after all.

Less than an hour later he was standing in front of his modest single-story house. It nestled snugly in the Oakland hills with a stellar view of the bay and San Francisco, which was why he'd paid a small fortune for it. That, and Danica had had her heart set on it. It was supposed to be the house where they lived happily ever after and raised their children.

He walked around to the side gate, pushed it open and made his way to the alarm keypad hidden beneath a faux dryer vent. He pushed in the code to open the garage door. The eerie creaking of the heavy wooden door as it rose grated on his nerves. Despite Raiden's healing, he was still one fucking bruise. He wanted to soak in the hot tub, take a few Vicodin, chase them with a couple of beers, and sleep for a week.

The sword he'd taped to his back warmed. Zach cursed at it. Reaching behind him, he pulled it out. Staring at it in his hand, he scowled.

Memories of Michael and his crazy mission erased any thoughts of rest and relaxation. It was just as well; he'd never been one who could just take it easy at will—another character flaw Danica routinely pointed out. He knew how to relax, he just liked to work more.

When he entered his house, stark walls greeted him. After he and Danica broke up he removed every remnant of her from the house—he wanted no reminder of her. Yet every time he entered his bleak house it was a constant reminder of what he'd had to give up.

He tossed the key and the sword onto one of the few pieces of furniture he had, an oak piece that had belonged to his grandmother. Zach kicked off the offensive clogs and padded his way down the hallway to his room. Despite his beat-to-hell body he moved quickly.

He dressed in comfortable jeans, a black T-shirt, and worn cowboy boots. A few Motrin later he realized his car was most likely still at the PD. He shrugged. It was a perfect day for a bike ride. Five minutes later he roared down the street on his Harley. It didn't get much better than the roar of a V-twin between his thighs, the power of the engine, the speed, the rush, the thrill of a precision piece of machinery.

He smiled. He could think of one thing that beat the thrill of a Harley ride, an altogether different kind of ride. He opened the throttle, his blood warming to the chase.

Twenty minutes later he rolled up in front of the Hope Chandler Museum of Ancient History. He'd only visited here once before.

Three years ago, to return his fiancées few belongings she had left at his house. She'd nearly torn him in half a second time. If was the only time in his life he hadn't returned a blow.

He'd stood unmoving as she lashed out at him with her fists and her words. He stood silent while her heart tore into a million little pieces. Pieces he alone could put back together by telling the truth. But he didn't. He couldn't. There was too much at stake. He wanted to explain that to her. To let her know she was collateral damage in a very deadly game, and that maybe she should be grateful she got out, or as she so bitterly corrected him, was forced out. Fired.

Zach breathed in a deep breath and slowly exhaled. He hung his helmet from one of the handlebars, then strode into the dark building. Quiet greeted him. The exhibition part of the building was closed for renovations. He walked farther into the cavernous hallway. He heard her voice long before he saw her. Farther down the hall, next room to the right. His booted footsteps landed imperceptibly on the black marble floor.

Her voice became louder, more defined. It was a strong voice, a voice that carried authority. It was also all female. He remembered the low throaty timbre of it when she begged him for more. She was insatiable in bed. He missed that. He missed a lot of things.

Zach stopped at the edge of the room. He'd heard she worked her way up from a night-grunt security guard to head of security for the building. She was dressed in a tailored dark pantsuit and low sensible heels, just as she was earlier today when she came to his hospital room. Her face, while still too piqued for his liking, was now fairly animated. She'd been a beauty, now she was but a mere shell of it. Her radiance had dulled. A dark hollowness filled her eyes. And he was responsible for it.

Zach sucked in a deep breath and slowly exhaled. Regret filled his soul.

Danica's skin warmed. Her heart rate cranked up several notches. She dismissed the feeling, trying to focus on her conversation with the man who had stood stalwartly by her these last three years. Asking nothing, offering only his shoulder.

She held her breath, and tensed, waiting for the unnerving feelings to pass. Seconds pounded by. Gone. Letting out a long breath when the world did not come crashing down around her, she relaxed.

The sensation returned. It built, too persistent to ignore.

*Zach.*

She felt him long before she saw him. She always could. It was an odd sixth sense she had when it came to Zach Garett. She knew the minute he entered the building.

Impossible!

Zach was in the hospital, weak as a puppy, where he'd been fighting for his life for three days. There was no way he could be here.

There! She felt it again. His presence. Stronger now.

Her heart rate fluttered and climbed. Her mouth became dry and her hands trembled. To hide that annoying fact she slid them into her pants pockets and continued her conversation with Mark Santos.

Zach's pull was too strong. Danica looked up and locked shocked eyes with the only man she'd ever loved. Her body surged and she leashed the impulse to rush to him. Then it locked. Frozen. Immobile. Instead she could only stare speechless at him. His haunted look shook her to her core. Something was very wrong. She felt Mark stiffen beside her.

Zach's body increased in size. A primal warning.

His penetrating stare shifted from Mark back to her. His lips twitched and she immediately knew his signature half smile would follow. She scowled, daring him. Mark turned when he realized her attention was no longer on him. Zach's eyes flashed in surprise before narrowing ominously. He stepped forward and into the large room being renovated for the Caladian exhibit.

"Well, well, well, Marcus, you certainly don't waste any time, do you?" Zach said, his voice low and husky. Danica gasped. Just two hours ago he could barely move. He'd had a trach tube in his throat and couldn't speak! With the exception of the small flesh-colored Band-Aid below his Adam's apple he looked the picture of health. Better actually. The dark stubble on his chin added a mercenary look to his hawk-sharp features. His deep tawny eyes glowed suspiciously, like a bird of prey fixated on its next meal. Her body warmed despite her anger at the man.

"What do you want, Zach?" she asked, trying to head off what looked like an impending dogfight. While she wouldn't mind seeing Zach get his ass whipped by Mark, she didn't want any disruption in the museum.

"Holy shit!" Mark said in good humor and surprise. He hurried past Danica toward his partner. "I can't believe you're standing here, man. I heard you'd be down for weeks. How the hell are you?" He extended his hand in friendship.

Zach's nostrils twitched and his eyes widened as if he were suddenly startled. The distinct odor of sulfur swirled around his partner. Mark, an Immortal?

Adrenaline rushed through Zach's body and before he gave thought to his action instinct took over. He leapt, clearing the ten-foot span that separated him and his deadly rival.

Zach's body crashed into Mark's, the velocity of it sending them both crashing into the wall a good eight feet behind Mark. Plaster cracked and fell in chunks to the floor.

Danica's screams sounded far off. Mark shoved him off, his strength surprising Zach. But then he understood. As a solider for hell he would possess strength no mortal man could claim. Zach grinned. Well, he might be mortal but he had righteousness on his side. He dove back into Mark, and would have pulled the sword and slit his throat right then and there, but he knew Danica would wig out, and no explanation on earth would calm her down. He shoved his arm under Mark's chin and dug his elbow in the bastard's throat. "I want you out of here now," he softly said. Surprisingly Mark nodded and in a gesture of surrender raised his arms. Zach didn't trust the bastard, but he didn't underestimate Mark either. The man was smart, and the last thing he would want to do at this point was tip Danica off. That was okay, Zach was going to give her an earful himself.

Danica grabbed Zach by the shoulders, shouting, "What the hell are you doing? Get out of here!"

Slowly Zach stood. He stepped back, away from Mark. Danica helped Mark to his feet. "Oh, my God! Are you all right?"

Mark swiped at his bloody lip after giving Zach a hard glare. Then being the actor he was, Mark slipped an arm around Danica's shoulder and said, "I'm fine."

Danica turned to glare at Zach. "Please leave," she softly said.

Without looking at her, his eyes trained on Mark's smug face, Zach said, "I will, but I'd appreciate it if you'd indulge me for a few minutes before I go."

Their gazes clashed. "I don't owe you one minute of my time."

"Maybe you should listen to the lady, buddy," Mark said, stepping in front of Danica.

Zach smiled and assumed a fighting stance. "Bring it on, brother."

Confusion riddled her features as Danica looked back and forth from one man to the other. "What the hell is going on here?" Danica demanded.

Mark laughed, his eyes sparkling, a dark undercurrent lurking just beneath. "You want to tell her, Zachary, or should I?"

Zach growled low. He turned his attention back to Danica but kept a sharp eye on his nemesis. "Danica, I need two minutes." He'd be damned if he was going to let Santos give his demonic version of what was going on, and besides, he wasn't sure Danica could handle the entire truth.

Danica left Mark and walked over to Zach. She pushed him back toward the entryway. "I'll give you two minutes in my office," she said, then turned and led the way down a long hall then another before they entered her small office tucked innocuously in the farthest corner of the building. Once in the room she slammed the door shut behind Zach then whirled around to face him. "What the hell do you want?"

Zach ground his teeth. His fists opened and closed, strength surged through his muscles. He could feel the pulse of it. His senses opened, acutely aware of everything around him.

He could smell Danica's essence. It mingled with her fear of him, and lurking just beneath it, passion.

"When did you and Mark become so close?"

"Nothing about me is any of your damned business."

Zach moved closer. Hostility raged. Not at her, but Mark. The minute he stepped within feet of the man he smelled it. *Sulfur.* A fucking Immortal! "Tell me, damn it!"

Danica blanched at his anger, and backed away, fear flashed in her wide eyes. "He's helping with security for the event we have planned. And whether you like it or not, he's my friend."

It cut deeply that she was afraid of him at that moment, but that was the least of his worries right now. Mark needed to go. Discreetly. That fact didn't faze him. Since the accident, he felt deeper, was stronger, and even if he hadn't got a whiff of the sulfur stink of Mark, signaling which side of the earth he was on, his gut told him Mark was pure evil. He knew that as surely as he knew the sword lying against the small of his back would be Mark's ride back to hell. "Get rid of him."

"Is that what you came here to tell me? Are you so jealous I've moved on?"

"You haven't moved on. I can see it in everything you do. It's in your eyes." He moved closer, his nostrils flaring. "I can smell it on you, Danica."

She slapped him. "Fuck you, Zach Garett."

He grabbed her hand. She tried to pull away but his strength surged. He opened her fist with one hand and pressed her palm to his cheek. For a moment he closed his eyes and inhaled the sweet scent of her. Her hand trembled. He opened his eyes to see hers moist with tears. One fell to her cheek.

He wiped it away with his thumb. "I never told you I was sorry."

Her features darkened, and she yanked her hand away. He could have kept her captive, but he didn't.

"You are the sorriest excuse for a man and a cop I've had the misfortune to meet. What do you want?"

Zach struggled with his emotions. Danica Keller was the only person on the earth who could make him forget words. She was in so many ways his Achilles' heel. He cursed Michael for using that fact against him.

*Michael.*

And what the hell was he supposed to tell her? The truth? He cringed. Damn it!

# CHAPTER THREE

"Spit it out, Zach. I have a shipment I need to oversee."

"The one from Caladia?"

Startled, she looked up at him. "How do you know about Caladia?"

"It's why I'm here."

Danica's heart constricted for one millisecond. She'd hoped for some unknown reason that maybe he was there for her. It was futile—Zach didn't have it in him to love. And her? After all this time seeing him again? He still screwed with her heart.

Her resolve galvanized. "Of course it is." Sarcasm dripped off her words. She whirled around to the door and jerked it open. "Get out, Zach, and don't come back."

He stepped past her and put his hand over hers on the knob. He squeezed and pushed forward, closing the door. His large body pressed against her back, his heat encompassing her like a warm blanket. She closed her eyes briefly, gritting her teeth and forcing the heat in her body to cool.

She stood flush against the closed door. His left hand touched her elbow, his fingertips brushing the fabric of her suit. He barely applied pressure, yet it felt as if they were skin on skin. Dormant passion flared in her brain like a red-hot sun whose rays sliced into her nerves, lighting her up.

Zach Garrett was a hard man, but his passion ran deep. How could she resist this dark moody man? The way his lips flickered when she walked into the room or the way he made her laugh with his dry humor? How could she resist a man who took foster kids by the dozens to As games?

She turned, wresting her hand from under his grip, her breath high in her throat. How could she not despise the man who lied to keep his job knowing she would lose hers? How could she allow a stone-cold murderer into her heart? Anger, frustration, and shame mixed into a toxic cocktail.

Danica slapped him with all the fury of a woman scorned. She watched the blanching of her fingerprints on his dark cheek rise. He didn't flinch. Instead he moved closer, his long hard body now pressed fully against hers. She felt the hot heat of his passion against her belly. A low growl rumbled in his throat. His hands dove into her hair, pulling the long tresses free from the bun at the nape of her neck. His lips slanted across hers. The contact sent her reeling backward against the door. The sound of her head thumping and her gasp of surprise did nothing to quell Zach's passionate attack. He pressed his body harder against hers, his groin digging into her.

She gasped for air and his tongue slid into her mouth, thick and hot. She arched in an attempt to push him away but it only served to fuel his fire. And hers. Passion flared between them, a real live wire. Her nipples tingled. Heat swept to the juncture between her thighs. Her fists relaxed. She pushed harder against him now, her lips opening for more, wanting, needing, demanding.

Zach gasped for breath, the rawness in his throat throbbing in tempo to the throb in his dick. God, she tasted sweet. His body ached for more, his heart for all. But he had nothing to give in return. He was a cold-blooded killer, and every time she looked at him he could see the horror of his deeds reflected in her eyes.

He shoved her away from him and stepped back to a safe distance.

Danica's full swollen lips, long hair in sexy disarray around her shoulders, and that wild hot look in her eyes he used to live for nearly did him in. He would gladly lie down and die for that look, but he couldn't. Not now, maybe never. They had the fucking world to save. He knew he'd lost his mind.

"I'm sorry, Danica, I—"

Her hysterical laughter stopped him. She pushed off the door then in a short jerky movement, worked her hair back into a respectable bun. Shaking her head, her laughter quieting, she moved past him to her desk where she sat down. "Fuck you, Zach Garett, and the horse you came in on. Get out of here before I shoot your ass."

"Hear me out first."

Sitting back in her chair, she put her feet up on her desk and clasped her hands behind her head. "What?"

"The shipment from Caladia, it has artifacts in it."

"No shit, Sherlock. In case you haven't noticed you're in a museum."

"There is a scabbard, with a jeweled star imbedded in it."

"So what if there is?"

"You can't give it to Zao."

"I have no intention of giving it to Zao." She swept her feet off the desk, sat up and frowned. "How do you know about Zao?"

Zach rubbed his temples. A sudden migraine erupted behind his eyes. "I can't explain." If he did she *would* shoot him. "I—just know." He stopped rubbing and looked at her through narrowed eyes. "What are your plans for it?"

Danica folded her hands on the desk and steepled her fingers. For a long moment she contemplated him. "The museum is going to loan it to Mr. Zao in exchange for a ten-million-dollar bequest."

"You can't, Danica. That scabbard *cannot* go to Zao from you."

"Sorry to disappoint, big guy, but that was part of the deal. I hand it over to him in a big ol' ceremony with the press and God to witness."

"Why you?"

Her brows furrowed.

Zach explained. "Why does it have to be you, the security head, to hand it over? Why not the curator?"

"I was told that was how Mr. Zao wanted it handled."

"What would you do if I told you Zao was going to use the scabbard for illegal purposes?"

Danica laughed. "What, is he going to go on a killing spree in Fremont with it?"

"Maybe."

Danica eyed him cryptically and sat forward. "Zach, I think they let you out of the hospital too soon."

He rubbed his throbbing temple and for a minute thought she might be right. He felt cold and clammy suddenly and the room teetered. Shaking the cobwebs from his head, he turned his gaze back to Danica, who sat calmly regarding him. The old Danica would have rushed to his side. This hard Danica, the one he'd created, sat stoic as an oak.

"Something happened to me, Dani. I can't explain it, but I have this thing inside me, warning bells. You're in danger, this museum is in danger, and it's tied somehow to a three-thousand-year-old scabbard."

"Four thousand years old. The only thing missing is the Sword of Caladia." In answer, the sword at his back warmed. Son of a bitch! Zach reached behind him and slowly withdrew the sword.

Danica stood, her eyes wide in wonder. Maybe seeing the sword would convince her. He held it in front of him. "I think this may be what goes into the scabbard."

Her eyes grew larger. She reached out to touch it. Heat flared in his hand. Zach pulled it away. Would it hurt her?

"Where did you get that?"

How did one tell a perfectly sane person you died, were on your way to burn in hell, then some guy named Michael plucked you from your fall, gave you a sword and told you to go save the world?

"The Immortals want the Star of Moria."

"The who want the what?" Danica laughed. "C'mon, Zach. You can do better than this fairy tale."

Zach's skin shivered. "The Immortals. We have to stop them. They want the star, it's the key to—a prison." He stopped short. His temple seared in pain.

Danica moved closer to Zach, still skeptical and more than a little wary. She put her hand to his brow; it was cool and damp. "What kind of medication are you on?"

"None."

"I don't believe you. From what I heard you were dead on the scene. Your larynx was crushed. They gave you a trach tube. Your body took a beating rolling around in the crash. And you're out three days later? No drugs? You couldn't speak this morning."

She shook her head. None of it added up. "Explain how you're here."

Zach's free hand shook as he reached out to touch her. She withdrew but kept a steadying hand on his shoulder to guide him to the chair in front of her desk. "Sit down, Zach."

He did and she unscrewed the cap off the bottle of water on her desk and handed it to him. He shook his head but she pressed it into his hand. He took a long drink. She watched as his Adam's apple jumped up and down with each swallow, the Band-Aid on his neck moving with it. No way could he not be on painkillers. The trauma to his head must have shaken a few brain cells loose. He was speaking like a crazy person. He obviously was not emotionally stable.

She glanced down at the sword in his hand. But how did she explain that?

He drained the bottle and set it down on her desk. "What the hell is going on, Zach, and don't feed me bullshit lines about Immortals."

As the words left her mouth he felt the pressure of *them* all around him. They were near. He could feel it. Waiting, wanting the sword, the scabbard, the star, and Danica.

A vision of Danica hanging naked and ripe with child in iron manacles, the fires of hell flashing around her sweaty, writhing body, pierced his consciousness. She cried out to him, her voice raw with emotion, begging him to save her and their child.

An overwhelming sense of duty filled him. Sensation filled his body, supercharging his cells, and he suddenly knew what he had to do.

His eyes rose to hers, the blue nearly black in the bright light of her office. "Your mother had the same port-wine birthmark on her inner thigh as you do."

Danica visibly whitened. "How do you know that?"

He just—knew. "And her mother and her mother before her."

As intimate as she had been with Zach, she had never revealed the fact she and her mother shared the same birthmark in such a private part of their anatomy. She'd always felt that was her mother's information to share.

"How do you know that?"

Zach shook his head again. "I just do." He stood, his body swaying. Danica reached out this time and steadied him.

"I need to see the scabbard."

Danica rubbed her suddenly pounding temples. She

made the decision to indulge him for several reasons, one being that Zach stood before her a healthy man even though just hours before he could not speak, and another, she was damn curious. Much more so than she should be. And knowing how involvement with Zach tended to go, she would live to regret the decision. "Fine, Zach, but understand the scabbard stays here."

As Danica opened the door to her office a sensation of doom struck Zach so hard his body took the hit, the percussion of it vibrating through him. "Danica!" he called.

She turned. Mark materialized almost as if from thin air and yanked her to his chest. Zach's adrenaline spiked and, with it, his muscles filled with blood, every sense sharpened on high alert. He growled low, regretting he hadn't killed Santos when he'd had the chance. The sword warmed at his back in agreement.

Zach locked his stare on Santos. The prick's eyes had morphed to hard onyx and he grinned at Zach. For the first time in the nearly three years he'd been partnered with him, Zach noticed the sharpness of Santos's incisors. Like a canine's. Fear for Danica filled his cells. He would die to protect her.

Danica yelped in surprise until she realized it was Mark. "You startled me." He continued to hold her, despite her efforts to pull away from him. "Let go of me, Mark." She yanked out of his grasp but he grabbed her back, pulling her farther from her office.

"I didn't want to tell you this, Dani, not this way," Mark said.

She twisted to see him but he kept her facing Zach even as the space grew between them.

"Tell me what? What the hell is going on?" She glanced back at Zach who looked winded, his color lighter. He looked to be in pain. His eyes, though, burned bright.

Mark raised his Sig and pointed it at Zach's heart. Danica had had enough of this pissing contest. "Put the damn gun down, Mark!"

He shook his head. His hand tightened on her arm. His gun hand steady. "I just got a call from Captain Leonard. Your ex is wanted for murdering a CI of mine."

Danica gasped and stopped struggling. Her gaze shot to Zach. He scowled. Her eyes narrowed. It wouldn't be the first time this man had killed.

"I'm taking you in, Garett," Mark said. He pushed Danica aside and waved his gun toward the doorway. "Come out, real slow. Hands up."

Zach straightened to his full height. He raised his hands and put them behind his head. Danica stood rooted to the floor, unable to grasp the depths of this man's dishonor. "You—bastard!" she hissed.

Her words had no impact on Zach; he didn't flinch. He stood rigid, his eyes riveted on Mark. She turned to look at Mark and what she saw chilled her to the bone. His features had paled, his dark eyes hardened to stone. And the subtle odor of . . . something unpleasant swirled around him. What the hell was going on?

She turned back to confront Zach. He moved lightning quick, dropping to his left knee and pulling that golden sword from behind his back where it was sheathed. It whizzed past her cheek. Mark screamed. The blade severed his thumb from his hand, the gun clattered to the marble. The appendage plunked next to it on the floor, leaving a bloody spray in its wake. Zach shot past her before she realized he had moved. He dove for the sword sticking straight into the wall behind them at the same time Mark did.

Zach grabbed the sword. Mark slammed him into the wall, and grabbed Zach's hand holding the sword. In a hard sweep he smashed Zach's hand against the plastered corner of the wall. Zach grunted, his fingers loosened, and the sword skittered across the floor toward Danica. She hurried toward it and picked it up. It felt warm in her hand. Alive.

"Stop!" she shouted.

Zach twisted out of Mark's grasp and elbowed him hard in the nose. Blood spattered in a high arch, staining the white wall and Zach's arms. Zach kicked Mark in the gut, the velocity of Mark's body cracking the plaster when he hit the wall. Zach turned toward Danica. Mark lunged off the wall and went for the gun at her feet. She kicked it away, then hurried after it. He skidded to a stop going the opposite direction.

Danica turned on both men, sword in one hand and pistol in the other. Calmly she took several steps backward, putting more distance between her and the two crazy-ass fiends. Cool as the evening fog, she leveled each weapon. One trained on each man.

"I want you both out of here. This minute. And I don't want to see either one of you ever again."

"Dan—" Mark started.

"*Don't.* I don't want to hear it. Get out!"

"He's under arrest," Mark said, looking at Zach. "If you let him go, I'll arrest you for aiding and abetting."

"You'll need backup for that."

She caught Zach's smile. "Don't try that on me, Garett. Once you leave here you're on your own. I hope this time IA nails your ass and the boys in Quentin finally get to make you their bitch."

"Dani, he's lying."

"Maybe." She shrugged. "But I have no problem with you taking the rap for all the times you didn't get caught."

"Danica, I'll go," Mark said, his voice suddenly weak. "I need to get to the hospital." He reached down and picked his thumb up from the floor.

Danica blanched at Mark's casualness. He'd just had his thumb sliced off and he acted as if he had a splinter. She'd always had a strong stomach but the absurdity of the scene made her belly queasy.

The least she could do was call an ambulance. "I'll call AMR," she offered.

Mark vehemently shook his head. "I'll drive myself." He turned then and sprinted down the hallway.

Zach turned to Dani and began his plea in earnest.

# Chapter Four

"Take me to the shipment."

Danica turned both weapons on him. "No."

Her fighting stance didn't impede him. He stepped closer. "Danica, please, you *must trust me.* We need to move. Now, before Santos comes back with friends."

"I'm not taking the fall for you again. Get out of here, Zach."

Zach stood still for a moment, thoughts crashing in his head. How could he convince this woman of this crazy-ass tale he had no explanation for? He swiped his hand across his face, unsure how to proceed with her.

But there were several facts he was crystal clear on.

First and foremost he needed to keep Danica away from Santos, and he needed to get his hands on the scabbard. What happened afterward he was unclear about, but he knew both he and Danica would be involved. He focused on Danica, who stood silent, angry, wielding two very dangerous weapons in front of him.

Zach looked down the long corridor that led to Dani's office. Miraculously it remained empty. It didn't really matter, he reasoned. The entire staff could show up at that moment and it would not change what he had to do. Get the scabbard. With Danica or without her.

He swooped her up into his arms and threw her over his shoulder. Danica's size and the fact her hands were full didn't stop her from kicking and screaming all the way down the hall.

"Danica, stop acting like a spoiled little girl."

"I'm going to stab you then shoot you!"

"Slide the sword down between my belt and back, and do the same to yourself with the Sig."

In classic Dani fashion she didn't listen. But at least she didn't slice and dice him either. And despite everything that had happened to him in the last seventy-two hours, Zach's strength mushroomed. He tightened his arm around Danica's legs. With his free hand, he grabbed the sword from her flailing hand and sheathed it behind him. Her pummeling fists on his back did nothing to deter him from snatching the nine mil and sliding it alongside the sword.

"Zach, you *will* regret this!"

He slapped her hard on her right ass cheek and squeezed the firm flesh. "Never."

For the moment she shut up.

Guided by instinct, Zach turned down one hall, pushed through a door, and strode down another hall until he stepped out onto the loading dock. He said a silent thank-you to whoever had orchestrated the lack of inquiring eyes or ears along the way. His luck ended, however, when the truck driver shifted the forklift into reverse, stopping several feet away.

Zach smiled at the man, who returned his gesture with raised brows.

Zach released his tight grip on his ex-fiancées bottom and let her slide down his body to the floor. As their hips met, he grinned when her angry eyes flashed at him.

"Danica, you know the curator wants the Caladian crate opened. Now, stop playing around," Zach chided. His reward for the charade? A murderous glare.

Her patience pushed to the limit, she steered him several feet away from the truck driver, who pretended not to be interested in their hijinks.

"I swear to God, Zach, if you don't knock this off, I'm going to start screaming."

"I need you to trust me, Dani!"

"Last time I trusted you I got fired!"

"Look, if I'm wrong about all of this and we're on a wild-goose chase, I'll go to the chief and tell him I lied."

She gasped at his confession and looked harder at him, searching his face for the lie she was sure he told. "Why would you do that?"

"Because it's the right thing to do."

"The right thing to do?" she shrieked. The truck driver coughed; she flashed him a look that said, mind your own damn business. Then she lit into Zach. "I haven't seen you for three years, and now you come waltzing back into my life and expect me to help just because you want me to? After you set me up to get fired?"

Zach lowered his voice and steered her away from the nosy driver. "Things are different now. And while I understand your reluctance to help me, you have to admit, there is some weird-ass stuff going on around here. Give me the benefit of the doubt, Danica. Help me and I swear on my sister's grave I'll do everything in my power to get you your job back."

"I don't want my job back!" she spat. "I don't want anything to do with Oakland PD." She shoved away from him. "Or you."

"Twenty-four hours, Dani. Give me twenty-four hours and I'll give you your life back."

She punched him as hard as she could in the chest. "Why did you do it?"

"Does it matter?"

She choked back a sob. "Yes, damn it, it does!"

"See this through with me, Danica, and when it's over I'll resign. I'll do whatever you want me to do." Zach stood rigid, hard, unyielding. Despite his refusal to give her answers to questions that had haunted her for years, his determination to see his crazy scheme through wore on her. That, and as angry as she was with him, she hadn't felt this alive in more than a thousand days.

"How can I trust a murderer?"

"I told you. I'll swear on my sister's grave. I'll resign and give up the info if you just do what I tell you."

Arms crossed, brows jammed together, Danica angrily tapped her foot on the floor. All this time she'd thought if the PD came crawling to her, begging her to come back, she would kick dirt in their faces. But given the chance, slight as it was . . . and even if the chance was contingent on helping the man who had more to do with her getting canned than not . . . Her heart rate accelerated. In her gut she wanted to be back on the streets of Oakland again—even if it meant working with Zach Garett for the next twenty-four hours.

"Promise me you won't kill anyone."

"I can't."

She shoved past him. He grabbed her arm, pulling her around to face him. "I promise not to kill anyone unless they try killing me first."

For a long moment Danica contemplated him. He looked so serious. More serious than the day he proposed to her. More serious than he had when he sat in a court-room and testified against drug dealers, murderers, and pedophiles. And more serious than on the anniversary of his sister's suicide when they visited her grave site.

She looked up at him and really took him in. His tawny eyes compelled her to rethink. He stared at her, unwavering in his cause. How could he just walk back into her life after three years of no contact and expect her to skip along with his half-baked schemes?

Her brows furrowed. But how did he know about her mother's birthmark? And the Caladian shipment? Then there was that sword . . .

"Danica, if I'm wrong what do you have to lose?"

"My job. Time wasted with you."

He moved closer, so close the warm percussion of his breath touched her cheek. He reached out and touched her shoulder. "Our time was never a waste."

Despite the alarms shrilling at capacity in her brain, and her heart twisting in indecision, she felt herself giving in to his pull.

"I swear to God, Zach, if you screw me again I'll kill you myself."

He smiled, the gesture lighting up his face. Her belly did a slow roll.

"You always were the bravest girl I knew," he said.

"Save it. What do you want from me?"

"The scabbard. Open that crate."

Danica nodded.

Although the packing slip was ambiguous, and didn't list the contents in exact terms, they went through the crate. Half an hour later with the entire container emptied, it was obvious there was no scabbard among the varied artifacts. Danica sat back on her heels. She called to the truck driver who was taking a smoke break and asked, "The manifest says there were two parts to this shipment. Where is the other crate?"

He shrugged and answered, "Fellow at the docks said customs tagged it for inspection."

"Is it customary to give this information to the people you're delivering to, or withhold it until asked?" Zach asked, all guise of pleasantries gone.

The teamster flicked his butt to the ground and crushed it under his boot. "My union says I only have to deliver."

Danica flashed Zach a glare then smiled at the driver. "Please ignore him, Roger, he's temporary."

"Do the shipments come in to Oakland or San Francisco?" Zach asked.

"Oakland."

Zach prodded Roger. "Dock number?"

"Sixty-six."

"We need to go, Danica."

"Right now?"

"Yes, right now."

"I can't just leave."

"Grab whatever credentials you need. I can't explain. I just know we need to get there before anyone else does."

Danica shook her head then pulled her Nextel out and alerted a number.

"Fredrickson."

"Jimmy, I need to leave the premises for a few hours, I need you to put this Caladian shipment in lockdown for Manfred."

"Will do."

"Who's Manfred?" Zach asked.

"The curator."

"Do you trust him?"

"Trust him how?"

"To not give the artifacts away?"

Danica laughed and shook her head. "Garett, I have no idea what happened to you in the crash but you have seriously lost it."

In answer his temple began to throb. He took Danica by the hand and pulled her behind him. "We need to get to the dock and open the other crate."

"First we have to wait for customs to go through it."

"How long does that take?"

"Depends on how backed up they are."

"Let's go see if we can hurry them along."

After a quick stop at her office for her purse, Danica said, "I'll drive. I'm not getting on the back of that bike of yours without a helmet."

"How did you know I rode the hog?"

"I just do."

And that was how it was between them. Even after

three years and a terrible breakup they were still as attuned to the other as if they were attached at the hip.

They exited through the back entrance. Just as Danica unlocked her Jeep the wail of sirens disturbed the quiet of the back parking lot. Danica caught Zach's gaze. "Let me drive," he said.

"No way. Get in."

As she turned east on Stevenson Boulevard heading toward 880, three squad cars and several unmarkeds squealed into the front lot before splitting, no doubt to cover all exits.

"I can't believe I let you talk me into this, Garett."

Despite the direness of their situation, Zach flashed her a disarming smile. "I can't believe I did either."

Well into the rush hour, they hit the diamond lane and blew past the commuters who refused to ride share.

It was easy getting on to the docks. Zach simply flashed his badge. They were met with little resistance at the customs office. When the customs official informed them the crate had been cleared and was in the holding area hope flared.

"If possible, sir," Danica said, "we'd like to check the manifest for the container."

The officer nodded and pulled it up on the computer then printed it out. Zach and Danica moved to a corner of the office and scanned the list. While several vessels, jewelry, pottery, and other miscellaneous items were listed, no scabbard was mentioned. "Officer," Zach said, stepping toward him. "We need to get into that container."

"I'm sorry, Detective Garett, but the holding area is on a time clock. The gates are locked."

"Open them."

The officer shook his head. "No can do. I don't have the lock code."

"Who does?"

"Dock security."

"Are they part of the customs office?"

"No, a private firm. And unless the cargo is in peril or there is some other type of emergency, we contracted for them not to open the area."

"Where can I find the security office?"

The officer started to protest but Danica spoke up. "Look, Officer, we're all on the same side here. There is what could be a crucial piece of evidence in that container. We need to get our hands on it, like yesterday. Please, time is of the essence."

Twenty minutes later Zach and Danica were carefully pulling packaged artifacts from the crate. It was obvious from the way the boxes were so intricately aligned, customs hadn't done a complete check, only a cursory look-see and X-ray. Probably had the dogs take a sniff as well.

Good.

"Zach, we need to make sure every item is replaced exactly as we found it."

"We don't have time for that. We need to get what we came for and get the hell out of here."

"But—"

"No buts, Danica. We need to get out of here while we can."

"But—"

He moved around the gaping crate and grabbed her arms. For once she didn't resist. "Call your curator, call his assistant, call anyone you want. Have them come take care of this mess."

Danica nodded, still unsure exactly why she had agreed to this wild-goose chase with the one person on earth whom she had sworn never to speak to again, much less abet in what was surely an illegal endeavor. She was curious, however, about the scabbard and even more curious about what the discovery would mean.

It wasn't until they got to the last container that Zach and Danica exchanged looks across the mess they'd made. Made of the same rough wood as the other boxes, this one's shape gave them hope. It was about a yard in length, and approximately eight inches high.

Zach pressed his palm to the lid. The sword at Zach's back hummed. Danica's eyes widened. So, she heard it too.

"I don't know what the hell you've gotten yourself into this time, Garett, but, God help me, it had better be good."

Together they lifted the container from the crate to the floor. With a small pry Zach opened the lid. Securely embedded in the container was a smoothly polished cypresswood box. It looked—ancient. Odd symbols were carved into the smooth wood. Instead of nails sealing the lid shut, intricate grooves sealed it.

Zach looked expectantly at Danica then back down at the cypress box. Together they lifted it from the protective box and set it on the floor. Excitement pulsed through her. Like anticipating a gourmet meal, Danica licked her lips. Zach looked up at her from his kneeling position. Wonder lightened his eyes to pure gold. He touched his thumb to a smooth divot on the corner. A small sound like a door quietly opening alerted them.

He slid the lid back, exposing what appeared to be—wool?

Danica's nose twitched. The smell was odd, and not completely unpleasant. "Wool?" she asked.

Zach touched his fingertips to the covering. A fleece. "It's soft."

Danica reached out and touched it, their fingers side by side. Heat emanated from the fabric. Zach lifted the object wrapped tightly in the wool. He could feel the heat intensify and the sword at his back mimicked it. Like two long-lost lovers the sword and scabbard yearned to meet again.

"Unwrap it," Danica softly said, realizing she was in the presence of something magnificent, something bigger than her, bigger than Zach. Bigger than life.

Carefully, Zach unwound the thick fleece. Their eyes widened as an ancient scabbard emerged. The gold was smooth but tarnished, yet the edges were honed to deadly sharpness, and several imperfections marred it. As it revealed itself they both gasped in awe. A simple yet spectacular six-pointed star of precious colored gemstones lay deeply imbedded at the wider opening. As Danica reached out and touched it, the warmth of the object, like something alive, filled her body in a soothing hypnotic fashion. Guided by an invisible hand, she turned the star counterclockwise and it moved, like a key, and cleaved to her hand. She held it up under the harsh light of the room.

"My God, it's beautiful." The stones glowed in blazing appreciation.

"The Star of Moria," Zach murmured. Danica's eyes widened in wonder as the gems glittered with fire in the light.

Deep voices echoed in the holding dock. Danica's heart thumped. She pressed the star protectively to her chest.

"It's Mark," Zach said.

"Impossible! He's at the hospital getting his thumb reattached!"

"It's him." Zach's heightened senses picked up the stink.

Zach held out his hand for the star. Danica shook her head and backed up. "It's safe with me."

"I know it is, but the star belongs with the scabbard." Grudgingly Danica knelt down next to the scabbard and gently replaced the star.

Zach quickly wrapped the scabbard in the wool then stood, tucking the package under his arm. He grabbed Danica's hand and pulled her out of the holding cell and started to run in the opposite direction of the voices. He wondered if Immortals were as aware of him as he was of them.

As they raced down the hallway, Zach tried one locked door after another. Unable to go farther, they were at the end of the long cavernous hall. Trapped.

Danica pulled the Sig from Zach's belt. "That won't work on Santos," Zach calmly informed her.

"Of course it will. If you remember correctly I was ranked sniper grade in the academy."

"It has nothing to do with your aim."

"Zach, you have some more explaining to do."

He handed her the fleece-wrapped package. He watched her eyes widen as she took it into her arms, and cradled it like a newborn. "My God, it . . . feels alive."

"It's your destiny, Dani."

Danica gasped and stared wide-eyed at him. He saw realization dawn, before fear clouded it. He drew the sword from his back and jammed it into the padlocked metal door behind them. The sound of slicing tumblers was music to his ears. He shoved open the door and pushed Danica through.

Zach pulled her along then slowed to keep pace with her. When he asked for the wool package back she shook her head. "Mine."

He smiled. Her possessiveness was a good sign. Did she feel the same urgency he did?

It didn't take long for them to maneuver through the dock buildings. As they hurried into the parking lot, Danica bit back a scream. Mark Santos along with two uniforms stood between them and her ride.

She hugged the scabbard pack to her chest. Zach pushed her behind him, pulled the sword from the small of his back, holding it before him in an attack stance. He didn't know the uniforms by name but he recognized them. He recognized the collective stench of sulfur that among the three of them was overwhelming. He also noticed the hard sheen in their eyes.

So, Santos had friends.

"Put it down, Garett," Santos called.

Danica gasped. "His thumb!"

Santos smiled, the gesture ugly. He lifted his right hand, and gave her a thumbs-up. "What can I say, Dani? I have a quick doctor."

*No way.*

Zach spoke. "I'm only going to warn the three of you once. Step aside and let us pass or—" He held the sword higher, the glow of the golden blade flashing under the parking-lot lights. "Be prepared to die, *permanently.*"

Santos shook his head. "Just give me the scabbard."

Danica gasped again and tightened her grip on the package.

"Come and get it," Zach challenged.

The uniform closest to him raised his service weapon.

Zach was never a man to be afraid of anything or anyone, and facing such unfair odds as he did now, with only a sword to protect them and Dani wielding a useless gun with one hand, he'd never felt so empowered.

"Get him," Santos directed his two men. The minute he opened his mouth, Zach's heightened senses picked up the coming command.

Holding the sword like a hammer, Zach lunged toward the uniforms. He dove then rolled on the asphalt in front of them. As he came up between them he jabbed the closest Immortal in the jugular, spun to his left and backhanded the Immortal who had unholstered his gun. Air hissed from his filleted neck. The warm spray of blood flicked across Zach's cheek. Both Immortals slid motionless to the ground.

Zach turned, the scent of blood sharp in his nose. Santos chased Danica, who shot at him as she ran, the bullets doing no more damage than gnat bites.

Danica stumbled and fell to the ground. With the fleece grasped to her chest she scooted backward as fast as her legs would move. Mark strode toward her and grabbed her by the front of her shirt, raising her off the ground. He turned with her in his right hand, just as Zach charged, his speed a blur. Danica kicked and pulled the scabbard from the fleece and stabbed at Santos with it. The attack had no impact.

Santos plucked the scabbard from Danica as easily as if he were removing a flower from a vase. She screamed and grabbed it back, Santos backhanded her, then twisted her around so her back pressed against his chest. He slid the scabbard around to the front of her throat pressing the razor edge into her skin. With every sense heightened, Zach came to an abrupt halt.

Santos laughed, the sound shrill, full of challenge. "A choice, my friend. The girl or the scabbard."

Danica squirmed and kicked at his knees. Santos shook her like a terrier would a rat, the scabbard never more than an inch from her throat. Zach's blood pounded, adrenaline infusing every cell in his body. "Let her go, Santos."

"Oh, come on now. You don't really think I'm just going to listen to you, do you? I want you to choose. The scabbard or the girl. You can't have both. Not while I'm alive."

Zach squatted down on his haunches. His eyes burned as he focused on the hand holding the scabbard. He gave the appearance he was weighing his choices. When in fact his choice was made the minute his nemesis touched the woman he loved. Zach sprang.

"Santos!" Zach roared. Zach let loose with the sword as Santos pressed the scabbard against Danica's throat.

The blade whizzed past his head, slicing his right ear off. Santos shrieked, dropping Danica and grabbing his bloody head. Zach rushed him, and shoved him to the ground.

While Zach had gained much in strength he hadn't realized how strong Santos was. They rolled on the asphalt fighting for possession of the scabbard. It scraped the asphalt, sparks jumping in the air. Santos's grasp held firm possession. Unable to pry his fingers from the metal, Zach slammed Mark's hand hard against the ground. The force of the blow loosened the star. It popped out and fell to the ground. Mark reacted with superhuman strength. He roared and shoved Zach off his chest and in so doing released the scabbard, but lunged for the star and snatched it up.

In his peripheral Zach saw Danica gather herself up from the ground, run to the sword and pick it up. She ran to her Jeep and started the engine. Zach grabbed Mark by the foot and yanked him hard toward him, then rushed him and rolled over on top of the bastard. As Danica pulled up, Zach pushed off the Immortal and grabbed for the prize.

Air.

Santos sprang up with the aplomb of a gazelle, and without looking over his shoulder bolted. Zach snatched the scabbard from the ground and took off after him. Sirens wailed close. Santos pulled away, heading straight for his unmarked car. He'd be on the radio calling in his location and a description of Danica's Jeep. And there damn sure was no way to explain the two sliced and diced cops.

Danica pulled up next to Zach as he ran. "Get in!"

He realized he had no choice. They needed to disappear.

And they needed a plan. He dove into the Jeep. She hit the gas, the sound of peeling rubber followed by the inevitable acrid smell launching them like a rocket through the parking lot. Several bullets tore through the canvas top. Zach shoved Danica's head down as they zigzagged out of the parking lot and onto the main drag.

In an insane feat, Danica got them back onto 880 headed north.

Her hands shook on the steering wheel. Her chest heaved as she gasped for breath. Realizing she was in a state of shock, Zach reached over to touch her to comfort her. She jerked her hand away. "Don't touch me!"

He looked down at his blood-spattered hand. In as calm a voice as he could manage, he said, "I guess the fact those two thugs were out for my blood doesn't matter."

"They were cops!"

"Dani—"

"Don't Dani me!" Her voice shook in rage and shock. Her body shook, her hands on the steering wheel shook. "You've just made me an accessory to murder! Capital murder!" She choked back a sob and shook her head. "Oh, my God, what have we done?"

"They aren't what they seem."

She continued to shake her head, hysteria edging her words. "What are they, Zach? What are you? And why the hell should I believe a word you say?" Her hands shook so hard the Jeep swerved before she righted it.

Zach put a steady hand on her right arm. "Because you know in your gut this is bigger than both of us. We're a part of it, a piece of the puzzle."

She flung his hand off her arm and abruptly pulled over

to the shoulder of the freeway and slammed on the brakes. She pulled the emergency brake and looked at him. Her skin had blanched to white and her eyes were huge dark orbs in her face. She was terrified. "I'm not going another foot until you explain everything to me."

Zach looked over his shoulder. "Danica, we can't stop. We need to get out of here."

Sirens wailed in the distance. "Go!" he yelled. She blanched at the force of his words. "I need you with me, Danica, but I can't force you."

He opened the Jeep door. "Stay away from Santos. He'll use you to get to me."

Tears blurred her vision. "That's bullshit," she yelled after him. "Everyone knows you hung me out to dry and don't give a shit about anyone but yourself."

Zach slammed the door shut. Danica sat stunned. Her body quaked, her brain raced. Confusion confounded her. Desperately she wrestled for a coherent logical thought. Had Zach abandoned her? And what about Mark? He'd tried to kill her!

She gasped when the driver door opened and Zach shoved her out of her seat. For a moment she wanted to jump out the other side and run to the nearest PD and turn him in. But—she couldn't. How could she? She'd shot Mark, for God's sake! He didn't even bleed. And she knew damn well she hadn't missed. Even running from him, her aim was true. It was like Mark was hyped up on PCP or something. His adrenaline gave him superstrength. But why the hell had he tried to kill her? Was he afraid she would go back to Zach? No, that was ridiculous. There was more to it. More she didn't want to know. Her body shook uncontrollably. Something was terribly wrong and she was smack-dab in the middle of it.

Anger pushed into her fear. Anger at Zach. How had she allowed this to happen? How the hell was she going to get out of this cluster-fuck Zach had got her into?

Zach shoved the Jeep into gear and gunned it onto the freeway. He glanced at her. "We need to hole up somewhere and figure out our next move."

"I don't want to be involved in a next move. Take me home."

"I can't take you home, not yet."

As Zach sped up 880 then to 980 East he formulated a plan. He had the sword and the scabbard. He needed to get the star back. But first he needed some downtime with Danica. To try and convince her. Hell, convince himself that they were doing the right thing. Another thought flashed in his brain. He cursed and looked over at Danica's rigid silhouette, and wondered how the hell they were going to convince the Oakland police department Santos was a rogue and those two Immortals playing cop were his accomplices. Shit, they needed to get out of Dodge.

"Does your friend Marcie still have that place out on the delta?"

She crossed her arms over her chest, and without looking at him said, "Maybe."

They entered the Caldecott tunnel. The eerie echo of the tires and the low glow of the lights illuminated the inside of the Wrangler. Fifteen minutes later when they turned south onto 680 Danica said, "You're going the wrong way."

"We'll need money. I'm going to stop in San Ramon and collect on a debt."

Danica didn't want to know what debt. In fact, all she wanted was to be left completely alone.

Almost two hours later with barely a word spoken between them, Zach punched in the code Danica gave him to the gate of a small private drive that dumped into the delta. The secluded house was on deep water, and if Zach remembered correctly, Marcie and her husband Troy had all the toys.

"How long will Marcie and her husband be gone?"

Danica shrugged. "Last week they were still down under with no immediate plans to return home."

Zach nodded as they passed homes butted up to the water in various stages of construction or renovation.

The small community had morphed over the years from blue-collar wharf rats to white-collar wharf rats. They had a knack for rotating in and out of one another's houses. It just depended on how fast you made your money, and how long you could hold on to it.

The heavy wrought-iron gates swung open and the Jeep rolled through. As delta minimansions went the Krupps' was one of the finest.

When the Jeep stopped in the wide circular driveway, Zach pulled the emergency brake, and turned to Danica, catching her angry gaze. He knew what she was thinking. And his blood surged.

He looked up to the second-floor balcony. They'd spent a lot of time in that room tearing up the sheets.

# CHAPTER FIVE

DANICA DISARMED THE ALARM and waved Zach into the garage where he pulled the Jeep in between the twin Bentleys. Looked like being a Krupp was profitable. Good for them. He'd always enjoyed their company, and after the ugly breakup, Marcie had come by his place, told him off then hugged him and wished him well, but not before she told him never to come near her friend again.

Inexplicably he reached behind to the small of his back and rested his hand on the sword. The hilt felt cool to his touch. He thought of the star in Mark's hands. His blood surged as the vision of him holding the scabbard to Danica's throat replayed in his brain. Zach would take extreme pleasure in relieving Mark of the star but before he did he would relish the moment he plunged the sword deep into Santos's Immortal heart.

Zach pulled the sword from its resting place and held it in the palm of his hand. The gold tempering aside, there was nothing extraordinary about it. Except . . . he narrowed his eyes and focused on the symbols etched on the blade just below the hilt. The same symbols as on the box the scabbard and star arrived in. What did they mean?

And how the hell was he going to get the star back from Santos? Just walk in and take it?

Zach traced his index finger along the edge of the blade; it was so sharp that when it sliced his skin, he was only aware of it after blood beaded at his fingertip. He nodded in silent alliance with the blade. He sucked the blood from his finger.

He had his answer. The only way to get the star was to draw blood for it.

As he entered the house through the garage with the sword in hand, he let out a long breath he hadn't realized he was holding. How the hell was he going to convince Danica they were destined to be together? And if by some remote chance that occurred, how was he going to get them both off for the cop killings? Shit. He clenched the sword and raised it skyward. "Thanks a lot, Mikey."

With great effort he cleared his thoughts of Michael and his mission, and instead stood in the wide circular entryway and took in his surroundings. The inside of the minimansion was as Zach remembered it: open, airy, classic Italian décor. Lots of potted plants and granite.

Zach crossed the granite floor, the tips of the live ferns wisping across his shoulders, silently giving him permission to be there, and walked toward the back of the house into the kitchen with what he knew was a panoramic view of the deep water. He smiled. Danica presented quite the pretty picture as she gazed out the big window. She'd removed her jacket and her ass was clearly defined in the black pants she wore. "Where is the safe?" he asked.

Danica started and turned around to face him, the

scabbard clasped to her heart. She gave him that look that said, *Don't bother me, I'm too busy hating you.*

"The safe, Danica?"

"In the pantry. There's a box of Wheaties. It's fake. Slide it to the side." She walked toward him slowly, as if she feared she'd go up in flames if she got too close. Zach cringed. Maybe she would, and after everything she'd been through he could not blame her in the least for wanting nothing to do with him. He wouldn't either. Grudgingly she handed the scabbard to him. "The combination is 714 plus the house number."

"What's the house number?"

"Go outside and check for yourself." She strode past him, her nose high in the air, her attitude imperious.

"I'm ordering pizza," Zach called after her.

Danica stopped, nodded and pointed to the drawer next to Zach. "In there, menus."

Zach smiled. "I remember."

"Good, then you remember what I like." She walked haughtily out of the room and debated whether to run as far and as fast as her legs would carry her from Zach, or stay and kill him.

Slowly she ascended the sweeping stairway. The adrenaline rush of the afternoon slowly subsided, as well as the shock of what she'd witnessed. She stopped midstep and squeezed her eyes shut then opened them. Her legs suddenly felt leaden as she continued up the stairway. Why didn't she call the cops? Right now. *This instant.*

Mark's sinister face flashed in her mind's eye. Fooled again! When had Mark gone bad? Had Zach rubbed off on him? No, as bad as Zach was, he'd never possessed the pure malevolence she saw in Mark's eyes tonight. She shivered.

Zach had saved her life. He'd gone for her, not the scabbard. She stopped at the landing, her heart racing. Was it possible Zach did care for her? The pounding in her chest intensified. It didn't matter what Zach had done tonight. He had not atoned for what he did to her in the past. And for that she could never forgive him.

No, what she wanted was for Zach to be gone from her life. Her comfortably numb state of the past three years was better than this crazy emotional roller coaster she'd been on today.

Then she wondered who the hell she was trying to convince. Even after all this time and even with all of the pain, resentment, and upheaval that came with any association with Zach Garett, Danica had always felt something more, something deeper. After she was fired and he walked out of her life, he never offered an explanation—nothing, only a cold indifference. There had been no concrete closure. They had unfinished business.

The Zach she knew, the man she loved, would *never* have stood silently by while she got the royal shaft. And knowing that? . . . Like a fool she'd always held out hope for him. Hoping that maybe somehow, someday, he would come through for her. He never had.

Never once in the three years since she last saw him had he made any attempt to contact her. Until today. And it wasn't because of her, it was because of some relic!

Jesus, what had he sucked her into? Why wouldn't he tell her? She knew why. It was another one of his nefarious doings. And now he had her as an unwilling accomplice. Did he have some half-baked scheme to sell the sword and the scabbard to the highest bidder? It had obvious value. Both Mark and Zach were willing to kill for it—Zach had, Mark nearly did. If Zach didn't come up with answers that made sense she was going to the cops.

She pressed her fingertips to her temples. Her heart hurt. She was so tired.

She just wanted to sleep forever. Danica hesitated as she stepped through the threshold to her bedroom. Memories of her and Zach in this room, in this bed, their hot sweaty bodies undulating, panting, and wanting more, evaporated as another vision crowded in: one of her sitting in the corner crying for hours, her eyes swollen shut, her throat raw, her heart broken, until finally Marcie, having had enough of her failure to engage with the living, burst into the room, grabbed her by the wrists, and tossed her sorry ass into a very cold shower. She was told not to come out until she was ready to live again.

Marcie had been right. Marcie was always right. Except when she'd told Danica she knew in her heart Zach was a good man. "Hah! Good man, my ass."

She strode into the room with a defiant sneer. Screw Zach Garett and screw the Oakland police department.

She stripped and turned the shower on as hot as she could stand it. It felt good, the hot pulse of water sluicing down her back, loosening tense muscles. She'd raid Marcie's closet for something decent to wear. As she lathered up a soft squishy sponge Danica smiled for the first time in three days. Maybe just for the hell of it she'd put something sexy on, and see how much information she could get out of Zach that way. He might be using her for reasons unknown, but she knew lust in a man's eyes when she saw it, and Zach stilled lusted after her. Would serve him right to feel a little pain while she got the information she wanted. Her skin flushed. And if she were honest with herself, since he kissed her in her office this afternoon she couldn't stop remembering how good he felt. She missed that physical connection they shared almost as much as she missed the man she thought loved her.

Zach was just pouring a glass of wine when he looked up and Danica walked, no, floated into the room. She'd lost weight since they broke up. But her curves were still there and the hip-hugger white sweats and midriff top she wore did nothing to hide them. In fact, as he watched her breasts softly bounce and her long hair fall in a veil around her, he thought she looked totally fuckable. His dick swelled in agreement.

"Put your tongue back in your mouth, Garett." She swiped the full glass of wine from under his nose and walked toward the deck. Lights twinkled on the water, little stars in their own universe. Letting out a long sigh she took a sip of the wine. The smooth cherry bouquet followed by an oak finish slid over her tongue, warm and rich. She swirled the wine in the glass, opened the slider then stepped onto the deck. Cool air wafted around her sultry body, her skin shivered. She leaned forward against the rail and sipped her wine again.

She stared off into the darkness, the only allusion to water the occasional silver cap of a ripple caught under the dock lights. Amazing. Here she was in a veritable

Garden of Eden and less than three hours ago she'd been in a fight for her life.

Her years as a cop had kept her head level and her emotions in check, but the adrenaline rush that went with it? It had only begun to fully subside in the shower. She told herself she would not make a rash decision until the rush ebbed and she could think straight.

And now it was time. She groaned. The mere thought of making sense of what happened today gave her a migraine. As unpleasant as the task was, she pushed through the barriers of denial and gave the events her full attention.

Zach had killed two cops. The circumstances might be otherworldly but a kill was a kill was a kill. And he had done it with no compunction. He had those two cops' throats slit before they'd fully drawn their weapons. He was a freaking rogue cop they had come to arrest, and instead they were dead.

And Mark? She didn't know what to think about Mark, except after today he obviously was not the friend she thought he was. No, there was something dark and sinister in him, a side of him she'd never seen. Hell, he'd tried to kill her! Self-loathing rose in her belly. Was she such a blind fool when it came to men?

But Zach had saved her . . .

Danica's mood shifted into high gear the minute he stepped onto the deck. Her nostrils flared and her skin flushed warm. He had that effect on her. His energy circled her, enveloping in its power, as if to say, *You can run from me but you can't hide.*

Ah, but she could run, and she could hide. If she really

wanted to. Danica turned to tell him she wanted the truth. Now. And to tell him he meant nothing to her, she was over him, she'd moved on, but then he was there, big, warm, overpowering. He whispered her name and slid his fingers deep into her hair.

"Don't, Zach," she whispered, even as her back arched and her sensitive nipples scraped against his chest.

"Let me touch you, Dani, just this once."

Just once? Her heart pounded. She wanted so much more. She moaned, "Just a kiss."

He pulled her head up to his, his lips warm, soft, and firm, pressed against hers. The sensation generated electric shards that zapped straight to her core. Good Lord, she had forgotten how good he could make her feel. Danica melted against him, allowing herself to enjoy the moment. And the moment felt so much better than the hell she'd been living in for the last three years.

And so she opened her mouth and let him in. He tasted as he always had. Sexy, dangerous, all male. His power and strength made her feel every bit female. He was possessive, marking her, letting all other males in the vicinity know who she belonged to.

His tongue swirled against hers. The hot liquid of his kiss stirred her. She hadn't allowed another man near her much less in her bed since Zach, and precious few before him.

His hands slid from her face to her shoulders. She managed to set her wineglass down on the flat rail. Because she missed the feel of him, she slid her hands up his waist and over the angled planes of his chest. His muscles bulged under her fingers. He was in impeccable shape and she marveled again how he had recovered so quickly from his accident.

Zach's hands slid around her bare waist and to the top of her ass. His fingers splayed and grabbed each lobe and pressed her hips against the ridge in his jeans. She broke her lips from his, and looked up into his eyes. They glittered hard in passion under the deck lights. Predatory.

Danica flinched, knowing heartache would follow if she proceeded.

He gave her no time to think. His mouth crushed down on hers again and this time she gasped. He sucked the breath from her. She trembled, the urgency of his kiss scared her. She had no intention of going past a kiss . . . But his assault left her hungry for so much more.

Zach's hands slid beneath her sweats. She moaned, she couldn't help it. His big warm hands massaging her ass so close to her core had her wet and hot. She pushed back against the railing, her arms bracing her. The wineglass tumbled into the water, and Zach's mouth ravaged her neck. Her back arched and her breasts smashed against his chest. His hands came up from her ass to her waist then around.

When they captured her naked breasts, Danica moaned and surged against his hands. He pushed up the midriff top and she almost died when his lips clamped down on a nipple. He groaned and pulled her tighter toward him. His free hand slid around her waist. With the exception of penetration they could not be physically closer.

"Zach," she breathed, "stop."

"I can't."

His hand slid down her waist, to her belly button then lower. She gasped again. Her nether parts twitched and clenched and she felt a warm wetness. His big hand cupped her mound and she undulated against him. *This was crazy.*

She jerked in his arms, wanting to stop but wanting more to continue. It had been so long.

And so she gave herself permission to indulge in this man. Just once. Just tonight.

His big hand splayed across her lower belly and pressed just as his teeth nipped at her throat. "I never stopped wanting you," he said. She hung suspended in his arms, a rag doll.

Neither had she.

His hand slipped between her pants and skin. She spread her legs in a wanton act of desire. She closed her eyes tight and gave in to her addiction to him. He rubbed her slick folds and Danica's knees buckled. He tightened his arm around her waist and as he brought her up closer to his chest he dipped a thick finger inside her. Danica cried out. The sublime pleasure of it all was too much. A sob welled up in her chest.

"Dani, I don't want to hurt you again," he whispered against her ear.

She tensed. Her hands pressed against his chest, his heart beat wildly beneath her palm. She looked up at him, the porch lights illuminating his sharp features. "You don't want to as in you are but can't help yourself?"

It was Zach's turn to tense.

*Bastard.*

Danica shoved off his chest, catching Zach by surprise. She ignored the dazed look of lust in his eyes and the growing bulge in his jeans. She moved past him into the house. Whirling around she faced him as he followed her into the kitchen.

"I want answers and I want them now!"

# Chapter Six

Not many things scared Zach, but explaining to Danica what was required of them turned his hair gray. He took a deep breath and slowly exhaled.

"I died three days ago."

"Oh, for heaven's sake." She threw her hands up in the air and turned and started for the foyer. Zach hurried behind her and grabbed her arm, spinning her around to face him. "Danica, I died in that crash. Not from the crash either, Mark, he hit me and crushed my larynx. I suffocated!"

Danica stood rigid in front of him, her arms crossed over her chest. He could see it in her face. She didn't believe a word he said.

"You saw Mark today. He tried to kill you! Could you smell him? The sulfur?"

Zach watched realization dawn on her face.

"He's an Immortal. One of the bad guys. He died too, four years ago, and he was headed straight to hell, but he was rescued by—by a dark force that promised him immortality if he fought for the dark side."

Danica unfolded her arms and stood speechless. Finally she said, "Zach, I'm calling 911 and have them 5150 you."

"I'm not crazy! I died! I was on my way to hell too! But Michael, he saved me, he gave me a second chance, Dani." He grasped her hands in his. "A chance to make all of my fuckups right."

When she did not pull away or interrupt he continued, hopeful she was at least listening with an open mind. "The sword, the scabbard, and the star, they are called the Trinity. They hold the key, the key to a prison, a prison for the watchers."

Danica continued to stand silently. But he knew from the expression on her face she didn't believe a word he said. He squeezed her hands. "Tell me this, Danica. Tell me you didn't feel a connection with the scabbard. And the star? *It came to you.*"

She pulled away from him. "No, it was—"

"You're the Starkeeper, Danica, just like your mother before you and her mother and her mother, all the way back in time. The one in charge of making sure the Immortals don't get it. With the Trinity they can literally unleash hell."

"Oh, well, I did a fucking bang-up job then, didn't I?"

"Dani, listen to me. They need all three pieces of the key. They only have one, and we're going to get it back."

She shook her head and pulled her hands from his death grip, then stepped back until the stairway landing stopped her. "No, you go get it. I'm going home."

"You gave me your word at the museum you'd give me twenty-four hours."

He watched her body tense, her hands ball into fists. She strode right into his face. "You have a hell of a lot of nerve talking to me about promises! You promised me the world and then sold me out so you could keep your job! I went to the wall for you! You lied to me. *Used me!*" She poked a finger in his chest. "For all I know you hooked up with me in the first place because I was IA, figuring your girlfriend would save your sorry ass when the time came."

Zach stood silent. He felt gut-punched. She'd hit the nail on the head. And he knew she knew it too. But what she didn't know was he fell in love with her.

"Danica—"

"You son of a bitch!" She pummeled his chest. "I hate you. I wish you'd burned in hell!"

He grabbed her arms, staying her attack. "None of that changes how I feel about you."

Danica wrenched free. He could have held her, his strength was superior, but he didn't want to hurt her. He'd done enough of that for two lifetimes.

In a low, controlled voice she said, "You listen to me, and hear my words, Zach Garett. I don't want anything—*nothing*—to do with you and your harebrained story. I don't care if it's true. I don't care about anything but putting as much distance between you and me as humanly possible. Now, I'm going to give you five minutes to get your sword and your scabbard and get out of here. If you don't, I'm calling the cops."

She turned and hurried up the stairway, slamming the door to her room behind her and locking it.

Danica threw herself on the bed, thoroughly wrought. Her heart couldn't break again. It was already in too many pieces. Yet somehow it managed to hurt. Zach had used her! Wooed her as a lover in order to have her bail his ass out in his next inevitable skirmish with IA! He'd even gone so far as to propose! God, she was a fool!

She pounded her fists into the pillows. In a fit, she pulled the case off and tore open the pillow; down soared into the air. She desperately wanted something to hurl across the room, or better yet at Zach.

Zach!

She grabbed the phone on the nightstand.

"You will *not* call the cops."

Zach stood in the doorway, filling it with his presence. She'd locked the door!

"How did you get in?" It didn't matter; she turned and started to dial.

Zach grabbed the phone out of her hand and threw it across the room. It shattered into pieces. And in a blur he was on her. She kicked at him. He flipped her over onto her belly, pressing his body flush against her, quelling her attack.

"God help me, Danica, you *will* help me. We, you and I, are up to our necks in this."

"Get off of me! I don't want to do this! I don't want to be with you!" she shrieked, trying to move him. Her efforts had no effect on him. He seemed stronger somehow, and it terrified her. She was at his mercy.

Thinking on the run, Danica stilled. Let him believe she would comply. She relaxed beneath him. Almost immediately she felt his body loosen. He rubbed his face in her hair. His hands loosened on her arms. But he didn't move away from her. She held her breath.

"Dani, don't do this to me." He inhaled her scent and she felt his body tighten. His fingers dug into her wrists.

Fear tore through her. Would he hurt her? He rubbed his face in her hair again, inhaling her scent. "I don't want to hurt you." The words more a plea than a statement. But he didn't say he wouldn't . . .

His instability frightened her more than his lucid anger.

Then he surprised her. Again. Carefully, as if she would break with too much pressure, he rolled her over then pressed her back into the mattress.

She opened her mouth to demand he let her go.

All thoughts of that evaporated when he pulled his head up from her shoulder and looked at her. She sucked in a deep breath. His eyes burned, the intensity searing in its harshness. A vein stood out on his forehead and his neck muscles corded in tension. His lips drew taut, exposing his teeth. She had the dizzying feeling she was witnessing something profoundly inhuman take over Zach's body. He closed his eyes and groaned. His fingers tightened around her wrists. When his eyes flashed open again, the hard bronze color shocked her. Every muscle in her body clenched and she knew she was in big trouble.

Summoning every ounce of calm she possessed, softly Danica said, "Let me go."

Slowly he shook his head. Damn him. He never made anything easy. She hesitated to take any action. The expression on his face left her speechless for a minute. While passion edged it, fear and regret filled in the lines. What the hell was he contemplating?

"Give it your best shot, Zach."

Immediately his features softened. His body loosened. "I could never hurt you, Dani." He moved off her to sit on the edge of the bed and dropped his head into his hands.

Slowly, Danica moved off the other side of the bed—her muscles tense, waiting for him to pounce. When she made it to the door and he hadn't moved, she stopped. For several long moments she watched him, knowing he was pulling another fast one on her. Yet she was unable to keep walking. And he remained silent. Still.

A deep heavy silence hung between them. Danica couldn't move. Too many uncertain thoughts slammed around in her head.

What—what if he was telling the truth? What if this day from hell *really was a day from hell*? Danica exhaled loudly. Zach didn't flinch. She rolled her eyes and stepped back into the room. "I swear to God, Zach, I know I'm going to live to regret this—"

He looked up. Hope sprang into his eyes.

"I have conditions."

He nodded.

"No sex! No relationship. If you promise me that, I'll help you get the star back. But that's where it ends. Period."

Zach stood and towered over her. "I'll agree if you agree all conditions are subject to change."

"No. You need to understand. I don't trust you. You've killed me over and over. I can't take any more. I want your promise you will not touch me. I want your promise you'll walk the other way when this is over and never look back."

Zach opened his mouth as if to argue, and thought better of it. He nodded and extended his hand.

"No touching."

"That's impossible."

"A lot is impossible now," an unfamiliar deep voice said from the shadows of the room.

Danica cried out in alarm. Zach stiffened, and pushed her protectively behind him, then turned to the tall dark-haired man who emerged from the corner of the room. It looked as if he'd come from the deck, but the slider was closed and Danica knew it was locked.

He was dressed in dark slacks and a black tailored shirt. A long dull scar ran from just below his left eye to his jaw-line. In the shadows she couldn't determine the color of his eyes, but she could see the glint in them.

Danica moved to Zach's side. While he didn't try to pull her back, his body language was explicit. *Come near her and you are a dead man.* "Who are you? How did you get in here?" Danica demanded, looking from Zach to the stranger for answers. Although Zach remained in battle stance he didn't appear threatened.

The stranger spoke. "Who I am is unimportant." He reached behind his back and withdrew the sword. "You're getting careless, Zach."

"How did you get that?" He'd locked it in the safe with the scabbard.

"As I said, you're careless."

Zach strode to him and held out his hand, demanding the weapon. The stranger stepped closer, into the light of the room. Sensing doom, Danica moved back toward the doorway.

In a swift movement the stranger plunged the sword deep into Zach's chest. Danica stood in shocked silence before her scream pulled her back into the reality of what had just happened. She rushed to Zach, who stood eerily erect and quiet. His hands grabbed the hilt. He looked at her, his eyes wide, incredulous. And Danica died a thousand deaths.

*This can't be happening.*

She looked back to his hands. Blood seeped between his fingers where they held the sword. A fast-forward of visions and thoughts whirled through Danica's mind. She reached out a hand to him, shock making her brain sluggish, her movements awkward, her speech stuttered.

Zach dropped to his knees, grasping the sword imbedded in his chest. "Danica." He closed his eyes. The soft hiss of his breath escaped, and in slow motion he fell onto his back to lie still on the carpet.

She dropped to her knees beside him, not knowing what to do. In a momentary flash she thought to call 911. But she knew it would be too late. The nearest firehouse was thirty minutes away.

She squeezed her eyes shut, telling herself this was just another nightmare. A dream. She was destined to cry over Zach Garett. Her mother had told her he would give her the greatest joy of her life as well as the deepest pain. Agony slashed her heart to shreds. Her eyes blurred with hot tears. For the second time in three days she knew Zach Garett would die. This time, there would be no miracle.

"Pull it out," the stranger told her.

She jerked her head back to look up at him, his silhouette distorted through her tears. Her fury knew no bounds. "You bastard! You killed him!"

She looked back at Zach. He lay still.

"You can save him," the stranger said. "Pull it out."

"He'll bleed out faster!"

Slowly she wrapped her fingers around the hilt over Zach's hand. His color had lightened, his skin deathly pale.

"Now, Danica Keller. Only you can save him. His life is in your hands."

Danica shook her head. She didn't want that power. Danica wiped the tears from her eyes and looked down at Zach. He opened his eyes. The tawny light had dulled. He asked nothing with them. No question, just a pragmatic resignation. He did not plead for his life. But it was in her hands.

A welling of hot tears bombarded her cheeks. Danica pushed them away with the back of her hand. She touched the hilt of the sword. Slowly she wrapped her fingers around it. Zach's life was in her hands, and as much as she thought she wanted him dead, she knew at that moment she wanted him very much alive. Despite everything he had done, despite everything he was, call her the fool of the century, but she wanted him to breathe the same air she did.

His hand wrapped around hers and he pushed the sword deeper. She cried out. "Let me go, Dani," he whispered.

"The hell I will, Zach Garett! You're going to live, you bastard! And you're going to take responsibility for everything you've done!"

She wrapped her hand around his and with both hands jerked the blade from his chest. A rush of warm blood poured over her fingers. He fell back onto the floor, silent.

Immobile. "Take your right hand and press it to his heart," the stranger directed. Danica started, having forgotten his presence. She didn't look up.

Gently, so as not to hurt him, Danica pressed her right hand to the bloody wound on Zach's chest. Then she pressed her left hand on top. No heartbeat. She felt— nothing. Nothing except the hot sting of tears in her eyes. "Zach," she whispered. "Wake up."

He remained motionless. Seconds turned into minutes. Her sobs began to rack her body in uncontrollable waves. She punched him and cried out his name. "Wake up!"

"Put your hands back over his heart," the stranger demanded.

Danica gave him a murderous look. "He's dead! You killed him!"

"Do as I say. Now!"

Through her tears she turned back to Zach, and pressed her hands to his heart as her own broke. She knew now she would never recover. Her life was not complete if this man beneath her hands was dead. She didn't want to live, she didn't want to exist on any level, if Zach Garett was gone to her.

Long minutes passed, her sobs grew louder, harsher, her throat felt raw. Blood pooled around her hands and her knees, the copper scent of it clogged her nostrils. Every day for the rest of her life when she looked at her hands she would see the stains of Zach's life blood.

Her hands flinched.

Oh, dear God!

Against all hope she felt it. A beat. Barely discernible, but there it was!

She leaned in closer, her ear to his nose. Breath. Barely, but a breath. A warm breath.

Another heartbeat, stronger this time. Then another even stronger, and another. She looked down at him in wonder, then up to the stranger. Zach's heartbeat thudded vigorously beneath her hands.

Raiden nodded and said, "Now your destiny is sealed. Go to the lake and retrieve the star." Then he turned and walked out of the room.

Danica had no idea what had just happened or how to explain it, and at this point she was beyond questioning.

"Dani?"

She looked down at the man she loved to hate and hated to love. "I'm here, Zach."

His eyes fluttered open. "What the hell just happened?"

"I have no idea."

# CHAPTER SEVEN

DANICA HELPED ZACH UP and onto the bed. Her body trembled with emotion and now her tears were joyful. Carefully she sat on the edge of the bed beside him. "My God, Zach! How do you feel?"

"Like I just got slammed in the chest with a hammer."

*No kidding.*

"Are you—okay? Can you breathe?"

Zach nodded and lay back onto the pillows. "I just need a few minutes."

He needed more than that. There was no way in his weakened condition they could leave the house anytime soon. "Zach, you need time to heal."

Zach's eyes softened at her concern. He reached out and touched her cheek. "Thank you," he softly said.

Her brows furrowed. His soft warm smile persisted.

"After everything I've done to you, you saved my life." His smile widened. "You're either a glutton for punishment or you still love me."

Emotion so full, so intense, so hard, mushroomed in her chest. Unsure how to handle it she squeezed his hand and said, "I don't ever want to experience anything remotely close to that again."

She caught his soft gaze, and refused to allow the building tears to further expose her vulnerability. She looked at the wound on his chest through the torn fabric of his shirt. From what she could see, for such recent damage it only looked red and swollen. She touched it in amazement. Zach flinched. She pressed her lips to it and kissed him. His body quivered and tightened and when she caught his gaze again, she read desire in them.

Her blood quickened. Her need to reconnect with him on a deeper level took hold of her. She kissed the thick column of his neck, trailing her lips up to his chin. Her lips hovered over his mouth, and she whispered, "Zach, you're covered in blood. Let me clean you up."

Gently she tugged at his hand and drew him from the bed and into the bathroom. Carefully she directed him to the bench near the vanity and guided him down to it. She reached past him and turned the water on in the large open shower stall. She turned back to him and her heart twisted. His color had lightened and he was soaked in blood. "Here," she said, and rolled up his shirt. Instead of having him raise his arms she grabbed the fabric at the neck and tore it down his chest.

She caught her breath at the full sight of his wound. She could see, while it was raw, it no longer bled. Tentatively she reached out and pressed her fingertips to it. Zach grabbed her hand and pressed it more firmly against him. Waves of charged electricity flowed between them. The friction heating. Yet soothing, healing. She felt the energy in his body regroup and build. His fingers clasped her hand tighter, his power built, his chest surged, his eyes glowed. His lips cracked a smile, and she knew at that instant, their bond was sealed. Their fate, their destiny, was forever forged. They would live and die as one.

With his free hand Zach grabbed a hank of her hair and pulled her lips down to his. She melted into him, the fusion of their meeting on this plain intensifying the charge. He stood, bringing her closer into him, and moved her backward and into the shower.

Hot water sprayed their flushed skin. Blood ran in rivulets between them to the shower floor, fading to pink before disappearing down the drain. Zach peeled Danica's clothes off. She rid him of his jeans.

Skin to skin, caught in the heat of each other's gaze, they stood silent. All of the pain, the anger, the heartache, the distrust was gone. Washed away just like the blood. Danica pressed her hand to Zach's belly, her gaze locked on his. She felt his body tremble beneath her palm. She smiled and pressed her other hand lower, brushing the tip of his penis. Zach hissed in a breath.

Liking very much the power she wielded over his body, Danica pressed her body to his. Wrapping her arms around his neck, she lifted her lips to his mouth and brought him down to her. Her body surged at the heat of his lips, and his tongue, and the way he took over. His hands dug into her butt cheeks, pressing her harder against him, his passion hard and full against her belly. His lips ravaged hers, his tongue swirled in her mouth, tasting, tempting, wanting all of her.

Time stood still, their two bodies molded, meshed, a perfect fit. The water cooled. But their body heat climbed off the charts.

Danica pushed him back against the tile wall of the

shower. His surprised look made her laugh. She grabbed the big sponge and lathered it up. "I'm not leaving. I'm going to lather you up."

She began at his throat and rubbed the thick creamy lather over his skin. Each time his hands slipped around her waist, pulling her against him, she pulled away. "My way, Zach."

Inch by inch she lathered his body, her hands swirling and kneading his skin. When she lathered his penis, and in bold up-and-down strokes washed him, Zach closed his eyes, gritted his teeth, and stood rigid against the tile wall. In perfect cadence to her hand his hips rocked against her, his passion mounting. It was all Danica could do not to mount him right then and there. The hard thick heat of him coming alive in her hands made her feel more womanly, more seductive, more sexy than she'd ever felt. Hot sparks of desire pricked at her womb. Her hips undulated in response, slipping and sliding up and down his thickness.

It was more than Zach could bear as well. He turned the tables on her. Pressing her against the wall, he growled low and took the sponge she'd just tortured him with and lathered it up. His big hands ran over her body, reveling in the silky softness of her skin. Her full breasts came alive in his hands. He pressed his cock against her hip, and suckled one cherry-tipped nipple. Danica arched and moaned beneath him. "I missed you so much, Zach."

His heart twisted. He'd been such a bastard. He didn't deserve her. And she sure as hell deserved better than him. He kissed her hard, wanting her to forget everything but here and now.

She answered his call, wrapping her arms around his neck, pressing her body harder against him. He let the hard spray of the water rinse off the soap. Then, not breaking the kiss, Zach picked her up in his arms. Leaving the water running, he stepped out of the shower and strode with them both dripping wet into the bedroom. He pressed her sultry body back onto the mattress. He paused, his gaze drinking in every line, every curve, every peak and valley of her body. He trembled as their gazes locked. Her eyes were soft limpid pools of love. She was his now and forever.

"Make love to me, Zach. Make love to me like there is no tomorrow." And she meant it, because in her heart she knew they faced a foe of superior strength and cunning, and more than that, Mark Santos had no conscience.

"Danica, I promise on my life, by this time tomorrow we'll have the star."

Danica's heart swelled and with every fiber of her being she wanted to believe him. She wanted a future with this man, but their present seemed so uncertain she could only live for each moment they shared.

She arched against his hands sliding up her waist to her breasts. His lips captured a nipple in his mouth. Danica moaned, unleashing everything she had to give to this man. His big hands cupped her breasts, his lips ravaging one then the other. Hot wet desire flooded her. Her fingers dug into his thick hair as she gasped for breath. Like two starved beings, ravenously they kissed, licked, bit and sucked, unable to consume enough.

He took her in one long fluid thrust. Danica cried out, the sublime experience nearly undoing her. The heat and strength of him filled her, electrical jolts like lightning sparked in her eyes, in her heart, in her womb.

Tied, bound together as one, Zach began the slow, long, deep fluid thrust of mating, a ritual as old and sacred as time itself.

Danica's arms tightened around Zach's neck, his lips pressed to hers, his kiss deep, protective, loving. This was where she was meant to be. Their bodies undulated; perspiration slicked their bodies, their limbs entwined.

Zach's blood quickened, his seed erupted. "Danica!" he cried out. Her thighs quivered and she followed him with a shattering orgasm. The cosmic energy of it exploded inside of them, shocking them both with its intensity.

Danica gulped for air, her body shuddering as the waves of the orgasm rippled through her body. Zach gathered her tighter in his embrace, burying his face in her damp hair.

"Jesus, Danica," he breathed, his chest heaving as he tried to catch his breath.

He felt her body tremble then her shoulders shake, her breasts, and then her hips.

She was laughing. He drew back to look at her ecstatic smile. Her laugher was music to his callused ears.

"Zach! We were damn good together before, but that was out of this world! Had I known, I would have had my way with you in the hospital!"

Relief flooded him. He rolled over onto his back and pulled her into the safe circle of his arms. He snuggled his nose in her hair and inhaled her sweet scent. "I've been trying to tell you . . ."

Danica chuckled and snuggled up tighter to him. She

yawned, the toll of the day taking a sudden hit on her. "Let's sleep, Zach, just for a minute . . ."

She closed her eyes and drifted off into the first peaceful slumber in three years.

Danica woke curled up in the circle of Zach's arms. Darkness filled the room. It was still night. Not moving for fear of waking him, she lay still, listening to the deep, even sounds of his breathing.

Gently she pressed her fingers to the wound on Zach's chest. It was gone! She raised up on an elbow and squinted in the low light of the room. Where only a few hours ago there had been a raw fatal wound, now smooth reddened skin replaced it. Amazing. Her brows knitted when she thought what they were up against. They had their work cut out for them. But instead of trepidation, righteous power surged through her veins. She and Zach were a team now and a formidable one at that. Mark Santos would have to pull all the stops to even come close to destroying them. She pressed a kiss to Zach's lips then slowly backed off the bed, careful not to wake Zach.

For a long moment she stared down at him. The sheet covered his lower half, his chest rose and fell in steady rhythm to his heartbeat. She smiled softly. His sharp features were slack in repose. She smoothed away a lock of his dark hair from his brow and wondered how a mother could shun a son's love. He'd always blown it off like it didn't matter, but she knew the gaping hole in his heart would never close.

"My God," she whispered.

With sudden clarity she understood his need to eradicate the streets of pedophiles and rapists. He wasn't about being a vigilante or cowboy disregarding the law, it was about saving the children. If the system couldn't protect them from the slimy bastards, then Zach would. Her heart swelled. The emotion bittersweet. Why hadn't he told her? She would not have liked it, but at least she could have understand what drove him, and perhaps even why he had sacrificed their love. After all, if he were off the streets, who would protect the children from the monsters?

Danica stepped back. Poor Zach, he probably didn't know himself. How could he tell her?

It didn't matter. Whatever Zach had done in the past was moot now. For the first time in her life a sense of purpose filled her. And no matter which road she traveled, it would be with the man she loved by her side.

Instead of throwing her off balance, the thought comforted her. Despite their bitter past, he'd never stopped loving her, and because of that she could forgive a lot.

Adrenaline juiced through her veins. They had their work cut out for them and she was up to the challenge. Quickly she went into Marcie's room and rifled for the second time that night for clothes. She slipped on a pair of Marcie's jeans and a lightweight sweater. On a mission, she went downstairs to Troy's office and opened his gun case. She loaded two .357 Magnums and took two boxes of hollow-tipped bullets from the drawer. She pulled out a backpack from the bottom drawer and stuffed the weapons and ammo inside. She also took a hunting knife and a pair of binoculars. Wanting to be prepared for anything Mark could throw at them, Danica hurried out to the garage and the vast workbench there. She stuffed the bag with wire cutters, saw, hammer, nails, and a wrench. She stood back and perused the plethora of tools that hung like trophies on a Peg-Board behind the workbench. A girl couldn't have enough tools.

After stuffing the bulging pack into the back of the Jeep, she couldn't ignore the growl in her stomach. Danica realized the poor pizza delivery guy must have gotten pretty frustrated waiting for them to open the door. She headed into the kitchen. There must be something she could fix.

Less than thirty minutes later, Danica walked upstairs with a tray. Soup and crackers would have to be enough. Setting it on the nightstand, she looked down at Zach.

Although his body twitched and he softly moaned as if having a bad dream, he still slept. To comfort him she pressed her hand to his brow; it was cool to the touch and she was happy to see his skin glowed a healthy pink beneath his tanned skin. His body quieted.

Quickly she got back to work. She picked the bloody sword up from the floor and wiped off his blood. She debated whether to put it in the Jeep now or wait for Zach. It warmed in her hand when her gaze turned to Zach still asleep in the bed, so she set it beside him on a pillow. Then she hurried back to the master bedroom and dug through Troy's dresser. While Marcie's hubby was the same height as Zach, he didn't have the bulk of muscles. She shrugged and took the largest T-shirt she could find, along with a button-down long-sleeved Ralph Lauren shirt and a pair of jeans. Gently she roused Zach. Time they didn't have was wasting.

He started. Wide-eyed, he popped up in bed, fists clenched, ready to fight.

Touching his shoulders, she softly said, "It's okay, sweetheart, it's just me."

Instantly his wild eyes cleared to lucid. "The lake. Raiden said the star is at the lake."

She nodded. "Let's eat then go."

Thirty minutes later the Jeep roared down Highway 4 toward the main interstate then to Lake County.

The night was dark and moonless, yet stars twinkled high in the stratosphere. Nervous energy charged Danica's cells. Her senses opened and she felt stronger, more capable, and more focused than at any other moment in her life. This was her purpose.

Zach reached over and took Danica's hand. He brought it to his lips and kissed her.

"Tell me everything, Zach."

"Promise me you won't jump out and try to admit me to the nearest nuthouse?"

She laughed. "They'd take me right along with you. At this point there is nothing that will surprise me."

Zach gave her a look that said, *Don't be so sure.*

"When we crashed, I died, no thanks to Santos. I was on my way straight to hell. I could feel the heat of it. The pain was excruciating and terrifying, yet I didn't fight it. I deserved it—"

"No, Zach!"

He smiled and squeezed her hand. "It's true, I did, but sometime during that fall a hand reached out and plucked me from the air. I ended up in a room. I thought I was in an IA, but it wasn't that, it was—someplace different. This guy who calls himself Michael, he knew things about me, Danica. Bad things. Then he told me I had a choice. Come back to earth and find the star and scabbard, protect the Starkeeper, and fight to the death to keep it from the Immortals. Or?" He looked at her. "Continue my descent to hell."

"I'm glad you chose to come back to me, Zach. I would have died that day without you."

"I couldn't not see you again."

"Was Michael the man who stabbed you?"

He shook his head. "No, that son of a bitch is Raiden, and I'm not sure who the hell he is, he just appears and tells me things. He's the one who healed me at the hospital and gave me the sword. Only the sword can kill an Immortal."

"What's an Immortal?"

"Mark and the two cops with him tonight, to begin with. I can smell them, Dani, sulfur. They stink. They, the Immortals, are the guys who made a different choice. They're promised immortality by something else. Something evil. They buy into it and fight for their lives to not go back to the flame."

"Why were you chosen?"

"According to Michael, I come from a bloodline of people who have the power of the sword to kill Immortals. I'm also one of the chosen to continue the line of the Starkeeper."

"What's a Starkeeper?"

"You are, Danica. As your mother before you, all the way back, to the firstborn daughter. The Starkeeper holds the secrets of the Trinity."

She shook her head, denial hitting her hard. This story—everything—it was so unbelievable. She retrieved her hand from his and pulled her knees up to her chest. She hugged her legs and shook her head. "I—I can't explain it, but for the first time in my life, I feel as if I have a purpose. Is this it? Is that why only I could save your life?"

"Yes."

"But my mother never told me—"

"Over the centuries the secret was lost. But the time has come for it to be resurrected. There are things happening I don't understand. I fought it, Danica, thought it was a crazy dream. But then Raiden showed up in my hospital room. He put his hand to my throat and healed me, just as you did after he stabbed me. I can't ignore that. Something is happening around us, and while I can't explain it, I know we need to get that star back from Mark, and in the process eliminate him."

Danica shivered.

"It's not murder—he's already dead. But I understand if you want to sit this one out. I can take care of Mark myself. In fact, I'd prefer you wait for me."

Her heart screamed no. Her gut told her there was no other way. "No." She reached for his hand on the steering wheel and squeezed it. "I'm not letting you out of my sight again."

Zach nodded. He swallowed down a huge lump in his throat and blinked back the hot sting in his eyes. He brought her hand to his lips and kissed her. "I love you, Danica Keller, and if it's the last thing I do I'll protect you with my life."

She moved toward him and kissed his cheek. "We're in

this together, and we'll survive it together. I'll be damned if I'll lose you a third time."

He flashed her a somber grin. "I'm going to hold you to that."

"Tell me where we're going."

"Raiden said 'the lake.' I know Mark has a place up near Clear Lake. I have a general idea and hope once we get up there I'll be able to pick up his scent."

"I know where it is."

Zach raised a brow and looked at her questioningly. "How is that?"

"He thought he had a chance with me and invited me up for a weekend. He wasn't happy when I showed up with Marcie."

Zach laughed. "I bet he loved that!"

"He ended up leaving us to a girls' weekend, said he had an emergency to take care of and asked us to just lock up."

"How far north?"

"It's on the lake, a mobile home park."

"Mobile home?"

"Don't knock it, the park is gorgeous and his place is set up like a swank condo, with all the toys."

"That kind of stuff impresses you?" Zach's voice carried an edge of jealousy.

Danica laughed. "Stop being an ass."

"Can we enter without being noticed?"

"Yes. There's a steep circular road that leads down to the park. We can park up on the road, and go down the bank, maybe one hundred feet down, and it'll bring us right to the back of his place. Or we can come in from the other side. But coming down the embankment will give us more cover, and we can most likely go in through the back bedroom window undetected."

Zach nodded. "I'm taking him out the minute I can."

"Is he stronger than you?"

"I think we're more evenly matched, but he knows his boundaries. I'm just learning what I'm capable of."

Danica nodded, a feeling of unrest shivering through her. Could Mark, with his superior experience, overcome Zach? Could she stop him? Could they?

An hour and a half later the Jeep rolled to a stop at the top of the bluff overlooking Lake Vista Mobile Home Park. Lights twinkled in the early morning light, the tiny community quiet. As soon as Zach exited the Jeep his nostrils twitched. "I can smell him."

Danica stepped up next to Zach and inhaled deeply. "Sulfur."

Zach grinned down at her, a dim streetlight illuminating her features. He took her face into his hands and kissed her. "Good girl. It's their stench. Whenever you smell it one is near. Remnants of hell, no doubt."

Danica nodded then pointed down to the soft lights in the shroud of brush and trees that separated them from the back of a mobile home. "I'm not sure if that's his place, but once we get down there I can get a fix on his unit."

Carefully, like mountain goats, the two zigzagged down the steep embankment. They weren't quiet as mice but they didn't sound like a herd of cattle either. Besides, the residents of Lake Vista Mobile Home Park were used to the sound of deer foraging for breakfast in the early morning hours.

When they hit flat ground they were several units south of Mark's. His stench was stronger.

A few minutes later, with the wire cutter she'd borrowed from Troy, Danica cut the thick screen open like a tuna fish can, then slid the window open. Easy. For a cop Mark wasn't very security conscious. But then, he was so arrogant, he probably had no fear of death. When Danica made to go in first, Zach pulled her back by the hips. He put his fingers to his lips and shook his head. *Me first* he mouthed.

Danica stepped back. He was the stronger of them and he held the now familiar sword in his hand and had no compunction to use it. "Good luck," she whispered.

Zach hoisted himself up and into the window. He gave her the three-minute sign. She nodded and watched his form disappear into the darkness of the unit.

Zach crept through the small bedroom, careful not to disturb any furniture. His vision was sharp, his hearing acute, and his sense of smell on alert. He smelled Mark but his scent was not as strong as it should be if he were in the unit. Alarm bells began to sound. What if he wasn't here?

A small scraping sound from behind him and outside caught his ear. Danica!

He rushed back to the bedroom, his speed so fast it would be a blur to a mortal. He nearly died when he saw Mark with an unconscious Danica in his arms hovering just above the ground. "Welcome to Hell on Earth, my friend."

Zach lunged through the window and Mark jumped up with Danica still in his arms. Zach turned and saw as clear as day Mark standing on the flat roof of the neighboring unit, dangling Danica by the foot over the sharp rocks of the side yard. "She won't be such a catch if I drop her on her face now will she, Garett?"

"If you harm one hair on her head, Santos, it will be the last thing you do."

"You think with just a few days of increased power, you can best me? Even with the sword you need the star more than you need your sweet Danica alive."

Mark laughed and in his gleefulness he reached into his pocket and held out the star. Taunting. "I have both. At mornings' end I'll have it all."

"You'll have nothing, not even your Immortal life!"

Mark laughed. "You'll discover soon enough you are no match for me." He slid the star back into his pocket and hoisted Danica up in front of him. She hung limp, unconscious in his arms like a rag doll. Mark pressed his hand against her belly. "Her womb is ripe. I have a hunger for her. If she bears my child then I will hold the power."

"You're too late."

Mark raised a brow and grinned, his teeth glittering like canines in the rising morning light. He pressed his hand more firmly into Danica's stomach. She moaned in pain. "I can undo what you have done."

She cried out, her body jerked against her captor's, and Zach saw blood. He sprang into the air and lunged at Mark, knocking him backward. Santos tossed Danica out into the air.

In a lightning move, Zach dove to catch her. She cried out, now conscious of her surroundings. Zach clutched her to his chest and rolled with her as they hit the sharp white rocks of the side yard. Zach stood and helped Danica to her feet.

Mark's laughter rang in their ears. "Danica, he played you again." He reached his arms out to her, his hands open, palms up. "Come to me. I'll love you unconditionally."

"Shut up, Santos," Zach warned.

"Did he promise to get your job back, Dani? Did he feed you a line about him going to hell but being saved? Then did he promise never to lie to you again?"

Zach felt Danica stiffen in his arms.

"Did you tell her, Zach, it was you who snitched her out to Captain Weber?"

Danica jerked out of Zach's grip and threw a hard look his way before she looked up to face Mark. "You're boring me, Mark. Tell me something I don't already know," she challenged.

Zach's heart stopped in mid-beat.

Santos was more than happy to indulge her. "Your lover boy told the captain you knew about the information IA was going to use to put Zach away. He said you paid the snitch for false information to jade the case. False information muddies up the big picture, doesn't it?"

Danica gasped and looked back at Zach. The pain in her eyes tore him in half. It was true. But he'd had his reasons.

Bravely she turned back to Santos. "That's old news."

Santos laughed. "Oh, really? Did Zach tell you how he maneuvered you between the sheets to seal the deal for when he needed an IA out?"

Danica swallowed hard. Zach felt like the biggest piece of shit on the face of the earth. He'd done many things in his lifetime he was not proud of. But his initial reason for getting intimate with Danica was his all-time low blow.

"Do you still want him, Dani?" Santos taunted.

"Finish the story, Santos," Zach said.

"There is no more."

"No? Tell her about the price on her head, and the death threats. Tell her about the package with all of the pictures of her. In her home, in the shower. *In my bed.*"

Danica gasped. "Death threats?"

Zach looked down at her stricken face. "When it looked like I was going down for killing Thomas Pike, an opportunity presented itself. And before I knew how it was going to play out, the pictures started to arrive. The last one had a picture of you naked, and asleep in bed, with your heart cut out. With the picture was a note. 'Back her off or she dies.'" Zach shrugged. Still not regretting he did what he thought he had to do to save her life. "So, I manipulated the evidence to make it look like you paid off an informant to testify in my defense. My attorney got a hold of it and, as you know, it killed the case against me."

"Did you kill Thomas Pike?"

"Yes."

"And I got fired for trying to prove you innocent?"

Zach's temper flared. He took her by the shoulders and squarely faced her. "I killed that pedophile piece of shit, Danica. When his scumbag attorney got him off, I went to tell the bastard I was watching him, and to let him know the minute he even looked at a minor I'd string him up. I found him sodomizing a nine-year-old. I snapped his fucking neck!"

Danica blanched at his rage. Not at her but for the

children. The injustice of it all. "Who sent the death threats?"

With her question, it all suddenly fell into place. Zach smiled. Finally, Danica would understand. He looked up at Santos who stood on the edge of the roof. "You're smarter than I gave you credit for, Mark. Nice setup."

"What are you talking about?" Danica demanded.

"Mark made the threats. He made them so I'd turn on you to protect you. You get canned, he gets me out of the picture, and the door opens for him."

"You!" Danica screamed at Mark. "Is that why you pursued me? Is that why you wouldn't leave me alone?"

Mark pulled the star from his pocket. "The time has come for the next generation of Starkeepers. You have no idea how close you came to my raping you, my sweet Dani. With my blood in the child's veins, the Immortals will have the power to set the Watchers free."

Zach pulled Danica against him and spread his hand across her belly. "You'll never poison her."

"Such a sentimental sight," Santos cooed sarcastically. "But you're too late, Garett. My power is stronger, older, more defined."

"No!" Danica screamed, grabbing her belly. Several lights in neighboring mobiles flashed on.

Like an avenging angel, Zach leapt into the air, the sword poised. Mark stood battle ready. The men leapt, lunged, and parried. They flew high into the air—somersaulting, striking, twisting, and kicking each other. The force of their blows was horrific. Danica stood in transfixed fascination and watched the two furious spirits fight to the death.

In a tangle of bodies they tumbled to the ground. Neither the force of the fall nor the sharp rocks digging into their skin impacted their bloodlust assault.

Accustomed to his power, Mark was quicker. He twisted out of Zach's grip then hauled him up by his feet and hurled Zach into the window he had slipped through only moments before. Mark dove in after him. Danica followed. The sound of crashing glass, wall beams splintering, and the thud of heads slamming into the floor, mingled with the heavy breathing of the two assailants, echoed through the place. Danica followed them, keeping a keen eye on Zach but also watching for an opportunity to snatch the star.

As she sprinted into the living room after the two, she skidded to a stop. Another man, and from the stench of him, an Immortal, caught the star Mark tossed to him, as Zach took that moment to plunge the sword deep into Mark's heart. He screeched as if the hounds of hell had been let loose. The sound caused every hair on her body to stand on end.

The Immortal next to him stood in stunned silence. Danica lunged at him and knocked him against the wall. As the star rattled across the tile floor, she scrambled toward it. But the Immortal came to his senses and slammed her to the floor, forcing her breath from her lungs. She blinked, spots flashing in her vision. His large body covered her but she could see, just beyond her reach, *the star.* She took a deep breath and stretched her fingers and touched the tip. Warmth radiated from the imbedded stones. Amazingly, as if it knew its place in the world, the star cleaved to her hand.

Wrapping her fingers around it Danica turned, and as she would with a Japanese throwing star, she jammed the sharp edges of the Star of Moria into the Immortal's eyes.

He screamed in pain. She shoved harder, twisting the razor-sharp tips deeper into the writhing body. The sickening smell of burning flesh assaulted her nostrils. The Immortal jerked back, she grabbed the star, and pushed away from him. The Immortal howled, clawing at his eyes, as he rose to his knees. Danica watched in fascinated horror as inch by inch, his skin turned to ash, as if an invisible bacteria ate him from the inside. In less than a minute his body was reduced to a heap of soot.

# CHAPTER EIGHT

"I HAVE IT, Zach!" Danica held up the star triumphantly to show Zach, who stood breathing heavily across the room, next to Mark's bloodied body.

Her triumph was short-lived.

"Danica," Mark called, his voice lower, weaker. Dying. His dark eyes pleaded. "Please. Help me."

Danica stood frozen for a moment before she stepped toward him. He sat on the floor, his back to the corner of a wall. The golden sword was buried to the hilt in his chest. Blood soaked his shirt, a small pool forming on the linoleum floor next to him. "You can save me, Dani. Please—" He reached a bloody hand out to her. "Heal me, you have the gift. I will reward you with eternal life."

She took another step closer. Her gaze caught Zach's. He stood rigid, but quiet beside her, watching expectantly.

She squatted down next to Mark, and keeping the star in her right hand she reached out her left hand and touched the hilt of the sword. Slowly she wrapped her fingers around it, and withdrew it.

Mark's face softened and he smiled. Blood ran in small rivulets from the right side of his mouth, dripping to his chest. "Dani." He closed his eyes. "Thank you."

Star in hand, her right hand joined her left, and she plunged the sword deeper into Mark's black heart, severing the chambers in half. His lifeblood sprayed out in a gush. Mark's eyes flew open in shock. Danica put all of her weight into the hilt. "You're welcome, Mark," she said between clenched teeth, then jammed it deeper. "Anytime."

Danica stood back, leaving the sword imbedded in Mark's chest. She wiped her bloody hands on her shirt and looked up to Zach who didn't know whether to kiss her or be shocked.

"He pissed me off," Danica said. She pointed the star at the carcass. "I'll let you get your sword."

Zach reached down and pulled it from Mark's quickly decaying remains. The odor of sulfur became almost unbearable. Danica turned away, covering her nose and mouth.

Cool feminine laugher ricocheted around the room. A harsh force swept across Danica's hand, taking the star. She cried out in pain, grabbing her wrist to her chest. It was then that her blood ran cold.

An enchantingly beautiful yet equally deadly apparition floated inches above the ground three feet in front of her. A woman, an angel, a devil—she wasn't sure which of the three or maybe a combination of all.

The room rumbled in her wake. The floor vibrated violently beneath her. The she-devil cried out and retreated to the corner of the room, her feet now barely touching the floor. When she did so, her form solidified.

She was even more enchanting in full human flesh. No longer suspended in midair, her gold and black robes hung perfectly about her noble shoulders. She stood regal, ethereal, and, Danica instinctively knew, lethal.

Her presence in the room was that of one thousand queens.

The rumbling increased in sound and velocity. Danica watched as the entity's violet-colored eyes widened then narrowed before returning to casual. The woman stood calmly as if no force on heaven or earth could unsettle her.

Suddenly another presence filled the room, this one darker, heavier, more powerful on a basic level, but without the seductive power the woman wielded. As it materialized the woman's eyes narrowed. Danica knew that look. It was the same one she reserved for Zach Garett when he upset her.

The entire unit shook, then steadied calmly.

Danica turned, following the apparition's stare, and gasped. A large man dressed completely in black stood behind her. Her eyes swept to his large feet, which did not touch the tile floor. Instead they hovered like the woman's had just moments before. His long black hair hung around his shoulders like a dark shroud. His face was strong and hard, the chiseled lines severe. His crystalline eyes burned with the brightness of ice.

The woman laughed, the sound rich, warm, tempting. "Michael, what took you so long?"

Danica scooted back against the wall and watched these two indomitable spirits dance.

"Sephora, I would have come sooner had you not been so coy."

She laughed again, the sound sexy, seductive. Even

Danica felt lured by its promise. Who was she? And Michael? He was larger than life and the energy emanating from him exuded thick hypnotic warmth. Sephora's energy was as strong too, but it was not good energy.

It was immediately obvious to Danica who the bad guy was. And she was the most beautiful creature Danica had ever set eyes on. She was hypnotizing. And from the look on Michael's face he was not immune to it.

Sephora held out her hand. The star glowed deep purple in her palm. "Have you come for this, my love?"

Michael smiled, the gesture pure pleasure. His eyes never touched on the star. Instead they locked with Sephora's. In a lightning-quick action Michael pulled a mighty sword from behind him, and before Danica realized what he was doing he cut Sephora in half, then he severed the hand holding the star from her arm. Snatching it before it fell to the ground, he slipped it inside the dark duster he wore.

What happened next stupefied Danica. There was no blood, only a soft glow from the internal parts of Sephora's body. The severed hand reattached to the arm. Then slowly, as if awakening from a long sleep, the two halves met, and melded again. Sephora stood before them whole, no sign of trauma.

Michael was not amused. Sephora walked toward him, her hips swaying seductively. "Your sword nearly killed me once. Now I am immune to it. Just as I am immune to you. Can you say the same for yourself?"

"The day hell freezes over is the day I take you again."

Her deep throaty laughter filled the room. "I can

arrange that." Then her features sharpened. Every hair on Danica's body stood on end. This woman was terrifying. Sephora pressed her body up against Michael. "The time has come, Michael, my people have atoned."

"They have atoned for nothing!"

She stepped back, away from him. "End your jealous revenge! Let my people go."

"Jealous? Of what, Sephora?"

"Of *feeling*, Michael. Of *living*. Your self-imposed prison is not ours!"

Sephora backed farther away from Michael before she turned her full attention on Danica. Her skin chilled and she felt very vulnerable. "For the rest of your life, my dear little Starkeeper, I will be near. You have what I want, and I will literally move heaven and earth." Sephora smiled and looked at Michael. "Or hell to possess it."

Next Sephora graced Zach—who had remained as still and transfixed as Danica—with her enigmatic smile. But to him she extended her hand. "I am Sephora, Queen of the Watchers, and Commander of the Immortals. We are of the same blood, Zachary Garett."

Zach remained motionless. Sephora looked askance at Michael, who stood with sword at the ready. "He can only deliver you from your evil. I can give you eternal life."

She touched Zach. He flinched; her fingers burned his skin. Sephora looked at Danica, who held her wrist. "You would come to love me as you love her."

Michael stepped toward Sephora, his feet still only an inch from the floor. Sephora laughed as her eyes noticed this fact. "Always so careful not to touch earth, are you,

Michael? Are you so afraid you'll lose that famous self-control of yours?"

Michael stood stalwart. Zach could see he would not be goaded into a war of words or, worse, prove he had control. Of what Zach had no clue, but he trusted Michael.

Sephora glanced at Danica before her amethyst-colored eyes flashed back at Michael. She smiled again but this time the gesture was pure malice. "Remember, Michael, I am all that you desire and more. I will use any and all means at my disposal to free my people—even tempting a fallen angel."

She rose above the floor as Michael had. Slowly her body turned to gossamer then disappeared, her sultry scent the only lingering reminder that she had been there.

Danica and Zach both gaped at Michael. He scowled. "Sephora is to be avoided at all costs."

"No shit," Zach whispered.

"Is what she said true?" Danica asked. "She and Zach are of the same blood?"

Michael nodded. "The result of the Watchers fornicating with mortals are Caladians. As a hybrid they are oftentimes made up of good and bad, of which Zachary is a prime example. A constant internal battle ensues until death. Then, a choice must be made. Caladians who choose Sephora turn into the strongest of Immortals. Those who choose the light? Live to fulfill their destiny on earth. And upon their next natural death go north."

"Was Santos a Caladian?" Zach asked.

Michael shook his head. "No, your dead partner was a purist. One born evil. Sephora especially enjoys recruiting them as they tumble into hell. They have no conscience, no remorse. No soul. They are the perfect fighting machine."

Michael reached into his pocket and handed Danica the star. "Take this, Starkeeper, and put it where no one would ever think to look. And protect the knowledge of the location with your life."

Zach moved between Danica and Michael. "What guarantee do I have she won't be followed?"

"I can shield her until the rise of the next full moon to find a home for the star, and another for the scabbard. The two shall never meet; should they end up in the wrong hands, humanity is doomed."

Danica's body quivered—her big blue eyes looked up at Zach as trustingly as a newborn baby's. She nodded. "I can do this, Zach. I *want* to do it."

Zach looked from Danica to Michael. "Can I go with her?"

"No. Only she will know the locations."

"So you're telling me after she hides these pieces of the Trinity, there's no way Sephora or an Immortal can track them down and life will be normal?"

Michael smiled. It almost made him seem . . . human. "There are two ways for the locations to be known. One is by accident. Which is why it is imperative the hiding place is well thought out."

"And the second?" Zach prompted.

Michael looked at Danica. "The Starkeeper."

"As in she tells someone?"

"Yes."

"But what if—"

"There are no ifs. Your daughter will be next to inherit the truth. And only she can pass it to her daughter."

Danica pulled at Zach's arm. "I can do this without you. I *need* to." She touched his hand and held his gaze. "Will you wait for me?"

Zach smoothed Danica's hair from her face, then took her head between his hands. Slowly he drew her lips to his and kissed her long, hard, then lovingly. Emotion built in his gut, spreading to his heart and filling it to capacity. Hot moisture stung his eyes. "I'll never stop waiting," he said against her lips.

He pulled slightly away from her and rested his forehead against hers. "Hurry back."

Danica smiled up at him and nodded. She looked past his shoulder to Michael, who stood dark and silent. He nodded. Clasping the star to her heart, she rushed past both men to retrieve the scabbard in the Jeep then on to fulfill her destiny.

# EPILOGUE

*Ten weeks later*

DANICA PULLED UP in front of Zach's house. For long minutes she stared at the Mediterranean-style home she and Zach had picked out together. The house with the view, the house full of love, the house where they would raise their children and live happily ever after. She should have known then that Zach was not capable of settling down. He had too much left to do, too many demons inside him and his own stubbornness to work through. She wondered now, after all they had been through, if the demons were gone, or if new ones possessed him?

The minute she'd set the star then the scabbard in their hiding place, a calm serenity filled her. Her life suddenly had a meaning that transcended her own feelings. She felt strong, sure, and ready to face whatever the world had to throw at her. And so when she returned from her quest the month before, she set the course for the rest of her life in motion. Now, it was time for reckoning.

She exited the Jeep and slowly walked to the wide wooden door. She raised her fist to knock, but it opened.

Zach stood on the threshold, clad only in a pair of

jeans, grinning ear to ear. He gathered her into his arms and hugged her so tightly to his chest she thought she would suffocate.

"Zach, you're hurting me," she managed to squeak out.

While he loosened his hold, he kicked the door shut with the heel of his right foot. He hoisted her up into his arms and strode with her down the hall to what she knew was the master bedroom. "Zach! We need to talk!"

"Talk while I'm undressing you."

He had her on the bed and her pants off before she could form a thought, much less tell him her news.

He rained kisses on her face, her throat, her belly. "Zach, I got my job back at the PD, with full back pay and benefits."

He stopped only long enough to flash her a smile, then resumed ravishing her body. His big warm hands swept up her waist and cupped her full breasts. He took a nipple in his mouth and she moaned, arching against him. The feel of his lips sucking at her more sensitive than normal. She smiled and put her arms around his neck, pulling him closer. He managed to rid himself of his jeans, and when he slid deep into her waiting warmth, she gasped, the feeling too good to describe. Emotion threatened to overflow. He held still inside her, the two and a half months that separated them doing nothing to quell their natural passion for each other. He smoothed her hair back from her face and gently kissed her. "God, I missed you, Dani. I don't think I can bear your leaving me again."

She looked up into his deep golden eyes. Her throat constricted when she saw his tears. "I love you, Zach Garett."

"I love you, Danica Keller."

He moved then, a long deep thrust. Danica sighed and smiled. "You'll be seeing more of me than you want to."

He moved deeply inside her again. "I'll never get enough of you."

"You might rethink that."

He stopped and looked at her. "Why?"

"Because in a few months I'll have to take maternity leave."

Zach grinned then threw his head back and laughed, the sound full of happiness. "Danica, I could not be more thrilled."

"I'm glad to hear that. Because I saw the doctor yesterday."

He smoothed her hair back and kissed her full on the lips. "And?"

She smiled. "Twins."

# DISCOVER DESIRE AFTER DARK

## WITH THESE BESTSELLING PARANORMAL ROMANCES FROM POCKET BOOKS!

### PRIMAL DESIRES SUSAN SIZEMORE

Only one woman can satisfy this Vampire Prime's every hunger…

### THIRTY NIGHTS WITH A HIGHLAND HUSBAND MELISSA MAYHUE

Transported back in time, a modern-day woman falls in love with a Highlander descended from the faerie folk—who can only be hers for thirty nights.

### IN DARKNESS REBORN ALEXIS MORGAN

Will an immortal warrior stay true to his people—or risk everything for the woman he loves?

### SOMETHING WICKED CATHERINE MULVANY

Wicked desires lead to insatiable passions—passions no vampire can deny.

### THE LURE OF THE WOLF JENNIFER ST. GILES

Be lured by a seductive shape-shifter whose dark allure is impossible to resist…

---